"The most important work of American fantasy since Stephen Donaldson's original Thomas Covenant trilogy."
—*Chicago Sun-Times*

"The best fantasy series now in progress."
—*Publishers Weekly*

Praise for Volume One: *SEVENTH SON*
"*Seventh Son* begins what may be a significant recasting in fantasy terms of the tall tale of America. . . . There is something deeply heart-wrenching about an America come true, even if it is only a dream, a fantasy novel. . . . The first volume of *The Tales of Alvin Maker* is sharp and clean and bracing. May its Maker grow."
—*Washington Post Book World*

Praise for Volume Two: *RED PROPHET*
"Harsher, bleaker, and more mystical than *Seventh Son*, *Red Prophet* superbly demonstrates Card's solid historical research and most of all, his mastery of the art of storytelling."—*Booklist*

Praise for Volume Three: *PRENTICE ALVIN*
"[*Prentice Alvin* is] Another thoughtful, involving, immensely appealing yarn, bubbling with folksy charm; Alvin shows no sign of running out of steam."
—*Kirkus Reviews* (starred review)

Praise for Volume Four: *ALVIN JOURNEYMAN*
"At long last, Card returns to what promises to be his most notable creation, The Tales of Alvin Maker. . . . This superb and welcome book continues the saga at the same high level as before, and is most highly recommended."—*Booklist* (starred review)

Praise for Volume Five: *HEARTFIRE*
"Another in Card's superior fantasy series about Alvin Smith. . . . Alvin continues to mature and gain confidence. . . . One more absorbing entry in this brilliantly conceived and fetchingly rendered series."
—*Kirkus Reviews*

TOR BOOKS BY ORSON SCOTT CARD

ORSON SCOTT CARD

THE CRYSTAL CITY

The Tales of
Alvin Maker VI

TOR®
fantasy

A TOM DOHERTY ASSOCIATES BOOK
NEW YORK

This is a work of fiction. All the characters and events portrayed in this book are either products of the author's imagination or are used fictitiously.

THE CRYSTAL CITY

Copyright © 2003 by Orson Scott Card

A Tor Book
Published by Tom Doherty Associates, LLC
175 Fifth Avenue
New York, NY 10010

www.tor.com

Tor® is a registered trademark of Tom Doherty Associates, LLC.

ISBN 0-812-56462-6
EAN 978-0812-56462-4

First edition: November 2003
First mass market edition: August 2004

Printed in the United States of America

0 9 8 7 6 5 4 3 2 1

To Chris and Christi Baughan
Evenly matched

Acknowledgments

So MUCH OF what a novelist does is made up at the moment of composition—details of milieu and character, questions that need to be answered, a secondary character's hopes and fears—that it is impossible, over the years between volumes of an ongoing series like this, to remember everything. As a result, there are contradictions between volumes (or even within a volume), threads that are left dangling, questions that remain unanswered.

Unless the novelist is fortunate enough to have a group of readers who are willing to collaborate by checking the current composition against what went before. In the online community that has formed at our Hatrack River Web site (*http://www.hatrack.com*) there were several generous and careful readers who volunteered to vet this manuscript for just such problems.

Undoubtedly there are still problems remaining. During my years as a professional proofreader and copy editor I learned that no matter how careful you are and no matter how many proofreaders and editors go over it, in a work of any length some problems will always get through. The errors that remain are entirely my fault, but the errors you don't see were corrected because of the work of Michael Sloan ("Papa Moose" on Hatrack), Noah Siegel ("Calvin Maker"), Adam Spieckermann, Anna Jo Isabell ("BannaOj"), "Kayla," and the most dedicated of all, Andy Wahr ("Hobbes").

In addition, Michael Sloan won a trivia contest at EnderCon in July of 2002, and the prize was to have a character named after you in a future book of mine. My intention—which everyone understood—was that this would be a "cameo," a momentary appearance of a character with the contest winner's name. But it happened that

Michael Sloan wrote a fascinating autobiographical note as his "thousandth post" on the Hatrack River forum that triggered some interesting possibilities in my mind, and as a result the character named for him—"Papa Moose," his online identity at Hatrack—became considerably more important in the story than either he or I had expected. Since his wife has long been nicknamed Squirrel, as a reference by the two of them to the famous moose and squirrel of television cartoon fame, I naturally gave that name to the character's wife. So the characters of Papa Moose and Mama Squirrel in this book are named, not for Rocket J. Squirrel and Bullwinkle Moose, but for two longtime readers of my work and contributors to the life of the Hatrack River community.

Oh, all right, I admit that I enjoyed having Rocky and Bullwinkle references in the book. If I could have George Washington beheaded in the first volume and have Alvin dream the plot of *Lord of the Rings* in a later one, why shouldn't I welcome a chance to allude to a masterpiece of comic fantasy from my childhood?

Roland Brown read the novel just after it was finished, and offered wise suggestions on the character of Old Bart and several other points, which I gratefully accepted.

My editor, Beth Meacham, and my publisher, Tom Doherty, deserve great thanks for their patience with my unpredictable delivery dates and for the wonderful things they do for and with my books after I turn them in. It was because Tom and Beth took a chance on this strange American fantasy series back in 1983—based on, of all things, an epic poem I wrote—that I was able to leave fulltime employment for the second time and return to the freelance writing life for the past twenty years.

Barbara Bova, my agent since 1978, has watched over my career assiduously, and she and her husband, Ben Bova—the *Analog* editor who discovered me back in 1976—have been dear friends all this time. This book, like all my others, exists because Barbara won for me a place in the commerce of books that allows me time enough to write.

Family members and friends have also read this book, chapter by chapter, as I wrote it, catching errors, reminding me of questions still unanswered, and making occasional suggestions that opened doors to my imagination. Erin and Phillip Absher, Kathryn H. Kidd, and my son Geoffrey were all of great help to me.

My wife, Kristine, remains my first reader, the one who receives my pages at her bedside when I finally crawl downstairs at three or five or seven A.M. after yet another late-night writing session. She also tends to the family and business matters that would, if I had to attend to them, seriously interfere with my ability to concentrate on my writing. The most important work of my life has been and continues to be my family, and she is my collaborator and partner in every aspect of that oeuvre.

And to Zina, our nine-year-old, my thanks for her patience with a father who vanishes for hours and days at a time, only to emerge with books she does not yet enjoy reading. So I'll leave her to the pleasures of Lemony Snicket, Harry Potter, *Avalon,* and the many other books that accompany her throughout her life, hoping someday to earn a place on that illustrious list.

I began writing this book on my laptop while my daughter Emily drove along I-40 toward Los Angeles. I continued writing at my cousin Mark's house in L.A., at my home in Greensboro, North Carolina, and on the highway between Greensboro and Buena Vista, Virginia, while Kristine drove the car. I finished the book in Avon, a town on Hatteras Island in the Outer Banks of North Carolina. I crossed a lot of water, but always on bridges.

Contents

1

Nueva Barcelona

IT SEEMED LIKE everybody and his brother was in Nueva Barcelona these days. It was steamboats, mostly, that brought them. Even though the fog on the Mizzippy made it so a white man couldn't cross the river to the west bank, the steamboats could make the trip up and down the channel, carrying goods and passengers—which was the same as saying they carried money and laid it into the laps of whoever happened to be running things at the river's mouth.

These days that meant the Spanish, officially, anyway. They owned Nueva Barcelona and it had their troops all over it.

But the very presence of those troops said something. One thing it said was that the Spanish weren't so sure they could hold on to the city. Wasn't that many years since the place was called New Orleans and there was still plenty of places in the city where you better speak French or you couldn't find a bite to eat or a place to sleep—and if you spoke Spanish there, you might just wake up with your throat slit.

It didn't surprise Alvin much to hear Spanish and French mingling on the docks. What surprised him was that practically everybody was talking English—usually with heavy accents, but it was English, all the same.

"Guess you learnt all that Spanish for nothing, Arthur Stuart," said Alvin to the half-black boy who was pretending to be his slave.

"Maybe so, maybe not," said Arthur Stuart. "Not like it cost me nothing to learn it."

Which was true. It had been disconcerting to Alvin to realize how easily the boy had picked up Spanish from a Cuban slave on the steamboat that brought them downriver. It was a good knack to have, and Alvin didn't have it himself, not a lick. Being a maker was good, but it wasn't everything. Not that Alvin needed reminding of that. There were days when he thought being a maker wasn't worth a wad of chawn tobackey on the parlor floor. With all his power, he hadn't been able to save the life of his baby, had he? Oh, he tried, but when it was born a couple of months too soon, he couldn't figure out how to fix its lungs from the inside so it could breathe. Turned blue and died without ever drawing air into it. No, being a maker wasn't worth that much.

Now Margaret was pregnant again, but neither she nor Alvin saw much of each other these days. Her so busy trying to prevent a bloody war over slavery. Him so busy trying to figure out what he was supposed to do with his life. Nothing he'd ever tried to do had worked out too well. And this trip to Nueva Barcelona was gonna end up just as pointless, he was sure of it.

Only good thing about it was running into Abe and Coz on the journey. But now they were in Barcy, he'd lose track of them and it'd just be him and Arthur Stuart, continuing in their long term project of showing that you can have all the power in the world, but it wasn't worth much if you was too dumb to figure out what to do with it or how to share it with anybody else.

"You got that look again, Alvin," said Arthur Stuart.

"What look is that?"

"Like you need to piss but you're afraid it's gonna come out in chunks."

Alvin slapped him lightly upside his head. "You can't talk that way to me in this town."

"Nobody heard me."

"They don't have to hear you to see your attitude," said Alvin. "Cocky as a squirrel. Look around you—you see any black folks actin' like that?"

"I'm only half black."

"You only got to be one-sixteenth black to be black in this town."

"Dang it, Alvin, how do any of these folks know they ain't one-sixteenth black? Nobody knows their great-great-grandparents."

"What do you want to bet all the white folks in Barcy can recite their ancestry back all the way?"

"What do you want to bet they made up most of it?"

"Act like you're afraid I'll whip you, Arthur Stuart."

"Why should I, when you never act like you're gonna?"

Now, that was a challenge, and Alvin took it up. He meant just to pretend to be mad, just a kind of roar and raise up his hand and that's that. Only when he did it, there was more in that roar than he meant to put there. And the anger was real and strong and he had to force himself *not* to lash out at the boy.

It was all so real that Arthur Stuart get a look of genuine fear in his eyes, and he really did cower under the threatened blow.

But Alvin got control of himself and the blow didn't fall.

"You did a pretty good job of looking scared," said Alvin, laughing nervously.

"I wasn't acting," said Arthur Stuart softly. "Were you?"

"Am I that good at it you have to ask?"

"No. You're a pretty bad liar, most times. You was *mad*."

"Yep, I was. But not at you, Arthur Stuart."

"At who, then?"

"Tell you the truth, I don't know. Didn't even know I *was* mad, till I started trying to mime it."

At that moment, a large hand took a hold of Alvin's shoulder—not a harsh grip, but a strong one all the same. Not many men had hands so big they could hold a blacksmith's shoulder afore and behind.

"Abe," said Alvin.

"I was just wonderin' what I just saw here," said Abe. "I look over at my two friends pretendin' to be master and slave, and what do I see?"

"Oh, he beats me all the time," said Arthur Stuart, "when no one's looking."

"I reckon I might have to start," said Alvin, "just so's you won't be such a liar."

"So it was playacting?" asked Abe.

It shamed Alvin to have this good man even wonder, specially after spending a week together going down the Mizzippy. And maybe some of that pent-up anger was still close to the surface, because he found himself answering right sharp. "Not only was it playacting," said Alvin, "but it was also our business."

"And none of mine?" said Abe. "Reckon so. None of my business when one of my friends reaches out to strike another. Guess a good man's gotta just stand by and watch."

"Didn't hit him," said Alvin. "Wasn't going to."

"But now you want to hit me," said Abe.

"No," said Alvin. "Now I want to go find me a cheap inn and put up my poke afore we find something to eat. I hear Barcy's a good town for eatin', as long as you don't mind having fish that looks like bugs."

"Was that an invitation to a meal?" said Abe. "Or an invitation to go away and let you get about your business?"

"Mostly it was an invitation to change the subject," said Alvin. "Though I'd be glad to have you and Coz dine with us at whatever fine establishment we locate."

"Oh, Coz won't be joinin' us. Coz just found the love of his life, a-waitin' for him right on the pier."

"You mean that trashy lady he was a-talkin' to?" asked Arthur Stuart.

"I suggested to him that he might hold out for a cleaner grade of whore," said Abe, "but he denied that she was one, and she agreed that she had plain fallen in love with him the moment she saw him. So I figger I'll see Coz sometime tomorrow morning, drunk and robbed."

"Glad to know he's got you to look out for him, Abe," said Alvin.

"But I did," said Abe. He held up a wallet. "I picked his pocket first, so he's got no more than three dollars left on him for her to rob."

Alvin and Arthur both laughed at that.

"Is that your knack?" asked Arthur Stuart. "Pickin' pockets?"

"No sir," said Lincoln. "It don't take no knack to rob Coz. He wouldn't notice if you picked his nose. Not if there was a girl making big-eyes at him."

"But the girl would notice," said Alvin.

"Mebbe, but she didn't say nothing."

"And since she was planning on getting what was in that wallet herself," said Alvin, "seeing as how you two already sold your whole cargo and she no doubt saw you get the money and divvy it up, don't you think she would have said something?"

"So I reckon she didn't see me."

"Or she did but didn't care."

Abe thought about that for a second. "I reckon what you're saying is I oughta look inside this-here wallet."

"You could do that," said Alvin.

Abe opened it up. "I'm jiggered," he said. Of course it was empty.

"You're jug-eared, too," said Alvin, "but your real friends would never point that out."

"So she already got him."

"Oh, I don't suppose she ever laid a hand on him," said Alvin. "But a girl like that, she probably doesn't work alone. She makes big-eyes . . ."

"And her partner goes for the pockets," said Arthur Stuart.

"You sound experienced," said Abe.

"We watch for it," said Arthur Stuart. "We both kind of like to catch 'em at it, iffen we can."

"So why didn't you catch them robbin' Coz?"

"We didn't know you needed lookin' after," said Arthur Stuart.

Abe looked at him with calculated indignation. "Next time you go to beatin' this boy, Al Smith, would you be so kind as to lay down one extra wallop on my behalf?"

"Get your own half-black adopted brother-in-law to beat," said Alvin.

"Besides," said Arthur Stuart, "you *do* need lookin' after."

"What makes you think so?"

"Because you still haven't thought about how Coz wasn't the *only* one distracted by her big fluttery eyes."

Abe slapped at his jacket pocket. For a moment he was relieved to find his wallet still there. But then he realized that Coz's wallet had been there, too. It took only a moment to discover that he and Coz had both been robbed.

"And they had the sass to put the wallets back," said Abe, sounding awestruck.

"Well, don't feel bad," said Arthur Stuart. "It was probably the pickpocket's knack, so what could you do about it?"

Abe sat himself right down on the dock, which was quite an operation, seeing how he was so tall and bony that just getting himself into a sitting position involved nearly knocking three or four people into the water.

"Well, ain't this a grand holiday," said Abe. "Ain't I just the biggest rube you ever saw. First I made a raft that can't be steered, so you had to save me. And then when I sell my cargo and make the money I came for, I let somebody take it away from us first thing."

"So," said Alvin, "let's go eat."

"How?" said Abe. "I haven't got a penny. I haven't even got a return passage."

"Oh, we'll treat you to supper," said Alvin.

"I can't let you do that," said Abe.

"Why not?"

"Because then I'd be in your debt."

"We saved your stupid life on the river, Abe Lincoln," said Alvin. "You're already so far in my debt that you owe me interest on your breath."

Abe thought about that for a moment. "Well, then, I reckon it's in for a penny, in for a pound."

"The American version of that is 'in for a dime, in for a dollar,' " said Arthur Stuart helpfully.

"But my mama's version was the one I said," retorted Abe. "And since I got exactly as many pennies and pounds as I got dimes and dollars, I reckon I can please myself which ones to cuss with."

"You mean that was *cussin'*?" said Arthur Stuart.

"Inside me there was cussin' so bad it'd make a sailor poke sticks in his own ears to keep from hearin' it," said Abe. "Pennies and pounds was just the part I let out."

All this while, of course, Alvin had been using his doodlebug to go in search of the thieves. First thing was to find Coz, partly because the woman might still be with him, and partly to make sure he hadn't been harmed. Alvin found his heartfire just as he was getting clubbed in the head in a back alley. It wasn't no hard thing to make it so the club didn't do him much harm. Put him down on the ground convincingly enough, so they wouldn't feel no need to give him another lick with it, but Coz'd wake up without so much as a headache.

Meanwhile, though, the woman and the man was strolling off as easy as you please. So Alvin searched them with his doodlebug and found the money fast enough. It was no great difficulty to make the man's pocket and the woman's bag unweave themselves a little, and it wasn't much harder to make the gold coins all slippery. Nor was it so hard to keep them from making a single sound when they hit the wharf. The tricky thing was to keep the coins from slipping through the cracks between the planks and falling into the slack water under the dock.

Arthur Stuart, of course, had enough experience and training now that he was able to follow pretty much what Alvin was doing. That was why he was stringing out the conversation long enough to give Alvin time to get the job done.

In a way, thought Alvin, we're just like that pair of thieves. Arthur Stuart's the stall, keeping Abe busy so he doesn't have a clue what's going on, and I'm the cutpurse and pickpocket. Only difference is, we're sort of *un*stealing what was already stolen.

"Let's go eat, then," said Arthur Stuart, "instead of talking about eatin'."

"Where shall we go to find food that we can stand to eat?" said Alvin.

"This way, I think," said Arthur Stuart, heading directly toward the alleyway where the coins had all been spilled.

"Oh, that doesn't look too promising," said Abe.

"Trust me," said Arthur Stuart. "I got a nose for good food."

"He does," said Alvin. "And I got the tongue and lips and teeth for it."

"I'll happily provide the belly," offered Abe.

They had him lead the way down the alley. And blamed if he didn't just walk right past the money.

"Abe," said Alvin. "Didn't you see them gold coins a-lyin' there?"

"They ain't mine," said Abe.

"Finders keepers, losers weepers," said Arthur Stuart.

"I may be a loser," said Abe, "but I ain't weepin'."

"But you're a finder now," said Arthur Stuart, "and I don't see you doin' no keepin'."

Abe looked at them a bit askance. "I reckon we ought to pick up these coins and search out their proper owner.

No doubt somebody's going to be right sorry for a hole in his pocket."

"Reckon so," said Alvin, bending over to pick up a few coins. Arthur Stuart was doing the same, and pretty soon they had them all. It was quite a bit of money, when you had it all together.

"Gotta carry it somewhere," said Alvin. "Why don't you put it into those empty wallets you got?"

Alvin fully expected that Abe would realize, when he started loading it in, that it was exactly the amount that had been stolen.

But he didn't. Because the money didn't fit. There was too blamed much of it.

Arthur Stuart started laughing and kept laughing till he had tears running down his cheeks.

"So now who's the weeper?" said Abe.

"He's laughing at me," said Alvin.

"Why?"

"Because I clean forgot that you and Coz probably wasn't the first folks they robbed today."

Abe looked down at the full wallets and the coins that Alvin and Arthur Stuart were still holding and it finally dawned on him. "You robbed the robbers."

Alvin shook his head. "You was supposed to think they just dropped your money and ran or something," he said. "But I can't pretend *that* when you go finding more money than they took."

Abe shook his head. "Well, I'm beginning to get the idea that you got you some kind of knack, Mr. Smith."

"I just know how to work with metals some," said Alvin.

"Including metal that's in somebody else's pocket or purse some six rods off."

"Let's go find Coz," said Alvin. "Since I reckon he's due to wake up soon."

"He's sleeping?" asked Abe.

"He had some encouragement," said Alvin. "But he'll be fine."

Abe gave him a look but said nothing.

"What about all this extra money?" asked Arthur Stuart.

"I'm not taking it," said Abe. "I'll keep what's rightfully mine and Coz's, but the rest you can just leave there on the planks. Let the thieves come back and find it."

"But it wasn't theirs, neither," said Arthur Stuart.

"That's between them and their maker on Judgment Day," said Abe. "I ain't gettin' involved. I don't want to have any money I can't account for."

"To the Lord?" asked Alvin.

"Or to the magistrate," said Abe. "I gave a receipt for this amount, and it can be proved that it's mine. Just drop the rest of that. Or keep it, if you don't mind being thieves yourselves."

Alvin couldn't believe that the man whose money he had just saved was calling him a thief. But after he thought about it for a moment, he realized that he couldn't very well pretend that he simply *happened* to find the money. Nor that it belonged to him by any stretch of the imagination.

"I expect if you rob a robber," said Alvin, "it doesn't make you any less of a robber."

"I expect not," said Abe.

Alvin and Arthur Stuart let the money dribble out of their hands and back down onto the planks. Once again, Alvin made sure that none of it fell through the cracks. Money wouldn't do no good to anybody down in the water.

"You always this honest?" said Alvin.

"About money, yes sir," said Abe.

"But not about everything."

"I have to admit that there's parts of some stories I tell that aren't strictly speaking the absolute God's-own truth."

"Well, no, of course not," said Alvin, "but you can't tell a good story without improving it here and there."

"Well, you *can*," said Abe. "But then what do you do when you need to tell the same story to the same people?

You gotta change it then, so it'll still be entertaining."

"So it's really for their benefit to fiddle with the truth."

"Pure Christian charity."

Coz was still asleep when they found him, but it wasn't the sleep of the newly knocked-upside-the-head, it was a snorish sleep of a weary man. So Abe paused a moment to put a finger to his lips, to let Alvin and Arthur Stuart know that they should let him do the talking. Only when they nodded did he start nudging Coz with his toe.

Coz sputtered and awoke. "Oh, man," he said. "What am I doing here?"

"Waking up," said Abe. "But a minute ago, you was sleeping."

"I was? Why was I sleeping here?"

"I was going to ask you the same question," said Abe. "Did you have a good time with that lady you fell so much in love with?"

Coz started to brag. "Oh, you bet I did." Only they could all see from his face that he actually had no memory of what might have happened. "It was amazing. She was—only maybe I shouldn't tell you all about it in front of the boy."

"No, best not," said Abe. "You must have got powerful drunk last night."

"Last night?" asked Coz, looking around.

"It's been a whole night and a day since you took off with her. I reckon you probably spent every dime of your half of the money. But I'm a-tellin' you, Coz, I'm not giving you any of my half, I'm just not."

Coz patted himself and realized his wallet was missing. "Oh, that snickety-pickle. That blimmety-blam."

"Coz has him a knack for swearing in front of children," said Abe.

"My wallet's gone," he said.

"I reckon that includes the money in it," said Abe.

"Well she wouldn't steal the wallet and *leave* the money, would she?" said Coz.

"So you're sure she stole it?" said Abe.

"Well how else would my wallet turn up missing?" said Coz.

"You spent a whole night and day carousing. How do you know you didn't spend it all? Or give it to her as a present? Or make six *more* friends and buy *them* drinks till you ran out of money, and then you traded the wallet for one last drink?"

Coz looked like he'd been kicked in the belly, he was so stunned and forlorn. "Do you think I did, Abe? I got to admit, I have no memory of what I did last night."

Then he reached up and touched his head. "I must have slept my way clear past the hangover."

"You don't look too steady," said Abe. "Maybe you don't have a hangover cause you're still drunk."

"I *am* a little wobbly," said Coz. "Tell me, the three of you, am I talking slurry? Do I sound drunk?"

Alvin shrugged. "Maybe you sound like a man as just woke up."

"Kind of a frog in your throat," said Arthur Stuart.

"I've seen you drunker," said Abe.

"Oh, I'm never gonna live down the shame of this, Abe," said Coz. "You warned me not to go off with her. And whether she robbed me or somebody else did or I spent it all or I clean lost it from being so stupid drunk, I'm going home empty-handed and Ma'll kill me, she'll just ream me out a new ear, she'll cuss me up so bad."

"Oh, Coz, you know I won't leave you in such a bad way," said Abe.

"Won't you? You mean it? You'll give me a share of your half?"

"Enough to be respectable," said Abe. "We'll just say you . . . invested the rest of it, on speculation, kind of, but it went bad. They'll believe that, right? That's better than getting robbed or spending it on likker."

"Oh, it is, Abe. You're a saint. You're my best friend. And you won't have to lie for me, Abe. I know you hate to lie, so you just tell folks to ask *me* and I'll do all the lyin'."

Abe reached into his pocket and took out Coz's own wallet and handed it to him. "You just take from that wallet as much as you think you'll need to make your story stick."

Coz started counting out the twenty-dollar gold pieces, but it only took a few before his conscience started getting to him. "Every coin I take is taken from you, Abe. I can't do this. You decide how much you can spare for me."

"No, you do the calculatin'," said Abe. "You know I'm no good at accounts, or my store wouldn't have gone bust the way it did last year."

"But I feel like I'm robbing you, taking money out of your wallet like this."

"Oh, that ain't my wallet," said Abe.

Coz looked at him like he was crazy. "You took it out of your own pocket," he said. "And if it ain't yours, then whose is it?"

When Abe didn't answer, Coz looked at the wallet again.

"It's mine," he said.

"It does look like yours," said Abe.

"You took it out of my own pocket when I was sleeping!" said Coz, outraged.

"I can tell you honestly that I did not," said Abe. "And these gentlemen can affirm that I did not touch you with more than the toe of my boot as you laid there snoring like a choir of angels."

"Then how'd you get it?"

"I stole it from you before you even went off with that girl," said Abe.

"You . . . but then . . . then how could I have done all those things last night?"

"Last night?" said Abe. "As I recall, last night you were on the boat with us."

"What're you . . ." And then it all came clear. "You dad-blasted gummer-huggit! You flim-jiggy swip-swapp!"

Abe put a hand to his ear. "Hark! The song of the chuckleheaded Coz-bird!"

"It's the same day! I wasn't asleep half an hour!"

"Twenty minutes," offered Alvin. "At least that's my guess."

"And this is all my own money!" Coz said.

Abe nodded gravely. "It is, my friend, at least until another girl makes big-eyes at you."

Coz looked up and down the little alleyway. "But what happened to Fannie? One minute I was walking down this alleyway with my hand on her . . . hand, and the next minute you're pokin' me with your toe."

"You know something, Coz?" said Abe. "You don't have much of a love life."

"Look who's talkin'," said Coz sullenly.

But that seemed to be something of a sore spot with Abe, for though the smile didn't leave his face, the mirth did, and instead of coming back with some jest or jape, he sort of seemed to wander off inside himself somewhere.

"Come on, let's eat," said Arthur Stuart. "All this talkin' don't fill me up much."

And that being the most honest and sensible thing that had been said that half hour, they all agreed to it and followed their noses till they found a place that sold food that was mostly dead, didn't have too many legs, wasn't poisonous when alive, and seemed cooked enough to eat. Not an easy search in Barcy.

After dinner, Coz got him out a pipe which he proceeded to stuff with manure, or so it smelled when he got the thing alight. Alvin toyed with putting out the fire, but he knew he wasn't given his makery gift just to spare himself the occasional stink.

Instead he took his leave, hoisted his poke onto his shoulder, made sure Arthur Stuart unwound himself from his chair before standing up, and the two lit out in search of a place to stay. None of the miserable fleabitten overpriced understaffed crowded smelly firetraps near the river. Alvin had no idea how long he'd be staying and he only had limited funds, so he'd want a room in a boarding house somewhere in the part of Barcy where decent people lived who aimed to stay a spell. Where a journeyman smith might stay, for instance, while he searched for a shop as needed an extra pair of arms.

He wasn't thirty steps out of the tavern where they'd dined afore he realized that Abe Lincoln was a-following, and even though Abe had even longer legs than Alvin's, there was no point in making him hasten to catch them up. He stopped, he turned, and only then did he realize that Arthur Stuart wasn't walking with *him*, he was with Abe.

It was disconcerting, how Arthur had learnt a way to keep Alvin from noticing his heartfire. Not that Alvin ever failed to find Arthur when he was looking for him. But it used to be Alvin always knew where Arthur Stuart was without even thinking, but ever since Arthur had figured out a bit of real makering—how to het up iron or soften it, which was no mean trick—it seemed he'd also figured out how to make Alvin not notice when he sort of drifted away and went off on his own.

But now wasn't the time for remonstration, not with Abe a-lookin' on.

"You decided Coz could be trusted with his own money tonight after all?" asked Alvin.

"Coz can't be trusted with his own elbows," said Abe, "but it occurred to me that you and Arthur Stuart here have become right good friends, and I'd be sorry to lose track of you."

"Well, it's bound to happen," said Alvin, "since the only way to get your profits back north is to buy passage and get aboard afore Coz falls in love again."

"You seem to be a wandering man," said Abe, "and not likely to have a place where a man can send you a letter. Me, though, I'm rooted. I don't make much money doing much of anything yet, but I know where I want to do it. You write to Abraham Lincoln, town of Springfield, state of Noisy River, that'll reach me right enough."

Alvin had no shortage of friends in his life, but never

had a man he liked so well upon such short acquaintance made it so plain that he liked him back. "Abe, I won't forget that address, and indeed I expect I'll use it. Not only that, but I do have a way that a fellow can write to me. Any letter posted to Alvin Junior in the care of Alvin Miller in the town of Vigor Church would reach me in due time."

"Your folks, I reckon."

"I grew up there and we're still on speaking terms," said Alvin with a smile.

But Abe didn't smile back. "I know the name of Vigor Church, and a dark story attached to the place."

"The story's dark enough, and also true," said Alvin. "But if you know the tale, you know there was some as didn't take part in the massacre of Prophet's Town, and didn't have no curse upon them."

"I never thought about it, but I reckon there had to be some as had clean hands."

Alvin held his hands up. "But that doesn't mean as much as it once did, because the curse has been lifted and the sin forgiven."

"I hadn't heard that."

"It isn't much spoken of," said Alvin. "If you want to learn the whole of the tale, you're welcome to visit my family there at any time. It's a welcoming house, with many a visitor, and if you tell them you're a friend of me and a certain stepbrother-in-law of mine, they'll serve you extra helpings and perhaps tell you a tale or two that you haven't heard afore."

"You can be sure I'll go there," said Abe. "And I'm glad to think tonight won't be the last I'll hear of you."

"You can't be any gladder than me," said Alvin.

With a handshake they parted yet again, and soon Abe's long legs were carrying him back toward the tavern with a stride that parted the flow of the crowd in the street like an upriver steamboat.

"I like that man," said Arthur Stuart.

"Me too," said Alvin. "Though I think there's more to him than making folks laugh."

"Not to mention being the best-looking ugly man or the ugliest handsome man I ever seen," said Arthur Stuart.

"Speaking of nothing much," said Alvin, "I wish you wouldn't do that trick of hiding your heartfire from me."

Arthur Stuart looked at him without blinking an eye and answered just as Alvin supposed he would. "Now that we're away from company, Al, ain't it about time you told me what our business is here in Barcy?"

Alvin sighed. "I'll tell you now what I told you back in Carthage when we set out on this journey. I'm going because my Peggy sent me here to Barcy, and a good husband does what his wife insists."

"She didn't send you to Carthage, that's for sure. She thinks you're gonna die there."

"When I die, I'll be dead everywhere, all at once," said Alvin, a little peeved. "She can send me to the end of the world, and I'll go, but at least I get to choose my own route."

"You mean you *really* don't know what you're supposed to do here? When you said that before I thought you were just telling me it was none of my business."

"It might well be none of your business," said Alvin, "but so far it's apparently none of my business, either. Back on the steamboat, I thought maybe our trip here had something to do with Steve Austin and Jim Bowie and the expedition to Mexico they tried to recruit me for. But then we left them behind and—"

"And freed two dozen black men as didn't want to be slaves."

"That was more you than me, and not a thing to be bragging on here in the streets of Barcy," said Alvin.

"And you still have yet to figger out what Peggy has in mind," said Arthur Stuart.

"We don't talk like we used to," said Alvin. "And there's times I think she tells me of an urgent errand in one place, just so I won't be in a different place where she saw some awful thing happening to me."

"It's been known to happen."

"Well, I don't like it. But I also know she wants our baby to have a living father, and so I go along, though I remind her from time to time that a grown man likes to know *why* he's doing a thing. And in this case, what the thing is I'm supposed to be doing."

"Is *that* what a grown man likes?" said Arthur Stuart, with a grin that was way too wide.

"You'll find out when you're growed," said Alvin.

But the truth was, Arthur Stuart might be full grown already. Alvin didn't know whether his father was a tall man, and his mother was so young she might not have been full grown. No matter how tall he might get, at age fifteen it was time for Alvin to stop treating him like a little brother and start treating him like a man who had the right to go his own way, if he so chose.

Which was probably why Arthur Stuart had gone to the trouble to learn how to hide his heartfire from Alvin. Not hide it completely—he'd never be able to do that. But he could make it so Alvin didn't notice him unless he was particularly looking, and that was more hidden than Alvin ever thought he'd be able to do.

Alvin did his share of hiding from folks, too, so he couldn't rightly begrudge the boy his privacy. For instance, there was no one who knew that Alvin not only didn't know what errand Margaret had in mind for him, he didn't much care, either. Or about anything else.

Because at the ripe old age of twenty-six, Alvin Miller, who had become Alvin Smith, and whose secret name was Alvin Maker; this Alvin, whose birth had been surrounded by such portents, who had been so watched over by good and evil as he was growing up; this same Alvin who had thought he had a great mission and work in his life, had long since come to realize that all those portents came to nothing, that all that watching had been wasted, because the power of makery had been given to the wrong man. In Alvin's hands it had all come to nothing. Whatever he made got unmade just as fast or faster. There was no overtaking the Unmaker in his dire work of unraveling the world. He couldn't teach more than scraps of the power to anyone else, so it's not as though his plan of surrounding himself with other makers was ever going to work.

He couldn't even save the life of his own baby, or learn languages the way Arthur Stuart could, or see the paths of the future like Margaret, or any of the other practical gifts. He was just a journeyman smith who by sheerest accident got himself a golden plow which he'd been carrying around in a poke for five years now, and for what?

Alvin had no idea why God had singled him out to be the seventh son of a seventh son, but whatever God's plan might have been at first, Alvin must have muffed it by now, because even the Unmaker seemed to be leaving him alone. Once he had been so formidable that he was surrounded by enemies. Now even his enemies had lost interest in him. What clearer sign of failure could you find than that?

It was this dark mood that rode in his heart all the way into Barcy proper, and perhaps it was the cloud that it put in his visage that made the first two houses turn them away.

He was so darkhearted by the time they come to the third house that he didn't even try to be personable. "I'm a journeyman smith from up north," he said, "and this boy is passing as my slave but he's not, he's free, and I'm blamed if I'm going to make him sleep down with the servants. I want a room with two good beds, and I'll pay faithful but I won't have anybody treating this young fellow like a servant."

The woman at the door looked from him to Arthur Stuart and back again. "If you make that speech at every door, I'm surprised you ain't got you a mob of men with clubs and a rope followin' behind."

"Mostly I just ask for a room," said Alvin, "but I'm in a bad mood."

"Well, control your tongue in future," said the woman.

"It happens you chose the right door for *that* speech, by sheer luck or perversity. I have the room you want, with the two beds, and this being a house where slavery is hated as an offense against God, you'll find no one quarrels with you for treating this young man as an equal."

⚞ 2 ⚟

Squirrel and Moose

ALVIN HELD OUT his hand. "Alvin Smith, ma'am."

She shook hands with him. "I heard of an Alvin Smith what has a wife named Margaret, who goes from place to place striking terror into the hearts of them as loves to tell a lie."

"She puts a bit of a scare into them as hates lying, too," said Arthur Stuart.

"As for me," said Alvin, "I'm neutral on lying, seeing as how there's times when the truth just hurts people."

"I'm none too fanatic about telling the truth, myself," said the woman. "For instance, I believe every girl ought to grow up in the firm belief that she's clever and pretty, and every boy that he's strong and good-hearted. In my experience, what starts out as a fib turns into a hope and if you keep it up long enough, it starts to be mostly true."

"Wish I'd known that fifteen years ago," said Alvin. "Too late to do much with this boy here."

"I'm pretty," said Arthur Stuart. "I figure that's all I need to get by in this world."

"You see the problem?" said Alvin.

"If you're Margaret Larner's husband," said the woman, "then I'll bet this pretty lad here is her brother, Arthur Stuart, who from the look of him is born to be royalty."

"I wouldn't cross the road to be a king," said Arthur Stuart. "Though if they brought the throne to me, I might sit in it for a spell."

By now they were inside the house, Alvin holding onto his poke, but Arthur surrendering his bag to the woman readily enough.

"Y'all afraid of climbing stairs?" she asked.

"I always climb six flights before breakfast, just so I can be closer to heaven when I say my prayers," said Alvin.

She looked at him sharply. "I didn't know you was a praying man."

Alvin was abashed. His lighthearted joke had apparently struck something dear to her.

"I've been known to pray, ma'am," said Alvin. "I didn't mean to talk light about it, if this is a praying house."

"It is," said the woman.

"Seems to me," said Arthur Stuart, "that it's also a house where folks are all named 'you,' cause they haven't heard about 'names' yet."

She laughed. "I've had so many names in my life that I've lost track by now. Around here, folks just call me Mama Squirrel. And let's have no idle speculation about how I got that name. My husband gave it to me, when he decided that he was Papa Moose."

"Always good to accept the hospitality of moose and squirrel," said Alvin, "though this is the first time I've been able to do it under a roof."

"This ain't no hospitality here," said Mama Squirrel. "You're paying for it, and not cheap, either. We've got a lot of mouths to feed."

It wasn't till they got to the third floor that they saw

what she meant. In a large open room with windows all along one wall, a sturdy brown-haired man with a look of beatific patience was standing in front of about thirty-five children who looked to be from five to twelve, who were sitting shoulder to shoulder on four rows of benches. About a quarter of the children where black, a few were red, some were white with hints of France or Spain or England, but more than half were of races so mixed that it was hard to guess what land on earth had *not* contributed to their parentage.

Mama Squirrel silently mouthed the words "Papa Moose," and pointed at the man.

Only when her husband took a step, which dipped and rolled like a boat caught in a sudden breeze, did Alvin notice that his right foot was crippled. There had been no attempt to find a shoe to fit his twisted foot. Instead the foot was sheathed and bound to the man's shin with leather straps, which also held a thick pad under his heel. But he showed no sign of pain or embarrassment, and the children did not titter or mock. Either the children were miraculously good or Papa Moose was a man of impenetrable dignity.

He was leading the children in silent recitation of words on a slate. He would print four or five words, hold them up so all could see, and then point to a child. The child would then rise, and mouth—but not speak aloud—each word as Papa Moose pointed at it. He would nod or shake his head, depending on correctness, and then point at another child. In the silence, the faint popping and smacking of lips and tongue sounded surprisingly loud.

The words currently on the slate were "measure," "assemble," "serene," and "peril." Without meaning to, Alvin found himself making them into some kind of poem or song. The words seemed to belong to him somehow. Of course, it helped that the first word, *measure*, was the name of Alvin's beloved older brother. *Assemble* was what he was trying to do, drawing together those who might be able to learn the knack of makery. But he had walked away from his community of makers in Vigor Church because he could not be patient with his own inabilities as a teacher. *Serene,* therefore, was what he most needed to become. And *peril*? He seemed to find it wherever he went.

Mama Squirrel led them up to the garret, which was hot, with a ceiling that sloped in only one direction, from the east-facing front of the house to the back.

"It's an oven up here on a hot day," said Mama Squirrel. "And it gets mighty cold in winter. But it keeps off the rain, which around here is no mean gift, and the beds and linens are clean and the floor is swept once a week— more often, if you know how to handle a broom."

"I been known to kill spiders with one," said Alvin.

"We kill no living thing in this house," said Mama Squirrel.

"I don't know how you can eat a blamed thing without causing something that was once alive to die," said Alvin.

"You got me there," said Mama Squirrel. "We got no mercy on the plant kingdom, except we're loath to cut down a living tree."

"But spiders are safe here."

"They live out their natural span," said Mama Squirrel. "This is a house of peace."

"A house of silence, too, judging by the school downstairs."

"School?" asked Mama Squirrel. "I hope you won't accuse us of breaking the law and holding a school that might teach blacks and reds and mixes how to read and write and cipher."

Alvin grinned. "I reckon there must be a law that defines a school as a place where children are required to recite aloud."

"I'm surprised at the breadth of your knowledge of the legal code of Nueva Barcelona," said Mama Squirrel. "The law forbids us to cause a child to read or recite aloud, or to write on slate or paper, or to do sums."

"So you only teach them to subtract and multiply and divide?" said Arthur Stuart.

"And count," said Mama Squirrel. "We're law-abiding people."

"And these children—from the neighborhood?"

"From this house," said Mama Squirrel. "They're all mine."

"You are a truly amazing woman," said Alvin.

"What God gives me, who am I to refuse?" she said.

"This is an orphanage, isn't it?" said Alvin.

"It's a boardinghouse," said Mama Squirrel. "For travelers. And, of course, my husband and I and all our children live here."

"I suppose it's illegal to operate an orphanage," said Alvin.

"An orphanage," said Mama Squirrel, "would be obliged to teach the Catholic religion to all the white children, while the children of color must be auctioned off by the age of six."

"So I imagine that many a poor black woman would rather leave her impossible baby at your door than at the door of any orphanage," said Alvin.

"I have no idea what you're talking about," said Mama Squirrel. "I gave birth to every one of these children myself. Otherwise they'd be taken away from me and turned over to an orphanage."

"From the ages, I'd say you had them in bunches of five or six at a time," said Alvin.

"I give birth when they're still very small," said Mama Squirrel. "It's my knack."

Alvin set down his poke, took a step closer, and enfolded her in a wide-armed embrace. "I'm glad to be paying for the privilege of staying in such a merciful house."

"My, what strong arms you have," said Mama Squirrel.

"Oh, now you done it," said Arthur Stuart. "He'll be bragging on them arms all month now."

"You wouldn't need any wood-chopping," said Alvin. "Of wood from trees as died naturally, of course. And no stomping any ticks or snakes as come out of the woodpile."

"The biggest help," said Mama Squirrel, "would be the hauling of water."

"I heard there wasn't no wells in Nueva Barcelona," said Alvin. "On account of the ground water being brackish."

"We collect rain like everybody else, but it's not enough, even without washing the children more than once a week. So for poor folks, the water wagon fills up the public fountain twice a week. Today's a water day."

"You show me what to tote it in, and I'll come back full as many times as you want," said Alvin.

"I'll go along with him to whisper encouragement," said Arthur Stuart.

"Arthur Stuart is so noble of heart," said Alvin, "that he drinks his fill, then comes back here and pisses it out pure."

"You two bring lying to the level of music."

"You should hear my concerto for two liars and a whipped dog," said Alvin.

"But we don't actually whip no dog," Arthur Stuart assured her quickly. "We trained an irritable cat to do the dog's part."

Mama Squirrel laughed out loud and shook her head. "I swear I don't know why Margaret Larner would marry such a one as you."

"It was an act of faith," said Alvin.

"But Margaret Larner is such a torch, she needs no *faith* to judge a man's heart."

"It's his head she had to take on faith," said Arthur Stuart.

"Let's go get some water," said Alvin.

"Not unless I get me to a privy house first," said Arthur Stuart.

"Oh, fie on me," said Mama Squirrel. "I'm not much of hospitaler, specially in front of an innkeeper's son and son-in-law." She bustled over to the stairs and led Arthur Stuart down.

Alone in the garret, Alvin looked about for a place to

store his poke while he lived in this place. There wasn't much in the way of hiding places there. The floorboards didn't fit tight together, so there was a chance someone might catch a glimpse of something if he hid the golden plow in the floor.

So he had no choice but to go to the chimney and pull out a few loose bricks. Not that they were loose to start with. He sort of helped them to achieve looseness until he had a gap big enough to push the plow through.

He pulled the plow from the sack. In his hand it was warm, and he felt a faint kind of motion inside it, as if some thin golden fluid swirled within.

"I wonder what you're good for," Alvin whispered to the plow. "I been carrying you asleep in my poke for lo these many years, and I still ain't found a use for you."

The plow didn't answer. It might be alive, in some fashion, but that didn't give it the power to speak.

Alvin pushed it through the opening into the sooty coolness of the chimney. There being no convenient shelf to set it on, and Alvin not being disposed to let it drop three-and-a-half stories to the hearth on the main floor, he had no choice but to wedge it into a corner. He had to let his doodlebug into the bricks to soften them up like cork while he pushed the plow in, then harden them up around the plow to hold it firmly in place. Then he closed the hole and bound bricks to mortar once again. There was no sign that this corner of the chimney had been changed in any way. It was as good a hiding place as he was likely to find. Depending on who was doing the looking.

Now his poke contained nothing but a change of clothes and his writing materials. He could leave it lying on his bed without a second thought.

Downstairs, he found Arthur Stuart just washing up after using the privy. Two three-year-old girls were watching him like they'd never seen handwashing before.

When he was done, instead of reaching for a towel—and there was a cloth not one step away, hanging from a hook—Arthur Stuart just held his hands over the basin.

Alvin watched as the water evaporated so rapidly that Arthur Stuart suddenly screeched and rubbed his hands on his pants. To warm them up.

"Sometimes," said Alvin, "even a maker lets things happen naturally."

Arthur Stuart turned around, embarrassed. "I didn't know it would get so *cold*."

"You can get frostbite doing it so fast," said Alvin.

"*Now* you tell me."

"How was I supposed to know you were too lazy to reach for a towel?"

Arthur Stuart sniffed. "I got to practice, you know."

"In front of witnesses, no less." He looked at the two girls.

"They don't know what I done," said Arthur Stuart.

"Which makes it all the more pathetic that you were showing off for them."

"Someday I'll get sick of you bossing and judging me all the time," said Arthur Stuart.

"Maybe then you won't come along on journeys I told you not to come on."

"That would be obeying," said Arthur Stuart. "I got no particular interest in doing much of that."

"Well then set your butt down and wait here and don't help me one bit while I go haul water from the public fountain."

"I'm not that easily fooled," said Arthur Stuart. "I'll obey you when you tell me to do what I already want."

"And I thought all you were was pretty."

This being water day, and the neighborhood having no shortage of people who could use some water beyond what their rain barrels held, Alvin didn't need to ask directions. Each of them held a couple of empty water jars. Alvin wasn't sure Arthur could carry them both full—but it would be better to have two half-full jars and balance the load on his shoulders than to have just one full one that he'd have to carry in front.

Alvin wasn't much impressed when they got to the

fountain. It was pretty enough, in a simple kind of way: a watering trough for animals around the base, and two spigots to let down water from the main basin. But the water in the trough was greenish, and swarms of skeeters hovered around the main fountain.

Alvin examined the water closer, and as he expected, it was all aswarm with tiny animals and plants and the eggs of skeeters and other kinds of insects. He knew from experience that water like this was likely to make folks sick, if they didn't boil it first to kill these things. But since they were invisible to most folks, who couldn't see so small, they wouldn't feel much urgency to do it.

He reckoned that Mama Squirrel's law against killing animals didn't apply this far from her house, and besides, what she didn't know wouldn't offend her. So he spent a few minutes working on the water, breaking down all the tiny creatures into bits so small they couldn't do no harm. Not that he broke them one by one—that would have taken half his life. He just talked to them, silently, showing them in his mind what he wanted them to do. Break themselves apart. Spill their inner parts into the water. He explained it was to keep folks from coming to harm by drinking. He wasn't sure just what these tiny creatures actually understood. What mattered was that they did Alvin's will. Even the skeeter eggs.

As if the skeeters understood that he'd just wiped out their progeny, they made him pay in blood for having cleaned the water. Well, he'd live with that, itch welts and all. He didn't use his knack to make himself comfy.

"I know you're doing something," said Arthur Stuart. "But I can't tell what."

"I'm fetching water for Mama Squirrel," said Alvin.

"You're standing there looking at the fountain like you was seeing a vision. Either that or trying real hard not to break wind."

"Hard to tell those things apart," said Alvin. "It gives visionaries a bad name."

"Get bad enough gas, though, and you can start a church," said Arthur Stuart.

They filled the jugs, taking their turns along with the other folks, some of whom looked at them curiously, the rest just minding their own business. One of the lookers, a young woman not much older than Arthur Stuart, bumped into Alvin as she reached to fill a jar. Then, her jar full, she walked up to Arthur with a bit of a swagger and, in a French accent, said, "Person rich enough to own a slave got no right to draw from this fountain. There is cisterns uptown for them with the money."

"We're not drawing for ourselves," said Arthur Stuart, mildly enough. "We're hauling this for Mama Squirrel's house."

The girl spat in the dust. "Hexy house."

An older woman joined in. "You pretty bad trained, boy," she said. "You talk to a white girl and never say ma'am."

"Sorry ma'am," said Arthur Stuart.

"Where we come from," said Alvin, "polite folks talk to the master."

The woman glared at him and moved away.

The teenage girl, though, was still curious. "That Mama Squirrel, is it true she has babies of all colors?"

"I don't know about that," said Alvin. "Seems she has some children that tan real dark in the sun, and some that just freckle."

"Personne know where they get the money to live," said the girl. "Some folks say they teach them kids to steal, send them into the city at night. Dark faces, you can't see them so good."

"Nothing like that," said Arthur Stuart. "See, they own the patent on stupid, and every time somebody in the city says something dumb, they get three cents."

The girl looked at him with squinty eyes. "They be the richest people in town, then, so I think you lie."

"I reckon you owe a dollar a day to whoever has the patent on no-sense-of-humor."

"You are not a slave," said the girl.

"I'm a slave to fortune," said Arthur Stuart. "I'm in

bondage to the universe, and my only manumission will be death."

"You gone to school, you."

"I only learned whatever my sister taught me," said Arthur Stuart truthfully.

"I have a knack," said the girl.

"Good for you," said Arthur Stuart.

"This was sick water," she said, "and now is healthy. Your master healed it."

Alvin realized that this conversation had taken far too dangerous a turn. To Arthur he said, "If you're done offending everybody in the neighborhood by talking face to face with a white girl, and not looking down and saying ma'am, it's time to haul this water back."

"I was not offended," said the girl. "But if you heal the water, maybe you come home with me and heal my mama."

"I'm no healer," said Alvin.

"I think what she got," said the girl, "is the yellow fever."

If anybody had thought nobody was paying attention to this conversation, they'd have got their wake-up when she said *that*. It was like every nose on every face was tied to a string that got pulled when she said "yellow fever."

"Did you say yellow fever?" asked an old woman.

The girl looked at her blankly.

"She did," said another woman. "Marie la Morte a dit."

"Dead Mary says her ma's got yellow fever!" called someone.

And now the strings were pulled in the opposite direction. Every head turned to face away from the girl—Dead Mary was her name, apparently—and then all the feet set to pumping and in a few minutes, Alvin, Arthur, and Dead Mary were the only humans near the fountain. Some folks quit the place so fast their jugs was left behind.

"I reckon nobody's going to steal these jars if we don't leave them here too long," said Alvin. "Let's go see your mother."

"They will be stole for sure," said Dead Mary.

"I'll stay and watch them," said Arthur Stuart.

"Sir and ma'am," said Alvin. "And never look a white person in the eye."

"When there's nobody around, can I just set here and pretend to be human?"

"Please yourself," said Alvin.

It took a while to get to Dead Mary's house. Down streets until they ran out of streets, and then along paths between shacks, and finally into swampy land till they came to a little shack on stilts. Skeeters were thick as smoke in some spots.

"How can you live with all these skeeters?" asked Alvin.

"I breathe them in and cough them out," said Dead Mary.

"How come they call you that?" asked Alvin. "Dead Mary, I mean."

"Marie la Morte? Cause I know when someone is sick before he know himself. And I know how the sickness will end."

"Am I sick?"

"Not yet, no," said the girl.

"What makes you think I can heal your mother?"

"She will die if somebody does not help, and the yellow fever, personne who live here knows how to cure it."

It took Alvin a moment to decide that the French word she said must mean *nobody*. "I don't know a thing about yellow fever."

"It's a terrible thing," said the girl. "Quick hot fever. Then freezing cold. My mother's eyes turn yellow. She screams with pain in her neck and shoulders and back. And then when she's not screaming, she looks sad."

"Yellow and fevery," said Alvin. "I reckon the name kind of says it all." Alvin knew better than to ask what caused the disease. The two leading theories about the cause of disease were punishment for sin and a curse from somebody you offended. Course, if either one was right, it was out of Alvin's league.

Alvin was a healer, of a kind—that was just natural for a maker, being sort of included in the knack. But what he was good at healing was broken bones and failing organs. A man tore a muscle or chopped his foot, and Alvin could heal him up good. Or if gangrene set in, Alvin could clean it out, make the good flesh get shut of the bad. With gangrene, too, he knew the pus was full of all kinds of little animals, and he knew which ones didn't belong in the body. But he couldn't do like he did with the water and just tell everything alive to break apart—that would kill the person right along with the sickness.

Diseases that made your nose or bowels run were hard to track down, and Alvin never knew whether they were serious or something that would just get better if you left it alone or slept a lot. The stuff that went on inside a living body was just too complicated, and most of the important things was way too small for Alvin to understand what all was going on.

If he was a *real* healer, he could have saved his newborn baby when it was born too young and couldn't breathe. But he just didn't understand what was going on inside the lungs. The baby was dead before he figured out a single thing.

"I'm not going to be able to do much good," said Alvin. "Healing sick folks is hard."

"I touch her lying on her bed, and I see nothing but she dead of yellow fever," said Dead Mary. "But I touch you by the fountain, I see my mother living."

"When did you touch me?" said Alvin. "You didn't touch me."

"I bump you when I draw water," she said. "I have to be sneaky. Personne lets me touch him now, if he sees me."

That was no surprise. Though Alvin figured it was better to know you're sick and dying in time to say goodbye to your loved ones. But folks always seemed to think that as long as they didn't know about something bad, it wasn't happening, so whoever told them actually caused it to be true.

Illness or adultery, Alvin figured ignorance worked about as well in both cases. Not knowing just meant it was going to get worse.

There was a plank leading from a hummock of dry land to the minuscule porch of the house, and Dead Mary fair to danced along it. Alvin couldn't quite manage that, as he looked down at the thick sucking mud under the plank. But the board didn't wobble much, and he made it into the house all right.

It stank inside, but not much worse than the swamp outside. The odor of decay was natural here. Still, it was worse around the woman's bed. Old woman, Alvin thought at first, the saddest looking woman he had ever seen. Then realized that she wasn't very old at all. She was ravaged by worse things than age.

"I'm glad she's sleeping," said Dead Mary. "Most times the pain does not let her sleep."

Alvin got his doodlebug inside her and found that her liver was half rotted away. Not to mention that blood was seeping everywhere inside her, pooling and rotting under the skin. She was close to death—could have died already, if she'd been willing to let go. Whatever she was holding on for, Alvin couldn't guess. Maybe love for this girl here. Maybe just a stubborn determination to fight till the last possible moment.

The cause of all this ruin was impossible for Alvin to find. Too small, or of a nature he didn't know how to recognize. But that didn't mean there was nothing he could do. The seeping blood—he could repair the blood vessels, clear away the pooling fluids. This sort of work, reconstructing injured bodies, he'd done that before and he knew how. He worked quickly, moved on, moved on. And soon he knew that he was well ahead of the disease, rebuilding faster than it could tear down.

Until at last he could get to work on the liver. Livers were mysterious things and all he could do was try to get the sick parts to look more like the healthy parts. And maybe that was enough, because soon enough the woman coughed—with strength now, not feebly—and then sat up. "J'ai soif," she said.

"She's thirsty," said the girl.

"Marie," the woman said, and then reached for her with a sob. "Ma Marie d'Espoir!"

Alvin had no idea what she was saying, but the embrace was plain enough, and so were the tears.

He walked to the doorway, leaving them their privacy. From the position of the sun, he'd been there an hour. A long time to leave Arthur Stuart alone by the well.

And these skeeters were bound to suck all the blood out of him and turn him into one big itch iffen he didn't get out of this place.

He was nearly to the end of the plank when he felt it tremble with someone else's feet. And then something hit him from behind and he was on the damp grassy mound with Dead Mary lying on top of him covering him with kisses.

"Vous avez sauvé ma mere!" she cried. "You saved her, you saved her, vous êtes un ange, vous êtes un dieu!"

"Here now, let up, get off me, I'm a married man," said Alvin.

The girl got up. "I'm sorry, but I'm so full of joy."

"Well I'm not sure I did anything," said Alvin. "Your mother may *feel* better but I didn't cure whatever caused the fever. She's still sick, and she still needs to rest and let her body work on whatever's wrong."

Alvin was on his feet now, and he looked back to see the mother standing in the doorway, tears still running down her cheeks.

"I mean it," said Alvin. "Send her back to bed. She keeps standing there, the skeeters'll eat her alive."

"I love you," said the girl. "I love you forever, you good man!"

Back in the plaza, Arthur Stuart was sitting on top of the four water jars—which he had moved some twenty yards away from the fountain. Which was a good thing, because there must have been a hundred people or more jostling around it now.

Alvin didn't worry about the crowd—he was mostly just relieved that they weren't jostling around some uppity young black man.

"Took you long enough," Arthur Stuart whispered.

"Her mother was real sick," said Alvin.

"Yeah, well, word got out that this was the sweetest-tasting water ever served up in Barcy, and now folks are saying it can heal the sick or Jesus turned the water into wine or it's a sign of the second coming or the devil was cast out of it and I had to tell five different people that *our* water came from the fountain *before* it got all hexed or healed or whatever they happen to believe. I was about to throw dirt into it just to make it convincing."

"So stop talking and pick up your jars."

Arthur Stuart stood up and reached for a jar, but then stopped and puzzled over it. "How do I pick up the second one, while I got the first one on my shoulder?"

Alvin solved the problem by picking up both the half-filled jars by the lip and putting them on Arthur's shoulders. Then Alvin picked up the two full ones and hoisted them onto his own shoulders.

"Well, don't *you* make it look easy," said Arthur Stuart.

"I can't help it that I've got the grip and the heft of a blacksmith," said Alvin. "I earned them the hard way—you could do it too, if you wanted."

"I haven't heard you offering to make me no apprentice blacksmith."

"Because you're an apprentice maker, and not doing too bad at it."

"Did you heal the woman?"

"Not really. But I healed some of the damage the disease did."

"Meaning she can run a mile without panting, right?"

"Where *she* lives, it's more like *splash* a couple of dozen yards. That mud looked like it could swallow up whole armies and spit them back out as skeeters."

"Well, you done what you could, and we're done with it," said Arthur Stuart.

They got back to the house of Squirrel and Moose and poured the water into the cistern. Mixed in with what they already had, the cleaned water improved the quality only a little, but that was fine with Alvin. People kept over-reacting. He was just a fellow using his knack.

Back at the house of Dead Mary—or Marie d'Espoir—nobody was following Alvin's advice. The woman he had saved was outside checking crawfish traps, getting bitten by skeeter after skeeter. She didn't mind anymore—in a swamp full of gators and cottonmouths, what was a little itching and a few dozen welts?

Meanwhile, the skeeters, engorged with her blood, spread out over the swamp. Some of them ended up in the city, and each person they bit ended up with a virulent dose of yellow fever growing in their blood.

⚔ 3 ⚔

Fever

SUPPER THAT EVENING was bedlam, the children moving
in and out of the kitchen in shifts with the normal amount
of shoving and jostling and complaining. It reminded Alvin of growing up with his brothers and sisters, only because there were so many more children, and of nearly
the same age, it was even more confusing. A few quarrels
even flared, white-hot in an instant, then promptly si-
lenced by Mama Squirrel flinging a bit of water at the
offenders or by Papa Moose speaking a name. The children didn't seem to fear punishment; it was his disap-
proval that they dreaded.

The food was plain and poor, but healthy and there was
plenty of it. So much, in fact, that both serving pots had
soup left in them. Mama Squirrel poured them back into
the big cauldron by the fire. "I never made but one batch
of soup in all the years we've lived here," she said.

Even the old bread and the half-eaten scraps from the
children's bowls were scraped into the big pot. "As long
as I bring the pot to a long hard boil before serving it

again, there's no harm from adding it back into the soup."

"It's like life," said Papa Moose, who was scouring dishes at the sink. "Dust to dust, pot to pot, one big round, it never ends." Then he winked. "I throw some cayenne peppers in it from time to time, that's what makes it all edible."

Then the children were herded upstairs into the dormitories, kissing their parents as they passed. Papa Moose beckoned Alvin to come with him as he followed the children up. It wasn't quick, following him up the stairs, but not slow, either. He seemed to bob up the stairs on his good foot, the clubbed foot somewhat extended so it stayed out of the way and, perhaps, balanced him a bit. It was wise not to follow too close behind him, or you could find out just how much of a club that foot could be.

They all lay down on mats on the floor—a floor well-limed and clean-swept. But not to sleep. One-hour candles were lighted all around the room, and all the children lay there, pretending to be asleep while Papa Moose and Mama Squirrel made a pantomime of tiptoeing out of the room. Naturally, Alvin glanced back into the room and saw that every single child pulled a book or pamphlet out from under their mat and began to read.

Alvin came back downstairs with Moose and Squirrel, grinning as he went. "It's a shame none of your children can read," he said.

Papa Moose held to the banister and half hopped, half slid down the stairs on his good foot. "It's not as if there were anything worth reading in the world," he said.

"Though I wish they could read the holy scriptures," said Mama Squirrel.

"Of course, they might be reading on the sly," said Alvin.

"Oh, no," said Papa Moose. "They are *strictly* forbidden to do such a thing."

"Papa Moose showed our ragged little collection of books to all the children and told them they must *never* borrow those books and carefully return them as soon as they're done."

"It's good to teach children to obey," said Alvin.

" 'Obedience is better than sacrifice,' " quoted Papa Moose.

They sat down at the kitchen table, where Arthur Stuart was already seated, reading a book. Alvin realized after a moment that it was written in Spanish. "You're taking this new language of yours pretty serious."

"Since you know everything there is to know in English," said Arthur Stuart, "I reckon this is the only way to get one up on you."

They talked for a while about the children—how they supported them, mostly. They depended a lot on donations from likeminded persons, but since those were in short supply in Barcy, it was always nip and tuck, allowing nothing to go to waste. "Use it up," intoned Papa Moose, "wear it out, make it do or do without."

"We have one cow," said Mama Squirrel, "so we only get enough milk for the little ones, and for a little butter. But even if we had another cow or two, we don't have any means of feeding them." She shrugged. "Our children are never noted for being fat."

After a few minutes the conversation turned to Alvin's business—whatever it was. "Did Margaret send you here for a report?"

"I have no idea," said Alvin. "I usually don't know all that much more about her plans than a knight does in a game of chess."

"At least you're not a pawn," said Papa Moose.

"No, I'm the one she can send jumping around wherever she wants." He said it with a chuckle, but realized as he spoke that he actually resented it, and more than a little.

"I suppose she doesn't tell you everything so you don't go improving on her plan," said Squirrel. "Moose always thinks he knows better."

"I'm not always wrong," said Papa Moose.

"Margaret sees my death down a lot of roads," said Alvin, "and she knows that I don't always take her warnings seriously."

"So instead of giving you warnings, she asks you to help her," said Squirrel.

Alvin shrugged. "If she ever said so, it would stop working."

"The woman is the subtlest beast in the garden," said Papa Moose, "now that snakes can't talk."

Alvin grinned. "But just in case she actually sent me here for a purpose, do you have anything to report to her?"

"Meaning," said Arthur Stuart, looking up from his book, "do you have anything you'd be willing to tell old Alvin here, so he can figure out what's going on?"

"Isn't that what I said?"

"There's all kinds of plots in this city," said Papa Moose. "The older children eavesdrop for us during the day, as they can, and we have friends who come calling. So we know about a good number of them. There's a Spanish group trying to revolt and get Barcy annexed by Mexico. And of course the French are always plotting a revolution, though it don't come to much, since they can't come to any agreement among the parties."

"Parties?"

"Them as favor being part of an independent Canada, and them as want to conquer Haiti, and them as want to be an independent city-state on the Mizzippy, and them as wish to restore the royal family to the throne of France, and two different Bonapartist factions that hate each other worst of all."

"And that don't even touch the split between Catholics and Huguenots," said Squirrel. "And between Bretons and Normans and Provençals and Parisians and a weird little group of Poitevin fanatics."

"That's the French," said Moose. "They may not know what's right, but they know everybody else is wrong."

"What about the Americans?" asked Alvin. "I hear English on the street more than French or Spanish."

"That depends on the street," said Moose. "But you're right, this city has more English-speakers than any other language. Most of them know they're just visitors here. The Americans and Yankees and English care about money, mostly. Make their fortune and head back home."

"The dangerous plotters are the Cavaliers," said Squirrel. "They're hungry for more land to put into cotton."

"To be worked by more and more slaves," said Alvin.

"And to restore some glory to a king who can't get his country back," said Squirrel.

"The Cavaliers are the ones who want to start a fight," said Papa Moose. "They're the ones who hope that a revolution here would make the King step in to bail them out—or maybe they're already sponsored by the king so he'd just use them as an excuse to send in an army. There's rumors of an army gathering in the Crown Colonies, supposedly to guard the border with the United States but maybe it's bound for Barcy. It's one and the same—if the King came in here, in control of the mouth of the Mizzippy . . ."

Alvin understood. "The United States would have to fight, just to keep the river open."

"And any war between the U.S. and the Crown Colonies would turn into a war over slavery," said Papa Moose. "Even though parts of the United States allow slavery, too. Free-state Americans may not care enough to go to war to free the blacks, but if they won the war, I doubt they'd be so stone-hearted as to leave the slaves in chains."

"Does all this have anything to do with Steve Austin's expedition to Mexico?" asked Alvin.

They both hooted with laughter. "Austin the Conqueror!" said Papa Moose. "Thinks he can take over Mexico with a couple of hundred Cavaliers and Americans."

"He thinks dark-skinned people are no match for white," said Squirrel. "It's the kind of thing slaveowners can fool themselves into believing, what with black folks cowering to them all day."

"So you don't think Austin and his friends amount to anything."

"I think," said Papa Moose, "that if they try to invade Mexico, they'll be killed to the last man."

Alvin thought back to his encounter with Austin, and, more memorably, with Jim Bowie, one of Austin's men. A killer, he was. And the world wouldn't be impoverished if the Mexica killed him, though Alvin couldn't wish such a cruel death on anyone. Still, given what Alvin knew about Bowie, he wondered if the man would ever let himself be taken by such enemies. For all Alvin knew, Bowie would emerge from the encounter with half the Mexica worshiping him as a particularly bloodthirsty new god.

"Doesn't sound like there's much useful for me to do," said Alvin. "Margaret don't need me to gather information—she always knows more than I do about what other folks aim to do."

"It kind of reassures me to have you here," said Squirrel. "Iffen your Peggy sent you here, stands to reason this is the safest place to be."

Alvin bowed his head. He would have been angry if he didn't fear that what she said was so. Hadn't Margaret watched over him from her childhood on? Back when she was Horace Guester's daughter Little Peggy, didn't she use his birth caul to use his own powers to save him from the dealings of the Unmaker? But it galled him to think that she might be sheltering him, and shamed him to think that other folks assumed that it was so.

Arthur Stuart spoke up sharp. "You don't know Peggy iffen you think that," he said. "She don't *send* Alvin, not nowhere. Now and then she *asks* him to go, and when she does, it's because it's a place where his knack is needed. She sends him into danger as often as not, and them as think otherwise don't know Peggy and they don't know Al."

Al, thought Alvin. First time the boy ever called him by *that* nickname. But he couldn't be mad at him for disrespect in the midst of the boy defending him so hot.

Papa Moose chuckled. "I sort of stopped listening at 'not nowhere.' I thought Margaret Larner would've done a better job of learning you good grammar."

"Did you understand me or not?" said Arthur Stuart.

"Oh, I understood, all right."

"Then my grammar was sufficient to the task."

At that echo of Margaret's teaching they all laughed—including, after a moment, Arthur Stuart himself.

During the day Alvin busied himself with repairs around the house. With his mind he convinced the termites and borers to leave, and shucked off the mildew on the walls. He found the weak spots in the foundation and with his mind reshaped them till they were strong. When he was done with his doodlebug examining the roof, there wasn't a leak or a spot where light shone through, and all around the house every window was tight, with not a draft coming in or out. Even the privy was spic and span, though the privy pot itself could still be found with your eyes closed.

All the while he used his makery to heal the house, he used his arms to chop and stack wood and do other outward tasks—turning the cow out to eat such grass as there was, milking it, skimming the milk, cheesing some of it, churning the cream into butter. He had learned to be a useful man, not just a man of one trade. And if, when he was done milking her, the cow was remarkably healthy with udders that gave far more milk than normal from eating the same amount of hay, who was to say it was Alvin did anything to cause it?

Only one part of the household did Alvin leave unhealed: Papa Moose's foot. You don't go meddling with a man's body, not unless he asks. And besides, this man was well known in Barcy. If he suddenly walked like a normal man, what would people think?

Meanwhile, Arthur Stuart ran such errands for the house as a sharp-witted, trusted slave boy might be sent on. And as he went he kept his ears open. People said things in front of slaves. English-speakers especially said things in front of slaves who seemed to speak only Spanish, and Spanish-speakers in front of English-speaking slaves. The French talked in front of anybody.

Barcy was an easy town for a young half-black bilingual spy. Being far more educated and experienced in great affairs than the children of the house of Moose and Squirrel, Arthur Stuart was able to recognize the significance of things that would have sailed right past them.

The tidbits he brought home about this party or that, rebellions and plots and quarrels and reconciliations, they added but little to what Papa Moose and Mama Squirrel already knew about the goings-on in Barcy.

The only information they might not have had was of a different nature: rumors and gossip about them and their house. And this was hardly of a nature that he would be happy to bring home to them.

All their elaborate efforts to abide by the strict letter of the law had paid off well enough. Nobody wasted any breath wondering whether their house was an orphanage or a school for bastard children of mixed races, nor did anyone do more than scoff at the idea that Mama Squirrel was the natural mother of any of the children, let alone all of them. Nobody was much exercised about it one way or another. The law might be filled with provisions to keep black folks ignorant and chained, but it was only enforced when somebody cared enough to complain, and nobody did.

Not because anybody approved, but because they had much darker worries about the house of Moose and Squirrel. The fact that the miracle water a few days ago had appeared in the public fountain nearest that house had been duly noted. So had the traffic in strangers, and nobody was fooled by the fact that it was a boardinghouse— too many of the visitors came and went in only an hour. "How fast can a body sleep, anyway?" said one of the skeptics. "They're spies, that's what they are."

But spies for whom? Some were close to the target, guessing that they were abolitionists or Quakers or New England Puritans, here to subvert the Proper Order of Man, as slavery was euphemistically called in pulpits throughout the slave lands. Others had them as spies for the King or for the Lord Protector or even, in the most fanciful version, for the evil Reds of Lolla-Wossiky across the fog-covered river. It didn't help that Papa Moose was crippled. His strange dipping-and-rolling walk made him all the more suspicious in their eyes.

There were more than a few who believed like gospel the story that Moose and Squirrel trained their houseful of children as pickpockets and cutpurses, sneakthieves and nightburglars. They were full of talk about how there was coin and silverware and jewelry and strange golden artifacts hidden all in the walls and crawlspaces of the house, or under the privy, or even buried in the ground, though it would take six kinds of fool to try to bury anything in Barcy, the land being so low and wet that anything buried in it was likely to drift away in underground currents or bob to the surface like the corpse of a drowned man.

Most of the stories, though, were darker still—tales of children being taken into the house for dark rites that required the eyes or tongues or hearts or private parts of little children, the younger the better, and black only when white wasn't available. With such vile sacrifices they conjured up the devil, or the gods of the Mexica, or African gods, or ancient hobgoblins of European myth. They sent succubi and incubi abroad in Barcy—as if it took magic to make folks in Barcy get humpty thoughts. They cursed any citizens of Barcy as interfered with anyone from that house, so those wandering children was best left alone—lessen you wanted your soup to always boil over, or a plague of flies or skeeters, or some sickness to fall upon you, or your cow to die, or your house to sink into the ground as happened from time to time.

Most folks didn't quite believe these tales, Arthur Stuart guessed, and them as did believe was too scared to do anything about it, not by themselves, not in a way that their identity might be discovered and vengeance taken. Still, it was a dangerous situation, and even though Mama Squirrel joked about some of the rumors, Arthur Stuart reckoned they didn't have any idea of how important their house was in the dark mythology of Nueva Barcelona.

It was a sure thing they never heard such talk directly. While he was still introducing himself as being the servant of a man staying at the house of Moose and Squirrel, people would be real cooperative but say nothing in his presence about that house. That was no help, so he soon started telling folks the equally true story that he was the servant of an American trader who came down the Miz-zippy last week, and then it didn't take much to get folks talking about strange things in Barcy, or dangers to avoid. And it wasn't just slave chat. White folks told all the same stories of Moose and Squirrel.

"Don't you think it's dangerous?" Arthur Stuart asked Alvin one night, as they were both in bed and going to sleep. "I mean, anything bad goes wrong, and folks are gonna blame these good people for it. Do they know what folks think of them?"

"I expect they do, but as with many warnings and ill portents, they get used to them and stop taking them serious till all of a sudden it's too late," said Alvin. "It's how cats stalk their prey, if you've noticed. They don't hide. They move up so slow and hold still so long that their prey gets used to them and thinks, well, it hasn't harmed me *so* far. And then all at once they pounce, no warning at all. Except there's been *plenty* of warning, iffen that poor bird or mouse had had the brains to just get up and move."

"So you see it my way. They gotta get out of here," said Arthur Stuart.

"Oh, sure," said Alvin. "They think so, too. The only difference of opinion is about *when* this great migration ought to occur. And how they're supposed to get some fifty children of every race out of town without nobody taking notice of just how far they've flouted the race laws. And what about money? Think they've got the passage for a riverboat north? Think they can swim Lake Pontchartrain and fetch up in some friendly plantation that'll be oh so happy to let a whole passel of free black children stay the night in their barn?"

Arthur was annoyed that Alvin made it sound like he was dumb to have wanted them to git. "I didn't say it'd be easy."

"I know," said Alvin. "I was exasperated at my own self. Because you know what I think? I think Peggy sent me here for exactly that purpose. To get them out of here. Only I didn't guess it till you thought of it."

"Three things," said Arthur Stuart.

"I'm listening."

"First. It's about time you realized what a brilliant asset I am on this trip."

"Shiny as a gallstone," said Alvin.

"Second. There's no chance this is what Peggy sent you for. Because if *that* was what she had in mind, she would've told you. And then you could have told them that she'd given warning, and they'd do whatever it took. As it is, they're just gonna fight you every step of the way, since they don't think you and me is so almighty smart that we can see how things are in Barcy better than they can."

Alvin grinned. "Hey, you're getting to be almost worth how much it costs to feed you."

"Good thing, 'cause I got no plan to eat less."

"Well, it'll still take you ten years to make up for how much I've wasted on you up to now when you wasn't worth a hair on a pig's butt."

"So this ain't what Peggy wants us to do," said Arthur Stuart, "and we can be pretty sure Papa Moose and Mama Squirrel don't want us to do it. So the way I see it, that makes it just about our number one priority."

"I'll talk to them."

"That always works."

"It's a start."

"And then you'll sing to them? 'Cause that might do more toward getting them to move out."

"So what's the third thing?" asked Alvin. "You said three things."

Arthur had to think for a second. Oh, yes. He wanted to ask Alvin why he hadn't done anything about Papa Moose's foot. But now it seemed pretty silly to ask. Because it wasn't as if Alvin hadn't noticed Moose's club foot. He'd have to be blind not to notice it. And it's not as if Alvin didn't know what he could or couldn't heal.

And besides, there was something else.

Wasn't Arthur supposed to be a prentice maker?

"Just my suggestion about singing to them," said Arthur.

Alvin grinned. "So you changed your mind about the third thing."

"For now," said Arthur Stuart. "I already used up all my brains thinking up how you ought to talk to Papa Moose and Mama Squirrel."

But there wasn't a chance to talk to Moose and Squirrel about it, because next morning five of the children were sick, screaming with pain, shaking with chills, burning up with fever. By nightfall there were six more, and the first ones had yellow eyes.

There wasn't any school now. The schoolroom became the sick ward, the benches all stacked up against the wall. None of the other children were allowed into the room. Instead they were sent outside to play among the skeeters. They could still hear the screaming out there. They could hear it in their minds even when nobody was making a sound.

Meanwhile, Papa Moose and Mama Squirrel were up and down two flights of stairs with water, poultices, salves, and teas. A couple of the herbs in the tea seemed to be a little help, and of course the water helped keep the fever down. But Alvin knew that even with the ones that had a rash, the salves and poultices did no good at all.

Of course he and Arthur Stuart helped—chasing up and down stairs with things so Papa Moose didn't have to, running errands in town, keeping food in the house, tending the fire, hauling the chamber pots to and from the sickroom. Moose and Squirrel didn't allow them to come inside, though, for fear of contagion.

That didn't stop Alvin from spending most of his concentration on the sick children. Having seen the disease at the end of its course in Dead Mary's mother, he knew what to look for, and kept repairing the damage the disease was doing, including keeping the fever down enough that it didn't harm them.

He also studied the sick children, trying to find out what caused the disease. He could see the tiny disease-fighting creatures in their blood, but he couldn't see what they were hunting down the way he could with gangrene or some other sicknesses. So he couldn't find any way to help them get rid of the cause of the disease. Still, he could see that it helped to keep the fever down and the seepage of blood under control. With Alvin tending to their bodies, the disease ran its course, but quickly, and never became dangerous.

And in the healthy children, whom he examined one by one, he found that most of them were already producing the disease-fighters, and he took such preventive action as he could.

What interested him, though, was the handful of children who did not get sick. Were they stronger? Luckier? What did they have in common?

Over the days of sickness in the house, Alvin checked on each of the ones who wasn't ill. They were of different races, and both sexes. Some were older, some younger. They did tend to be the ones who read the most—he always found them curled up in some corner of the house, always indoors with a book in their hands, now that Papa

Moose wasn't patrolling to make sure none of them could be caught reading. But how could reading keep them from getting sick? Bookish people died all the time. In fact, they tended to be more frail, more easily carried off by disease.

Meanwhile, it was Arthur Stuart who kept his eyes open outside the house. The yellow fever was beginning to spread through the town, but the early cases all showed up in the area around the fountain. It was inevitable that people began to say that the "miracle water" had brought the fever back to Barcy. Many who still had any of it threw it out. But others were just as convinced it was the only cure, which God had sent in advance, knowing that the yellow fever was coming to smite the wicked.

Arthur Stuart was glad, for the first time he could remember, that white folks around here didn't pay all that much attention to a half-black young man carrying water with his master. So far nobody had linked him or Alvin to the miracle water. But that didn't mean somebody might not remember how he sat there in the plaza, waiting for his master to come back from some Swamptown shack where Dead Mary had said her mother might have yellow fever. No, said she *did* have it. The first victim of this epidemic.

And it occurred to Arthur that however much danger the house of Moose and Squirrel might be in, Dead Mary would face much worse, and much quicker, now that the yellow fever was back.

When this thought came to him he was in the market down in the old town, choosing whatever was cheap but still edible. He debated with himself for a moment—what was more urgent, to get food back to Alvin, or go check on the girl?

What would Alvin choose?

Well, that made it easy. He always went for the dramatic over the sensible—or rather, he chose whatever would cause him the most inconvenience and danger.

Arthur had already bought a sack of yams, and not a

light one. It not only got heavier as he walked, but it made it so he couldn't run—nothing was more sure to get him stopped than to be a half-black boy running with a sack of something on his back. Everybody knew that slaves on their masters' business always moved about as slow as they could get away with, without somebody pronouncing them dead. So when a boy of color was running, it was sure to be a crime in progress.

So he walked, but quickly, and followed, as best he could find it, the path he'd seen Alvin's and Dead Mary's heartfires trace through the swamps. He knew he didn't see heartfires anywhere near as well as Alvin did, and once they got a few hundred yards off, or mixed in with a lot of other folks, it was hopeless. But Alvin's heartfire he could follow, it was so bright and strong, and not only that, when he followed Alvin he could see, like a sort of backwash, something of where he was, the terrain he was moving through. And he had traced along with Alvin and Dead Mary all the way to her mother's house. He had seen her heartfire flicker and grow strong, even if he didn't understand what Alvin had done.

Now it took a bit of splashing around and slapping at skeeters before he finally got to the plank bridge leading to Dead Mary's house. He stood this side of the plank and clapped his hands. "Hello the house!" he called. "Company!" Which was wrong, of course—he was supposed to call out, "Alvin Smith's servant here!" Or, if the world had not been so ugly, "Alvin Smith's brother-in-law!" Then again, he didn't know if Alvin had ever so much as told Dead Mary his name. Maybe names wouldn't mean a thing here.

And they didn't. Because no one was home.

Or if they were, they weren't answering.

He walked swiftly across the bridge and pushed open the door, half fearing that he might find them dead, murdered by fearful people. But he knew that couldn't be so—iffen some mob blamed Dead Mary for the plague and wanted to kill her for it, they'd have burned down the house around them.

The house was empty. Cleaned out, too—or else they didn't own a blame thing. Most likely they had realized their peril and fled. He didn't need to tell *them* how Dead Mary was regarded in this town.

He shouldered his sack of yams and retraced his route back into the city. Staying away from crowded streets and especially from the plaza with the public fountain, he made his way back to the house of Moose and Squirrel, scratching at skeeter bites the whole way.

He emptied the sack of yams into the bin in the kitchen, an action which Alvin, who was stirring the soup, greeted with a raised eyebrow. Which made Arthur Stuart feel guilty about how few of his errands he had finished.

"What?" asked Arthur Stuart. "It's not like I had a lot of money, and besides, I got worried about Dead Mary and her mother, and so I went out to check on them."

"I expect they were gone," said Alvin.

"You expect right," said Arthur Stuart.

"But that's not why I raised my eyebrow at you."

"Too lazy to wave?"

"You don't just dump out a sack of yams. They need washing. Or peeling."

"Why should I, when you can just talk the dirt right off the skins, or the skins right off the yams?"

"Because knacks weren't given to us for frivolous purposes."

"Oh, like the time you made me work half a summer making a dugout canoe when you could have made a canoe out of it in five minutes."

"It was good for you."

"It was a waste of my time," said Arthur Stuart. "And it nearly got you shot by that bear hunter."

"Old Davy Crockett? I ended up kind of liking that fellow."

"Peeling the yams wouldn't stop you from healing those kids upstairs the way you been doing."

Alvin turned slowly. "How do you know that?" said Alvin. "How do you know what it costs me to do that work?"

" 'Cause it's easy for you. You do it like breathing."

"And when you run up a hill, how easy is it to breathe?"

"Maybe I'd know what healing was like if you ever tried to teach me."

"You only just started hotting up metal."

"So I'm ready for the next step. You're working so hard on healing those children, I know you are. So tell me, show me what to do."

Alvin closed his eyes. "You don't think I wish you could?" he said. "But you can't help if you can't see what's going on inside their bodies. And Arthur Stuart, I tell you, you got to be able to see pretty small."

"How small?"

"Look at the thinnest, smallest hair on your arm," said Alvin.

Arthur Stuart looked.

"That hair is like a feather."

Arthur Stuart tried to get his rudimentary doodlebug inside that hair, to get the feel of it like he got the feel of iron. He could almost do it. He couldn't see the featherness of it, but he could sense that it wasn't smooth. That was something.

"And each strand of that feather is made of lots of tiny bits. Your whole body is made of tiny pieces, and each one of them is alive, and there's stuff going on inside those pieces. Stuff I don't understand yet. But I get a sense of how those pieces are supposed to work, and I kind of . . . you know . . ."

"I know," said Arthur Stuart. "You tell them how you want them to be."

"Or . . . sort of show them."

"I can't see that small," said Arthur Stuart.

"Bones are easier," said Alvin. "Bones are more like metal. Or wood, anyway. Broken bones, I bet you could fix those."

Immediately Arthur Stuart thought of Papa Moose's foot. Was that a problem with bones? Was Alvin maybe hinting something to him?

"But the yellow fever," said Alvin. "I barely know what I'm doing with that, and I think it's out of your reach so far."

Arthur Stuart grinned. "So what about yams? Think I could get the dirt off yams?"

"Sure. By scrubbing."

"What about taking off the skins?"

"By peeling *only,* my friend."

"Because it's good for me," said Arthur Stuart, and not happily.

"Because if you do it any other way, I'll just put the skins and dirt right back on them."

Arthur Stuart had no answer to that. He sat down and held a yam in his hand. "All right, which is it? Peel or wash? Cause I ain't doing both."

"You asking me?" said Alvin. "You know what a bad cook I am. And I don't think Squirrel wants me to toss these yams into the permanent soup. I think they'd kind of take over the flavor for the next couple of years."

"So we'll roast them," said Arthur Stuart.

"Suits me," said Alvin.

And it occurred to Arthur Stuart that Alvin hadn't grown up watching Old Peg Guester wash and peel taters and yams for twenty or thirty people at a time. All this was new to Alvin. Of course, if Arthur Stuart had his druthers, he'd rather be an expert on healing people with fevers or club feet.

"So I'll wash them," he said.

"And meanwhile," said Alvin, "I'll keep snapping beans from the back garden, while my doodlebug works on the body of the most recent person to get the fever."

"Who's that?"

"You," said Alvin.

"I'm not sick," said Arthur Stuart.

"Yes you are," said Alvin. "Your body's already fighting it."

Arthur Stuart thought about that for a minute. He even tried to see inside his own body but it was all just a confused mass of strange textures to him. "Is my body going to win?"

"Who do you think I am, Dead Mary?"

So it was on to snapping beans and scrubbing yams, while Arthur Stuart wondered what had made him sick. Somebody cursed him? He walked into a house that had fever in it a week ago? Dead Mary touched him? Yams?

Where *was* Dead Mary? Hiding in the swamp? Traveling to some safe, familiar place? Or skulking somewhere, hoping not to get killed by those who thought her knack caused the diseases that she warned about?

Or was she already dead? Her body burnt somewhere? Her mother too? Caught by superstitious fools who blamed them for something they had no part in causing?

Every terrible thing in the world was caused by a whole combination of things. But everybody wanted to narrow it down to one cause—and not even the real one. Much better to have one cause—one person to punish. Then the unbearable could be borne.

So why is it, Arthur Stuart wondered, that Alvin and Margaret and I and so many other decent people manage to bear the unbearable without having to punish anyone at all?

Though come to think of it, Alvin *did* kill the slave-catcher who killed Arthur's and Peggy's mother. In a fit of rage he slew the man—and regretted the killing ever since. Alvin hadn't flailed around at any old victim; he got the right man, for sure. But Alvin, too, had needed someone to blame for the unbearable.

What about me, then? I talk big, I have a mouth like no half-black boy ought to have, my birth being so shameful, the rape of a slave woman by her master. Haven't I had unbearable things happen? My mother died after carrying me to freedom, my adopted mother was murdered by the catchers who came to take me back to my owner. People tried to bar me from school even in the north. Being nothing but a third-rate prentice maker in the shadow of the greatest maker seen in this world in many lifetimes. So much that I've lost, including any hope of a normal life. Who'll marry me? How will I live when I'm not Alvin's shadow?

Yet I never want to lash out and punish anybody, except with words, and even then I always pretend that it's a joke so nobody gets mad.

Maybe that's how God will get out of it, when he gathers us at his judgment seat and tries to explain why he let so many awful things go on. Maybe he'll say, "Can't you take a joke?"

More likely, though, he'll just tell the truth. "I didn't do it," he'll say. "I'm just the one who has to clean up your mess." Like a servant. Nobody ever says, How can we make things easier on God? No. We just make messes and expect he'll come around later and clean it all up.

That night in bed, Arthur Stuart sent out his doodlebug. He searched for Papa Moose's heartfire and found him easily enough, sleeping lightly while Mama Squirrel kept watch over the children.

Arthur Stuart wasn't used to examining people's bodies, and he had trouble keeping his doodlebug inside the boundaries. But he began to get the knack of it, and soon found the club foot. The bone was clearly different from the other tissues—and the bones were a mess, broken into dozens of pieces. No wonder his foot was so crippled.

He might have begun to try to put the pieces back together, but it wasn't like looking at them with his eyes. He couldn't grasp the whole shape of each bone fragment. Besides, he didn't know what the bones in a normal foot were supposed to look like.

He found Papa Moose's other foot and almost groaned aloud at his own stupidity. The good foot had just as many bones as the bad one. The club foot wasn't the way it was because the bones were broken. And when Arthur went back and forth between them, comparing the bones, he realized that because Papa Moose's foot had been twisted up his whole life, none of the bones were the right shape any more to fit together like a normal foot.

So it wouldn't be a matter of just getting the bones back into place. Each one would have to be reshaped. And no doubt the muscles and ligaments and tendons would all be out of place, too, and the wrong size. And those tissues were very hard to tell apart. It was exhausting work just trying to make sense of them. He fell asleep before he understood much of anything.

⚔ 4 ⚔

La Tia

THE RUMOR MILL went on. The yellow fever only added to it—who's sick, who's dead, who fled the city to live on some friend's plantation until the plague passed.

The most important story, though, was no rumor. The army that the King had been assembling was suddenly ordered back home. Apparently the King's generals feared the yellow fever more than they feared the military might of Spain.

Which might have been a mistake. The moment the threat of invasion disappeared, the Spanish authorities in Nueva Barcelona began arresting Cavalier agents. Apparently the Spanish had been aware of the plots all along— they heard the same rumors as everyone else—and had only been biding their time before striking.

So it wasn't just the yellow fever that was decimating the English-speaking population of Nueva Barcelona. Plenty of Americans and Yankees and Englishmen were taking ship out of the city—Americans in steamboats up the river, Yankees and Englishmen in clippers and coastal traders heading out to sea, bound for New England or Jamaica or some other British destination.

Cavaliers weren't finding it any easier than the French. The Pontchartrain ferry and all the other passages out of the city were being watched, and those who carried royal passports from the Crown Colonies were forbidden to leave. Since the Cavaliers were the largest single English-speaking group, this left a lot of frightened people trapped in Nueva Barcelona as the yellow fever made its insidious way through the population.

Wealthy Spanish citizens headed for Florida. As for the French, they had nowhere to go. The borders had been closed to them from the time Napoleon first invaded Spain.

The result was a city full of fear and anger.

Alvin was shopping in the city, which was getting harder these days, with the fever making farmers more reluctant to bring in their produce. He was looking through as ratty-looking a bunch of melons as he'd ever seen when he became aware of a familiar heartfire making toward him in the crowd. He spoke before turning around. "Jim Bowie," he said.

Bowie smiled at him—a big, warm smile, which made Alvin check to see if the man's hand was on his knife. Nowhere near, but that didn't mean much, as Alvin well knew, having seen the man in action.

"Still here in Barcy," said Bowie.

"I thought you and your expedition would be long gone."

"We almost made it before they closed the ports," said Bowie. "Cuss the King for making such a mess of things."

Cuss the King? As if Bowie weren't part of an expedition committed to spreading the power of the King into Mexican lands.

"Well, the fever will pass," said Alvin. "Always does."

"We don't have to wait for that," said Bowie. "Word's just come down from the Governor-General of Nueva Barcelona. Steve Austin's expedition can go ahead. Any

Cavaliers who are with us can get passage out on a ship bound for the Mexican coast."

"I reckon that gave recruitment a big boost."

"You bet," said Bowie. "The Spanish hate the Mexica worse than they hate Cavaliers. I reckon it has something to do with the fact that King Arthur never tore the beating hearts out of ten thousand Spanish citizens to offer as a sacrifice to some heathen god."

"Well, good luck to you."

"Seeing you in the market here, I got to say, I'd feel a lot better about this expedition iffen you were along."

So you can find a chance to stab me in the back and get even for my humiliating you? "I'm no soldier," said Alvin.

"I been thinking about you," said Bowie.

Oh, I'm sure of that.

"I think an army as had you on their side would have victory in the bag."

"There's an awful lot of bloodthirsty Mexica, and only one of me. And keep in mind I'm not much of a shot."

"You know what I'm talking about. What if all the Mexica weapons went soft or flat-out disappeared, as once happened with my lucky knife?"

"I'd say that was a miracle, caused by an evil god who wanted to see slavery expanded into Mexican lands."

Bowie stood there blankly for a moment. "So that's how it is. You're an abolitionist."

"You knew that."

"Well, there's folks who are just agin slavery and then there's abolitionists. Sometimes you can offer a man a good bit of gold and he don't mind so much how many slaves another fellow owns."

"That would be someone else," said Alvin. "I don't have much use for gold. Or expeditions against the Mexica."

"They're a terrible people," said Bowie. "Bloody-handed and murderous."

"And that's supposed to make me want to go fight them?"

"A man don't shrink from a fight."

"This man does," said Alvin. "And you would too, if you had a brain."

"The Mexica won't stand up to men as knows how to shoot. On top of that, we're bound to have thousands of reds from other tribes join with us to overthrow the Mexica. They're tired of having their men sacrificed."

"But you'd restore slavery. They didn't like that either."

"No, we wouldn't enslave the *reds*."

"There's lots of black former slaves in Mexico."

"But they're slaves by nature."

Alvin turned away and picked a half-dozen melons to put in his poke.

Bowie poked him hard in the arm. "Don't you turn your back on me."

Alvin said nothing, just offered a couple of dimes to the melon seller, who shook his head.

"Come on now, this is for kids in an orphanage," said Alvin.

"I know who it's for," said the farmer, "and the price of melons today is ten cents each."

"What, it took so much more work to raise these? They plated with gold inside?"

"Take it or leave it."

Alvin pulled some more money from his pocket. "I hope you're proud of profiting from the neediness of helpless children."

"Nobody helpless in *that* house," murmured the farmer.

Alvin turned away to find Bowie standing in his way.

"I said don't turn your back on me," Bowie murmured.

"I'm facing you now," said Alvin. "And if you don't take your hand off your knife, you'll lose something dear to you—and it ain't made of steel, no matter how you brag to the ladies."

"You don't want me as your enemy," said Bowie.

"That's true," said Alvin. "I want you as a complete stranger."

"Too late for that," said Bowie. "It's friend or foe."

Alvin walked away with his poke full of melons, but as he went, he hotted up the man's knife blade. Also the buttons on the front of his pants. In a few moments, the threads around the buttons burned away and Bowie's pants came open. And when he reached for his knife, the sheath burst into flame. Behind him Alvin could hear the other shoppers laughing and hooting.

That was probably a mistake, he thought. But then, it was a mistake for Bowie to show his face near Alvin again. Why did men like that refuse to accept defeat and keep challenging someone they knew had the better of them?

Arthur Stuart woke up in the middle of the night with his bowels in a state. It felt sloshy, so it wasn't something that could be relieved by the soundless passing of gas and then pretending to be asleep if Alvin noticed. So, resigned to his fate, he got up and carried his boots downstairs and put them on by the back door and then slogged on out into the sultry night to the privy.

It was about a miserable half-hour in there, but each time he thought he was done, he'd start to get up and his bowels would slosh again and he'd be back down on the seat, groaning his way through another session. Each time of course, thinking he was through, he'd wipe himself, so by the end he felt like his backside was as raw as pounded flank steak. At least the cows are lucky enough to be dead before they get turned into raw meat, he thought.

Finally he was able to get up without hearing more sloshing or feeling more pressure, though that was no guarantee he wouldn't reach the top of the three flights of stairs and have to go clomping back down. He worried, of course, that maybe this had something to do with yellow fever, that Alvin might not have made him healthy enough, that it was coming back.

Though when he thought about it, he reckoned it probably had more to do with the street vendor who sold him a rolled pie this afternoon that might not have been cooked as much as it ought.

He flung open the privy door and stepped outside.

Someone tugged at his nightshirt. He yelped and jumped away.

"Don't be afraid!" said Dead Mary. "I'm not a ghost! I know Africans are afraid of ghosts."

"I'm afraid of people grabbing at my nightshirt when I come out of the privy in the middle of the night," said Arthur Stuart. "What are you doing here?"

"You're sick," she said.

"No joke," he agreed.

"But you will not die this time," she said.

"And just when I was beginning to wish I could."

"So many people are going to die. And so many of them blame me."

"I know," said Arthur Stuart. "I went out to warn you, but you and your ma were gone."

"I saw you go there and I thought, this boy is coming to give warning. So tonight I think, maybe you're the one who can give us some food. We're very hungry."

"Sure, come on in the house," said Arthur Stuart.

"No no," she said. "It's a strange house. Very dangerous."

Arthur Stuart made a disgusted face at her. "Yeah, so the stories they tell about *you* are lies, but the stories they tell about this house are all true, is that it?"

"The stories they tell about me are *half* true," said Dead Mary. "And if the stories about this house are half true, I won't go in, no."

"This house has no danger for you, at least not from the folks that live there," said Arthur Stuart. "And now I've been standing outside the privy this long, I'm beginning to notice how bad it stinks here. So get your ma and come on inside where the air is breathable. And make it quick or I'll be out here in the privy again and then who's going to feed you?"

Dead Mary considered for a moment, then picked up

her skirts and scampered off into the wooded darkness near the back of the property. Arthur Stuart took the opportunity to move farther away from the privy and closer to the kitchen.

A few minutes later, he had a candle lighted and Dead Mary and her mother were gobbling slightly stale bread and bland cheese and washing it down with tepid water. Didn't matter how it tasted, though. They were swallowing it down so fast they probably couldn't tell bread from cheese.

"How long has it been since you last ate?" said Arthur Stuart.

"Since we hid," said Dead Mary. "Didn't have no food in the house though, or we would have took it."

"All the time flies bite me," said her mother. "I got no blood now."

She did have a few welts from skeeter bites, now that Arthur Stuart looked at her. "How you feeling?" he asked her.

"Very hungry," she said. "But *not* sick, me. That all done. Your master, he make me well."

"He's not my master, he's my brother-in-law."

Dead Mary looked at him sideways. "So Alvin married an Africaine? Or you have married his sister?"

"I'm adopted," said Arthur Stuart.

"So you're free?"

"I'm no man's slave," said Arthur Stuart. "But it's not exactly the same as being free, not when everybody says, You're too young to do this and you're too young to do that and you're too black to go here and you're too inexperienced to go there."

"I'm not black," said Dead Mary, "but I rather be a slave than what I am."

"Being French ain't so bad," said Arthur Stuart.

"I mean one who sees who is sick."

"I know," said Arthur Stuart. "I was joking. Course, like Alvin says, if you have to tell folks you was joking, it wasn't much of a joke, was it?"

"This Alvin," said Dead Mary. "What is he?"

"My brother-in-law," said Arthur Stuart.

"Non, non," said the mother. "How he make me so better?"

Suddenly Arthur was suspicious. They come in the middle of the night and ask questions about Alvin. Perfectly good explanations for all of it—why *not* be curious about Alvin!—but it could also be somebody had set out to trap Arthur Stuart into telling more than he should.

"I expect you can ask him yourself in the morning."

"Got to be gone by morning," said Dead Mary. "Before light. People watch this house. They see us, they follow us, they kill us. Hang us for witches, like in New England."

"They haven't done that in New England in years," said Arthur Stuart.

"Your Alvin," said the mother. "Did he touch this bread?"

Alvin had, in fact, bought the baguettes. So Arthur hesitated a moment before saying, "How should I know?" He knew that the hesitation was more of an answer than his words. And without knowing why, he wanted to snatch the bread back and send them on their way.

As if she had read his desire, or perhaps because she thought her mother had been too obvious, Dead Mary said, "We go now."

"Inmediatement," echoed her mother.

"Thank you for the food," said Dead Mary.

Even as she was thanking him, her mother was putting a couple more baguettes into her apron. Arthur would have stopped her—that was supposed to be part of breakfast in the morning—but he thought of them out in the swamps for days with nothing to eat and little to drink and he held his tongue. He'd go fetch more baguettes in the morning.

He followed them out the door.

"Non," said the mother.

"You shouldn't go with us," said Dead Mary.

"I'm not," said Arthur Stuart. "I got to go sit in the privy again. So you best move fast, cause I don't want the ensuing odor to offend your delicate sensibilities."

"What?" said Dead Mary.

"I'm gonna let fly in the privy right quick, ma'am, so hightail it if you value your nose."

They hightailed it, and Arthur Stuart went back to groaning over the privy pot.

It began with a few stones thrown against the house late the next night, and a muffled shout that no one inside understood.

Next morning, a group of men marched back and forth in front of the house carrying a coffin, calling out, "Why ain't nobody sick in there!"

Since Papa Moose and Mama Squirrel were still nursing three children who had been seized by the fever despite Alvin's preventive healing, it was tempting to invite the men inside to see that their claim was a lie. But everyone knew that showing three sick children wouldn't be much of an answer, when in this neighborhood more children were dying than anywhere else in Barcy, while not one child in the house of Moose and Squirrel had been carried out in a box.

It wasn't because Alvin had confined his ministrations to the children of the orphanage. He had searched out other heartfires in other houses, and had saved many. But it took time, working one by one, and while he saved many, far more died beyond his reach, ones he had not even looked at. There were limits to what he could do.

No longer did he pretend to run errands or do chores. The baguettes Arthur Stuart had shared with Dead Mary and her mother were the last he bought; and when he slept it was because he could stay awake no longer. He dozed fitfully, waking from nightmares in which children died under his hands. And the worst nightmare of all, a vision of Dead Mary's mother filled with invisible disease, walking about giving people the yellow fever just by bumping into them or speaking to them or whispering in their ear. Tousling the head of a child, she'd move on and the child would drop dead behind her. And each dead person would turn to Alvin and say, "Why did you save her and let her walk around to kill us all?"

Then he'd wake up and search out more heartfires dimmed by disease and try to repair their ravaged bodies.

It never occurred to him not to reach first for those nearest to where he was at the moment. But the result was that deaths from the fever increased in direct relationship to one's distance from the orphanage. It was as if God had put a blessing on the place that spilled over to neighboring houses.

Or, as the marchers outside the house were broadly hinting, it was as if the devil was protecting his own.

That night there were more stones, and marchers with torches, and drunks who threw bottles that crashed. Children woke up and cried, and Papa Moose and Mama Squirrel led them into the back rooms of the house.

Still Alvin lay on his bed, reaching out with his doodlebug to heal and heal, concentrating now on children, saving all that he could.

Arthur Stuart dared not interrupt his work—or wake him, if by chance he was asleep. He knew that somehow Alvin blamed himself for the plague—he understood the grim relentlessness of Alvin's labors. This was personal; Alvin was trying to undo some terrible mistake. That much he had hinted at before he went completely silent. And now Alvin was silent, and Arthur Stuart was on his own.

Arthur had no power to heal anyone. But he had learned some makering, and thought now to use it to protect the house. It was something Squirrel said that triggered his action: "What I'm a-feared of are the torches. What if they try to burn us out?"

So he reached out to the torch-bearing men and tried to get a sense of the fire. He had worked in metal before, but little else. Wood and cloth were organic and hard to get into, hard for him to feel and know. But soon he found that what was burning was the oil the torches had been soaked in, and that was a fluid that made more sense to his half-blind groping doodlebug.

He didn't know how fire worked, so he couldn't stop the burning. But he could dissipate the fluid, turn it into gas the way he had turned metal into liquid. And when he had vaporized it, the torch would soon go out.

One by one, the torches nearest the house began to go dark.

It wasn't until Papa Moose said, "What's happening? God help us, why are the torches going out?" that Arthur Stuart realized that he might be doing something wrong.

There was fear in Papa Moose's voice. "The nearest torches are going out."

Arthur Stuart opened his eyes and looked. He had blacked out about a dozen of the torches. But now he saw that the remaining torchbearers had backed away from the house, and the street was now littered with the discarded sticks, scattered about like the bones of some long-dead creature.

"If they ever wanted proof that this house was a cursy place, this was it," said Mama Squirrel. "Whoever came near, his torch went out."

Arthur Stuart was sick at heart. He was about to confess what he had done when the crowd began to move away.

"Safe for tonight," said Papa Moose. "But they'll be back, and more of them, what with one more miracle to report."

"Arthur Stuart," said Mama Squirrel. "You don't think Alvin would be so foolish as to douse their torches like that, do you?"

"No ma'am," said Arthur Stuart.

"Let's get the children back to bed, Mama Squirrel," said Papa Moose. "They'll be glad to know the mob is gone."

Only after they left the room did Arthur Stuart see

through the window the dark shape of one man lingering in the street, not particularly watching the house, but not leaving it, either. From the way the man moved, shambling like a bear, with pent-up energy, he thought he recognized him. Someone he had met recently. Someone on the riverboat. Abe Lincoln? Coz?

Tentatively he reached out to the heartfire. Not being deft, like Alvin, he didn't know how to merely graze the man, glance at him. One moment he was seeing him as a distant spark, and the next moment he was filled with the man's self-awareness, his body-sense, what he saw and felt and heard, what he hungered for. Filled with hate he was, and rage, and shame. But no words, no names—that wasn't a thing that was easy to find. Peggy could see such things, but not Arthur Stuart, and not Alvin, so far as Arthur knew.

It was hard to pull himself back out of the fiery heart of the man, but he knew now who it was, for in the midst of all the turmoil, one thing stood out—a constant awareness of the knife at his hip, as if it were the man's best and truest hand, the tool that he relied on before all others. Jim Bowie, without doubt.

With all that malice in him, there was no doubt Jim Bowie was there for mischief. Arthur Stuart couldn't help but wonder if he still harbored his old grudge from the river. But then, why didn't he remember his fear, as well?

Maybe he needed a reminder. Arthur Stuart couldn't make the knife disappear as Alvin had, but he could do something. In moments he had the thing het up enough that Bowie was bound to feel it. Yes, there it was—Bowie whirled around and ran full-tilt away from the orphanage.

What Arthur Stuart couldn't figure out was why, as he ran, Bowie kept a tight hold on the front of his pants, as if he was afraid they'd fall down.

Alvin was asleep, not knowing where dreams left off and the living nightmare of his failure to save more lives began. But in the midst of his restless slumber he heard a voice calling to him.

"Healer man!"

It was a commanding voice, and a strange one. Whoever called him in his sleep, it was not a voice that he had heard before. But it seemed to know him, to speak out of the center of his own heartfire.

"Wake up, sleeping man!"

Alvin's eyes opened as if against his will. There was the faintest light of dawn outside the attic, visible only through the window at the end of the long room.

"Wake up, man who keeps a golden plow in the chimney!"

In a moment he was out of bed, across the long room, standing with his hand pressed against the brick. The golden plow was still there. But someone knew about it.

Or no. That must have been a dream. He had fallen asleep after healing a child four streets over. The mother had also been dying, and he meant to heal her afterward. Had he done it, before sleep took him?

He cast about wildly, then with more focus, searching. There was the child, a boy of perhaps five years. But where the mother should have been, nothing. His body had failed him. The child was alive, but an orphan now. Sick guilt stabbed at him.

"Take your gold out of the chimney, healer man, and come down to talk to me!"

This time it could not be a dream. So strong was the voice that he obeyed almost as if it had been his own idea. In a moment, though, he knew that it was not.

Yet there was no reason not to obey. Someone knew about the golden plow, and so it was not hidden anymore. Time to get it out of the chimney and carry it with him again in his poke.

It took time and most of his concentration, tired as he was, grieved and guilty as he felt, to get the bricks apart and soften the golden plow to let it fall into his hand. It quivered there, vibrant as always, alert, yet seeming to want nothing. It made his hand tremble as he pulled it through the gap in the bricks and brought it close to him. His heart warmed when the plow came near. Whether it was the plow that caused it, or the emotion of greeting a friend and traveling companion, he didn't know.

"Come down to me, healer man."

Who are you? he asked silently. But there was no answer. Whoever called him out of his own heartfire either could not hear his thoughts or did not wish to answer him.

"Come down and break bread with me."

Bread. Something about bread. It meant more than mere eating. She wanted more from him than to share a meal.

She. Whoever called him was a woman. How did he know?

With his plow in its poke, along with his few other belongings, Alvin went down the stairs. Papa Moose saw him as he passed the third floor, Mama Squirrel as he passed the second, and when he got to the bottom floor they were right behind him.

"Alvin," said Squirrel. "What are you doing?"

"Where are you going?" asked Papa Moose.

"Someone's calling me," he said. "Look after Arthur Stuart till I come back."

"Whoever's calling you," said Squirrel, "are you sure it's not a trap? Last night they came with torches. Some strange power put the torches out as they came near the house, and now you can be sure the house is watched. They'd love to lure us out."

"She's calling me as a healer," said Alvin. "To break bread with her."

Arthur Stuart appeared in the kitchen door. "It's the woman you healed in the swamp," he said. "She came two nights ago, with Dead Mary. I gave them bread, and they asked if you had bought it."

"There it is," said Squirrel. "Terrible power, what Dead Mary has."

"Knowing something may be a terrible burden to bear, but it holds no danger to them as aren't afraid of truth. And it's not Dead Mary calling me."

"What about her mother?" asked Arthur Stuart.

"I don't think so," said Alvin.

"Do you think it couldn't be no come-hither, then?" asked Squirrel. "Do you think that you're so powerful such things have no hold on you?"

"A come-hither," said Alvin. "Yes, I think that's likely."

"So you mustn't go," said Arthur Stuart. "Good people don't use such spells to draw a man. Or to make the awful sacrifices such a spell must take."

"I suspect that all it took was the burning of some bread," said Alvin. "And I go or not, as I choose."

"Isn't that how everyone feels, when they've had a come-hither set on them?" asked Papa Moose. "Don't they all think up good reasons for obeying the summons?"

"Maybe so," said Alvin, "but I'm going."

He was out the door.

Arthur Stuart dogged his heels.

"Go back inside, Arthur Stuart."

"No sir," said Arthur. "If you're going to walk into a trap, I'm going to see it, so I can tell the story to folks later, about how even the most powerful man on earth can be dumb as a brick sometimes."

"She needs me," said Alvin.

"Like the devil needs the souls of sinners," said Arthur Stuart.

"She's not commanding me," said Alvin. "She's begging."

"Don't you see, that's how a compulsion would feel to a good man? When people need you, you come, so when someone wants you to come, they make you think you're needed."

Alvin stopped and turned to face Arthur Stuart. "I left a child orphaned last night because I couldn't stay awake," he said. "If I'm so weak I can't resist my own body, what makes you think you can talk me into being strong enough to resist this spell?"

"So you know it isn't safe."

"I know that I'm going," said Alvin. "And you're not strong enough to stop me."

He strode on, out into the deserted early-morning street, as Arthur Stuart trotted at his side.

"I was the one put them torches out," said Arthur Stuart.

"No doubt," said Alvin. "It was a blame fool thing to do."

"I was a-feared they meant to burn down the house."

"They mean to, no doubt of it, but it'll take them a while to work up the courage," said Alvin. "Or to work up the fear. Either one, if it gets strong enough, will make them put the house to the torch. You probably did no more than tip them to the side of fear. Put it out of your mind."

"You have to sleep," said Arthur Stuart, "so put your own troubles out of *your* mind, too."

"Don't talk to me like you understand my sins."

"Don't talk to me like you know what I do and do not understand."

Alvin chuckled grimly. "Oh, that mouth you've got."

"You can't answer what I said, so you're going to talk about my saying it."

"I ain't talking about nothing. I told you not to come with me."

"It was Jim Bowie last night," said Arthur Stuart. "Last man who stayed behind when the mob run off."

"He invited me to join their expedition. Told me if I wasn't their friend, I was their foe."

"So he's maybe goading on the mob, to try to force you into joining?"

"A man like that thinks that fear can win loyalty."

"Plenty of masters with a lash who can testify it works."

"Don't win loyalty, just obedience, and only while the lash is in the room."

They were moving out of the city of painted buildings and into a different New Orleans, the faded houses and shacks of the persecuted French, and then beyond them into the huts of the free blacks and masterless slaves—a world of cheap and desperate whores, of men who could be hired to kill for a piece of eight, and of practitioners of dark African magics that put bits of living bodies into flames in order to command nature to break her own laws.

The black folks' way was as different from the knacks of white folks as was the greensong of the reds. Alvin could feel it around him in the heartfires, a kind of desperate courage that if worst came to worst, a person could sacrifice something to the fire and save what was most dear to him.

"Do you feel it?" he asked Arthur Stuart. "The power around you?"

"I smell the stink," said the boy. "Like folks here just spill their privy pots onto the ground."

"The soil wagons don't come here," said Alvin. "What choice they got?"

"Don't feel no power, me," said Arthur Stuart.

"And yet you're talking like the French of this place. 'Don't feel no power . . . *me?*' "

"That don't mean nothing, you know I pick up what I hear."

"You're hearing them, then. All around you."

"This be blacktown, massa," said Arthur Stuart, affecting the voice of a slave. "This be no Veel Francezz."

"French slaves run away as sure as Spanish ones, or slaves of Cavaliers."

Now black children were coming out of the houses, their mothers after them, tired women with sad eyes. And men who looked dangerous, they began to follow like a parade. Until they came to a woman sitting by a cookfire. Not a fat woman, but not a thin one, either. Voluptuous as the earth, that's what she was, but when she looked up from the fire she smiled at Alvin like the sun. How old was she? Could have been twenty from the smooth bronze skin. Could have been a hundred from the wise and twinkling eyes.

"You come to see La Tia," she said.

A smaller woman, French by the look of her, came forward from behind the fire. "This be the Queen," she said. "You bow now."

Alvin did not bow. Nothing in La Tia's face suggested that she wanted him to.

"On your knees, white man, you want to live," said the French woman sharply.

"Hush now, Michele," said La Tia. "I don't want no kneeling from this man. I want him to do us a miracle, he don't have to kneel to me. He come when I call him."

"Everybody have to come, you call them," said Michele.

"Not this one," said La Tia. "He come, but I don't make him. All I do is make him *hear* me. This one choose to come."

"What do you want?" asked Alvin.

"They gonna be burning here in Barcy," said the woman.

"You know that for sure?" asked Alvin.

"I *hear* that. Slaves listen, slaves talk. You know. Like in Camelot."

Alvin remembered the capital city of the Crown Colonies, and how rumors traveled through the slave community faster than a boy could run. But how could she know that he had been there?

"I had your skin on that bread," she said. "Most gals like me, they don't see it, so small that skin. But I see it. I got you then. While the fire burn, I got whatever you have in there. I see your treasure."

She could see more in his heartfire than Alvin could see in hers. All he could see was the health of her body, and some strong fears, but also an intense sense of purpose. But what the purpose was, he couldn't know. Once again, his knack was not as much as he needed it to be, and it stung.

"Don't you fret, mi hijo," she said. "I ain't gonna tell. And no, I don't mean that thing you got in your poke.

That ain't your treasure. That belongs to its own self. Your treasure is in a woman's womb, far away and safe."

To hear it in words like that, from a stranger, stabbed him in the heart. It brought tears to his eyes, and a weakness, almost a giddiness to his head. Without thinking, he sank to his knees. That was his treasure. All the lives he had failed to save in Barcy, they were that one life, the child who had died those years ago. And his redemption, his only hope, his—yes, his treasure—it was the new child that was so far away, and beyond his reach, in someone else's charge.

"Get up," whispered Arthur Stuart. "Don't kneel to her."

"He don't kneel to me," said La Tia. "He kneel to his love, to the saint of love. Not Lord Valentine, no, not him. The saint of a father's love, St. Joseph, the husband of the Holy Mother. To him he kneeling. That be so, no?"

Alvin shook his head. "I'm kneeling because I'm broke inside," he whispered. "And you want this broke man to do something for you, and there's nothing I can do. The world is sicker every day and I got no power to heal the world."

"You got the power *I* need," said La Tia. "Maria de los Muertos, she tell me. You make her mother whole, she."

"*You're* not sick," said Alvin.

"The whole of Barcy, *she* be sick," said La Tia. "You live in a house about to die from that sick. This blacktown, she about to die. The French people of Barcy, they be about to die. The sick of angry people, the sick of stupid people all afraid. Gotta have somebody to blame. That be you and that crazy Moose and Squirrel. That be me and all us who keep Africa alive, we. That be all them French folk like Maria de los Muertos and her mama. What they gonna do when the mob decides to blame the fever on somebody and burn it out? Where they gonna go?"

"What do you think *I* can do? I got no control over the mob."

"You know what I want, you."

"I don't."

"You maybe don't *know* you know, but you got them words burnt in your heart by your mama all them years ago, when you little, you. 'Let my people go.' "

"I'm not Pharaoh and this ain't Egypt."

"Is *too* Egypt and I reckon you ain't Pharaoh, you *Moses*."

"What do you want, a plague of cockroaches? Barcy already got that, and nobody cares."

"I want you to part the sea and let us across on dry land in the dark of night."

Alvin shook his head. "Moses did that by the power of God, which I ain't got. And he had someplace to go, a wilderness to be lost in. Where can *you* go? All these people. Too many."

"Where you send them slaves you set free from the riverboat?"

That flat out stunned Alvin. There was no way that story could be known here in the south. Was there?

Alvin turned and looked at Arthur Stuart.

"I didn't tell nobody," said Arthur. "You think I'm crazy?"

"You think I need somebody tell me?" said La Tia. "I saw it inside you, all on fire, you. Take us across the river."

"But you ain't talking about no two score slaves here, you talking about blacktown and the orphanage and— Frenchtown? You know how many that is?"

"And all the slaves as want to go," said La Tia. "In the fog of night. You make the fog come into Barcy from off the river. You let us all gather in the fog, you take us across the river. You got red friends, you take us safe to the other side."

"I can't do it. You think I can hold back the whole Mizzippy? What do you think I am?"

"I think you a man, he want to know why he alive," said La Tia. "He want to know what his power be for.

Now La Tia tell you, and you don't want to know after all!"

"I'm not Moses," said Alvin. "And you ain't the Lord."

"You want to see a burning bush?" asked La Tia.

"No!" said Alvin. She might be able to conjure up some kind of fireworks, but he didn't want to see it. "And it wouldn't work to cross the river anyway. How would we feed the people on the far bank? It's swamp there, mud and snakes and gators and skeeters, just like here. Ain't no manna in the wilderness there. My friends among the reds are far to the north. It can't be done. Least of all by me."

"Most of all by you," said La Tia.

They stood there in silence for a moment.

Arthur Stuart spoke up. "Usted es tia de quien?"

"I don't speak no Spanish, boy," said La Tia. "They call me La Tia cause them Spanish people can't say my Ibo name."

"We don't say her name neither," said the smaller woman. "She be our Queen, and she say, Let my people go, so you do it, you."

"Hush, child," said La Tia. "You don't tell a man like this what to do. He already want to do it. So we help him find his courage. We tell him, go to the dock and there he find him hope this morning. There he find a brother like Moses did, make him brave, give him trouble."

"Oh good," said Alvin. "More trouble." But he knew that he would do her bidding—go to the dock, at least, and see what her prophecy might mean.

"Tonight at first dark, there be fog," said La Tia. "You make fog, everybody know to come."

"Come where?" said Alvin. "Don't do it. We can't cross the river."

"We leave this place one way," said La Tia, "or we leave it another, we."

As they hurried away, with blacks watching them on either hand, Arthur Stuart asked, "She mean what I thought she meant?"

"They're going to leave or they're going to die trying," said Alvin. "And I can't say they're wrong. Something ugly's building up in this city. They were itching for war before this yellow fever. Steve Austin's been gathering men who like to fight. And there's no shortage of others who'll fight when they're afraid. They all mean to have some killing, and La Tia's right. There's no staying here, not for any of the people they might turn on. If I find a way to get Papa Moose and his family out of Barcy, they'll turn on the free blacks or the French."

"How about a hurricane? You done a flood to stop the slave revolt in Camelot, but I think this time you could do it with wind and rain," said Arthur Stuart.

"You don't know what you're asking," said Alvin. "A bad blow in this place, and we'd kill the very folks we ought to save."

Arthur Stuart looked around him. "Oh," he said. "I guess they're all pretty much on low ground."

"Reckon so."

White faces watched them from the windows of poor shacks in Frenchtown, too. La Tia's words had gone out already. They were all looking to Alvin to save them, and he didn't know how.

Story of my life, thought Alvin. Expectations built up all around me, but I got neither the power nor the wisdom to fulfil any of them. I can make a man's knife disappear and I can melt the chains off a bunch of slaves but it's a drop of blood in a bucket of water, you can't even find it, let alone draw it out again.

Drop of blood in a bucket of water.

He remembered how Tenskwa-Tawa made a whirlwind on a lake, put his blood into the waterspout, and saw the future in the walls of it as he and Alvin rose up in the air inside.

He remembered that it was in the visions inside that column of swirling water that he saw the Crystal City for the first time. Was it something in the distant past, or something in the future? What mattered was not that dream of what might have been. It was the process by which Tenskwa-Tawa shaped the water to the form hc wanted, and held it there, seeming to whirl at great speed, but really holding absolutely still.

Blood in the water, and a whirlwind, and walls as clear and smooth as glass.

5

Crystal Ball

LONG BEFORE HE reached the dock, Alvin began to scan the heartfires of the throngs of people ahead of him. He could not see into them the way Margaret could, knowing things about them, their past, their future. But he could see whose heartfire burned bright, and whose merely smoldered hot and dark; who was strong and who was weak, who fearful and who courageous.

There were many that he recognized, having been in town for so many weeks. He easily found Steve Austin and Jim Bowie, not together at the moment, and not really much alike. He knew Austin was a dreamer, Bowie a killer. The dreamers always seem to think their dream is worth the price that others will pay. They also delude themselves that they will control whatever evil they use to try to bring about their dream.

But soon his reflections on Austin and Bowie were stopped cold by a bright familiar heartfire that was just about the last one he expected—or wanted—to find here in Barcy.

His younger brother Calvin.

Calvin had been the closest companion of Alvin's childhood. They had been inseparable, and whatever Alvin did, Calvin had to try. Alvin, for his part, rarely succumbed to the temptation to tease his brother, but instead included him and watched over him.

What neither had counted on was Calvin's jealousy. He, too, was a seventh son of a seventh son—though Calvin was seventh only because the firstborn, Vigor, had died in crossing the river Hatrack on the very day, in the very hour that Alvin was born. So whatever gifts were conferred by that powerful position of birth, Calvin's were never as great as Alvin's.

But to have a knack that was less than Alvin's was no great disappointment, surely—most human beings suffered from the same deficiency. And Calvin's were remarkable enough.

The problem was that Calvin had never worked at his knack. He had expected to be able to do whatever Alvin did, and when he couldn't, he grew sullen and angry. Angry at Alvin, which was ridiculous and unfair, Alvin thought. And said.

Calvin didn't have much of an ear for argument or criticism. He couldn't bear it, and avoided it, and so the brothers who once had been close had spent the last few years with little contact. It didn't help that Margaret disliked Calvin. Or perhaps not that—perhaps she merely feared him, and didn't want him to be near Alvin.

And yet here Calvin was. The coincidence was too pointed. Calvin had probably been sent here. And the only person likely to do such a sending was Margaret. Had she decided that Calvin's presence was actually good for Alvin right now? More likely she through it necessary to accomplish whatever her purpose was.

As he drew nearer to the dock, Alvin felt the moment when Calvin noticed *his* heartfire. There was a quickening in his heart. The old love still burned there. Calvin might be annoying, disappointing, and sometimes even a bit frightening. He might have done some dark deeds that made his heartfire seem hooded and flickery sometimes. But he was still that young boy that Alvin delighted in through the best hours of his childhood, before he understood the dark enemy that sought his life.

Before Calvin began to be seduced by that same enemy.

So Alvin's pace quickened through the crowded streets, and he jostled people now and then, though none thought to challenge him once they saw his height and the size of his blacksmith's shoulders.

Behind him Arthur Stuart trotted to keep up. "What is it? What's happening?"

And then they emerged from the street and saw the endless row of ships and riverboats tied up along the dock, the stevedores loading and unloading, the cranes lifting and lowering, the passengers milling about—few arriving, many leaving—the vendors shouting and pushing, the thieves and whores skulking and strutting, and in the midst of them all, standing alone and gnawing on a baguette, was Calvin.

He had finally reached his adult height. Not as tall as Alvin, but lankier, so he looked more like a tall man, while Alvin looked like a big one. His hair was light in the sunshine. And his eyes twinkled when he saw Alvin approaching.

"What are you doing here, you great oaf!" cried Alvin, reaching out to embrace his brother.

Calvin laughed and hugged him back. "Came to save you from some dire peril, I gather, though your wife wasn't more specific than that."

"It's good to have you here," said Alvin. "Even if neither of us has any idea why we're here."

"Oh, I know why we're here," said Calvin. "I just don't know why Peggy sent us."

"So . . . are you going to tell *me*?"

"We're here because it's time for us to get over petty jealousies and work together to really change the world."

They hadn't been talking for a whole minute, and already Alvin was grinding his teeth a little. Petty jealousies? Calvin was the only one who had ever been jealous, and Calvin was the one who decided to leave Vigor Church and head off for wherever he'd been—France and England, Alvin knew, and Camelot, and Philadelphia once, and a lot of other places that he didn't have any idea of. Calvin was the one who decided to stop working on trying to train his knack, who had to learn everything on his own.

Apparently he'd learned it all and was ready to take his place as Alvin's equal. But Alvin had no delusion that they'd be working together. Calvin would cooperate if he felt like it, and not, if he felt like not.

And when he really bollixed it up, Alvin would step in to try to undo whatever madness Calvin had gotten into.

No, no, that's not fair. Give the kid a chance.

The man, I mean.

Or maybe that's what I mean.

"All right," said Calvin. "Maybe we *aren't* over our petty jealousies."

Alvin realized that he'd left Calvin's declaration unanswered. "What jealousies?" he said. "I was just trying to think how best to divide our labors."

"Why not think out loud?" asked Calvin. "Then maybe I'll have a chance to think of an idea, instead of just waiting for yours."

He said it with a smile, but Alvin almost laughed in reply. So much for petty jealousies being put behind them.

"Where's that French fellow you were traveling with a few years back?"

"Balzac?" said Calvin. "Back in France, writing subversive novels that make Napoleon look like an ass."

"And Napoleon permits it?"

"We don't know yet. Balzac hasn't actually published any of it."

"Is it any good?"

"You'd have to decide that for yourself," said Calvin.

"I don't read French," said Alvin.

"Too bad," said Calvin. "That's where all the interesting writing is going on right now."

Go ahead, thought Alvin. Assert your superiority. You *are* my superior when it comes to speaking French, and I don't mind. Good manners would suggest you not rub my nose in it. But then, you think I always rub my skill at makery in *your* face, so . . . fair is fair.

"Hungry?" asked Alvin.

"I ate on the boat," said Calvin. "In fact there wasn't much else to do but eat. Nothing but fog on the river."

"Didn't it stay to the western shore?"

Calvin laughed. "Every now and then I'd play around with it a little. Whip up a little extra fog using the river water. Surround the boat in fog. I suppose we looked strange to anybody on shore. A little cloud floating down the river with the sound of a steam engine coming from it."

Alvin felt the familiar contempt rise in him. Calvin persisted in using his knack for foolishness and showing off.

Not that Alvin didn't know a little bit about the impulse. But at least he tried to control it. At least Alvin was ashamed when he caught himself showing off. Calvin reveled in it. He seemed oblivious to Alvin's scorn. Or maybe it was Alvin's scorn that he wanted to provoke. Maybe he wanted a quarrel.

And maybe he'd get one. But not over this, and not right now. "Sounds fun," he said.

Calvin looked at him with amusement. "I guess you've never whipped up a little fog?"

"From time to time," said Alvin. "And cleared some away, when I found the need."

"Some noble cause, I'm sure," said Calvin. "So, what dire problem are you working on saving, and what part do you think I'll play in it?"

Alvin explained things as best he could—the yellow fever, how Alvin had been healing as many people as he could. The rumors about the orphanage. Jim Bowie's little mob. La Tia and the desire of the oppressed people of

Barcy to get out before the bloodshed began.

"So, what'll it be? Take all these boats?"

"We don't have a lot of sailors among the French and the slaves and the free blacks and the orphans," said Alvin.

"We could persuade the crews to stay with them."

"La Tia has some idea of my parting the river. Like Moses and the Red Sea. Only I guess it would be more like Joshua and the crossing of the Jordan. How the water piled up on the righthand side as the Israelites crossed over to the western shore."

"And you don't want to do that."

"Makes no sense," said Alvin. "First, that's a lot of water, and it would have to go somehow. No doubt it would end up flooding the whole city, which wouldn't exactly make things better. And when we got to the other side, what's there? Fog and swamp. And some mighty suspicious reds who won't be glad to see us. And let's not forget, several thousand people to feed."

Calvin nodded. "I ain't too surprised, Al. I mean, everybody else has a plan, but you can see how they're all fools and their plans are no damn good."

Alvin knew that if he called Calvin on trying to pick a fight, the boy would look at him with big innocent eyes and say, Whatever do you mean, Al? They *are* all fools and their plans *are* no damn good.

"They ain't fools," said Alvin. "Especially considering I didn't have no plan at all. Until I was on the way here, and I remembered something I saw Tenskwa-Tawa do."

"Oh, yeah, Lolla-Wossiky, that old one-eyed likkered-up red."

To speak of the great Prophet that way made Alvin's blood boil, but he said nothing.

"Of course I suppose he doesn't drink much *now*," said Calvin. "And didn't you fix his eye? Course, we don't know what all he's doing on the other side of the fog. Maybe they're brewing good old corn mash and getting drunk every Thursday." He laughed at his own humor.

Alvin didn't.

"Oh, you old stick-in-the-mud," said Calvin. "Everything's serious with you."

Just the people that I love, thought Alvin. But he didn't say anything more about that. "What I saw Tenskwa-Tawa do," said Alvin, "was mix his blood with water and turn it into something solid."

Calvin nodded. "I don't know about red knacks."

"They don't have knacks," said Alvin. "They sort of draw their powers from nature."

"Now, that's plain dumb," said Calvin. "We're all human, aren't we? Reds can marry whites, can't they? So what would their children have, half a knack? What would half a knack look like? And they could half draw their power from nature?"

"Here I thought you didn't know about red knacks," said Alvin, "and you turn around and insist that their knacks are just like ours."

"Well, if you're going to be quarrelsome," said Calvin, "I'm gonna be sorry I came."

That would make two of us, Alvin refrained from saying.

"So you think you can do this thing old Lolla-Wossiky did," said Calvin. "And then what? You make the river solid? Like a bridge, and the rest of the water flows under it?"

"All the other problems are still there," said Alvin. "No, I was thinking something about Lake Pontchartrain."

"Where's that?"

"Just north of the city. A huge briny lake, but it's shallow. Good for catching shrimp and crawfish, and there's a ferry across it, but it doesn't get used much, because there's nothing worth going to on the other side. Most folks either take a boat upriver or a ship downriver. But at least on the other side of Pontchartrain there's farms and food and shelter and no angry reds wondering what we're doing coming across into their land."

"But there's a whole passel of angry farmers wondering

why you're bringing three thousand people, including free blacks and runaway slaves, right through their cotton plantations," said Calvin.

Now *this* was an argument worth having, thought Alvin. Not just fight-picking, but something that actually mattered.

"Well," said Alvin, "I reckon if we had thirty runaways folks might get angry with us. But we come across with three thousand, and I reckon they might decide against fighting us and just feed us and hurry us on our way."

"They might," said Calvin. "Or they might send for the King's soldiers to come and teach you proper discipline."

"And the King's soldiers might find us in a fog somewhere," said Alvin.

"Aha," said Calvin. "I knew that fog would turn up as *your* idea."

"I thought you wanted me to include your ideas in this plan," said Alvin, grinning because it was either that or punch the boy's nose.

"As long as you remember they're mine," said Calvin.

"Cal," said Alvin, "ideas aren't like land or poems or babies or something. If you tell me an idea, and I like it, then it's my idea too, and *still* yours, *and* it also belongs to everybody else on God's green earth who thinks it's a good one."

"But I thought of it first," said Calvin.

"Well, Cal, if we're getting sticky about it, when it comes to fog, I reckon God thought of it long before you and me was born."

"And I guess you're gonna make me whip up all this fog while you get to do the glamorous stuff with the water."

"I don't know," said Alvin. "I've never covered a city in fog. And you've never mixed blood and water and turned it into glass. So if we both just do the thing we already know how . . ."

Calvin laughed and shook his head. "So you've got my part all figured out."

"Tell you what," said Alvin. "I'll do the fog *and* the water, and you can get back on the boat and go live your own life as you've been doing for the past six years."

"So you don't need me," said Calvin. "I guess Peggy was wrong again."

"There's parts of you I need, all right," said Alvin. "The part that wants to use his knack to help get a bunch of innocent or at least mostly innocent people out of Barcy before the killing starts, I need *that*. But the part of you that wants to pick fights with me and distract me from what I've got to do, that part can go stick its head up a horse's butt."

Calvin just laughed. "I bet the horse would like that even less than me."

"You're right," said Alvin. "I was forgetting that horses got rights, too."

"Ease up, old Al," said Calvin. "Don't you know when a body's teasing you?"

"I reckon I do," said Alvin. "You think you're a quick dog teasing a slow bull. But what you don't seem to realize is, sometimes the dog ain't that quick and the bull ain't that slow."

"Threatening me?" said Calvin.

"Reminding you that I don't got all the patience in the world."

"Don't even have patience enough for *me*? Your beloved little brother?"

"A man could have eight barrels full of patience for you, Cal, and you'd just have to keep goading him till you saw what happened when it turned out he needed nine."

"Sometimes I rile people, I admit it," said Calvin. "But so do you."

"I reckon I do," said Alvin, thinking of Jim Bowie.

"So you'll make a bridge over this Paunchy Train?"

"I thought you spoke French."

"Paunchy Train is supposed to be *French*?" Calvin laughed. "Oh . . . oh, now I get it. Pont Chartrain."

He said it with an exaggerated French accent so his mouth looked all pursed up like he'd just et a persimmon.

Alvin couldn't help himself. He put on his dumb American act. "Pone Shot Train? I just can't ever hold my mouth right to speak them hard French words."

It was like the best of the old times, tossing words back and forth. "That was the best French accent I ever heard from a journeyman blacksmith."

"Aw shucks, Cal," said Alvin. "I reckon you done made me want to haul my poke over to Paree."

"Iffen you wash yourself proper, I'll take you to meet Bonaparte himself," said Calvin.

"No thanks," said Alvin. "I met him once and I'm done with him."

All at once the playfulness fled from Calvin's face and Alvin could see his heartfire flare with anger. "Oh, excuse me, I forgot you already did everything long before little Calvin come along."

"Oh, don't be a . . ."

"Don't be a what? What were you going to call me, big brother?"

"I met him when I was a kid, and I didn't like him. You met him, and apparently you did. What of it? He was here in America. It was before he overthrew the monarchy. What am I supposed to do, pretend that I didn't meet him, just so you don't get provoked? Are you the only one entitled to have met famous people?"

"Oh, just shut up," said Calvin, and he stalked off in another direction.

Since Calvin was perfectly capable of finding Alvin's heartfire whenever he wanted, Alvin didn't fret about it. He just headed home, wishing that Margaret had decided that he needed a different helper. Like, say, Verily Cooper—there was a good man, and he didn't pick foolish fights. Or Measure. Alvin could have used *any* of his brothers better than Calvin.

But the truth was, Alvin had no idea whether he could sustain a good fog *and* do the thing with the water, not at the same time—not reliably. Promising as Arthur Stuart was, he was still flailing about with makery, and Alvin would be lucky if he could teach Arthur to raise steam from a teapot, let alone a full-fledged fog. So he needed Calvin. A good thick fog wouldn't be just to hide them on the other side. It would cover the whole city tonight. It would keep people from finding them till they were all across the lake and safely gone.

Margaret was right to send him, and Alvin would just have to swallow hard and not let Calvin make him mad.

Arthur Stuart's big accomplishment of the day was coming up with fifteen cloth bags that the older children could use to carry food for the journey. Papa Moose and Mama Squirrel were supervising the loading of the bags, arguing back and forth about what they'd need. Papa Moose was determined that they should carry spare clothing, while Mama Squirrel wanted nothing but food.

"They'll get hungry before they get nekkid," she said.

"But no matter how much we carry with us, we'll run out of food soon, and if we're going to have to forage or buy food anyway, we might as well carry spare clothing so the children don't have to travel in rags."

"If we can afford to buy food we can afford to buy clothes, and we'll need the food first."

"We can pick *food* off trees and glean it out of fields."

"Well, if you're talking about stealing, Papa Moose, we can take clothes off clotheslines."

"If we're lucky enough to find clothes that fit."

"There's not a child in this house who fits the same clothes for six months in a row."

And on and on it went. Meanwhile, to Arthur Stuart's amusement, they were unloading each other's bags almost as fast as they were loading their own. The children seemed to be used to seeing this sort of thing and most of the bags were in another room, where the children were carefully loading them with food they were carrying out of the kitchen. Apparently they were voting with Mama Squirrel.

"Don't like none of our clothes nohow," said one of the children to Arthur Stuart. "Druther travel nekkid."

At that moment a cry from the kitchen sent them all running to see.

Papa Moose lay on the floor, doubled up, holding his crippled foot and crying out with great groans of pain.

"What happened?" said Arthur, amid the clamor of the children.

"I don't know, I don't know," said Mama Squirrel.

Arthur Stuart knelt down by Papa Moose, moving some of the children out of the way as he did. He took the man's ankle and foot in his hands and began unwinding and unfastening the straps that bound it in place and held on the pad at the heel. Almost at once the groaning stopped—but not because the pain had eased, Arthur Stuart soon realized. Papa Moose had fainted.

No one even heard the knock at the door—if there was one. The first they knew that they had a visitor was when he spoke.

"This is what comes of having a kitchen built right onto the house."

Arthur Stuart looked up. It was Alvin's younger brother Calvin.

Calvin shook his head. "Burn himself on the stove?"

"Don't know," said Arthur Stuart.

"Hasn't Alvin taught you anything?"

Arthur Stuart seethed, but stuck to the subject. "It's something with his foot."

Calvin knelt down across from Arthur and began to examine Papa Moose. "This looks like a club foot," said Calvin.

Arthur Stuart looked up at Mama Squirrel, raising his eyebrows to say, Isn't it wonderful to have a real doctor here to tell us what we already knew.

Mama Squirrel was not, however, in the mood for sarcasm. "Who are you, sir? And get your hands off my husband's foot."

Calvin looked up at her and grinned. "I'm Calvin Maker, the brother of a certain journeyman blacksmith who's been living in your house, I think."

Now that really did make Arthur Stuart mad. Calling himself a maker, as if that was his profession, when Alvin didn't make no such claim, and him ten times the maker Calvin would ever be!

But Arthur held his tongue, since there'd be nothing gained by going to war with Calvin.

"I'm getting the lie of the bones in his foot. The muscles have grown up all wrong around the bones." Calvin palpated the foot some more, then pulled off the thick stockings.

"What are you doing?" demanded Mama Squirrel.

"I can't believe Alvin's been in this house so long and didn't do a blamed thing about your husband's foot."

"My husband gets along just fine on his foot the way it is."

"Well, he'll get along better now," said Calvin. "Got everything back in place." He stood up and offered his hand to her. "It'll take him some getting used to, but in a few weeks he'll be walking better than he ever has in his whole life."

"A few weeks?" said Mama Squirrel, ignoring his hand. "Maybe you're all proud of your miracle working, but you might have thought to ask if this was a convenient day to go fixing up his foot. We've got miles to walk tonight! And for weeks to come."

"And he was going to do that with a club foot?" said Calvin.

Arthur Stuart knew, from the slight snideness now creeping into Calvin's tone, that he was irked by Mama Squirrel's lack of gratitude.

"Some folks," said Mama Squirrel, "is so proud of their knacks that it just don't occur to them that other folks might not want them to do their public demonstrations on *them*."

"Well, then," said Calvin, "I'm pretty sure I remember

how the club foot was. I think I can put it back."

"No you can't," said Arthur Stuart.

Calvin looked at him with cool, amused hostility. "Oh?"

"Because his foot had already been changed before you got here," said Arthur Stuart. "That's what made him cry out with pain and fall down. Something moved all the bones around while the foot was still all strapped up. And that was a good five minutes ago."

"How interesting," said Calvin.

"So you see," said Arthur Stuart, "the bones the way you found them when you knelt down here, that ain't how they was."

Calvin shook his head sadly. "Arthur Stuart, does Alvin know you've been trying to heal this poor man without him even asking?"

"I've done no such thing!"

"If you knew how his foot was before, and how it was different when I got here, that says you been doodling around in there," said Calvin. "Don't deny it, you've always been a bad liar."

"How do *you* know what I've always been."

"Oh, then I suppose you're a *good* liar," said Calvin. "Not a thing I'd have expected a body to be proud of, but there you go." Calvin went to the door and looked out into the back yard. "Mind if I use your privy? It's a long time since I left the riverboat as brought me here, and I could use a pissoir."

Mama Squirrel gestured for him to go ahead. As soon as he was gone, she knelt again beside Papa Moose. "He did it, didn't he?" she said. "Before he even walked in the door."

"He likes to make grand entrances," said Arthur Stuart. "And he loves to show Alvin up, if he can."

"Daring to cause my husband so much pain. Do you think we don't know what Alvin is? Do you think we couldn't have asked him to fix that foot iffen we'd wanted it done?"

"Calvin's never going to admit he done it," said Arthur Stuart. "So you might as well work on helping him learn to walk with his foot this way. Have you got the other shoe to this pair?"

"Other shoe? Pair?" Mama Squirrel snorted. "He's never bought a *pair* of shoes in his life."

"Well, is this the only shoe he's got?"

"He has another, for Sundays."

"Let's get it on his other foot."

"They don't match."

"One shoe on and one foot bare match a good bit worse," said Arthur Stuart.

Mama Squirrel sent a couple of children to go look for Papa Moose's Sunday shoe. Then she turned back to Arthur Stuart. "I don't reckon you'd know how to wake my husband up."

"I don't mess around inside people's heads *or* feet," said Arthur Stuart. "Besides, Calvin didn't do all that good a job. It's still a mess inside his foot, even if it is shaped mostly right on the outside. I think when Papa Moose wakes up, there's gonna be a lot of pain."

"Best let him sleep then," said Mama Squirrel. "I just. I . . . ever since I knowed him, I never seen Papa Moose laid out like that. In all these things that've been happening, I never been scared till this moment."

"When Alvin gets himself back here, he'll make it OK," said Arthur Stuart.

"Oh, I hope so, I sure do," said Mama Squirrel.

"We might as well get back to loading up the pokes," said Arthur.

And in moments, the children were back to loading up with food. The extra clothing, all unloaded now, was left in a pile in the parlor. "For the poor," said Mama Squirrel.

Arthur wondered if she had some definition of the word *poor* that didn't include her and her huge hungry family.

Alvin sat on the damp bank near Dead Mary's house, his bare feet in the water, watching a gator glide by. The gator had given him a passing thought—Alvin saw it in his heartfire, that flash of hunger. But Alvin asked him to search somewhere else, and the gator obligingly moved along.

Well, to put it precisely, Alvin put the idea of the gator getting its guts ripped out into its mind, and associated it with the sight of Alvin, and the gator flat-out skedaddled.

It's a good thing to be able to scare away gators, thought Alvin. I could go into it fulltime and make a profession of it. They could call me Gator Al, and they'd always ask me how come I never wore gator-skin boots or a gator-skin belt, and I'd say, How can I get me a gator skin, iffen the gators won't come close to me?

Sounded to him like a better job than his current employment, which right now looked like having the responsibility for saving the lives of hundreds of people without a clue of how to actually do it.

He'd poked himself a couple of times with his knife to draw blood, which was a kind of embarrassing thing to do in the first place. It made him feel like he was just a couple of steps away from a Mexica sacrifice. He let the blood drip into the murky water and then felt it dissipate and vanish.

He had done this once, on the *Yazoo Queen,* but not with river water. It was with drinking water, already pure. The blood had nowhere to go, it mixed with the water immediately and Alvin had been able to shape it as he wanted. But how to make something out of an almost infinite body of water, filled with impurities?

More blood? Open a vein? An artery?

How about opening a gator's artery, how about that?

No, he knew that wouldn't do at all. The maker is the one who is part of what he makes. If there was one thing he knew, it was that.

But he'd spent his childhood getting nearly killed by water over and over again, till his Pa was plumb scared to let Alvin have a cool drink from a stream for fear he'd drown or choke.

Stop thinking, he told himself. This ain't science, like feeling head bumps or bleeding a patient. This is serious, and you gotta keep your mind open in case an idea comes along—you want there to be some room for it to fit in.

So he occupied himself with clearing the water around him. It wasn't hard—he was good with fluids and solids, at purifying them, asking whatever belonged there to stay, and whatever didn't to go. The skeeter eggs, the tiny animals, the floating silt, all the creatures large and small, and above all the salt of this briny tidewater—he bid them find somewhere else to go, and they went, till he could look down into the water and under the reflection of the trees spreading overhead he could see his bare feet and the muddy bottom.

It was an interesting thing, looking into water, seeing two levels at once—the reflection on the surface and what was underneath it.

He remembered being there in the midst of the whirlwind with Tenskwa-Tawa, and in the walls of solid water he saw not just some reflection or whatever was in the water, but also things deep in time, hidden knowledge. He was too young to make much sense of it at the time, and he wasn't sure anymore what he actually remembered or merely remembered that he remembered, if you know what I mean.

He could hear a kind of wordless song, he sat so still. It wasn't in his own mind, either. It was another song, a familiar one, the song that he had heard so many times in his life as he ran like wind through the woods. The greensong of the life around him, of the trees and moss, the birds and gators and fish and snakes, and the tiny lives and the momentary lives, all of them making a kind of deep harmony together that became a part of him so that he could hear himself as nothing more than a small part of that song.

And as he listened to the greensong and as he looked down into the water, another drop of blood fell from his hand and began to spread.

Only this time he let his doodlebug spread out with his blood, following that familiar liquid, keeping it warm, letting it bind with the water as if it was all part of the same music. There were no boundaries to contain it, but he held on to the blood, kept it as a part of himself instead of something lost, as if his heart were still pushing it through his veins.

Instead of having outside boundaries imposed on the blood, he set his own limits to its flow. This far, he told his blood, and no farther. And because it was still a part of himself, it obeyed.

At the limits the blood began to form a wall, become solid, become like a very thin sheet of glass. Then, working inward, the blood formed itself into a latticework that drew the water around it into complicated whorls that never ceased moving, but also never left their orbit around the impossibly thin strands of blood.

The water moved faster and faster, a thousand million tiny whirlwinds around the calm threads, and Alvin reached down with his hands on both sides of the sphere of solidified water and lifted it out of the clear water of Lake Pontchartrain.

It was heavy—it took all his strength to lift it, and he wished he hadn't made it so large. It was far heavier than the plowshare he carried in his poke. But it was also strangely inert. Even though he knew the motion of water inside the sphere was incessant, to his hands it felt as still as stone. And as he looked into it, he saw everything at once.

He saw his own labor to be born, straining to emerge into the world, his mother's wombwalls pressing against him as he pushed back; he heard her cries and saw her surrounded by the canvas walls of a covered wagon that rocked and slid and pitched and yawed in the current of a river gone to flood. And now he was outside that wagon and he saw a great fallen tree floating like a battering ram straight at the wagon, straight at him, this passionate angry hopeful unborn infant, and then heard a great loud cry and saw a man leap onto the tree and roll it over, over, so it struck only a glancing blow against the wagon and careened off into the rainstorm. . . .

And now he saw a young girl reach out to the face of a just-born infant who had not yet drawn breath because a caul of flesh covered his whole face like a terrible mask. She pulled the caul back and air rushed into the baby's mouth and he began to cry. The girl put the caul away as tenderly as if it were the heart of a Mexica sacrifice, and he felt how the baby and the caul remained connected, and he knew that this was Little Peggy, the child five years old when he was born, who was now his wife, with almost nothing of that ancient, dried-up caul left in her keeping, because she had rubbed bits of it between her fingers and turned each bit to dust in order to draw the power of Alvin's own knack out of it, to use it to save his life.

But now, he thought. What about now?

Whether the heavy sphere responded to his question or simply showed him the desire of his heart, he saw himself kneeling in the water at the shore of Pontchartrain, dripping blood heavily into the inland sea, and watching as a crystal path hurtled forward across the lake, six feet wide, as thin as the skiff of ice on a basin left in the window on the night of the first freeze of autumn. And in ones and twos the people began to step out onto this crystal bridge and walk along with the surface of the water holding them up, a dozen, scores, hundreds of them, a great long chain of people. But then he realized that the line was slowing down, stopping, jostling, as more and more of them looked down into the crystal at their feet and began to *see* the way Alvin was seeing now.

They would not go forward, so captured were they by the crystal visions in the water. They took too long, too many minutes, as the blood continued to flow out of him.

And then all of a sudden in the glass he saw himself faint and fall onto the bridge and at once it began to break up and crumble and all the people fell into the water and screamed and splashed and . . .

Alvin dropped the crystal sphere and it fell into the water with a splash.

He thought at first that it had dissolved instantly upon breaking the surface, but when he reached down into the water at his feet, there it was.

He picked it back up again.

I thought the things the crystal water showed me would be true, he thought. But that can't be true. Margaret wouldn't have sent me here to them if I didn't have the strength in me to make this bridge hold until the last soul had crossed over.

He looked at the ball of crystal he held in his hands. I can't leave this thing here, he thought. But I can't take it with me, either. It's too heavy, not with the plow, not with all I've got to do.

"I will carry it, me," said a soft voice behind him.

He saw her reflection in the face of the crystal, and to his surprise the round surface did not distort her image.

He wasn't seeing her *on* the crystal, he was seeing her *in* it, and all at once he knew far more about her than he had ever thought he could know about a person. "You're not French," he said. "You and your mother are Portugee. She has a knack with sharks. They took her on voyage after voyage because of it, to keep the sea monsters at bay, only one of them used her for something else and she got pregnant with you and so she threw herself from the ship and rode the back of a shark to shore and gave birth to you at the very mouth of the river."

"She never told me, her," said Dead Mary. "Might be so, might not."

Alvin rose to his feet, still standing in the water, and turned to hold the sphere out to her. "It's heavy," he said.

"I can bear any burden," she said, "if I take it freely." And it was true. Though she staggered a little from the weight, she held the ball to her and didn't let it fall.

"Don't look in it," said Alvin.

"It's in front of my face," she said. "How can I not look?" And yet she didn't look. She closed her eyes tightly. "Bad enough to know what I already know about people," she said. "I don't want to know all this else."

Alvin peeled off his shirt and draped it over the sphere. "I'll take it now," he said.

"No," said Dead Mary. "You need all the strength you have for tonight's work."

All the children were sitting on the floor in every room on the main floor. The older ones all had a poke to carry, stuffed with every scrap of food in the house. Arthur Stuart admired how they all obeyed Mama Squirrel, without all that much fussing from her or from them.

What he didn't know was what they were going to do about Papa Moose. He lay on the kitchen floor, wide awake now, but with his eyes tight shut, saying nothing, making no groan, showing no wince, but still a streak of tears ran from both eyes down into his hair and ears. Arthur Stuart longed to help him, knew that all the little bones were shaped wrong and didn't fit, pinching here and there, the ligaments and tendons sometimes too short, sometimes too long for the place they were supposed to be. What he didn't know was how to get them to change into something closer to what was right.

The kitchen door opened and Alvin stepped in. Alvin wore no shirt, and Arthur Stuart noticed how much slacker he looked than he did in the days when he actually did a blacksmith's work every day. But slack as he was, compared to Arthur's own self, Alvin was still massive, breasting the air like a great ship with full-bellied sails.

Before Arthur Stuart could wonder what he'd done with his shirt, Dead Mary came in behind him carrying something with Alvin's shirt draped over it.

Calvin hadn't bothered them a bit after causing Papa Moose all this pain. But now that Alvin was here, he appeared on the instant, striding through the front rooms of the house, calling out to his brother. "Alvin, you come in good time! You should see the mess your stepbrother-in-law done caused here, meddling in this good man's foot."

Arthur Stuart didn't bother to answer, knowing that Alvin knew Calvin too well to believe his account.

Alvin walked up and stood over Papa Moose. He closed his eyes; Arthur Stuart thought for a moment he could feel Alvin's doodlebug warm his own inside the remade foot. Looking at no one, Alvin spoke softly. "On this night of all nights I need all my strength, and now you make me spend it on something that could have waited another week or another year."

"Then wait," said Mama Squirrel hotly. "You think he ain't man enough to bear it? Oh, he can. I'll carry him if I have to, me and some of the bigger boys. My Moose, he don't want to cost us what we can't afford to pay. He'd die for these children, Alvin, you know he would."

They all knew he would.

"But I need him walking," said Alvin. "I need his strength. I'll spend some of mine on him, and later he can spend some of his on me."

Arthur Stuart tried so hard to keep up with what Alvin was doing. But it was too quick. Alvin was too skilled at this. Bones that weren't shaped right suddenly were. Tendons that wrapped themselves all wrong slid like snakes into place. In no more than a minute it was done, and Papa Moose cried out.

No, it wasn't a cry. It was a great sigh of relief, so sharp and sudden that it sounded like a shout.

"God bless you sir," said Mama Squirrel.

Papa Moose stood up and promptly fell back down the moment he tried to take a step.

"I don't know how it's done," he said. "I can't walk on these two feet. My right leg feels too long."

"Lean on me," said Mama Squirrel. He did, and managed to stand.

"Go to Frenchman's Dock," said Alvin. "You and all the children. I'll be there afore you."

"Me too?" asked Dead Mary.

"Go to your mother and arrange a wheelbarrow from among the French, to tote that thing. I got another shirt."

"Me?" asked Arthur Stuart.

"To La Tia, and tell her to get all them as is going down to Frenchman's Dock at nightfall."

When all were gone, it left only Alvin and Calvin there in the house of Moose and Squirrel, which was, after all, just a big old empty house when it didn't have all them children in it.

"I suppose I've done a dozen things wrong," said Calvin with a crooked grin.

"I need a fog from you," said Alvin. "To cover the whole city. Except right at Frenchman's Dock."

"I don't know where that is," said Calvin.

"Don't matter," said Alvin. "You make the fog everywhere else, and I'll push it away from where I don't want it to go. Just don't push back at me."

He didn't say: For once.

"I can do that," said Calvin.

"I'm glad Margaret sent you," said Alvin. "And I'm glad you came."

Arthur Stuart stood outside the kitchen door until he heard those words. He could hardly believe that Alvin acted like Calvin hadn't meddled and fussed and picked quarrels, not to mention the mess he made with Papa Moose.

There was only one meaning Arthur Stuart could get from it. Alvin didn't believe Calvin *had* caused the problem with Papa Moose. And that meant Alvin believed Calvin's lie and thought Arthur Stuart had caused the problem with Papa Moose's foot.

Burning with resentment at Calvin, at the way a real brother could instantly supplant a half-black oughta-be-a-slave step-brother-in-law in Alvin's heart, Arthur Stuart took off at a run to find La Tia and get the show on the road.

◈ 6 ◈

Exodus

CALVIN STOOD ON the levee that kept the Mizzippy from pouring over its banks to flood the city of Nueva Barcelona. A couple of hundred masts stuck up from the water like a curiously bare forest, as the seagoing vessels were towed up and down the river by steam-powered tugboats. Dozens of columns of smoke and steam joined to cast a pall over the city as the sun sank toward the horizon.

It had been a sultry, hazy day. Already everything got blurry only a mile off. The air was so wet that sweat could hardly evaporate. It ran down Calvin's neck and back and legs, and when he mopped his brow with a handkerchief, it came away dripping wet.

Nobody'd mind if he cooled things off a little.

Around him the air suddenly gave up some of its heat, sending it upward. The moment the air cooled just a couple of degrees, the water vapor began to condense a little, just enough to form a cloud, not enough to make rain or dew. It wasn't easy to maintain the temperature at just that point, and Calvin had to jostle the temperature up and down a little till he got it right.

But once the fog was nicely formed, he began to reach out farther and farther, cooling the air, condensing the invisible humidity into visible fog.

He turned a slow circle, watching as his fog spread out over the city. This was power—to change the look of the world, to blind the eyes of men and women, to block the light and heat of the sun, to allow slaves and oppressed people to sneak to freedom. Poor Alvin, always fencing his power about with rules—he never felt the sheer joy of it like Calvin did.

It was like being rich, but spending money like a poor man. That was Alvin, wasn't it? A miser, hoarding his enormous power, using it only when he was forced to, and for trivial purposes, and according to rules that were devised to allow weaker men to control strong ones. I have no use for such rules, thought Calvin. I don't choose to wear chains, still less to forge my own.

So I'll help you, Alvin, because I can and because I love you and because I don't mind being part of your noble causes when it suits me. But I make up my own mind on all things. Collect your disciples and try to teach them some clumsy imitation of makery, like that sad boy Arthur Stuart, whose true knack you stole from him. But don't ever count *me* as one of your disciples. I spent too many years of my life worshiping you and tagging along behind you and begging for your attention and your love and your respect. Those were my childhood days. I'm a man now, and I've held my own with a great emperor and I've slain an evil man that you hadn't the courage to kill, Alvin.

It's not enough to have power, Alvin. You have to have the will to use it.

Street after street, the fog crept through the city, dimming the light of the setting sun and hiding passersby.

Slaves felt the cool clammy fog pass around them, or looked out windows and watched as buildings across the street disappeared, and they thought, Today we cross over Jordan to the promised land.

In Frenchtown the children and grandchildren of the founders of this place, whose city had been stolen from them, looked out of their shanties and thought, You can't keep us here no more, Conquistadores. You can take our city, but that's only land. You can't hold onto us when we've a mind to go.

In Swamptown, the poorest of the poor—free blacks and down-and-out whites—saw the fog and gathered up their few possessions for the journey ahead. La Tia, Dead Mary, some sorcerer from up north, they didn't care whom they were following. It couldn't help but be better than here.

But in the rest of the city, in fine houses and the humbler homes of the working class, in hotels and whorehouses and along the dock, where people already cowered in fear of the yellow fever, afraid to go out into the streets—they saw the fog roll through and it looked like a biblical plague to them. I'm not going out in that weather, they thought. I'll send a slave out on my errands. I'll leave the streets to the poor and those whose business is so pressing they'd risk death to carry on with it.

Only in the taverns, where drink brought a few hours of courage and uncontained passion, did the fear burn into hatred. Someone brought this yellow fever on us. It was them French witches, that Dead Mary and her mother, didn't Dead Mary claim the plague for her mother first?

It was those wicked race-mixing abolitionists Moose and Squirrel, they're the ones brought this down on us, cursing the city because they hate us for keeping black folk in the place where God meant them to be. You want proof? All around that house folks is dying of the fever, but not a soul in that crowded house is sick, not a body has been brought out.

"Not Moose and Squirrel, no sir," said a powerful-looking man who carried a knife at his hip the way other men might carry a pistol. "Their house, but it's a traveling man staying there, him and his half-black catamite he uses like a witch does a cat. His name is Alvin and he has a sack full of gold he stole from the smith he was prenticed to. I tell you he brought this fever here. He and his catamite was seen at the public fountain where that magical water was drawn."

They listened spellbound to the man. They itched for action, these men. They had come to Barcy to take part in a war, but the dread of fever had sent the King's army back into their holes, and here they were with nothing to do. Their fingers flexed into fists. The drink burned in them. They could do with a good hanging. Take a man and his slave boy and drag them to a tree or lamppost and hoist them up and watch them clutch and twitch and pee themselves while they strangled on the end of a rope. That was a good use of this foggy night. There'd be no witnesses, and maybe it would stop the fever, and even if it didn't, a hanging was still a good idea now and then, just to get your blood up, and none of this nonsense about an innocent man. Wasn't nobody in this world hadn't earned hanging five times over, if their hearts were only known.

Out of the tavern and into the street they staggered and lurched, shouting threats and brags. A few carried torches against the fog and night as darkness fell over the city, and as they moved near the waterfront, they were joined by the drunk, the angry, the fearful, and the merely curious from other taverns. Where are you going? Off to hang us a traveling wizard and his boy.

The slaves skulking through the streets dodged into alleys or into the shadows of doorways as the mob passed. But they weren't looking to hang the first black man they found. They had a specific man in mind tonight, thanks to that man with the big knife at his belt. They'd find him at the house of Moose and Squirrel—who probably needed hanging too, there being no shortage of rope in Barcy.

*　　*　　*

Arthur Stuart saw at once that the name "Frenchman's Dock" was meant as a cruel irony. Compared to the miles-long dock along the Mizzippy, this shabby jetty on Lake Pontchartrain was pathetic. Several dozen shrimpboats were tied up to it, and more were coming in, the shrimpers shouting and answering to help each other find their way in the fog. All of them spoke in French, a language in which Arthur was becoming quite fluent, though he suspected the French he was learning here in Nouveau Orleans was not quite the same French that Calvin would have heard in Paris.

There was no room on that busy wharf for fifty children, so Moose and Squirrel kept their family loitering back around the fish houses, trying to stay out of the way. Many of the shrimpers had already heard what was happening tonight. Either they'd come along or not, but there was no debating or discussing it. Everyone stepped around the children and made no comment about their presence there. Even if they wouldn't follow Dead Mary out of the city, they wouldn't dare stand in her way, either.

Blacks began arriving, too, staying even farther out of the way. Like the children, they carried bags and sacks, but it was a sad thing to see how little they had, considering that most of them were carrying all they owned in the world. The blacks who did get in some shrimper's path were met with a growl or a bark to get out of the way; it was clear that even among the oppressed French, blacks had a lower status still.

Flies hovered and swarmed everywhere, there being plenty to feast on for them amid the shrimp offal discarded all along the shore. Skeeters, too, and Arthur Stuart could imagine that with all the people gathering here those little bloodsuckers would probably drink their fill till they bloated up and exploded. He could imagine the sound of it, like distant gunfire, the pop pop pop of busted skeeters.

Only he didn't want them sucking blood out of these children.

He tried to get his doodlebug inside a skeeter, but it

wouldn't hold still. And besides, he wasn't looking to perform surgery on it, he wanted to talk to it the way Alvin would, telling it to go away. But he couldn't find the heartfire. It was just too small and faint. Even the heartfires of the big fat lazy flies were almost invisible to him. All the same, he tried talking to the skeeters inside his own mind. "Go away," he said silently. "Nothing to eat here." But if they heard him, they didn't pay him no mind.

A couple of boats ran into each other in the fog, and there was much shouting and cursing. It was silly, Arthur Stuart thought, to put up with fog here, where it wasn't needed. And fog was more like metal or water, he could get inside it and work with it. Arthur Stuart stirred up a little air, drawing a little breeze in from the lake, blowing the fog back toward the city where it was needed.

Arthur was pleased that it didn't take long for the air to clear. The sunset now blazed red in the west, while the fog hung thickly only a street or two back from the water. The shrimpers quickly got their boats tied up and their catch loaded off and dragged into the fish houses. Then thcy disappeared into the streets, some of them with shrimp carts to sell the catch, the others probably heading for their families, to bring them to Frenchman's Dock for the escape.

There being no more need for clear vision now, Arthur Stuart let the breeze die down, and the fog drifted back out over the water a little. Stillness came with it, a heavy silence in which footfalls were muffled and voices became whispers.

As it became fully dark, Arthur began to worry about folk losing their way, or somebody stumbling into the water, so he woke up the breeze again to clear the air near the shore. In the distance, he could hear shouting, and after a while, he realized that it was probably the noise of a mob moving through the streets of Barcy. He worried about folks who was trying to make their way through the streets, but the fog was the best help they could get, and there wasn't nothing Arthur Stuart could think of to add to it.

As the fog cleared and the faint light of the stars and a sliver of moon illuminated the shore, Arthur Stuart realized that the man sitting crosslegged in the shallow water was Alvin.

At once Arthur strode forward, but said nothing, because Alvin seemed to be concentrating. Arthur came up beside him and saw that Alvin held a knife in his hand, with the tip of the blade under the water. He was slicing into the soft skin on the side of his left heel, under the place where the leg bone joined on.

Blood began to flow out in a slow trickle into the water.

Almost by habit now, Arthur Stuart tracked the blood in the water, feeling its dissipation. But then it stopped dissolving, and instead began to form a rigid structure, gathering water around a delicate latticework, thickening and hardening the water into something not at all like ice, and very much like thin, delicate glass.

The area of hardened water extended to about six feet on either side of Alvin, then narrowed gradually as it extended out over the lake. When it narrowed to about as wide as Alvin's arms could reach on both sides, it stopped narrowing and went on and on, straight north. Arthur could sense it moving forward. But he could also see that it was all connected to Alvin's living blood, still flowing out into the water and thrusting the lacy inner structure of this crystal road farther and farther out. The bridge was growing from the base, not the tip.

"Can you see it, Arthur Stuart?" whispered Alvin.

"Yes."

"And on the other end, do you think you can anchor it there and hold it firm?"

"I can try."

"It's taking more blood than I hoped," said Alvin, "but less than I feared. I'm not sure I'll know when it's long enough. I have to concentrate on what I'm doing here. So I need you to lead the way across, because you can see it. And when you get to the end, anchor it and stop it from growing. I'll feel it at this end. I'll know that you're doing it, and I'll know when it's done."

"Now?" said Arthur Stuart.

"If we're going to get all these people to walk across in one night, I think now's a good time to start."

Arthur Stuart turned around and beckoned to Moose and Squirrel. They didn't see him. So he called out, but not loudly. "Papa Moose! Mama Squirrel! Can you bring the children?"

With Papa Moose leaning on Mama Squirrel and one of the older boys, they came down to the water's edge. When they arrived, Arthur Stuart stepped out onto the crystal.

To the others it seemed that he stood on water. They gasped, and one of the children began to cry.

"Come closer," said Arthur Stuart. "See? It's smooth where it's safe to walk. It's not water any more. It's crystal, and you can walk on it. But stay to the middle. Hold hands, stay together. If someone falls in, pull him back up. It's strong enough to hold you, see?"

Arthur looked straight down into the crystal as he stomped his foot a couple of times.

What he saw there made him freeze.

It was his mother, flying, a newborn baby strapped in front of her. Flying over the trees, heading north, to freedom.

And suddenly she could fly no farther. Exhausted, she tumbled to the earth and lay there weeping. She would kill the baby now, Arthur Stuart realized. Rather than let it be taken back into slavery, she'd kill the baby and herself.

"No," he murmured.

"Arthur Stuart," said Alvin sharply. "Don't look down into the crystal."

Arthur tore himself away and was surprised to find Moose and Squirrel and their family all watching him, wide-eyed.

"Nobody look down into the bridge," said Arthur Stuart. "You'll think you're seeing things, but they're not really there. It's not a thing to look at, it's a thing to walk on."

"I can't see the edges," said Mama Squirrel. "The children can't swim."

"They won't have to," said Arthur Stuart. "Let's get the little ones in between the older ones. Everybody hold hands."

"The youngest can't walk so far," said Papa Moose.

Someone pushed her way through the family to the water's edge. La Tia. "Don't you fret about that. Got plenty of strong arms here to carry them as can't walk." She called out several names, and strong young men and women stepped forward, most of them black, but some French or of other European nations. "It's all right, babies," La Tia said to the children. "You let these big folk carry you, you be all right. You tell them be happy," she said to Mama Squirrel.

"It's all right," said Squirrel. "These are our friends now, they're going to take us out across this bridge Alvin's done made for us."

Some of the children whimpered and a few cried outright, but they hung on all the same, doing their best to obey despite their fear. Arthur Stuart walked farther out onto the bridge, taking care to stay right in the middle. The worst thing he could do would be to stumble off the edge. They'd all be terrified then. "Come to me," he said. "We have to move quick, once we get started."

"I stay right here," said La Tia, "I keep it all moving, I make everybody help each other. You go, you. We follow."

Arthur turned around and walked a good twenty paces out onto the bridge. Then he stopped and turned around. Several of the older children were following him tentatively. He strode back to them and took the leading child by the hand. "All hold hands," he said. "Stay right in line. It's a long walk, but you can do it."

"Listen to the music," said Alvin. "Listen to the music of the water and the sky, all the life around you. The greensong will carry you forward."

Arthur Stuart knew the greensong well, though he could never find it on his own. As soon as Alvin spoke of it, though, he became aware of it, as if it had always been there, and he'd just not bothered to notice it before. He stepped on out, holding the hand of the child behind him, and set a pace that he thought everyone would be able to keep to.

In the darkness, he couldn't see the bridge stretching out before him—his eyes told him only that he was walking out into the middle of a trackless lake. But his doodlebug felt the bridge as clear as day, reaching on and on, out and out, and he walked with confidence.

At first he couldn't stop his mind from fretting about all that could go wrong. Somebody falling off. Losing the way somehow. Getting to the end of the bridge and finding that it didn't quite reach the other shore. Or having the bridge get softer and wetter the farther it got from Alvin. Or the bridge bending in on itself, making a spiral that led nowhere. All kinds of imaginable disasters.

But the rhythm of the step, step, step and the sound of the lapping water and the calls of birds began to still that relentless fretting. It was the familiar rhythm of the greensong. He let it come over him like a trance. His legs began to move, it seemed, of themselves, so he no longer thought about walking or even moving, he simply flowed forward as if he were a part of the bridge, as if he himself were a breeze on the night air. The bridge was alive under him. The bridge was part of Alvin, he understood now. It was as if Alvin's hands bore him up, as if the water and wind drew him along.

He only sometimes noticed that he himself was singing. Not just humming, but singing aloud, a strange song that he had always known but had never noticed before. The child behind him picked up the melody and murmured it along with him, and the child behind her, until Arthur

Stuart could hear that many voices carried the song. No one was crying or whimpering now. He could hear adult voices farther back. But all of them were faint, only threads amid the fabric of the great wide song that Arthur heard from the wind and the waves and the fish under the water and the birds in the sky and from animals waiting for them on the other side and from all the people on the bridge, a half mile of them, a mile of them.

Faster and faster Arthur Stuart walked without realizing he was speeding up, but the children did not complain. Their legs carried them as fast as they needed to go. And the adults carrying children found that the little ones did not grow heavy. The babies fell asleep clinging to their bearers, their breath whispering in rhythm with the song. On and on they strode, the far shore coming no nearer, it seemed.

And as they were all caught up in the greensong, it seemed that the bridge turned into light. They could all see the edges of it now, and could feel how the greensong throbbed within it. Each footfall on the crystal bridge caused the song to surge a little stronger for a moment and made the bridge glow a little more clearly in the night. And Arthur Stuart realized that they were becoming part of the bridge, their steps strengthening it, thickening it, making it stronger for those coming after. And since the bridge was part of Alvin himself, they also strengthened him, or at least made it so the creation of the bridge drained him less than it might have.

Arthur could feel Alvin's heartbeat in the crystal bridge. And he realized that the light they all saw rising from the crystal was a pale reflection of Alvin's own heartfire.

It seemed to be forever, that crossing. And then, suddenly, there was land ahead of him, and it felt as if it had taken no time at all.

He reached forward with his doodlebug and saw that the bridge did not reach the land yet. So, without slowing down his stride, Arthur Stuart sent his doodlebug leaping beyond the end of the bridge to find where the rim of the water lapped the mud and he said to the bridge—to Alvin: Here it is. Here's the edge. Come to this spot and no farther.

The bridge leapt forward. It was what Alvin had been waiting for, for Arthur's doodlebug to show the way, and in moments the bridge was anchored into the land.

Arthur Stuart did not speed up, though he wanted to run the last few hundred yards. There were people behind him, hands linked. So he kept the same pace, right to the end, and then drew the child behind him up onto the shore.

He continued to lead her into the trees, talking to her as he went. "We'll go up into the trees," he said to her. "The others will follow. Keep moving, move in and off to the right, so there's room for everyone else. Keep holding hands, all of you!"

Then he let go of her.

As he did, the greensong let go of *him*.

He staggered, almost fell.

He stood there gasping for a moment in the unwelcome silence.

The line of people on the bridge stretched out for miles, he could see, and all of them moving swiftly, faster than he would have thought possible. Even Papa Moose now strode easily, boldly, no one helping him.

He saw how Moose and Squirrel, too, stumbled when they let go of the line. But they immediately took charge of the children, not forgetting their responsibility.

Nor will I forget mine, thought Arthur Stuart. He scanned the nearby area for the heartfires of small creatures. Unlike the skeeters, he easily found the snakes and, not so easily, awoke them and sent them slithering away. Danger here, he told them silently. Go away, be safe. Sluggishly they obeyed him. It exhilarated him. He suspected that some part of Alvin's power still rested on him, enabling him to do more than he had ever found possible before. Or perhaps traveling on Alvin's bridge, surrounded by the greensong, had woken senses inside Arthur Stuart that had always slept.

Will we all be makers, having crossed this bridge?

Here and there he caused water to drain away from a bog, so that the land where the people would have to stand was all firm. And from time to time he reached back out across the water, following the bridge with his doodlebug, trying to see how Alvin was doing. The bridge remained strong, and that meant Alvin's heartfire blazed brightly. But his body was too far away for Arthur Stuart to find him, so he could not tell whether he was becoming weak. Nor could he find the far shore to count the people there, so he could not even guess how many more would come.

It was his job to make sure there was room for them all, enough firm, safe ground that they could gather.

Many of them sat down, then lay down, and with the echoes of the greensong still singing in their hearts, they dozed in the faint moonlight, their dreams infused with the music of life.

Calvin couldn't help being curious. And it's not as if he had to stay on the levee to keep the fog in place.

In fact, the fog could pretty much look after itself, at this point. And with all the angry, frightened heartfires flowing through the streets of Barcy, Calvin couldn't see any particular reason to stay by himself. Who knew what mischief these mobs might be up to? And since he was a maker, wasn't it his job to keep such mischief from happening?

One mob was moving through Frenchtown, getting more and more furious as they found house after house empty. Another mob, consisting mostly of dockside drunks, was looking for slaves to throw into the water. Finding none, they started throwing in whatever passersby spoke English with a foreign accent or not at all. Which wasn't too logical, seeing how this wasn't even an American city.

All Calvin could see of this was the anger in the heart-fires and, of course, the panic in those being tossed into the river.

The angriest mob, and the one moving with the most sense of purpose, was moving directly toward the orphanage where Alvin had been unable to resist showing off by one-upping Calvin's fixing of the man's foot. What was the big deal, Calvin wanted to know. When was he supposed to have learned anatomy? Of course, Alvin knew everything—everything except how the world actually worked.

So let him sit there by that briny lake and flow his heartfire out as a bridge for the scum of the earth to walk on. Wasn't that just like Alvin? Making a show of being humble and the servant of all. But since Jesus said that the person who wanted most to be ruler was the one who was servant of all, didn't that tell something about Alvin, after all? Who was the ambitious one? Calvin was perfectly willing to stay in the background—which was the attitude a maker ought to have, as Alvin always said. But with Alvin it was do as I say, not as I do.

Calvin jogged easily along the foggy streets—sober, decent folk were all indoors, fearful of the sudden fog and the sound of distant shouting. There were soldiers marching, too. The Spanish were ostensibly looking for a riot to quell, but the officers carefully found the quietest streets, since there was neither honor nor safety in confronting a mob. If you shoot, it's a massacre; if you don't shoot, you're likely to get a brick in the head.

So it wasn't hard to avoid the soldiers, and soon Calvin found himself on the fringes of the mob just when it reached the house of Moose and Squirrel. He wasn't that interested in most of the people—a mob was a mob, and all the faces were as ugly and stupid as always when people turn their decision-making over to someone else. Brutal puppets, that's all they were. What Calvin wanted was the hot, dark heartfire that was leading them and goading them on.

Glass was shattering as bricks and stones went through the windows of the house. Several men with torches were trying to set the house on fire, but the air was so moist and heavy that it wasn't working.

The leader, who carried a big heavy knife at his hip, was taunting the would-be firestarters. "Y'all never set a fire before? Babies burn theirselves up all the time, but you can't even get a dry wooden house to burn!"

Calvin sidled up. "Reckon sometimes you gotta do a thing yourself."

The man turned to him and sneered. "And have the Spanish find some informant to testify against me? No thanks."

"I didn't mean you," said Calvin. He reached out and pointed toward the roof. While he was pointing, he hotted up the wood just under the peak of the gable, so sudden and hot that it burst into flames.

A cheer went up from the crowd, everyone being too drunk, apparently, to notice that the fire had started about as far as possible from where the torchwielders were doing such a pathetic job. But the mob's leader wasn't drunk, and that's the only person Calvin was looking to impress.

"You know something?" said the man with the big knife. "I think you look a powerful lot like a certain thief and fraud name of Alvin Smith as was living in that boardinghouse only this morning."

"You're speaking of my beloved brother, sir," said Calvin. "Nobody gets to call him names but me."

"Beg your pardon, sir," said the man. "I'm Jim Bowie, at your service. And if I'm not wrong, you just proved to me that Alvin ain't the only dangerous man in his family."

"Don't get no ideas about siccing this mob on me," said Calvin. "My brother plain hates to kill folks, but I got no such compunction. You turn the mob on me, and they'll all blow to bits as if they'd swallowed a keg of gunpowder. You first."

"What's to stop me from killing you right here?" said

the man. And then, suddenly, he got a panicked look on his face. "No, I was just joking, don't do nothing to my knife."

Calvin laughed in his face. "Want to see the house go up real spectacular?"

"You're the artist," said the man.

Calvin found his way into the structure of the house, the thick heavy beams and posts that formed its skeleton. He hotted them up all at once—and so hot did he make them that they didn't so much burn as melt. The outer layer of each piece of wood burnt so fast that as the ashes peeled away it looked as if somebody had just flumped a busted pillow on the ground and released a hundred thousand feathers all at once.

The house collapsed, sending up such a cloud of smoke and ash and hot, searing air that it burned the hair and eyebrows and eyelashes right off the men in the front row. Their skin was also burned, and some were blinded, but Calvin didn't feel any particular pity. They deserved it, didn't they? They were a murderous, house-burning mob, weren't they? The ones who was blind now, they'd never join a mob again, so Calvin had flat cured them of their violence.

"You look to be a useful man to have as a friend," said the man with the knife.

"How would you know?" said Calvin. "You haven't seen me with any of my friends."

The man stuck out his hand. "Jim Bowie, sir, and *I'd* like to be your friend."

"Sir, I don't reckon you have many friends in this world, and neither do I. So let's not pretend to love each other. You have something you want to use me for, and I'm perfectly willing to consider being used if you can let me see what's to gain from it, and why it's a good and noble undertaking."

"They ain't no good and noble undertakings. Everybody I know of gets undertaken has to be dead first and doesn't seem to enjoy it."

Bowie was grinning.

"What do you want from me, Mr. Bowie?"

"Your company," said Bowie. "On an expedition. A job your brother turned down on account of I think he was scared."

"Al ain't afraid of anything," said Calvin.

"Anybody isn't scared of the Mexica might as well shoot out his own brains, cause they ain't worth keeping."

"The Mexica?"

"Some of us think it's time civilization came back to Mexico."

Civilization . . . like this? Calvin watched the remaining mobbers cavorting and gamboling in front of the hot glowing embers and laughed.

"A mob's a mob," said Bowie. "But the Mexica are evil and need destroying."

"No doubt they do," said Calvin. "But why is it *your* job?"

"I got tired of waiting on God."

Calvin grinned at him. "Maybe we got something to talk about. I never been to Mexico."

Alvin felt someone nudge him, shake his shoulder.

"Sun coming," said a woman's voice.

La Tia, that's who it was.

"Everybody already pass over," said another woman. Dead Mary's mother.

"What's your name?" Alvin murmured. "I don't know your name."

"Rien," she said.

Dead Mary reached out and took his bleeding hands in hers. "Get up, you wizard you. Get up and cross over the bridge of your blood."

He tried to rise, with her helping, but at once he felt faint and his legs gave way under him. He fell face forward onto his hands and even his elbows buckled, and his face struck the surface of the crystal bridge. The heavy weight of the plow made the poke slide off his shoulder. It made the whole bridge shimmer with life, and Alvin felt himself suffused with warmth. With peace. It was all done. He could sleep now.

At once the bridge began to give way under him.

"No!" cried La Tia. "Hold up that bridge! You can't sleep now!" She reached down and lifted the poke from the surface of the bridge. At once the shimmering stopped, and Alvin could concentrate again. No, it wasn't time to rest, was it?

"The army coming, boy!" La Tia said. "They know they slaves gone now, morning coming and nobody doing they chores. This ain't no drunken mob today, no. This be soldiers, and we got to cross over!"

It wasn't just her words filling him with strength, though. He could feel the power of charms she bore. He always saw the small magics of spells and hexes and could stop them if he wanted, so he had gotten used to the idea that they had no effect on him.

But now he was grateful for the strength that flowed into him as she draped a charm around his neck.

"I have to stay here," he said softly, "or the bridge won't hold."

"You had to stay here to make the bridge," said La Tia. "But don't you feel your brother put in his blood from the other side?"

Alvin cast his awareness through the whole length of the bridge and now realized that his own heartfire was not alone in it. His was the overwhelming light within the crystal, but there was another heartfire there, too, and not a weak one, either. Arthur Stuart had taken hold of the bridge and had put his own blood into the water to join him.

La Tia and Dead Mary's mother—Rien, was it?—supported him on either side, while Dead Mary pushed her wheelbarrow out onto the bridge to lead the way. Already the last of the people was out of sight in the fog. But the fog was thinning, and the first rays of dawn were lighting the eastern sky. Arthur Stuart might still be on the job, but Calvin wasn't.

Behind them Michele, La Tia's friend and doorkeeper, was laying down charms on the bridge. They did not cause the shimmer that the plow had brought. Rather they felt like salt dropped on ice.

"That burns," said Alvin. "I can't have that."

"Got to keep them enemies back," said La Tia. "They my fear and fire charms she laying down."

"This bridge was made to welcome people. The crystal is meant to open their eyes. You can't put darkness and fear onto it and hope to have it stay."

"You know what you know," said La Tia. "You do a thing I never see, so while I stand on your blood, I do what you say." She called back over her shoulder. "Michele, you pick up all this stuff, you, you make it a ring on the shore, hold them back a little!"

Michele ran back to land and laid the charms in a great semicircle to keep the soldiers at bay as long as possible.

"To them it be like a fire," said La Tia. "Hate and fear, they make it into a fire."

Blood still dripped from Alvin's hands as he walked. Dead Mary set down the barrow and tried to take one hand and bind it up to stop the bleeding, but Alvin pulled away. "Got to keep my blood going into the bridge," he said. "Arthur can't hold it up alone."

"So this thing you make, it don't stay made?" said Dead Mary.

"First time I done it," said Alvin, "and I don't think I done it right. But maybe it can never stay. Maybe you can't build nothing out of this that lasts."

"Stop making him talk," said Rien. "You keep pushing, Marie, you keep showing us the way."

"I know the way," said Alvin.

"But what happen to us when you faint, yes? What?"

Alvin had no answer, and Dead Mary continued to push her barrow on ahead.

They weren't all that far when they heard Michele run

up from behind. "Soldiers come, and a lot of other men, very angry. The fire hold them back for now, but they got their own peeps and slinks and they get through soon. We got to run."

"I can't," said Alvin.

But even as he said it, he heard the greensong that had helped the others cross so quickly, and now that he wasn't concentrating on holding the bridge alone, he could let it into him, let it strengthen and heal him a little. He hushed them. "Hear that?" he said. "Can you hear?"

And after a while, yes, they could. They stopped talking then, and Alvin stopped leaning on them, and soon he and the four women were walking swiftly, faster than they thought they could, with longer strides than any of these women had ever taken. Long before they reached the other side of Pontchartrain they overtook the last of the people, and when Alvin got there, the song grew stronger in their hearts as well, and they stopped straggling and picked up their pace.

It was good that they did, because Alvin felt it like a blow when the first of the soldiers charged onto the bridge. It was his heartfire they were treading on, and where the people's feet had been light, the soldiers' boots were heavy, and as they ran along the narrow bridge Alvin heard them fighting the greensong like the cacophony of two marching bands playing wildly different tunes.

It weakened him and slowed him down, just a little at first, but more and more as they drew nearer. Hundreds of them, carrying muskets. At the far end of the bridge, someone was trying to get a horse out onto the crystal—a horse pulling a light piece of field artillery.

"I can't hold that up," gasped Alvin.

"Almost there," called Dead Mary. "I can see the shore!" She started to run.

But there was no fog on this side of Pontchartrain, so seeing the campfires on the far shore did not mean they were truly almost there. Alvin slowed, staggered. Again he had to lean on the women until they were almost dragging him along. Again he felt alone, abandoned by—or perhaps merely oblivious to—the greensong. But with each weakening of his own strength under the burden of the approaching army, he could feel another strength move in under his blood in the skeleton of the bridge. Arthur Stuart was already reaching far beyond his strength, but Alvin had no choice but to rely on his strength until all were safe.

Just when it seemed that the bridge was lengthening infinitely before them, they closed the last hundred, the last fifty, the last dozen steps and staggered onto the shore. Dead Mary had set down her barrow on the bank and now hovered around, eager to help.

There lay Arthur Stuart, prostrate in the sand, Papa Moose and Mama Squirrel kneeling beside him, their hands on him, Papa Moose praying, Mama Squirrel singing the first words Alvin had ever heard anyone put to the greensong, words about sap and leaves, flowers and insects, fish and birds and, yes, squirrels all climbing along in the nets of God.

Arthur Stuart's hands were extended, his wrists bleeding onto the bridge, and his fingers digging down into the face of the crystal. He shouldn't have been able to do that, to push his skin and bone into Alvin's crystal bridge, but here it was partly Arthur Stuart's, and right around his bleeding fingers it was almost entirely his bridge, so it followed his need.

Alvin sank down beside him and rested his hands and head on Arthur's back. "Arthur, you got to let go now, you got to let go first. When I let go of it the whole weight of it will fall on you, and you can't bear it, you got to let go first."

Arthur seemed not to hear him, so deep was he in his trance of concentration.

"Pull his hands out of the bridge," Alvin said to the others.

But Moose and Squirrel couldn't do it, and La Tia and Dead Mary couldn't do it, and Alvin whispered into his ear, "They're coming and we can't bear them up, the bridge can't hold such a harsh load, you got to let go, Arthur Stuart, I can't hold it any longer and if you try to hold alone it'll kill you."

Arthur Stuart finally managed to make an answer, barely audible. "They'll die."

"I reckon so," said Alvin. "Them as can't swim. They'll die trying to bring slaves back into slavery. It ain't your job to keep alive such men as would do that."

"They're just soldiers," said Arthur Stuart.

"And sometimes good men die in a bad cause, when it comes to war."

Arthur Stuart wept. "If I let go I'm killing them."

"They chose to come up on a bridge that was built for freedom, with slavery and killing in their hearts."

"Bear them up, Alvin, or I can't let go."

"I'll do my best," said Alvin. "I'll do my best."

With a final cry of anguish Arthur Stuart tore his blood-covered hands out of the crystal. Alvin felt his heartfire vanish from the substance of the bridge, and in that moment he withdrew his own.

It lingered for a long moment, held by the blood alone.

And then the bridge was gone.

"Bear them up in the water!" cried Arthur Stuart. And then he fell into something between a faint and a deep sleep.

Papa Moose and Mama Squirrel drew him back from the water's edge and bandaged his wounds, while Dead Mary and her mother did the same for Alvin's hands and feet.

Alvin barely noticed, though, because he was trying to find the heartfires of the soldiers. He could not save them all. But those with brains enough to let go of their weapons, to pry off their boots, to try to swim, them he could keep afloat. But those who didn't try, and those that wouldn't let go of the things that made them soldiers, he hadn't the strength to help them.

La Tia grasped what he was doing and stepped to the

water's edge, where the bridge had once been. She reared her head back and pinched a powder into her open mouth. Then she looked out over the water and cried out in a voice that could be heard for miles across the lake, a voice as loud as thunder, a voice that made wide ripples race forward across the water.

"Drop your guns, you! Try to swim! Take off your boots! Swim back!"

All heard, and most heeded, and they lived. Three hundred soldiers went out onto that bridge that morning, along with one horse hitched to a fieldpiece. The horse had no way to save itself, but it took Alvin only a moment to sever the harness that held it to that murderous load. The horse came out alive; the fieldpiece stayed behind under the water. All but two score men finally swam to shore, gasping and half drowned but alive. But not one gun and not one boot made it back.

Only then, with the last of their enemies safe who was willing to be saved, Alvin let go of consciousness.

The north shore teemed with thousands of people, of every age and color and several languages. They desperately needed someone to tell them what to do, and where to go if they were to find drinkable water and food to eat. But not one of them proposed awakening Alvin or Arthur Stuart. The man and boy who made a crystal bridge out of blood and water—such power struck them all with awe, and they would not dare.

Back in Barcy, Calvin saw what was happening with Alvin's heartfire, how deeply he slept, how weak he was.

I could kill him right now. Just open up a hole in his heart and fill his lungs with blood and he'd be dead before anyone else realized what was happening and no one would know it was me, or if they did, they'd never prove it.

But I won't kill him today, thought Calvin. I'll never kill him. Even though he kills me all the time, with his judgments and condemnations, his condescensions and his lessons and his utter ignorance of who I am. Because I'm not like Alvin.

He refrains from purposely killing people because he thinks it's wrong, under some arbitrary law. While I refrain from killing people, not out of obedience, but of my own free will, because I'm merciful to those who hurt me and despitefully use me.

Who's the Pharisee here? And who's the one like Jesus? Even though nobody else will ever see it that way, that's the truth, as God is my witness.

⚒ 7 ⚒

Errand Boy

VERILY COOPER AWOKE in the old roadhouse in the town of Hatrack River. It was the place where Alvin Maker was born, and where he returned twelve years later to serve his prenticeship to the blacksmith there.

It was that prenticeship that brought Verily Cooper there. The old smith had died a while ago, and since his wife had died before him, their children were now in possession of a will that gave them "one plow of pure gold, stolen by a prentice named Alvin, son of Alvin Miller of Vigor Church." Margaret Larner's father, Horace Guester, had written to Verily as soon as rumors of the will began to spread through town. Verily was the only lawyer old Horace trusted, and so here he was to try to prevent some hare-brained judge from issuing a writ demanding that Alvin produce the plow.

If only the plow didn't exist.

But it did exist, and the smith had never owned it. Alvin had forged it himself in the Hatrack River smithy. It was Alvin who had somehow turned it to gold, and it was only greed that made the old smith claim that Alvin stole it from him.

It would be an open-and-shut case, if not for the local prejudice that for many years had made Alvin out—at least among those who never knew him—to be six kinds of scoundrel. In vain had Horace insisted to all and sundry that the smith never owned that much gold, that his daughter would never have married a thief, and that everyone knew the smith was a notorious liar and sharp-dealer. It would come to court, and the judge, who had to stand for reelection this fall, might well issue a writ based on popular prejudice rather than law.

And that's why Verily Cooper, attorney-at-law, was here once again to plead Alvin's case in court. This time, fortunately, Alvin himself was not incarcerated. He was off somewhere doing his wife Margaret's bidding—as if he didn't have work of his own to do.

Not fair, not right. Judge not, lest somebody think you're jealous of Alvin's wife, for heaven's sake.

It was full dark outside. Why in the world had he woken up now? He didn't particularly need to micturate. There must have been some kind of noise. Some drunk refusing to leave the roadhouse at closing time?

No. Now he heard a stamping of horses and the voice of the stableman as he led a team off to be walked and watered and fed and stabled for the night. It was rare for the coach to push on in the darkness. But when Verily stepped to the window and opened it, sure enough, there it was, lanterns blazing—enough of them that from a distance it might be mistaken for a forest fire.

Curiosity would never let him go to sleep without finding out who had arrived at such an untimely hour.

He was not altogether surprised to find, sitting at the kitchen table, Alvin's wife Margaret, just settling in to have a bowl of her father's justly famous chicken stew.

"You," she said.

"And I'm delighted to see you, as well, Goody Smith." If she was going to be rude to him, he could reply by giving her the "courtesy" of calling her by her husband's name instead of her own.

She squinted her eyes at him. "I'm tired and I was surprised to see you up, but you have my apology, Mr. Cooper. Please accept it."

"I do, Mistress Larner, and you have mine as well."

"Nothing to apologize for," she said. "I haven't been a teacher in years, so I hardly deserve the name Larner any more. And I'm proud to have my husband's occupation as my title, since his work is all the work that's left to me."

Old Horace walked up behind her and rubbed her shoulders. "You're tired, Little Peggy. Save conversation till morning."

"He might as well know it now. I expected not to see him till morning, but as long as I've woken him, I might as well ruin the rest of his night."

Of course she had known he was in Hatrack River. Even if Horace hadn't written to her about his arrival, she would have known, the way she knew anything she cared to, what with her gift as a torch. It always bothered him more than a little, that she knew just by looking at him what lay in his future, but never took the trouble to tell him.

"What is it you want me to know?" said Verily.

"Alvin needs your help."

"Alvin unchose me as his traveling companion years ago," said Verily. "But I'm still helping him—that's why I'm here."

"Something more urgent than this."

"Then send somebody else," said Verily. "If I don't settle this business with the will and the plow right now, it's going to come back to haunt him."

"Right now," said Margaret, "he's got about five thousand people who have just escaped from Nueva Barcelona. More than half are runaway slaves or free blacks, and most of the rest are despised French folk, so you can imagine how eager the Spanish are to have them back under their thumb."

"So I'm going to do what, recruit an army and we'll all fly down there like passenger pigeons to save them just in the nick of time?"

Horace Guester clucked his tongue. "It's not impossible, you know."

"It is to me," said Verily. "That's not my knack."

"Your knack," said Margaret, "is making things fit together."

"Sometimes."

"Alvin can keep these people safe while they travel," she said. "What he needs most desperately is a place that they can travel *to*."

"I assume you've got a place in mind."

"Alvin made a friend down in Nueva Barcelona," said Margaret. "A failed storekeeper from the western reaches of Noisy River. His name is Abraham Lincoln."

"And he has land?"

"He's well-liked in his part of the country. He can help you find some land."

"Free of charge, I hope," said Verily. "My practice hasn't been such as to make me a wealthy man. I keep working pro bono for my friends."

"I don't know how it will be paid for," said Margaret. "I only know that if you don't go to see Mr. Lincoln, there are few paths that lead anywhere but to disaster for Alvin and the people in his care. But if you do go . . ."

"Let me guess—there *might* be some path that leads to safety."

"First things first," said Margaret. "He needs a place that will take in these homeless folk and board them and bed them for a time. There's no place in the slave lands that will have them, that's certain."

Verily sat down at the table and leaned his chin on his hands and stared into her eyes. "I'd rather stay here and get Alvin shut of this will once and for all time. Why don't *you* go and talk to this Mr. Lincoln?"

She sighed and stared into her bowl. "Mr. Cooper, I have spent five years of my life trying to persuade people to do the things that would avoid a terrible, bloody war. With all my years of talking, do you know what I accomplished?"

"We ain't had a war yet," said Verily.

"I postponed the war by a year or two, maybe three," she said. "And do you know how I did that?"

"How?"

"By sending my husband to Nueva Barcelona."

"He put off a war?"

"Without knowing what he did, yes, the war was delayed. Because of an outbreak of yellow fever. But then he went on and did this—this impossible escape. This rescue, this liberation of slaves."

Horace chuckled. "Sounds like he finally got him the spirit of abolition."

"He's always had the wish for it," said Margaret. "Why did he have to pick now to find the will? This escape of slaves—it will lead to war as surely as ever."

"So he eliminated one cause of war, and then brought about another," said Verily.

Margaret nodded and took a bite of soup. "This is very good, Papa."

"Forgive me for thinking like a lawyer," said Verily Cooper, "but why didn't you foresee this before you sent him down?"

She was chewing, so Old Horace answered. "She can't see that clear when it comes to Alvin. Can't see what all he's going to choose to do. She can see some things, but not most things, when it comes to him. Which I think is a plain mercy. A man who has a wife can see *everything* he does and thinks and wants and wishes, well, I think he might as well kill himself."

Horace was joking, and so he laughed, but Margaret didn't take it as a joke. Verily saw her tears drop into the stew.

"Ho, now," he said, "that's already salted well enough, I can swear to that, I had some for supper."

"Father is right," she said. "Oh, poor Alvin. I should never have married him."

Verily had actually had that thought occur to him several times in the past, and since he knew she could see into his heartfire, he didn't bother trying to lie and reassure her. "Maybe so," he said, "but as you already know, Alvin's a free chooser. He chose you the way most folks choose a mate, not seeing the end, but wanting to find his way to it with his hand in yours."

She placed her hand on his and gave him a weak smile. "You have a lawyer's way with words," she said.

"What I said is true," said Verily. "Alvin chose you because of who you are and how he feels about you, not because he thought you'd always make right choices."

"How he feels about me," she said, and shuddered. "What if he finds out that I sent him to Nueva Barcelona knowing that by going there, he'd cause the deaths of hundreds of souls?"

"Why does he have to find out?" said Verily. But he knew the answer already.

"He'll ask me," said Margaret. "And I'll tell him."

"He caused the plague of yellow fever, is that it?"

"Not on purpose, but yes."

"And you knew he would."

"It was the only thing that would stop the war that the King already planned. His invasion of Nueva Barcelona would have forced the United States to invade the Crown Colonies in order to keep the King from sealing off their access to the sea. But the yellow fever prevented the King's army from approaching the city. By the time the fever is gone, so will be all the King's agents inside the city. That road to war is closed."

"So at the cost of those who die of the fever," said Verily, "you saved the lives of all who would have died in the war."

She shook her head. "I thought it would. But Alvin reopened the door without realizing it, and the war that will come now is every bit as bloody."

"But you delayed it a few more years," said Verily.

"What good is that?"

"It's two or three more years of life. Of loving and marrying and having babies. Of buying and selling, of plowing and planting and harvesting, of moving and settling. It will be a different world in two or three years, and those who die in the war will have had that much more life. It's not a small thing, those years."

"Maybe you're right," said Margaret. "But that won't keep Alvin from hating me for sending him down there to cause hundreds of deaths in order to postpone hundreds of thousands of others."

"Hush now," said Horace. "He's not going to hate you."

But Verily wasn't sure. Alvin wasn't one to appreciate being manipulated into committing what he would see, no doubt, as a terrible sin. "Why couldn't you just tell the man and let him decide for himself?"

She shook her head. "Because every path that included me telling him led to him doing something else to prevent the war—and all those things would have failed, and most of those paths ended with him dead."

She burst into tears. "I know too much! Oh! God help me, I'm so tired of knowing so much!"

Horace was sitting beside her in a moment, his arm around her shoulder. He looked at Verily, who was about to try to offer comfort. "She's tired, and you were wakened out of your sleep," said Horace. "Go to bed, as she will too. Tomorrow is time enough for talk."

As usual, Horace knew just the right thing for everyone to do to be content. Verily got up from the table. "I'll go and do what you asked," he said to Margaret. "You can count on me to help find a place for Alvin's people."

She nodded slightly, her face still hidden in her hands.

That was all the good-night he was going to get, and so he headed back along the hall toward his room. At first he was filled with irritation at having to set aside his plan to free Alvin from the smith's litigious heirs. But by the time he got to his room he had already let go of that. It wasn't his case any more. He had other work now, but it hadn't yet begun. And so, when he lay back down in his bed, it took him little time to sleep, for at the moment he had no worries.

In the morning, he didn't see Margaret after all. There was a note waiting for him on the floor of his room, giving the name of Abraham Lincoln's town and how to get there.

At breakfast the old innkeeper looked grave. "I'm worried about the baby," said Horace. "She started throwing up last night. She's worn herself out and she's sick as a dog. She's asleep now, but if she loses this baby too, I swear I don't know but what she'll lose her mind."

"So I should go on without talking to her?"

"Everything you need to know is on that paper."

"I doubt *that*," said Verily.

"All right then," said Horace with a wan smile. "Everything she *thinks* you need to know."

Verily Cooper matched his smile, then went back to his room to get his things together for the long westward ride. If he'd only stayed in Vigor Church instead of coming here to Hatrack River, he'd have only one-third the journey now. Sometimes it felt to him as though he'd spent most of his life traveling, and never quite got to anywhere that mattered.

Then again, that might be as good a description of what life was supposed to be as anyone ever thought of. The only real destination was death, and our lives consisted of finding the most circuitous and pleasant path to get there.

He was on horseback and on his way hours before noon, so the sun was still at his back. It would be nice when they finally got the railroad through clear to the Mizzippy. If they laid enough tracks, a man wouldn't even need to keep a horse. But for now it was either ride the horse or struggle to keep the horse from going crazy on a flatboat or a steamboat and he wasn't inclined to try either.

He thought, as he rode, about how Alvin and Margaret were the two most powerful, gifted, blessed people on this continent, without question, and yet Margaret was desperately sad and frightened all the time, and Alvin wandered about half-lost and melancholy, and not for the first time Verily thought it was a good thing to be a man of relatively ordinary gifts.

⚔ 8 ⚔

Plans

NUEVA BARCELONA FINALLY had something to take the
people's minds off the yellow fever. Folks were still dying
from it, and you can bet their families weren't losing track
of the fever's vicious progress through the city, but a
whole bunch of men who had felt completely helpless in
the face of the epidemic were now given a task that would
cover them with honor for doing what they'd been longing
to do since the first outbreak of the plague:

Get out of town.

It was the first move that the rich made, whenever the
fever struck—they packed up their families and went to
the plantation in the country. But regular folks didn't have
that option, and rather despised the rich because they did.
No, *real* men stuck around. They couldn't afford to get
their families out of the city, so they had to stay with
them and risk watching their wives and children get sick
and die. Not to mention the risk of dying themselves. Not
much of a way to die, moaning with fever till you became

one of those corpses the body wagons picked up on their sad passage through the streets.

So when word spread that Gobernador Anselmo Arellano was calling for volunteers to go upriver and bring home all the runaway slaves—and kill the white renegades who had helped them—well, there was no shortage of volunteers. Especially among that element of the city that was commonly known as "drunk and disorderly."

Not everybody thought them particularly brave or honorable. Few whores, for instance, gave them their fifteen minutes free just because "I'm a soldier and I might die." Nobody knew better than prostitutes just how few men were more than talk. This wasn't an army that was likely to stand up long if they got any resistance. Hanging helpless, unarmed French folk, that was all they'd be good for, and then only if the French didn't do anything dangerous, like slapping them or throwing rocks.

That's what Calvin was hearing in the taverns along the dock as the "soldiers" assembled for shipment upriver. The commander was the governor's son, Colonel Adan, who, as longtime head of the Nueva Barcelona garrison, was grudgingly appreciated for being less brutal than he could have been. But Calvin could easily imagine the despair the poor colonel must have felt upon seeing this sorry lot that had assembled to take ship.

Yet maybe they weren't so sorry. Most of them were drunk—but tomorrow they wouldn't be, and they might look like better soldiers by then. And it wasn't as if the enemy would be hard to find. Five thousand slaves and French people, moving at the pace of the slowest child—it wasn't going to be hard to locate them, was it? And what kind of fight could they put up? Oh, Colonel Adan probably felt just fine about things.

He might feel differently if he actually believed those ludicrous reports about a bridge made out of clear water that disappeared when his soldiers were out on it, causing a score of deaths and a lot of splashing and spluttering.

Perhaps he was so used to pathetic excuses from his men for their failures that it never occurred to him that this one might be true.

What will Alvin do, Calvin wondered. Probably not fight. He puts far too high a value on human life, poor fellow. It's not as if half these oafs won't get themselves killed in some meaningless fight or just by falling into the river one drunken night.

Well, whatever he does, I won't be there to help.

Though Calvin was not against helping if it didn't put him out of his way. That's why he had searched out Jim Bowie this morning and arranged with him to lead Calvin to Steve Austin. They met in a saloon two streets back from the water, which meant it was relatively quiet, with no jostling. There were a few other men there, though none that Calvin cared much about. Either he'd get to know them later or he wouldn't. Right now all that mattered was Austin and his Mexican adventure.

Austin was going on about how he owed it to help the governor return the slaves to their place before going on his expedition. "It won't take long," said Austin. "How far can a bunch of runaways get? We'll probably find them crying on the north shore of Pontchartrain. Hang a few, whip a lot, and drag 'em on home. *Then* it's on to Mexico."

Calvin only shook his head.

Austin looked from him to Bowie. "I need fighters," he said, "not advisers."

"I'd give him a listen, Steve," said Bowie.

"Colonel Adan's little slave-catching venture is doomed," said Calvin. "Don't be with them when they go down in flames."

"Doomed? By what army?"

In answer, Calvin simply softened the metal in their mugs until they collapsed, covering the table with ale and cold soft metal. With not a little of it flowing onto their laps.

All the men sprang up from the table and began brushing ale off their laps. Calvin avoided smiling, even though they all looked like they'd peed in their trousers. He waited while Austin realized that the metal pools on the table were the former mugs.

"What did you do?"

"Not much," said Calvin. "For a maker, anyway."

Austin squinted at him. "You telling me you're a maker?"

Another man muttered, "Ain't no makers."

"And your ale is still in your cup," said Calvin cheerfully. "I ain't much of a maker. But my brother Alvin, he's a first-rater."

"And he's with them," said Jim Bowie. "Tried to get him to join up with us, but he wouldn't do it."

"When Colonel Adan's army finds those runaways," said Calvin, "*if* he finds them, I wouldn't be a bit surprised if all their weapons turn into pools of metal on the ground."

"Or plumb disappear," said Bowie. "I seen him do it. Hard and heavy steel, and it was gone, like *that*." He snapped his fingers.

Austin moved to a dry table and called for more ale. Then paused a moment to inquire, "I trust we'll be allowed to finish these drinks?"

Calvin grinned.

Soon they were all seated at the new table—except for a couple of Austin's men who found urgent business to attend to in some place where somebody wasn't melting metal cups just by thinking about it.

"Mr. Austin, do you think I could be useful on your expedition to Mexico?" asked Calvin.

"I do," said Austin. "Boy, howdy."

"And I've got me a hankering to see what that tribe is like. My brother, see, he thinks he knows all about reds. But *his* reds is all peaceful like. I want to meet some of them Mexica, the ones who tear the beating heart out of their sacrifices."

"Will it satisfy you if you see some of them dead?

'Cause we ain't going there to meet them, we're going there to kill them."

"All of them?" said Calvin. "Oh my."

"Well, no," said Austin. "But I reckon the common folk'll be glad enough to be shut of these human-sacrificing heathens."

"I'll tell you what," said Calvin. "I'll go with you to the end of your expedition, and help you all I can. Provided that you leave for Mexico by tomorrow morning."

Austin leaned back and laughed. "So you think you can come here and start dictating when we'll leave."

"Not dictating a thing," said Calvin. "Just telling you that any expedition to Mexico that sets out tomorrow, with all its men, I'll join. And any that doesn't, I won't. You didn't make your plans with me in mind, and you're free to go on and carry them out without me."

"Why are you so all-fired eager to keep us from helping catch them runaways?"

"Well, first, my brother's with them, like I said. Since your men are probably the most dangerous in Barcy right now, I'm making my brother a little bit safer by keeping you all out of it."

"That's what I figured," said Austin. "So what's to say that as soon as Colonel Adan is gone upriver, you won't just disappear?"

"Second reason is more important," said Calvin. "If you go upriver with Colonel Adan, your men will get just as messed up as anybody else. My guess is that once Alvin's through with them, you'll never get them to invade their grandma's privy, let alone Mexico."

"I don't know if your brother's all that dangerous."

Calvin got up, leaned over to their first table, and brought back a congealed swatch of metal that had once been a mug. "Can you just keep this in mind for a little while, so I don't have to melt any more of them?"

"All right," said Austin, "of course he's dangerous, and I'm obliged to you for warning us."

"And the third reason is, I don't like sitting around

waiting. If the expedition starts tomorrow, I'll be with it. If it doesn't, I'll get bored and go off and find something entertaining to do."

Austin nodded. "Well, I'll think about it."

"Good," said Calvin.

"But you still didn't answer my question about how do we know you'll actually be there tomorrow."

"I gave you my word," said Calvin. "You can't make me go if I don't want to, but I tell you that I want to, and so I will. You get no better guarantee than that. You don't have to trust me. You can do what you want."

"How do I know I won't have nothing but trouble from you along the way, trying to run everything? The way you're bossing me around now?"

Calvin rose from his chair. "I can see, gentlemen, that some of you are more interested in being the big boss than in overcoming whatever powers these Mexica get from all the blood they spill. I apologize for wasting your time. I hear that the Mexica castrate the big boss before they cut out his heart. It's an honor you're welcome to."

He started for the door.

Austin didn't call him back. No one ran after him.

Calvin didn't hesitate. He just kept on walking. Out into the street. And still no one ran after him. Well, doggone it.

No, there *was* somebody. Jim Bowie—Calvin recognized his heartfire. And he was stopping and throwing a—

Calvin ducked down and to the left.

A big heavy knife quivered from the wooden wall right where Calvin's head used to be.

Calvin leapt up, furious. In a moment, Jim Bowie was there, grinning. Calvin ripped out a long string of French profanities—eloquent enough that a couple of people nearby, who spoke French, looked at him with candid admiration.

"What's got your dander up, Mr. Maker?" said Jim Bowie. "Of course I aimed right at your head. Your brother would have made my knife vanish in midair."

"I have more respect for cutlery," said Calvin. Though truth to tell, he could no more make a knife disappear in mid flight than he could stop the world from spinning. He could work with mugs because they mostly sat on the table, very very still.

"The way I see it," said Bowie, "you ain't half the maker your brother is, but you want us to think that whatever he can do, you can do. And if that makes you mad to hear me say it, as it seems to be doing—"

"I'm not mad," said Calvin.

"Glad to hear it," said Bowie. "I'm laying it out the way I laid it out to Steve Austin. I wanted your brother because he would have guaranteed our success. He wouldn't do it, and instead he got himself five thousand runaways to feed and no place to take them. Fine with me. But you, you *want* to come with us, and I think it's because you want a chance to show off you're just as good as your brother, only you're not, and when that fact becomes plain and evident, I think a lot of good boys from this expedition are gonna be dead because they counted on you."

Calvin wanted to blast him into pieces on the spot. But he had his own rules, even if they weren't Alvin's. You don't kill a man just for saying something you don't want to hear, even if it is a pack of lies.

So Calvin only nodded and walked on toward the dock. "Well," said Calvin, "I reckon that's a wise choice. You run on back to Steve Austin and tell him I said good luck."

Bowie, however, did not turn and go back. A good sign. "Look, Mr. Calvin, I'm here to ask you to come back. We just got to know—what can you do? Turning a bunch of pewter mugs into mush is thrilling, of course, but we need to know what you can *do*. You saw my knife coming early enough to dodge it, but you couldn't destroy it in flight, which suggests that Mexica bullets aren't gonna disappear in midair either. So before we take you along with your brag and your bossiness—and I mean that in the nicest possible way, those being traits I'm proud of in myself—before we take you along, we got to know: What exactly can you do that'll be of practical help in our fighting?"

"That fog yesterday," said Calvin. "That was mine."

"Easy enough to claim you caused the weather. Me, I've been running winter ever since my old pap left me the job in his will."

In reply, Calvin cooled the air right around them. "I think we got us a fog starting up right here, right now."

And sure enough, the moisture in the air began to condense until Bowie couldn't see anything else in all the world but Calvin's face.

"All right," said Bowie. "That's a useful knack."

"My knack isn't fog-making," said Calvin. "Or weather, or any other one thing."

A fish flopped up out of the water onto the dock. And another. And a couple more. And pretty soon there were scores of fish flopping around on the wooden planks right among the passersby. Naturally, some of the fishermen on the dock started picking them up—some to throw the fish back, others to try to keep them to sell. An argument immediately sprang up. "Those fish must be sick, you can't sell them!" To which the reply came, "He don't feel sick to *me,* a fish this strong!" Whereupon the fish flapped out of the man's arms and back into the water.

"If you ever need fish," said Calvin.

"Oh, yeah, sure," said Bowie. "But can you do it if there ain't no river?"

For a moment Calvin wanted to slap him. Couldn't he recognize a miracle when he saw one? He would have made a perfect Israelite, complaining at Moses because all they had was manna and no meat.

Then Bowie grinned and clapped him on the shoulder. "Can't you tell when you're being joshed, man? Of course you can come. Nobody has a dodge-the-knife-from-behind knack *and* the fog-making knack *and* the knack of making fish jump out of the water right up onto the dock."

"So I pass your test?" said Calvin, letting a little pissed-offedness seep into his voice.

"Sure enough," said Bowie.

"But do you pass mine?"

No sooner had Calvin said this than he felt a knife blade poking into his belly. He hadn't seen it coming, not in Bowie's heartfire and not in his body. All of a sudden there was a knife in his hand.

"If I wanted you dead," said Bowie, "would you have had time to stop me?"

"I reckon you got a knack a man can respect," said Calvin.

"Oh, that ain't my knack," said Bowie. "I'm just dang good with a knife, that's all."

Alvin woke only because he had to pee. Otherwise he could have slept for another ten hours, he was sure of it. There wasn't a deep enough sleep in the world to give him back his strength.

But when he got up, he found that he was surrounded by duties impossible to avoid. Things he had to do before he could even void his bladder. Only his mind wasn't clear, and his eyes were still bleary with sleep, and as people bombarded him with questions he found that he couldn't bring himself to care about the answers.

"I don't know," he said to the woman demanding to know where they were supposed to find breakfast in this godforsaken place.

"I don't know," he said to the man who tremulously asked, in broken English, whether more soldiers would come in boats.

And when Papa Moose came to him and asked if he thought there was fever on this side of the lake, Alvin barked his "I don't know" so loudly that Papa Moose visibly recoiled.

Arthur Stuart was lying nearby, looking like a gator sunning itself on the shore of the lake. Or a dead man.

Alvin went and knelt by him. Touched him, because that way he could see his heartfire without exerting himself. He had never been so tired before that merely looking into somebody's heartfire felt like an impossible burden to him.

Arthur was all right. Just tired. At least as worn out as Alvin. The difference being that nobody was pestering Arthur Stuart with questions.

"Let this man be," said La Tia. "You see he bone tired, him?"

Alvin felt hands on his arm—small hands, thick arm—trying to raise him up. His first impulse was to shrug them off. But then a soft voice said, "You hungry? You thirsty?" It was Dead Mary, and Alvin turned to her and let her help him rise to his feet.

"I got to pee," he said softly.

"We set folks to digging latrines," she said. "We got one not far off, you just lean on me."

"Thank you," he said.

She led him along a short path through the underbrush till he came to a reeking pit with a plank across it. "I think this wouldn't be hard to find in the dark," he said.

"Bodies got to do what bodies got to do," she said. "I leave you alone now."

She did, and he did all his business. A lot of leaves had been piled up for wiping, and a couple of buckets of water for washing, and he had to admit he felt better. A little more awake. A little more vigorous. And hungry.

When he came back to the shore, he saw that La Tia was doing a good job of keeping folks calm. She had a line of people waiting to talk to her, but she answered them all with patience. But it's not like she had a plan, nor was she organizing things for the journey ahead. Nor did it seem that anybody was working on the problem of food.

Alvin looked along the shore, which was teeming with people for half a mile in either direction. He also scanned for gators, which would have no qualms about snatching any child who strayed too close to shore. None here so far; and now he felt strong enough that scanning for heart-fires took no noticeable effort.

Mama Squirrel and Papa Moose were not too far off. Alvin started to make his way over to them. At once he found Dead Mary at his side, offering her arm.

"I'm too big to be leaning on you," said Alvin.

"You already did, and I was strong enough," she said.

"I'm feeling better." But then he did lean on her, because his balance wasn't all that good yet, and the sand on the shore was irregular and treacherous, the damp grass just inland of it slippery and creased with ditches and rivulets. "Thank you," he told her again. Though he still tried not to put any weight on her.

Papa Moose strode up to him—strode, his legs showing no sign of his old limp. "I'm sorry I plagued you the moment you woke up," said Papa Moose.

"I'm glad to see you're doing better your own self," said Alvin. "And walking well."

Papa Moose embraced him. "It's a blessing from God, but I still thank the hands that did God's work on me."

Alvin hugged him back, but only briefly, because he had work to do. "Mama Squirrel," he said, "you packed up a lot of bags of food."

"For the children," she said defensively.

"I know it's for the children," said Alvin. "But I want you to consider—if folks get desperate enough, how long do you think you can keep those bags from getting hauled away? There's farms with plenty of food not too far inland, but we need to travel together. Share this food now, at least with all the children who aren't from your house, and I can promise you more food by nightfall—for everybody."

Mama Squirrel weighed this. He could see that it plain hurt her even to think of sharing away what her children would need. But she also knew that it would hurt to see other children starve, when hers had plenty. "All right, we'll share it out with children. Bread and cheese, anyway. Nothing we can do with raw potatoes and uncooked grain right now."

"Good thinking," said Alvin. He turned to Dead Mary. "Do you think you can get La Tia to spread the word among the blacks, and you and your mother among the French, that children should be brought here to line up quietly for food?"

"You dreaming, you think they all line up quietly," said Dead Mary.

"But if we ask, some will," said Alvin.

"Asking is easy," said Dead Mary. She took off at a trot, holding up her skirt to hop over obstructions on the way.

People were pretty orderly in line, after all—but those adults that had no children were getting loud and angry. As Alvin walked against the flow of children and their parents queuing up for the food, one of the men with no children called out to him from the trees. "You think we don't got hungry, mon?"

"Thank you for your patience," Alvin answered.

A stout black woman called out, "Starving to death don't look like freedom to me!"

"You got a few good hours of life left in you," called Alvin. That won him some laughter from others, and a huffy retreat from her.

Soon he was with La Tia again, and Dead Mary and her mother. "We need to organize," he said. "Divide people up into groups and pick leaders."

"Good idea," said La Tia. Then she waited for more.

"But I don't know any of these folks," said Alvin. "You got to do the dividing of the folks as speak English." He turned to Dead Mary and her mother. "And you have to divide up the French. And each group of ten households, tell them to choose a leader, and if they can't choose one without bickering, I'll pick one for them."

"They don't like me," said Dead Mary.

"But they know you," said Alvin. "And they fear you. And for right now, that's good enough. Tell them I asked you to do it. And tell them that the sooner we get organized, the sooner we'll all get away from Pontchartrain and get fresh water and good food. Tell them I won't eat till they all eat."

"You get mighty hungry, maybe, you," said La Tia.

It took longer than Alvin expected. It seemed such a simple task, but the sun was well past noon when La Tia and Dead Mary reported that everyone was organized. They had their groups of ten, and then out of each five leaders, one was chosen to head a group of fifty, and out of every two leaders of fifty, one was designated the leader of a hundred.

The way things worked out, that gave them ten leaders of a hundred households that sat down on the shore of Pontchartrain as the Council, to plan the trek with Alvin, La Tia, Dead Mary, and Arthur Stuart, who was finally awake. Rien, Mary's mother, was one of the leaders of a hundred—chosen by the people, to her surprise—and Papa Moose and Mama Squirrel weren't counted in anybody's group, since their household was so extravagantly large.

People fancied titles, Alvin knew, so he designated the leaders of hundred as "colonels," the leaders of fifty as "majors," and the leaders of ten as "captains."

"Reckon that makes you 'general,' " said Arthur Stuart.

"It makes me 'Alvin,' " said Alvin. "You can be general."

"*I* be general," said La Tia. "Not this boy. Who gonna follow this boy, him?"

"You will," said Alvin, "when I leave."

La Tia wanted to answer him sharply, but she held her tongue and listened while Alvin explained to the Council.

"We got no place to go," said Alvin. "I can get us north into farm country, and we'll work out a way to get food without leaving any farmers' families to starve. But the longer we keep marching around the countryside, the bigger the armies they can raise up to destroy us. We've got to get out of slave-owning country, and there's only one way to do that."

"By sea," said Dead Mary. "We need boats."

"Boats do us no good without willing crews," said Alvin. "Anybody here know how to navigate?" No one did. "But that was a good idea, all the same," said Alvin. "And I appreciate you making suggestions. That goes for everybody. No such thing as an idea that shouldn't be suggested, at the right time and place."

"Where we go, then?" asked La Tia.

"Well, General La Tia," said Alvin—not smiling at the title, which made her preen just a little, "only one place we *can* go, where white men won't follow."

"Don't take us to red land!" said Rien.

"We can't stay there," said Alvin, "but maybe Tenskwa-Tawa will let us pass through. Maybe them red folks'll help us with food and shelter. But my point is, I know Tenskwa-Tawa, and so I'm the one that's got to go and talk to him and see whether we can use his land as our road north. Can't send nobody else. So you folks is gonna have to follow General La Tia."

"But I don't know the way."

"Go north for a while, and then find a road that leads west to the Mizzippy," said Alvin. "Be resourceful. What white folks along the way won't tell you, black folks will."

"But what if an army comes?" said Dead Mary. "We got no fighters here, except maybe a few of the French men. We got no guns."

"That's why General La Tia has to consult with Arthur Stuart here."

"I don't got any guns," said Arthur.

"But you know what to do with any guns that are raised against us," said Alvin. "Every plantation you come to, you got to be there, Arthur, to make sure no guns get fired. At night, you got to make sure there's fog keeping bad folks from finding us. You got to follow the heartfires to make sure no one strays."

"No," said La Tia. "I can do that. I know how to do that, you can't lay so much on that boy, him."

Arthur nodded gratefully. "Watching heartfires ain't as easy for me as for you, Alvin. And making fog—that's what Calvin done, not me."

"But it's not hard," said Alvin. "I'll teach you today. And there's another thing. You're the only one speaks *all* the languages, Arthur. You got to make sure everybody's understanding everybody else."

"Heck, Alvin, half the time I don't even understand *you*."

Everybody laughed at that, but in truth they were all frightened—of the dangers on the road, but, even more, of their own inexperience. It wasn't the blind leading the blind, really. More like the clumsy leading the clumsy.

"And one more thing," said Alvin. "There's gonna be lots of complaining. That's fine, you just keep your patience, you leaders—all of you, make sure they know. Listen to everything, don't get angry. But if somebody raises a hand of violence against a leader—you can't stand for that. You understand me? Person raises a hand against a leader, he's out of the company. He's not one of us any more. Because we can't be afraid of our own people. We have to know we can trust everybody to be gentle with each other."

"How we gonna throw out this angry hitting man?" said La Tia. "Who gonna do that?"

"The general will ask some strong men to put the offender out of the camp," said Alvin. "And then Arthur will see to it he doesn't find his way back."

"What if he got family, him?"

Alvin sighed. "General La Tia, you'll always find a good reason not to punish a man. But sometimes you got to punish a man to save a dozen other men from needing punishment. And sometimes you have to have a hard heart to do what needs doing."

Arthur snorted softly.

"Arthur knows," said Alvin. "But when I'm not here, it's not my job. The decisions are yours. You make them, you make them stick, or you don't, and then you live with the consequences. Either way, you live with them."

"That why you going?" asked La Tia.

"That's right," said Alvin. "Just when things get hard, I leave."

He stared her down. When she looked away, it occurred to him that maybe that didn't happen to her very often. Giving way like that.

"When you leaving?" asked one of the colonels.

"Not till we've had our first meal," said Alvin. "Not till we're all bedded down for the night. Inland. Dry and away from these skeeters."

Margaret walked up the stairs into the attic room where she had slept as a child. It was a storeroom now. Father kept a room on the main floor for her, when she visited. She had tried to get him to rent it out like any other room in the roadhouse, but he wouldn't do it. "If other people pay to sleep in it," he said, "it ain't your room."

It was the room where Alvin had been born twenty-five years ago. Father probably didn't remember that. But every time she walked into that room on the main floor, she saw that scene. Alvin's mother lying on the bed, in desperate pain but even more desperate grief, for her first-born son, Vigor, had been swept away by the Hatrack River scarcely an hour before.

Peggy—"Little Peggy" then, since her mother was alive, and doing the midwifery—had a job to do. She rushed to the woman lying on the bed and laid hands on her womb. She saw so many things in that moment. How the child was lying in the womb. How the mother was clamped down and couldn't open up to let the child out. Her mother had done a spell with a ring of keys then, and the womb opened, and out came the baby.

She had never seen a baby whose heartfire told such a dire story. The brightest heartfire she had ever seen—but when she cast her eyes into the paths of his future, there were none at all. No paths. No future. This child was going to die, and before he ever made a single choice.

Except . . . there was one thing she could do. One tiny dim pathway leading out of all the dark futures, but that one opened out into hundreds, into thousands of glorious futures. And in that one narrow gate, the one that led to everything for this child, she saw herself, Little Peggy Guester, five years old, reach out and take a caul of flesh from the baby's face. So she did it, and all the deaths fell away, and all the lives became possible.

I gave him life. In that room.

But just the once. She took the caul and saved it, and later brought it up here into the attic, to her room, and hid it in a box. And as the baby grew up into a little boy, and then a bigger boy, she used tiny pinches of the caul to access his own knack, which he was too young and inexperienced to understand.

Not that Peggy knew much better. She learned as she went. Learned to do her work of saving his life. For when she removed the caul from his face, thousands of bright futures opened up for him. But on every one of those paths, he died young. And each time she saved him from one of those deaths, another death opened up for him farther down the road.

Alvin the miller's son had an enemy.

But he also had a friend who watched over him. And gradually, as more and more paths showed him reaching adulthood, she began to see something else. A prim and austere woman, a schoolteacher, who loved him and married him and kept him safe.

There in that attic room, holding one of the last shreds of the caul in her hand, she realized that the prim, austere schoolteacher was herself.

I do love him, she thought. And I'm his wife. I have his baby inside me.

But I can't keep him safe.

In fact, I harm him as much as anyone now. I have no more of his caul. And it wouldn't matter if I did. He deeply understands his knack. He knows more about the way the whole universe works than I ever will; even when I look inside him, I can't understand what and how he sees.

So instead of watching over him, I use him. I found my own purpose in life, to fight slavery but also prevent the terrible war that I see in everyone's heartfire. I have gone everywhere and done everything, while he floundered, unsure of what he ought to do.

And why was he unsure?

Because I have never told him.

I know the great work he is supposed to do. But I can't tell him, because once he sets his foot on that road, there is no saving him. He will die, and die brutally, at the hands of men who hate him, betrayed by some that he loved. A bitter, sad death, with his great work unfinished. And without her even there beside him. In some paths he is alone; in others, he has friends with him. Some of those friends die, some live. But none can save him. In fact, it's his death that saves them.

But why? Why should he die? This is a man who could stop bullets by melting them in the air. He could simply walk through a wall and leave the room where they corner him. He could drop them all through the floor. He could blind them all, or fill them with unreasoning panic to make them run away.

And yet on every path, he does none of those things. He accepts the death they bring him. And I can't bear it. How could Alvin, so full of life and joy, ever choose to embrace death when he always has it in his power to live?

She knelt in the little attic window where, as a five-year-old, she had stood to watch Alvin's family ride away into the west, to the place where they built a mill that became the foundation of the town of Vigor Church. And she realized: If Alvin wishes he could die, I can't pretend that it has nothing to do with me.

A man with a wife and children doesn't want to die. Not if he loves them, and they love him. Not if he has hope for the future. If I just love him enough, I could save him. I've always known that.

Yet what have I done? I sent him to Nueva Barcelona. Knowing that if he went, he would indirectly cause the deaths of hundreds of people. Save thousands, yes, but hundreds would still be felled, and it won't help that it was my responsibility. In fact, it will hurt. Because he'll cease to trust me. He'll think I love something else more than him. That I will expend his trust in a greater cause.

But it isn't true, Alvin. I love you more than anything.

I just didn't love you the way you wanted to be loved. I loved you like that little five-year-old girl, keeping you safe. Helping turn you away from terrible futures. Giving you the freedom to make all the good choices you've made as a grown man.

And then taking away your freedom by not telling you all that I knew about the consequences of your actions. She could hear him telling her: A man isn't free if he doesn't know all that could be known about his choice.

But if I told you, Alvin, you wouldn't have done the things that had to be done. You would have tried to intervene and save everybody. And I saw those paths. It wouldn't have worked. You would have failed, and quite probably would have died right then, with your great work undone.

Instead you've turned it into something wonderful. I didn't see these paths. When you use your power you always open doors into the future that didn't exist before. So I didn't see that bridge you made across the water, I didn't see these five thousand heartfires you brought with you out of the city and into the wilderness. So it worked out well, don't you see?

Except that he'll say, "If my power opens doors to paths you didn't see, why didn't you trust me to find my own way in Barcy?"

Or maybe he won't say it. There are paths where he doesn't say that.

She reached down and laid her hands on her own belly, above the womb where her baby's heart was beating. A healthy baby, with a heartfire as bright and strong as she could have reasonably hoped for.

But nothing like Alvin's heartfire had been. An ordinary child.

Which is all she could have hoped for. An ordinary child—talented in this, having a knack with that, but all within the realms of the expected. This little boy will have no enemy pursuing him every day of his life. And instead of watching him every waking minute as I watched Alvin for so many years, I can be a natural mother to him. And to his brothers and sisters, God willing.

God and Alvin willing, that is. Because he may never come to me again. When he knows how I used him, how I deceived him, what I caused him, unknowingly, to do. How I did not trust him to make his own choices.

She sat down with her back to the window and cried softly into her apron.

And as she wept, she wondered: Did my mother weep like this, when my two older sisters died, each one just a baby? No, I know what those tears are like. Even though my first baby didn't live long enough for me to get to know him, I laid that little body in the ground and I know at least something of what she went through, laying her babies in their graves.

Nor do I weep the way my mother *would* have wept, if she had known about my father and his love for Mistress Modesty. I kept that secret from her because I saw the terrible consequences of her learning the truth, how it would destroy them both.

No, the way I weep now is the way my father would have wept, if he had known that his betrayal of my mother was sure to be discovered, and he could do nothing to prevent it. My sin was not adultery, to be sure. I've been faithful to Alvin that way. But it was a betrayal nonetheless, a violation of the deep trust between a man and the woman he has taken to be half his soul, and to be half of hers.

Bitter tears of anticipated shame.

And with that thought, the tears dried up. I weep for myself. It's myself I'm pitying here.

Well, I won't do it. I'll bear the consequences of what I did. And I'll try to make the best of what is left between us. And maybe this baby will heal us.

Maybe.

She hated all the maybes. For on this matter, as so many others, the fog that blocked so many of Alvin's futures from her view obscured what would happen. She could know exactly what would happen in the whole life of some shepherd she passed in her carriage, but her husband, the person whose future mattered most to her, remained so dangerously exposed and yet tantalizingly hidden.

All her hopes were in the hidden parts of his heartfire. Because the paths that were not hidden gave her no cause for hope. There'd be no happiness for her on any of those roads. Because a life without Alvin in it held no hope of joy for her.

Calvin stood on the dock and watched the riverboats pull out, one by one. Colonel Adan had done his planning well. The steamboats pulled out on schedule, and there was no danger of collision.

Unfortunately, there were also men determined to get out of this city whether they were part of the official expedition or not. So in the midst of the attempt to order the steamboats into a convoy for the passage upstream, two big rowboats swung out into the river, with six men pulling at the oars of each and another dozen or so under arms, many of them foolishly standing up and huzzahing their own bravado.

Calvin laughed aloud to see them. What fools. So eager for death, and so sure to find it.

Sooner, in fact, than Calvin himself anticipated. Though in retrospect, it seemed almost inevitable. Too much order always seemed to bore God or Fate or Providence or whoever decided such things. There was always a little chaos just to liven things up.

Sure enough, one of the rowboats, with its pilot yelling for a steamboat to get out of the way, tried to insert itself between the big riverboats. But steamboats don't stop quickly, and half-drunken rowers don't maneuver well when they try to cross the wake of a steamboat. The captain of the steamboat saw the danger, and some of the Spanish soldiers on board fired at the rowers.

That provoked the armed men in the other rowboat to stand up and fire a volley at the Spanish soldiers. Not a shot hit home, for the obvious reason that so many muskets firing in the same direction at once had such a recoil that the boat rocked over and capsized. Some of the men came up sputtering. Some came up screaming. Some didn't come up—apparently unable to remove their boots in the water or get rid of all the lead balls they carried in their ammunition pouches.

How short life is for fools, thought Calvin. They go out on the water with no thought about how to get ashore if the boat should fail them.

Meanwhile, panicked at the warning shots the Spanish had fired, and some of them thinking that a Spanish cannonball had sunk the other rowboat, the rowers on the first boat tried to change direction. Trouble was, they hadn't agreed on which direction to change to, and so the oars interfered with each other and the rowboat was swept by the current right back into the bows of the big riverboat.

The collision broke half the oars and turned some of them into spears that pierced the bodies of their erstwhile masters. Some of the men jumped into the water; those that didn't were borne under when the steamboat pushed the rowboat over.

It was bedlam on the docks, with some people trying to help the swimmers ashore, and a couple even diving in to help save some of the drowning men. Smaller rowboats quickly put out to help with the rescue. But most of the people were laughing and hooting and catcalling, having a grand old time at the expense of those fools. And while he didn't do any of the catcalling, Calvin had to admit he was one of the laughers.

Alvin would probably have tried to use his knack somehow to save the fools who couldn't swim. Maybe dissolve their boots or something. Or grow them gills—he could probably do it, just to show off.

But even if Calvin had been able to think of something like that quick enough, and even if he had enough control to do anything useful at such a distance, he wouldn't have tried. The world was no poorer for the loss of a few such fools. Indeed, it was downright generous of these "brave" drunk nitwits to improve the breeding population of Barcy by removing themselves from it.

All fools on the river today, thought Calvin. Because the ones following such careful plans were going to end up looking just as stupid as these clowns, when Alvin was done with them. They probably wouldn't be dead—it *was* Alvin, after all—but what they most certainly would *not* be was successful.

Which was probably about how the expedition to Mexico would turn out, too, Calvin cheerfully recognized. These arrogant men, thinking that because they were white they could easily defeat the Mexica. They would probably fail, too. And because it was the Mexica they were facing, and not Alvin Maker, a good number of Steve Austin's boys would probably end up dead.

But not Calvin. He might go along with the plans of fools as long as they looked useful, or at least entertaining. But he would never turn his life over to someone else's plan. His own plans were the only plans he ever followed.

Not like Alvin, letting his wife tell him what to do. Speaking of fools.

IT TOOK SOME doing, but they found the nicest dresses in the whole company that would fit them, and decked out Dead Mary and her mother, Rien, so they could pass for slave-owners. Slightly shabby, perhaps, but it wasn't completely impossible that they would have a mammy slave like La Tia seemed to be and a sturdy young man like Arthur Stuart.

It's not like strangers would be rare in this country, either. Ten years ago the only white folks here was trappers or fugitives. But when most of the reds who didn't want to live white crossed over the Mizzippy, it opened up this land to settlement. Around here, if your house had been standing for five years, you were an old-timer. So nobody'd be too surprised to see two ladies of a family they didn't know—or so they hoped.

Alvin refused to go to the door of the plantation house with them. "What good does it do for you to see how I'd do it? I'm a white man, and not a word I say would be useful to you after. I'll be watching in case anything goes wrong, but you've got to do it yourselves."

La Tia and Arthur Stuart waited just off the porch as Dead Mary and Rien stepped up to clap hands and call someone to the door. Soon it was opened by an elderly black man.

"Good evening," he said gravely.

"Good evening," said Dead Mary. She was doing the talking because her French accent was not so pronounced as Rien's. And because she could do a better job of faking high-class conversation. "Sir, my mother and I would like to speak to the master of the house, if we may."

"Master of the house away," said the old man. "Mistress of the house poorly. But the young master, he here."

"Could you fetch him for us, then?"

"Would you like to come and rest inside, where it's shady?" asked the old man.

"No thank you," said Mary. She had no intention of getting out of sight of Arthur Stuart or La Tia.

Soon the old man returned, and brought with him a young man who could not have been much over fourteen years old. Behind him hovered a white man of middle age. Not the master of the house, and not a slave, so who was he?

Mary addressed the young man. "My name is Marie Moore," she said. They had agreed an English last name would be better for her, suggesting that her father had simply married a Frenchwoman. "My mother is shy about speaking English."

It was the middle-aged man who leapt to answer. "Parley-vous français, madame?"

"Mr. Tutor," said the boy, "they come to see *me*."

"*Came*, young master," said Mr. Tutor.

"This is not my lesson right this very moment, if you please." So the boy was faking being high class just as much as Mary. He turned back to her with an irked look on his face, but quickly changed it to an expression of dignity. "What do you wish? If you wish to have water or a bite to eat, the kitchen's around back."

This was not a good sign, that he was treating them like beggars, when he should take them for slave-owning gentry like himself.

Fortunately, Mr. Tutor saw the gaffe at once. "Young master, you can't ask ladies to go around back as if they were servants or beggars!" To Mary and Rien he said, "Please excuse his lapse. He has never met a visitor at the door before, and so—"

"They're not ladies," said the boy. "Look at their dresses. I've seen better dresses on slaves."

"Master Roy, you are being impolite, I fear."

"Mr. Tutor, you forget your place," said Roy. He turned back to Mary. "I don't know what you want, but we got nothing to contribute to any cause, and if I were you I'd be careful, cause the story is that a whole passel of folks crossed over Pontchartrain last night. Rumor's been spreading all over and they say they're a lot of runaway slaves. We've got ours locked down today just in case they get some bad ideas, but you'll never keep those two under control if they get ideas."

Mary smiled and put on her archest high-class voice. "There's danger about, and yet you do not invite two ladies inside because our dresses are not new enough to suit you. Your mother will be pleased when all the neighbor ladies hear how we were turned away at your door because the young master of the house was so proud." She turned her back on him and started down the stairs. "Come along, Mother, this is not a polite house."

"*Young* master!" said Mr. Tutor, in great distress.

"You always think I do wrong, but I tell you I *know* they're a bunch of liars, it's my *knack*."

Mary turned around. "You say that you have a knack for discerning a lie?"

"I always know," said Roy. "And you and your mother got liar written all over you. That's rude to say, I know it, but Father has me go with him when we buy horses or slaves or anything expensive, because I can always tell him when the man is lying when he says, This is as low as I'll go, or, This horse is right healthy."

"You must be quite a help to your father," said Mary.

"I am," said the boy proudly.

"But not all lies are alike. My mother and I have fallen on hard times, but we still pretend to be ladies of substance because that allows us to uphold our dignity. But I would be surprised if we were the first ladies to come to this house planning to deceive you about our rank in the world."

The boy grinned sheepishly. "Well, you got that aright. When her friends come to call, the lies come thicker and faster than hail in a storm."

"Sometimes you should let a harmless lie stand, sir, without naming it so, for the sake of good manners."

"I could not have said that better," said Mr. Tutor. "The young master is still so *young*."

"They can *see* that I'm young," said Roy, irritated again. To Mary and Rien he said, "Why don't you ladies come on inside, then, and we'll see about maybe something to drink, like . . . lemonade?"

"Lemonade would be lovely," said Mary. "But before we accept your kind invitation, we heard that your name is Roy, but not your family name."

"Why, we took our name from what we grow. Roy Cottoner, and my father is Abner Cottoner, after some general in the Bible."

"And in French," said Mary, "*your* first name means 'king.' "

"I know that," said Roy, sounding irritated again. He was quite an irritable boy.

They followed him into the house. Mary had no idea if they were doing things properly—should Mother go first, or should she?—but they figured Roy wouldn't know, and besides, they were already tagged as impostors, so it wouldn't hurt if they got a few things wrong.

"Master Cottoner," said Mary.

Roy turned around.

"Our servants are thirsty. Is there . . ."

He laughed. "Oh, them. Old Bart, our houseboy, he'll show them around back to the cistern."

Sure enough, the elderly black man was already closing the front door behind him as he headed out to where Arthur Stuart and La Tia were waiting. Mary wished she had more confidence in Arthur Stuart's knack. But Alvin seemed to have confidence in him, so how could Mary refuse to trust in his abilities?

Roy led them into a parlor and invited them to sit down. He turned to Mr. Tutor. "Go tell Petunia we need lemonade."

Mr. Tutor looked mortally offended. "I am not a servant in this house, sir."

"Well what do you think, I should go tell them myself?"

Mary suspected, from what she knew of manners, that that was indeed what he ought to do, but Mr. Tutor merely narrowed his eyes and went off to obey. Mary was just as happy to have him out of the room.

She watched as Roy took a pose in the archway. It looked studied and unnatural, and she suspected that he was imitating the way he'd seen his father stand when company came. On a full-grown man, the stance would have seemed languid and comfortable.

"Master Cottoner," said Mary. "We have, as you guessed, come to ask for aid."

"Father isn't here," said Roy. "I got no money."

"It happens that we don't need money. What we need is permission to bring a large group of people onto your land, and feed them from your larder, and let them sleep the night."

Roy's eyes narrowed, and he dropped his pose. "So you *are* from those people who crossed Pontchartrain."

"We are indeed," said Mary. "There are five thousand of us, and we'd rather have your help offered freely. But if we have to, we'll just take what we need. We have hundreds of hungry children among us, and we don't mean for them to go hungry."

"You get out of my house," said Roy. "You just get out of here."

For the first time, Mother spoke. "You are young," she said. "But it is the essence of dignity to pretend to desire what you cannot prevent."

"My father'll shoot you down like dogs when he gets home."

"Roy!" A woman's voice came from the hall, and a frail-looking woman came into view behind him, wan and bedraggled from sleep, a robe drawn around her shoulders. "Roy, in my house we will be polite."

"They're a bunch of runaways from Barcy, Mama! They're threatening to take food and such from us."

"That's no reason not to be polite," said the woman. "I am Ruth Cottoner, mistress of this house. Please forgive my ill-mannered son."

"You shouldn't apologize for me, Mama, not to thieves and liars!"

"If I weren't so ill, I'd have reared him better," said Ruth sadly.

Then she pulled up a musket that she had been holding behind her leg. She aimed it straight at Rien and before Mary could even scream, she pulled the trigger.

The gunpowder fizzled and sparked, and a double handful of smallshot dribbled out the end of the barrel.

"How odd," said Ruth. "My husband said it was loaded and ready to fire."

Arthur Stuart appeared behind her. "It was," he said. "But sometimes guns just don't do what you tell them."

She turned around to face him, and now for the first time there was fear on her face. "Whose slave are you! What are you doing in my house!"

"I'm no man's slave," said Arthur Stuart, "nor any woman's neither. I'm just a fellow who doesn't take kindly to folks pointing muskets at my friends."

La Tia appeared behind him. "Ma'am," she said, "you lay down that foolish gun and sit." La Tia was carrying a tray with a pitcher of lemonade and six glasses. "We gonna have a talk, us."

"You leave my mother alone!" shouted Roy. And he

made as if to shove at La Tia. But Arthur Stuart was already there and caught his wrists and held him.

"You will die for laying a hand on my son," said Ruth.

"We'll all die someday," said Arthur Stuart. "Now you heard the lady. Set."

"You have invaded my home."

"This ain't no home," said Arthur Stuart. "This is a prison, where sixty black people are held captive against their will. You are one of the captors, and for this crime you surely deserve terrible punishment, ma'am. But we ain't here to punish nobody, so maybe you best be keeping your thoughts of punishing us to yourself. Now *set*."

She sat. Arthur propelled Roy to another chair and made sure he, too, sat down.

La Tia put the tray on the small serving table and began to fill the glasses with lemonade. "Just so you know," said La Tia, "we notice that some fool has lock all the black folk into their cabins. In the heat of the day, that be so mean to do."

"So I let them all out," said Arthur. "They're drinking their fill at the pump right now, but pretty soon they'll be helping our company find places to camp on your lawns and in your barns, and setting out a supper to feed five thousand. It's like being in the Bible, don't you think?"

"We don't have food enough for so many!" said Ruth.

"If you don't, we'll impose on the hospitality of some of your neighbors."

"My husband will be back any time! Very soon!"

"We'll be watching for him," said Arthur. "I don't think you need to fret—we won't let him accidentally hurt somebody."

Mary couldn't help but admire how cool he was, as if he was enjoying this. And yet there was no malice in it.

"He'll raise the county and have you all hanged!" said Roy.

"Even the women and children?" asked Arthur Stuart mildly. "That's a dangerous precedent. Fortunately, we *aren't* killers, so we won't hang *you*."

"I bet Mr. Tutor's already run for help," said Roy smugly.

"I take it Mr. Tutor is that soft-bodied white man who has read more books than he understood."

Roy nodded.

"He's standing out in the yard with his pants down around his ankles, while some of the illiterate black folks are reading to him from the Bible. It seems they heard him make a big deal about how black folks couldn't be taught to read because their brains wasn't big enough or they got baked in the sun or some such theory, and they're proving him wrong at this moment."

"You were busy out there," said Rien.

"I'm a sick and dying woman," said Ruth. "It's cruel of you to do this to me in the last weeks of my life."

Arthur looked at her and smiled. "And how many weeks of freedom were you going to give any of your slaves, before they died?"

"We treat our servants well, thank you!" said Ruth.

As if in answer to her, Old Bart came into the room. He didn't walk slowly now. His stride was bold and quick, and he walked up to Ruth and spat in her lap. At once Roy leapt up from his chair, but Old Bart turned to him and slapped him so hard across the face that he fell to the floor.

"No!" cried Mary, and her mother also cried out, "Non!"

"We don't hit nobody," said La Tia softly. "And no spitting, neither."

Old Bart turned to her. "The folks out back, they all wanted to do it, but I said, Let me do it just the once for all of us. And they chose me for the job. You know this boy already done had his way with two of the girls, and one of them not even got her womanlies yet."

"That's a lie!" shouted Roy.

"My son is not capable of—"

"Don't you try to tell black folks what white folks is capable of," said Arthur Stuart. "But we're done with all that now. We ain't come here, sir, to bring vengeance or justice. Just freedom."

"You bring me freedom, and then say I can't use it?" said Old Bart.

"I know what you doing," said La Tia. "You a house slave, you try make them field slave forget you sleep indoors on a bed, you."

Old Bart glared at her. "Every day I got them treating me like dirt, they in my face all the time, you think a indoor *bed* make up for that? I hate them more than anybody. Me slapping him stead of killing him, that what *mercy* look like."

Arthur Stuart nodded. "I got respect for your feelings, sir. But right now I don't care about justice nor mercy neither. I care about getting five thousand people safe to the Mizzippy. And I don't need to have the whole country stirred up by a bunch of stories about slaves slapping the children of their former masters."

"They ain't gonna tell no slapping story," said Old Bart. "They gonna tell that we *killed* this white boy and *raped* that white woman, and cut that stupid teacher all up. So as long as they gonna tell it, why not do a *little* of it?"

Ruth gasped.

"You already done all you gonna do," said Arthur Stuart. "I told you why. So if you raise a hand against anybody else while we're here, sir, I'll have to stop you."

Old Bart smiled patronizingly at Arthur Stuart. "I'd like to see you try."

"No you wouldn't," said Arthur.

Mary tried to defuse the situation. She rose from her chair and approached Ruth Cottoner. "Please give me your hand," she said.

"Don't touch me!" cried Ruth. "I won't give my hand to an invader and a looter!"

"I know something about disease," said Mary. "I know more than your doctor."

"In Barcy," said Arthur Stuart, "everybody came to her to know if they was gonna get better when they was sick."

"I'll do no harm," said Mary. "And I'll tell you the truth of what I see. Your son will know if I'm lying."

Slowly the woman raised her hand and put it in Mary's.

Mary felt the woman's body as if it became part of her own, and at once knew where the cancer was. Centered in her womb, but spread out, too, eating away at her inside. "It's bad," she said. "It started in your womb, but it's everywhere now. The pain must be terrible."

Ruth closed her eyes.

"Mama," said Roy.

Mary turned to Arthur Stuart. "Can you . . . ?"

"Not me," said Arthur Stuart. "It's too much for me."

"But Alvin, don't you think he—"

"You can ask him," said Arthur Stuart. "It might be too much for him, too, you know. He ain't no miracle worker."

"You have some kind of healer with you?" said Ruth bitterly. "I've had healers come before, the charlatans."

"He ain't mostly a healer," said Arthur Stuart. "He only does it kind of, you know, when he runs into somebody who needs it."

Mary let go of the woman's hand and walked to the window. Already the people were walking onto the land in their groups of ten households and fifty households. Blacks from the plantation were guiding them to various buildings and sheds, and there were noises of pots and pans, of chopping and chattering coming from the kitchen.

Among the swarming people, it was easy to pick out Alvin. He was as strong as a hero out of legend—Achilles, Hercules—and as wise and good as Prometheus. Mary knew he could heal this woman. And who could then accuse them of stealing, if he paid her back with years and years of life?

Verily Cooper's thighs always got sore when he rode. Sore on the outside, and sore in the muscles as well. There were people who throve on riding, hour after hour. Verily wasn't one of them. And he shouldn't have to be. Lawyers prospered, didn't they? Lawyers rode in carriages. On trains.

Riding a horse you had to think all the time, and work, too. The horse didn't do it all, not by any means. You always had to be alert, or the horse would sense that no one was in control and you'd find yourself following a route to whatever the horse happened to smell that seemed interesting.

And then there was the chafing. The only way to keep the saddle from chafing the insides of your thighs was to stand in the stirrups a little, hold yourself steady. But that was tiring on the muscles of your legs. Maybe with time he'd develop more strength and endurance, but most days he didn't take such long rides on horseback. So it was raise yourself in the stirrups until your thighs ached, and then sit and let your thighs chafe.

Either way your legs burned.

Why should I do this for Alvin? Or for Margaret Larner? What do I actually owe them? Haven't I given *them* most of the service since I've become their friend? What do I get out of this, exactly?

He was ashamed of himself for thinking such disloyal thoughts, but he couldn't help what entered his head, could he? For a while he'd been a friend and traveling companion to Alvin, but those days were gone. He'd tried to learn makery with the others in Vigor Church, too, but even though his own knack was to see how things fit and change them enough to make them fit exactly right—which, as Alvin said, was one of the key parts of making—he still couldn't do the things that Alvin could.

He could set a broken bone—which wasn't a bad knack to have—but he couldn't heal an open wound. He could make a barrel fit so tight it would never leak, but he couldn't open a steel lock by melting the metal. And when Alvin left his own makery school to go a-wandering, Verily couldn't see much reason to stay and continue the exercises.

Yet Alvin asked him to, and so he did. He and Measure, Alvin's older brother—two fools, that's what they were. Working to teach others what they hadn't learned themselves.

And not making much money at lawyering.

I'm a good lawyer, Verily told himself. I'm as good at law as I am at coopery. Maybe better. But I'll never plead before the Supreme Court or the King's Bench or any other lofty venue. I'll never have a case that makes me famous—except defending Alvin, and then it was Alvin who got all the notoriety, not that Verily minded that.

And here his attention had wandered again, and the horse was not on the main trail. Where am I this time? Will I have to backtrack?

Just ahead the road he was on crossed a little stream. Only instead of a ford, as most such roads would have, there was a stout bridge—a covered one, too—only ten feet long, but well above the water, and showing no signs of weakening even though as Verily knew, all the covered bridges on this road had been built by Alvin's father and older brothers, so no other travelers would lose a beloved son and brother because some insignificant river like the Hatrack happened to be in flood on the very day they had to cross.

So the horse had taken a turn somewhere and now they were headed, not direct west to Carthage and on into Noisy River from there, but northwest to Vigor Church. It would be a little longer getting to Abe Lincoln that way, but now that Verily thought of it, this was the better way. It would give him a place for respite and resupply. He might hear news. And maybe the love of his life would be there, ready to introduce herself and take him away from all these complicated things.

Alvin's got him a wife and a baby on the way, and what do I have? Sore legs. And no clients.

What I need is to find a lawyer in Noisy River who needs a good courtroom lawyer in his practice. I think I know how to partner with another lawyer. I'll never be a partner to Alvin Maker. He's his own best partner, except perhaps for his wife, and as far apart as they always are, it's hard to call that much of a partnership either.

I'll take a look at Springfield, Noisy River, and see if it looks like home.

And I won't go through Vigor Church. The love of my life is *not* there. For good or ill, it's my love of Alvin Maker that shapes my life, and I was sent to serve him in Springfield. I'll take no circuitous side trip.

He turned his horse and did not go far before he found the fork in the road where the horse had taken the wrong turning. No, be honest, he told himself. Where *you* took the wrong turning, hoping to flee like Jonah from your duty.

Arthur Stuart watched Alvin close, hoping to learn how to heal this kind of disease. He hadn't caught the details of how Alvin fixed up Papa Moose's foot, but he grasped the main lines of it. This woman's cancer, it was going to be harder. Once Dead Mary had pointed out what was going on in her body, then Arthur had been able to find it, but it was hard to see the boundaries of the cancer, to know where the good flesh left off and the bad began. And there were lots of little spots of it scattered here and there inside her—but there were some he wasn't sure about, whether they were cancer or not.

So when Alvin came into the house and greeted him and La Tia and Rien and Dead Mary, Arthur Stuart could hardly wait to take him to Mistress Cottoner.

Alvin bowed over her hand, and gravely shook the hand of the boy as well, though Roy was sullen about it.

Then Alvin asked if he might sit beside her and take her hands, "because this goes easier if I'm touching you, though I can do it without if you prefer."

In answer, she placed her hands in his. And there, sitting in the parlor, with all the noise of the business of camp outside, and some of it inside, too, as people bounded in from time to time, demanding a decision from La Tia or Rien, Alvin set to work changing her inside.

Arthur Stuart tried to follow along, and this time Alvin was moving slowly and methodically. Almost as if he were trying to make it clear for Arthur—and maybe he was. But always the most important details seemed to elude him. He'd see what Alvin was looking at, and he'd feel how he was seeking out the boundary between good flesh and bad. But how Alvin knew when he had it right, that's what Arthur Stuart just couldn't fathom.

But some things he *could* see. How, when Alvin broke down the sick flesh, he made it dissolve into the blood to be carried away. How he made sure to connect everything up inside when the cancerous parts were gone. How he left her strong.

"I feel sick," she murmured.

"But not in pain," Alvin whispered back.

"No, no pain."

"I'm almost done. Your body is helping me find all the wrong places. I couldn't do it without your own body's help. You know how to heal yourself, not in your mind, but in the flesh and bone and blood. It just needed a little . . . direction. You see? There's no miracle here. My knack is no more than finding what your body already wants to do but can't figure out for itself, and . . . showing the way."

"I don't understand," she said.

"The sick feeling will pass when the last of it comes out of you at stool," he said. "By morning at the latest. Maybe sooner."

"But I won't die?"

"Can't you feel it?" said Alvin softly. "Can't you feel how right things are inside you now?"

She shook her head. "The pain's gone, that's all."

"Well, that's something, ain't it?" said Alvin.

She began to weep.

At once Roy rushed to her, put a hand on her shoulder, and looked in anger at Alvin and Arthur Stuart. "She never cries! You made her cry!"

"She's crying in relief," said Arthur Stuart.

"No she's not," said Alvin.

"You hurt her!" said Roy.

"She's crying because she's afraid." He looked to Mistress Cottoner. "What are you afraid of, ma'am?"

"I'm afraid that when you go, it'll come back."

"I can't promise you it won't," said Alvin. "But I don't think it will. But if it ever does, you send me a letter. Send it to Alvin the Miller's son, at Vigor Church in the state of Wobbish."

"You can't come back here," she said.

"Damn right he can't," said Roy. "I'll be bigger then, and I'll kill him!"

"No you won't," said Mistress Cottoner.

"Will so. Stealing all our slaves! Don't you see, Mother? We'll be poor!"

"We still have the land," said his mother. "And you still have your mother. Isn't that worth something to you?"

Her steady gaze must have said something to the boy that Arthur Stuart just didn't understand, because the boy burst into tears and ran from the room.

"He's young," she said.

"We've all been guilty of *that* sin," said Alvin. "And some never get over it."

"Not me," she said. "I was never young."

Arthur Stuart reckoned there was a whole story behind that, but he didn't know what it was. If his big sister Peggy had been there, *she* would've knowed, and maybe she could have told him later. Or if Taleswapper had ever been here and learned her story and wrote it in his book, then maybe he'd understand. As it was, though, he could only guess what she meant when she said she was never young.

Or what Alvin meant when he answered her, "You're young *now*."

"For a few hours, maybe," she said.

Alvin opened his hands to let hers go. But she moved

quickly and caught him by the wrists. "Oh, please," she said. "Not yet."

So he sat there a while longer and held her hands in his.

Arthur Stuart couldn't watch it for long. There was no healing going on now. Alvin wasn't doing a blame thing with his knack. He was just holding hands with a woman who looked at him like he was God or a long-lost brother or something. It made Arthur Stuart feel like something was wrong. Like his adopted sister, Peggy, was somehow being betrayed by this. Those aren't your hands to hold, Ruth Cottener, he wanted to say.

But he said nothing, and went outside, and saw how La Tia was quietly making decisions and keeping things moving without raising her voice. She even laughed sometimes, and got smiles and laughs from those who came to her.

She saw him, and called to him. "Come here, you!" she said. "I don't got enough Spanish to understand this man!"

So Arthur Stuart got back into the business of camp, and left Alvin alone in the house with a woman who was half in love with him. Well, why shouldn't she be? He just saved her life. He just looked inside her body and saw what was wrong and fixed it up. You have to love somebody who does that, don't you?

It was no riverboat they boarded for the Mexico expedition. Steve Austin must have found somebody with mighty deep pockets, because what they had was a three-masted lateen-rigged schooner, good for the coastal trade, and with oar ports like a galley ship because the Gulf of Mexico was so often calm. There were full blown cannon on this ship, and fieldpieces to take ashore when they got there. Artillery, by damn!

Calvin's respect grew for Steve Austin's ability to get things done. Naturally, there were plenty of people willing to put up money to conquer Mexico—if they believed the expedition could actually succeed. And since there was almost no chance that it would—not with just one ship and a hundred or so minimally obedient "soldiers"—the fact that he got so much money behind this project meant that Steve Austin knew how to *sell*.

That's something I need to learn, thought Calvin. I'll watch this man and learn how he persuades people to invest money in insane projects. That would be a useful knack to have.

The ship turned in the river with the help of a couple of lines still attached to shore, so there'd be no chance of it getting out into the perpetual fog on the far bank and being lost. Then they cast free and began the long, stately voyage to the Mizzippy's mouth.

Not far below Barcy, the fog on the right bank thinned and well before they reached the open sea the fog was gone. That was interesting. The fog must not be attached to the river, it must be attached to the boundary of the land that Tenskwa-Tawa intended to protect. Which made Calvin wonder if there was fog along the coast, too, and fog between the Mexica lands and the lands that Tenskwa-Tawa had taken under his protection.

Or was Tenskwa-Tawa somehow allied with the Mexica? Did Tenskwa-Tawa maybe do some of this human sacrificing, too? And if he does, does Alvin know about it? What an interesting thought. All this high-mindedness about opposing slavery and trying to prevent a bloody war, and all the time he's best friends with a red prophet who chums up with the heart-ripping savages of Mexico.

Not that Calvin didn't know it all along. Alvin pretended to be virtuous and only use his power for "good," but he didn't know what "good" was any more than Calvin did or anyone else. Whatever story he believed in, whatever "us" he was protecting against "them," Alvin had to think that whatever he was doing was noble, but it wasn't. It never was. Alvin was just like everybody else, doing what he wanted that he thought he could get away with, using whatever power came to hand, and stepping on whoever got in his way.

At least Calvin knew that about himself. Didn't have any illusions.

He looked out over the sun-shimmered water as the breeze caught the sails and bellied them and allowed the ship to zigzag its way out to sea. So smooth and clean, this ocean, so bright and dazzling. Downright blinding, when the sun reflects on the little waves and the light gets thrown into your eyes. All so clean, with the little white clouds parading along in the bright blue sky.

But underneath the water was murky, the bottom was filth, and creatures crawled there, devouring whatever they could, and getting scooped up into shrimpers' nets like God coming down to punish the sinners. Only there wasn't any punishment, and there weren't any sinners, just hungry brutal animals that got caught, and hungry brutal animals that got left behind.

Alvin tries to live on top of the bright blue sea. But not me.

Around him the other soldiers of the expedition were laughing and joking and boasting about what they'd do in Mexico. But Calvin had a pretty good idea that when it came right down to it, Steve Austin's plan consisted of getting ashore somewhere and then using Calvin's powers to impress potential allies and terrify the Mexica. These laughing, boasting men—they were hirelings, every one. And there weren't many hirelings who rented out their courage along with their bodies. As long as nobody was shooting at them, as long as they didn't see their comrades turned to corpses, they'd be brave. But when trouble started, they'd be gone.

Well, why not? So will I.

Poor Steve Austin. All this money, just to carry some cannons to the Mexica.

Then again, he might just win. After all, he had Calvin Maker, the man with power who wasn't ashamed to use it.

Wasn't it Calvin who kept the wind blowing, nice and steady, and always in a direction they could use? Not a soul on board suspected that it was him. But when you've got *me* aboard, you don't need those oar ports.

It was evening, and everyone had eaten. Thick fog now surrounded the Cottoner plantation on every side, though in the middle the air was clear and they could see stars.

Arthur Stuart was proud of having learned how to shape the fog. It was hard to realize that only a couple of weeks ago, he had just been learning how to soften iron, and it was so agonizingly slow. But he was like a toddler who struggles to take a couple of steps, and then two weeks later is running headlong through the house and yard, bumping into everything and having a grand old time.

Fog or clear air. Arthur Stuart could decide.

"It's just fog," Alvin told him when he got so excited. "You didn't make a new moon or move a mountain."

"It's *weather,*" said Arthur Stuart. "I'm making weather."

"You're making a fence around some people who need protection," said Alvin. "Don't start showing off, and don't start trying to decide who gets rain and who doesn't. Once you get a storm started, it's mighty hard to slow it back down again."

"I'm not gonna start no storm," Arthur Stuart said scornfully. "You know me all these years, and you think I'm Calvin?"

Alvin grinned. "I ain't confused on that point. But you ain't never gonna be able to tell me, It ain't my fault, I didn't know!"

"So you're gonna teach me *everything*?"

"Everything I think of."

"Who taught *you*?"

"My own stupid mistakes."

"So if stupid mistakes have done so much for *you,* how come you won't let me study from the same teacher?"

Alvin had no answer to that, just a laugh.

And then it was time for Alvin to go.

"You have to sleep," said Dead Mary to him. "Don't go till morning."

"Night time's the best for me," said Alvin. "And I'll sleep as I go."

Dead Mary looked confused.

"It's a thing he learned from the reds," said Arthur Stuart. "He runs in his sleep. We got some of that last night, crossing the lake. Didn't you hear it?"

"*Hear* it? What does running in your sleep sound like?" She laughed, thinking Arthur Stuart was joking.

But in a moment she had forgotten Arthur again. She was back to watching Alvin, and it occurred to Arthur that watching Alvin was pretty much what she did, whenever she wasn't actually compelled to do something else. She didn't look at him in that emotional way Ruth Cottoner had. It was something else. Perfect raptness. Complete intensity. As if she wanted to own him with her eyes.

Ruth Cottoner, that was love, all right, love made of gratitude and relief and fear and trust in this man who had saved her. But Dead Mary, she loved him, too, but it was something else. It was purposeful. She hadn't yet got what she wanted. But she meant to get it.

I can't know that, thought Arthur Stuart. I'm not Peggy, I'm no torch to see inside folks' heartfires.

And anyway, Peggy wouldn't send Alvin into a place where some other woman was going to fall in love with him.

Then again, for all Arthur Stuart knew, women were always falling in love with Alvin and he had always been too young and dumb to notice. He remembered a few times, sure. Never amounted to much. It's not like Alvin ever flirted back.

But this time Alvin didn't seem to see how she looked at him. Because maybe she was more subtle. After all, Arthur hadn't seen it himself until just now, just tonight. So maybe Alvin didn't notice how her gaze was always attached to him, how she listened to every word, how she worshiped him. But notice it or not, it had its effect on him. He kept turning to her. He'd be speaking to somebody else, but he kept glancing at her, as if checking to make sure she'd heard him. As if he expected her to get some joke that only the two of them knew.

Only there was no joke between them, there was nothing, there hadn't been *time* for anything, Arthur Stuart had been there, hadn't he? Almost always, except that very first time they met, when she led him to that cabin in the swamp to heal her mother.

This Dead Mary, all she ever sees in every man she meets is whether he's sick or not, and if he's gonna die of it. But in Alvin, what does she see? The man who can make her nightmares *not* come true.

No, she sees power. To change the world, change the future.

Or maybe it's just them strong blacksmith's arms and shoulders.

And what do I care, anyway? It's not like Alvin's going to fall for *her*. He doesn't even look at other women than Peggy—if he ever did I'd know it. So what difference does it make to me?

It's not like Alvin's the only man around here who can do things. I may not be able to heal folks, but I held up the other end of Alvin's bridge, and that ain't nothing. I kept Ruth Cottoner's musket from firing. I made the *fog*.

What am I thinking? She must be five years older than me. And white, and French. Though I *can* speak French now pretty good. And I'm *half* white, and what difference should it make, anyway, once we get out of slave country?

No. I'm a child in her eyes, and a half-black one at that, and most of all, I'm Alvin's prentice maker, and he's the real thing, so why *should* she ever look at me?

Good thing Alvin's going, though. Good thing he's got errands to run. Wouldn't want to have a lot of distraction, when they had so much to do.

Alvin didn't make a big deal about going. He'd done

all he said he'd do. La Tia and Arthur and Dead Mary and Rien knew their jobs—Dead Mary and Rien to distract the folks in the big house until Arthur Stuart and La Tia could get the slaves free and learn what all they had to know. It wouldn't always be like this, of course, with the man of the house gone and the slaves all locked down in their cabins and the overseer drunk and easy to keep asleep. And there'd be no healings of sick women, with Alvin gone. But they'd manage.

And the last thing Alvin wanted was for all the thousands of refugees from Barcy to see a lot of fuss about him going. Especially not if anybody was going to get emotional and plead with him to stay. That would fill the camp with uncertainty. As it was, the people who had actually done all the important work today were still with them. And when folks started asking where Alvin was, they could say, He's scouting on ahead, he'll be back soon.

So when it came time for Alvin to step away, most people didn't even notice that he'd done it.

Only Arthur Stuart, and he didn't run up to Alvin and say any last words, just gave him a grin and watched him shoulder his poke, slip into the trees, and move on into the fog.

When he looked away from where Alvin had faded from view, nobody else even seemed to have noticed.

Except Dead Mary. She was ostensibly talking with her mother and a couple of Frenchmen about something, but her gaze was fixed on the place where Alvin had last been visible.

It's love, thought Arthur Stuart. Girl is crazy with love. Or *something*.

It took a while for folks to settle down. They hadn't got much sleep, so you'd think they'd all be tired, and the children *had* fallen asleep about as soon as their stomachs were full. But there was conversation and wonderment and worry, plenty to keep things humming for an hour or so after the meal and the cleanup were over.

Arthur knew he needed sleep as much as anyone, maybe more. But first he checked to make sure the fog was in place. That was his first job, and if he failed at that, what would he be worth? So he walked the perimeter of the camp one last time. A couple of the blacks just released from slavery on the Cottoner plantation saw him and came and gave him thanks, but he refused, and just said he didn't give them anything God didn't give them first, and then excused himself to finish checking on things.

When he got back to the big house, most everyone was asleep. And it occurred to him that he hadn't arranged so much as a blanket for himself.

No matter. The grass was dry and the air was warm and he didn't mind the insects. He found an empty patch of ground not far from the edge of the fog, where nobody else was sleeping, and he sat down and started rubbing the bottoms of his feet with grass, which he found was soothing after a day's walking. His shoes were somewhere near the house, he remembered now. He'd get them in the morning, or do without. Shoes were good to have in winter, but they were a bother to have to carry around all summer, when mostly you wanted to feel the ground under your feet.

"So he's gone," said Dead Mary.

Arthur hadn't even noticed her approach. He cursed himself. Alvin always knew who was nearby. And Arthur Stuart *could* see the heartfires, the near ones anyway. He just wasn't used to looking. There were hundreds around him now, all sleeping. He hadn't been paying attention.

"And you are the maker now," said Dead Mary.

"Prentice maker," said Arthur Stuart. "If that. My real knack is learning languages."

She said something to him in a language that sounded partly like Spanish and partly like French.

"I got to learn them first," said Arthur. "It's not like I already got all possible languages inside my head."

She laughed lightly. "What is it like, traveling with him all the time?"

"Like being with your brother-in-law who sometimes treats you like a kid and sometimes treats you like a person."

She smiled and shook her head. "It must be wonderful, to see him do these noble things."

"He usually does no more than one noble deed afore dinner, and then he's done for the day."

"You're teasing me," she said.

"You want to know what it's like?" said Arthur Stuart. "Just ask your ma how thrilling it is every time she sees you find out whether somebody's sick, and whether they'll die of it."

"How could you ever get used to something like this?"

"I'm not trying to get used to it," said Arthur. "I'm trying to learn to do it."

"Why? Why do you need to know, when *he* can do it so much better?"

Didn't she have any idea how hurtful it was to say such a thing? "Well, it's a good thing I did learn something, don't you think?" he said. "Or we'd have to have a bunch of watchmen out tonight, and in this group, how many reliable guards do you think we'd find?"

"So you really made the fog? He didn't do it?"

"He started it, to show me how. I made the rest."

"And you can do it tomorrow?"

"I hope so," said Arthur Stuart, " 'cause we got to leave this fog behind. If we stayed a second night here, this plantation wouldn't have anything left to eat and the Cottoners would starve."

"They won't starve—they don't have all those slaves to feed now, remember?" She lay back on the grass. "If I could travel with him, I would be happy every minute of every day."

"Don't work that way for me," said Arthur Stuart. "About every other day, I stub my toe or eat something that makes me queasy. Otherwise, though, it's pretty much ecstasy."

"Why do you tease me? All I'm doing is telling you what's in my heart."

"He's a married man," said Arthur Stuart. "And his wife is my sister."

"Don't be jealous for your sister," said Dead Mary. "I don't love him that way."

Yes you do, thought Arthur Stuart. "Glad to hear it," he said.

"Can you help me?" she said.

"Help you what?"

"This globe of crystal water he made, that I've been carrying with me—"

"As I recall, you had a couple of boys who were sweet on you pushing that wheelbarrow most of the day."

She waved his tease away. "I look in it and what I see frightens me."

"What do you see?"

"All the deaths in the world," she said. "So many I can't even tell who is doing the dying."

Arthur Stuart shuddered. "I don't know how the thing works. Maybe you only see what you've been trained to see. You already know how to see death, so that's what you see."

She nodded. "That makes sense. I was going to ask you what *you* see."

"My mother," said Arthur Stuart. "Flying. Carrying me to freedom."

"So you were born in slavery."

"My mother spent all her strength and died of it, getting me away."

"How brave of her. How sad for you."

"I had family. A couple of families. A black one, the Berrys, they pretended they were my real parents for awhile, so folks wouldn't tag me as a runaway. And the Guesters, the white family that actually raised me. Alvin's mother-in-law, Old Peg, she adopted me. She meant it, too. Though I reckon Alvin's been more my father than Peggy's father was. He's an innkeeper, and a good man. Helped a lot of slaves get to freedom. And he always made me feel welcome, but it was Alvin took me everywhere and showed me everything."

"And all before you were twenty."

"I don't reckon we're done yet," said Arthur Stuart.

"So you can tease me, but I can't tease you?"

"I didn't know you were teasing."

"So you don't speak *all* the languages." She laughed at him.

"If you don't mind, maybe it's time for sleep."

"Don't be mad at me, Prentice Maker. We have a lot of work to do together. We should be friends."

"We are," said Arthur Stuart. "If you want to be."

"I do."

He thought, but did not say: Just so you can use me to stay close to Alvin, I reckon.

"Do you?" she said.

Does it matter what I want? "Of course," he said. "This is all going to work better if we're friends."

"And someday you'll help me understand what I see in Alvin's globe?"

"I don't even understand what I see in my soup," said Arthur Stuart. "But I'll try."

She rolled onto one arm and leaned toward him and kissed his forehead. "I will sleep better knowing you're my friend and I can learn from you."

Then she got up and left.

You might sleep better, thought Arthur Stuart, but I won't.

✦ 10 ✦

Mizzippy

ALVIN FOUND IT hard to hear the greensong in this place. It wasn't just the disharmony of field after field of cotton tended by slaves, which droned a bitter, complaining monotone under the songs of life. It was also his own fears and worries, distracting him so he couldn't listen to the life around him as he needed to.

Leaving Arthur in charge of all the makery that this exodus required was dangerous, not because there was any ill will in the young man, but because there was simply so much he didn't know. Not just about makery, either, but about life, about what the consequences of each action were likely to be. Not that Alvin was any expert himself—nor was Margaret, for even she saw many paths and wasn't sure which ones led to good places in the end. But he knew more than Arthur Stuart did simply by virtue of having lived years longer, with a watchful eye.

Worse, the actual authority in the camp was held by La Tia, and—to a lesser extent—by Dead Mary and her mother. La Tia he had only met the day before the crossing of the lake. She was a woman who was used to being more powerful than anyone around her—how would she deal with Arthur Stuart when Alvin wasn't there to look after him? If only Alvin could see into people's hearts. La Tia was fearless, but that could mean either that she had no guile or that she had no conscience.

And Dead Mary. It was obvious she was enamored of Arthur Stuart—the way she watched him, enjoyed his company, laughed at his wit. Of course the boy would never see that, he wasn't used to the company of women, and since Dead Mary wasn't a flirt or a tart, the signs would be hard for him to recognize, being so inexperienced. But what if, in Alvin's absence, she did something to make it obvious after all? What would Arthur Stuart do, unsupervised, in the company of a woman who might be a great deal more experienced than he was?

He also had misgivings about bringing along the slaves from the plantations where they stopped along the way. But as La Tia said, when he suggested they might not want to swell their numbers: "This a march of freedom, man! Who you gonna leave behind? These folk need less freedom? Why we the chosen ones? They as much Israelites as us!"

Israelites. Of course everybody was comparing this to the exodus from Egypt, complete with the drowning of some of "Pharaoh's" army when the bridge collapsed. The fog was the pillar of smoke. And what did that make Alvin? Moses? Not likely. But that's how a lot of the people felt.

But not all. There was a lot of anger in this group. A lot of people who had come to hate all authority, and not just that of the Spanish or the slaveowners. The anger in Old Bart, the butler in the Cottoner house—there was so much fury in his heart, Alvin wondered how he had managed to contain it all these years. Old Bart was still in control of himself, and had calmed down considerable since he'd had a chance to see how big a job it was, getting all these folks safely through slave country. Didn't hurt that he'd seen Arthur Stuart and La Tia use powers he'd never seen black folks using—and that there was plenty of white folks in the company who was doing what Arthur Stuart and La Tia told them. It was already a new world.

But then they'd come to a new plantation where slaves had suffered worse than they did on the Cottoner place, and Old Bart's anger would rekindle, and the others from his old plantation would see the fire in him and it would stir it up in them, too. That was just human nature, and it made the situation dangerous.

How many others were there, with bits of authority like Old Bart's? Not to mention the ones that would like to make trouble just because they liked stirring things up. It's not like they'd get to say, at each plantation, We're gonna free all of you what's nice and forgiving, anybody who's got any nastiness in them, or is too angry to act peaceful, you're gonna stay here under the lash.

Like Moses, they'd take everybody that had been in bondage. And like Moses, they couldn't guess if some of them might find some way of making a golden calf that would destroy the exodus before they got to the promised land.

Promised land. That was the biggest worry. Where in the world was he going to take them? Where was the land of milk and honey? It's not as if the Lord had appeared to Alvin in a burning bush. The closest he'd ever come to seeing an angel was the dark night when Tenskwa-Tawa—then a perpetually drunken red named Lolla-Wossiky—appeared in his room and Alvin had healed his blind eye. But Lolla-Wossiky wasn't God or even an angel like the one that wrestled with Jacob. He was a man who groaned with the pain of his people.

And yet he was the only angel Alvin had ever seen, or even heard about, unless you counted whatever it was that his sister's husband, Armor-of-God Weaver, had seen in Reverend Thrower's church back when Alvin was a child. Something shimmering and racing around inside the walls of the church, and it like to made Thrower crazy to see whatever it was he saw, but Armor-of-God could never make it out. And that was as close to seeing a supernatural creature as anyone of Alvin's acquaintance had ever come.

Oh, there had been miracles enough in Alvin's life, plenty of strange doings, and some of them wonderful. Peggy watching out for him throughout his childhood without his even knowing it. The powers he had found inside himself, the ability to see into the heart of the world and persuade it to change and become better. But not one of them had given him the knowledge of what he ought to be doing from one moment to the next. He was left to muddle through as best he could, taking what advice he could get. But nobody, not even Margaret, had the truth—truth so true that you *knew* it was true, and knew that what you knew was bound to be right. Alvin always had a shadow of doubt because nobody truly knew anything, not even their own heart.

With all this running through his mind, over and over again, reaching no conclusion, he soon found that his legs were tired and his feet were sore—something that hadn't happened to him while running since Ta-Kumsaw had first taught him to hear the greensong and let it fill him with the strength of all the life around him.

This won't do, he realized. If I run like a normal man, I'll cover ground so slowly it will be more than one night before I reach the river. I have to shut all this out of my mind and let the song have me.

So he did the only thing he could think of that would shut all else out of his mind.

He reached out, searching for Margaret's heartfire, which he always knew as well as a man might know his own self. There she was . . . and there, just under her own heartfire, was that glowing spark of the baby that they had made together. Alvin concentrated on the baby, on finding his way through its small body, feeling the heartbeat, the flow of blood, the strength coming into the baby from

Margaret's body, the way his little muscles flexed and extended as he tested them.

Exploring this new life, this manling-to-be, all other worries left Alvin and then the greensong came to him, and his son was part of it, that beating heart was part of the rhythm of the trees and small animals and grass and, yes, even the slave-grown cotton, all of it alive. The birds overhead, the insects crawling in and on the earth, the flies and skeeters, they were all part of the music. The gators in the banks of languid rivers and stagnant pools, the deer that still browsed in the stands of wood that had not yet made way for the cotton fields, the small herbs with healing and poison in them, the fish in the water, and the hum, hum, hum of sleeping people who, in the nighttime, became part of the world again instead of fighting against it the way most folks did the livelong day.

So it was that he was not tired, not sore, but alert and filled with vigor and well-being when he reached the shores of the Mizzippy. He had crossed many a wagon track but nothing so fine as to be called a road, for in these parts the best road was the water, and the greatest highway of all was the Mizzippy.

Though it was night, there were stars enough, and a sliver of moon. Alvin could see the broad river stretching away to the left and right, each ripple in the water catching a bit of light. Halfway across, though, there was the perpetual fog that guarded the west bank from the endless restless ambition of the Europeans.

There was no doubt that Tenskwa-Tawa knew Alvin was coming. His sister-in-law, Becca, was a weaver of the threads of life. She would have noticed Alvin's thread and how it moved over to be at the boundary between white men and red. Tenskwa-Tawa would have been told. He would know that if Alvin came here, straight toward the river, and not traveling north or south along it, it meant he wanted to cross the water. It meant he wanted to talk.

It wasn't something Alvin did often. He didn't want to be a bother. It had to matter, before he'd come. And so

Tenskwa-Tawa would trust his judgment and come to meet him.

Or not. After all, it's not as if Tenskwa-Tawa came and went at Alvin's bidding. If he was busy, then Alvin would have to wait. It hadn't happened yet, or not much of a wait, anyway. But Alvin knew that it *could* happen, and was prepared to wait if he needed to. For a while.

But if Tenskwa-Tawa didn't come at all, what would that mean? That his answer was no? That he would not let these five thousand children of Israel—or at least children of God, or maybe Tenskwa-Tawa saw them as nothing more than the children of their powerless parents, but human beings all the same—was it possible he would not let them pass? What would Alvin do then?

He looked toward his left, not with his eyes, but searching for the heartfires of the northbound expedition that had left Barcy that afternoon to bring these runaway slaves back home. Good—they hadn't made much progress on the first day, and were still far off. There was a lot of anger and discomfort in the group, too, as drunks vomited and former drunks suffered from headaches and men who wished they were drunk grumbled at the tedium of the journey and the poor quality of the pleasures aboard a military boat.

Even farther was the ship that carried Calvin. Plenty of anger on that ship, too—but of a different kind, a sort of bitter sense of entitlements long delayed. Calvin had found a like-minded bunch, people who felt the world owed them something and was slow to pay up. Were they really going to Mexico? Was Calvin so foolish as to put in with that mad expedition? Wherever they went, he knew they'd cause trouble when they got there.

Mostly, though, Alvin wondered how he was going to cross the river.

Building a bridge for just himself didn't seem to have much point to it. But it was a long swim, and a hard one to do wearing all his clothes and carrying a golden plow—which would make a pretty good anchor but a mighty poor raft.

So he began to make his way up the river. The trouble was that close to the water, all was a tangle of trees and brush, while farther back, he couldn't see whether there was any boat tied up. This wasn't hospitable country for farming or fishing, and it was doubtful anybody lived too close. And there were gators—he could see their heartfires, dimmed a bit by sleep, except the hungry ones. Wouldn't they just like a piece of manflesh to digest as they lay on the riverbank through the heat of the day tomorrow.

Don't wake up for *me,* he murmured to a nearby wakeful gator. Keep your place, I'm not for you today.

Finally he realized there was going to be no boat unless he made one.

So he found a dead, half-fallen tree—no shortage of those in this untended land—and got it to let go of its roots' last hold in the earth. With a great splash it fell into the water, and after a short while, Alvin had shorn it of all the branches he didn't want it to have. The tree had been propped up there, mostly dead, for long enough that it was dry wood, and floated well. He gave it a bit more shaping, and then picked his way between bushes and stepping on roots until he was near enough to the log that he didn't have to splash far in the water to reach it.

Mounting it was a bit of a trouble, since it was inclined to roll, and it occurred to Alvin that it probably wasn't much different in appearance from the great tree that had been swept downstream on the Hatrack River flood the day that he was born. What killed my brother Vigor is now my vehicle to cross.

But thinking about the past reminded him of all those years of childhood, when it seemed that every bad accident that befell him was related somehow to water. His father had remarked upon it, and not as some kind of superstition about coincidence, either. Water was out to get him, that's what Alvin Senior said.

And it wasn't altogether false. No, the water itself had no will or wish to harm him or anything. But water naturally tore and rusted and eroded and melted and mudded up everything it passed over or under or through. It was a natural tool of the Unmaker.

At the thought of his ancient enemy, who had so often brought him to the edge of death, he got that old feeling from his childhood. The sense that something was watching him from just out of sight, just on the edge of vision. But when he turned his head, the watcher seemed to flee to where the new edge of his vision was. Nothing was ever there. But that was the problem—the Unmaker *was* nothing, or at least was a lover of nothing, and wished to make everything into nothing, and would not rest until it all was broken down and swept away and gone.

Alvin stood against him. A futile, pathetic weakling, that's what I am, thought Alvin. I can't build up faster than the Unmaker tears down. Yet he still hates me for trying.

Or maybe he doesn't hate me. Maybe he's a wild creature, hungry all the time, and I simply smell like his prey. No malice in it. Wasn't tearing down just a part of building up? All part of the same great flow of nature. Why should he be the enemy of the Unmaker, when really they worked together, the maker and unmaker, the maker making things out of the rubble of whatever the unmaker tore down.

Alvin shuddered. What had he been about to do? What had he been thinking about?

There was a heartfire near him. A hungry one indeed. That gator that he had told to stay away. Apparently it changed its mind, what with Alvin standing there thigh-deep in the Mizzippy, resting his hands on a floating log and burdened with a heavy poke slung over his shoulder.

Alvin felt the jaws snap shut on his leg and immediately drag him downward, a sharp tug that jerked his feet out from under him and put him under the water.

He fought to keep his body's reflexes from taking over——flailing arms all panicking to try to swim up for air wouldn't do him much good with a gator holding onto one leg.

The gator jerked its head this way and that, and Alvin felt his thigh bone pull hard away from the hip socket. Next try and the gator would have him disjointed.

Alvin reached into the mind of the gator to persuade it to let go. A simple thing, to tell some feeble-brained animal how to see the world. Not food, not prey, danger, go away.

Only the gator had no interest in his story. What Alvin felt there in its heartfire was something old and malicious. It wasn't hungry. It just wanted Alvin dead. He could feel it hungering to tear him apart, a frenzy building inside it.

And he could feel other heartfires coming. More gators, drawn by the thrashing in the water.

Why wouldn't this gator respond?

Because you're in the water, fool.

No, I've been in water a thousand times with no danger, and—

No time to settle this now. If I can't do it by persuasion, I'll do it another way.

Alvin reached down with his doodlebug and stopped up the gator's nostrils and told it that it needed air and couldn't breathe.

Didn't matter. The gator didn't care.

And now Alvin knew that he was fighting something a good deal more dangerous than a gator. Animals wanted to live, and they never forgot that. So when this gator didn't care that it couldn't breathe . . .

Another jerk. Alvin felt his hip joint come apart inside. Now it was just some ligaments and muscles and his skin holding his leg onto his body. The gator would have those torn apart in no time.

The pain was terrible, but Alvin shut his mind to that. He hadn't come all this way, through all the dangers that he'd faced, to die in a river the way the Unmaker had tried to kill him so many times before.

Alvin pulled the poke down from his shoulder and jammed the heavy end of it into the gator's mouth.

With one end of the living plow between its teeth, the

gator tried to snap at it. That meant releasing its grip on Alvin's leg. He couldn't just pull the leg free, though— with the bones disconnected his muscles didn't work right and the leg wouldn't obey him. Nor could he reach down and pull his leg free, because he needed to use both hands to hold the plow. For all he knew it was the Unmaker's plan to get the plow away from him and lose it at the bottom of the river, and Alvin wasn't going to do that. He'd put a good part of himself into that plow, and he was blamed if he was going to let go of it without more of a fight than *this*.

The other gators were getting close. Alvin got inside the nearest one and tried to lead it to attack the gator who was holding onto him. But while this second animal wasn't filled with malice, it also wasn't responding to him. It was afraid to obey him. The Unmaker could cry fear into the animal's heart louder than Alvin could speak hunger to it. It retreated. All the other gators waited in a semicircle, all about fifteen feet away, watching the struggle in the water.

The gator was still trying to gnaw at the plow, and each time it bit down, Alvin worked the plow deeper and deeper between its jaws. The plow was thicker than Alvin's leg. And finally, with the teeth no longer gripping him, he was able to twist his body and his injured leg came free.

In that moment the gator made its move, to try to get away with the plow in its mouth. But Alvin was ready. He flopped onto the gator's back and embraced its whole head in a great bear hug, clamping the jaws tightly around the plow.

That did bother the gator. The plow was too big for its jaws to close with the plow between them, and with Alvin holding on so tightly it could neither swallow nor open its mouth enough to let go of the thing. On top of that, its nostrils were still closed, and even though Alvin had caught plenty of breaths during the struggle, the gator had been going some minutes without taking in any air. How long could a gator's lungs hold out?

A long time, Alvin learned, as he held on, squeezing tighter and tighter.

After a while, he realized that the gator was no longer thrashing.

Still he held on.

Yes, there it was. One last twitch, one feeble attempt to rise to the surface and breathe.

And in that moment, Alvin unstopped its nostrils. Because he was blamed if he was going to let the Unmaker force him to kill a perfectly innocent gator who wouldn't have done nobody any harm except the Unmaker forced it to.

Alvin rose up, balancing on his one good leg, lifting the gator's head above water. At once it began to thrash weakly, sucking air into its partly open mouth and its nostrils. Then Alvin flung it across the log. Its mouth hung open for one long moment and Alvin snatched the poke, with the plow in it, back out of the gator's mouth. Then he shoved the gator back into the water and this time when he told it to go away, it heard him, and feebly began to swim away.

The other gators leapt upon the weakened one and dragged it under the water.

No! shouted Alvin into their minds. Let it go. Go away. Let it go.

They obeyed.

And as they swam away, Alvin thought, for just a moment, that swimming alongside them was a reptilian creature that was not a gator at all, but rather a fiery salamander, its glow damped by the murky water of the Mizzippy.

Was that what Thrower saw in his church, when Armor-of-God saw him cower in terror at whatever was circling the walls? Or was it just a trick of my eyes because the pain is . . . so . . . bad.

Alvin dragged his bad leg and the poke with the plow up onto the shore and lay there, panting.

And then he realized that even this would be a victory

for the Unmaker. He didn't want me to cross that river. Therefore I must cross, and without delay, or he still wins.

With the water to help bear the agonizing weight of his disjointed leg, Alvin half hopped, half swam to the log and put the plow on top of it and dragged his own body on. It took more than his physical strength—he had to use his power to keep the thing from rolling with him on it. But finally he was fully atop the log, and he paddled it out into the current of the river.

Ahead of him the wall of fog waited. It was safety. If Alvin made it there, he'd be under the influence of Tenskwa-Tawa, and he had all the power of the red people behind the making of that fog. The Unmaker surely couldn't go there.

Alvin kept going, despite the fog of pain that threatened to plunge him into unconsciousness. He couldn't concentrate well enough to make the paddling go faster or easier. Nor could he spare the attention to tend to his disjointed hip. He just kept paddling and paddling, knowing that the current was sweeping him ever leftward, farther downstream than he wanted to go.

The fog closed around him. And with the wave of relief that swept over him, he finally slipped into unconsciousness.

He woke to find a black man bending over him.

The man spoke in a language that Alvin didn't understand. But he had heard it before. He just couldn't remember where.

Alvin was lying on his back. On dry land. He must have made it across.

Or maybe somebody on the river found him and brought him to the other shore.

It was hard to care.

The man's voice became more urgent. And then his meaning became very clear as large, strong hands pulled on his injured leg and another pair of hands shoved at his upper thigh, scraping bone on bone in a blinding flash of agony. It didn't work, the bone wouldn't go back into the socket, and as they let his leg slide back into its out-of-joint position the pain became too great and Alvin fainted.

He woke again, perhaps only moments later, and again the man spoke and gestured and Alvin raised one feeble hand. "Wait," he said. "Wait for just a moment."

But if they understood his words or his gesture, they gave no sign. He saw now that there were several of them, and they were determined to get his hip back together, and nothing he said was going to stop him.

So, with desperate hurry, he scanned through his own body, finding the ligaments that were blocking the way, and this time when they pulled and pushed, Alvin was able to arrange things so the top of the thigh bone slid past the obstructions. For a moment it balanced on the lip of the socket, and then with a jolt slipped back where it belonged.

Alvin fainted again.

When he awoke he was in a different place, indoors, and no one was with him, though he heard voices in a strange language—not the same language—outside.

Outside what?

Open your eyes, fool, and see where you are.

A cabin. An old one, in need of fresh mud to chink the holes in the walls. Long out of use, apparently.

The door opened. A different black man entered. And now Alvin saw that he looked familiar. He was dressed in a costume that consisted of feathers and animal skins arranged to give the impression, but not the reality, of decorated nakedness. Not like a red man. But perhaps like an African. Perhaps dressed as he would have dressed in his homeland, before he was carried away into slavery.

But Alvin had seen him before, on the deck of a boat.

"I am learn English," said the man.

That's right, the slaves on the boat spoke little English. Some spoke Spanish, and most spoke the language of the Mexica, but both those languages were a mystery to him.

"You were on the *Yazoo Queen,*" said Alvin.

The man looked baffled.

"Riverboat," said Alvin. "You."

The man nodded happily. "You on boat! You put I . . .we . . . off boat!"

"Yes," said Alvin. "We set you free."

The man threw himself to his knees beside Alvin's mat and then bent over to embrace him. Alvin hugged him back. "How long have I been here?" he asked.

The man again looked baffled. Apparently Alvin had taken him beyond the limits of his English.

Alvin tried to sit up, but the man pushed him back down.

"Sleep sleep," said the man.

"No, I've had enough sleep," said Alvin.

"Sleep sleep!" insisted the man.

How could Alvin explain to him that while they'd been talking and hugging, Alvin had checked over his leg, found all the injuries—the sore spots in the joint, the places where the gator's teeth had torn the skin—and fixed them?

All he could do was raise the leg that had been dislocated and show that it could be moved freely. The man looked at him in surprise, and tried to get him to lay his leg down, but Alvin instead showed him that where the gator had bitten him, there were no scars.

The man suddenly laughed and tugged at the blanket still covering Alvin's other leg. Apparently he thought Alvin was joking by showing him the leg that had never been injured. But when this one, too, turned out to be unharmed, the man stood up and slowly backed away.

"Where are my clothes?" Alvin asked.

In reply the man darted for the door and pushed on out into daylight.

Alvin got up and looked around in the semi-darkness of the cabin, but it wasn't his clothes he was looking for. The poke was gone, and with it the plow. Had it slipped off the log into the Mizzippy? Or had it stayed with him until he reached whatever shore he was on, and now these men had it?

He cast about him with his doodlebug, looking for the warm glow of it. But it wasn't like a heartfire, a bright spark in a twinkling sea. The plow was living gold, yes, but gold all the same, with no one place in it that held the fire of life. If Alvin knew where to look for it, he always found it easily. But he had never searched for it without knowing where it was already.

Finally he pulled up the blanket and wrapped it as a skirt around his waist. They may not believe he could heal so fast, but he wasn't going to let their caution or his modesty keep him from finding what was lost.

He stepped out into bright daylight—morning light, so maybe he hadn't slept all that long. If it was morning of the same day. Why should he have slept longer? He'd been perfectly refreshed by the greensong just prior to his fight with the gator. And the fight hadn't lasted all that long. A few thrashes and it was done. Why had it worn him out so bad in the first place? Apart from the pain and loss of blood and the energy it took to help them put his hip back in place, it shouldn't have taken that much out of him. No, this had to be the same morning. He hadn't lost a day.

He was noticed very quickly, and black men came rushing to him. These had to be the men that he and Arthur Stuart had freed from slavery aboard the *Yazoo Queen*— the men that Steve Austin had been planning to use as interpreters and guides in Mexico, since they had once been slaves there. So they had no reason to do him harm.

"My poke," he said. "A homespun sack, I wore it slung over my shoulder, it was heavy." He pantomimed putting it on and taking it off.

At once they understood him. "Gold spirit!" cried the one who had talked to him just moments before in the house. "Gold she fly!" He ran a few steps, then beckoned for Alvin to follow.

He found the plow, out of the poke, floating in the air

about a yard above the ground. Three black men sat forming a perfect triangle, looking up at the plow, each with one hand extended toward it.

Alvin's guide called to them as they approached, and slowly the three rose up, but without ever letting their hands stop reaching for the plow. It remained equidistant between them and three feet off the ground. Carefully they turned and began to walk toward Alvin.

"No take," said the guide. "She no let."

Alvin realized that the plow simply wouldn't let itself be taken by another hand. It kept its distance from reaching hands.

Except Alvin's. He approached it, reached out, and it didn't retreat. Instead it almost leapt into his hands. Of course, that involved letting go of the blanket, but seeing how these folks was as near naked as could be Alvin just said, "You got my clothes anywhere, please? And what about the poke I carry this plow in?"

With lots of smiles and bobbing heads, he found himself being dressed—they actually tried to lift up both his legs at the same time to put them into his trouser legs.

"No!" he said firmly. "I been dressing myself since I was little." He carefully set the plow down in the damp grass. Must have been a heavy dew. Or it rained in the night. Anyway, the moment he set it down, they rushed forward, reaching for the plow, causing it to rise into the air.

"Gold she fly!" the guide admonished him.

"It's a plow," said Alvin. "It's meant to set on the dirt." In fact, it was meant to bite into the earth and churn it up, breaking up clods and baring the soil to the heat of the sun. And in that moment Alvin understood the nature of the plow. All this time he'd been thinking of what it was made of, the living gold, but it was a plow *first*, before it turned to gold, and it was long overdue to be put to its proper use. Just because a thing was made of metal which, if you melted it down, would be worth a lot of money, didn't mean it wasn't still the kind of thing it was made to be.

Dressed, holding the poke in his hand, Alvin simply drew the mouth of it over the plow there in the air, then slung the poke over his shoulder. It went docilely into place, just like always.

The men sighed to see it.

And then another black man approached, carefully holding something on a mat of leaves. It shimmered in the bright sun like crystal, and Alvin recognized it at once. If he had had any doubt that these were the same men he and Arthur Stuart had freed from the *Yazoo Queen*, it was gone now, because the crystal cube he held was made with a drop of his own blood in water on the *Yazoo Queen*. He had given them two such cubes, to use as tokens to show to the reds on the other side of the river. They would know that such things could only be made by Tenskwa-Tawa himself or one that he had taught, and it would win them safe passage. Apparently it had worked.

"Now," said Alvin. "Where am I, and where's Tenskwa-Tawa?"

"Profeta Roja," said one of the men. "Ten-si-ki-wa Ta-wa." The way he pronounced it sounded more like the way reds said the Prophet's name. Well, speaking other languages wasn't Alvin's knack, that was already settled and he wasn't going to be embarrassed about calling his friend by the wrong name all these years.

"Ten-sa-ka-wa Ta-wa," he muttered.

One of the men tried to correct him, but Alvin gave up right away. Tenskwa-Tawa had been answering to that name for years and if he minded, he'd've mentioned it by now.

"We stay," said the guide. "Wait-for."

So Tenskwa-Tawa was coming. Well, Alvin could wait as well as the next man—especially now he was dressed and had the plow back. It also reassured him to find out that the plow could take care of itself, somewhat. A plow that flies from your hand when you reach to take it would be hard to put over a fire and melt down. Though that wasn't to say some powerful hexery might not do the trick. Still, it wasn't a thing a thief could easily do. Alvin might fret a little less about the plow, knowing.

Alvin spent what was left of the morning trying to learn the names of some of these men, but it turned into a game of laughing at his bad pronunciation. For all he knew they weren't telling him names at all, but making him say ugly cuss words in their language.

There was food at noon, but this, too, was strange and unfamiliar. A thin flat bread like a flapjack, only thinner, smeared with a spicy paste that might have contained mashed beans but then might not. It was good, though. Burned a little, and drinking water didn't help, but they had some pawpaw fruit sliced up in a basket and a bite of that took away the sting. And after a while he got used to the burning and kind of liked it.

After the meal, Alvin went walking to try to orient himself. He found that the whole troop followed him along like children in a small town, following a stranger. He wasn't sure whether they were protecting him or keeping watch to make sure he didn't run away or were simply curious what he'd do next.

He found that they were on a wide, flat island near the right bank of the Mizzippy. The fog, which was on their side of the river, ended at the shoreline, sharp as butter cut with a knife. And canoes were drawn up on the shore of the river channel that separated the island from the main shore. So these men weren't prisoners here. Alvin was relieved at that. He imagined, though, that choosing this big island as their dwelling place might have been some kind of compromise that Tenskwa-Tawa reached between those reds who didn't want to make any exceptions to the law that only reds could live west of the river, and those that believed runaway slaves were in a different category from white men with guns and axes.

Tenskwa-Tawa arrived that afternoon with a great deal of to-do. All of a sudden a whole passel of reds started hooting and hollering like they was going to war—Alvin had heard that sound before, when he was taken captive by warriors, before the Mizzippy was set as a dividing line. It was a terrible sound, and for a moment he wondered whether the reds on this shore had been using their years of peace to prepare for bloody war. But then he realized that the hooting and ululating was the red equivalent of yee-haw, hosanna, huzzah, hallelujah, and hip-hip-hooray.

Tenskwa-Tawa emerged from the woods on the far shore of the channel, and the reds surrounded him and led him down to a large canoe. They carried him so he wouldn't even get his feet wet and set him in the canoe, then leapt in and paddled furiously so he shot across the water like a skipped stone. Then he was lifted up again and carried to shore and set down right in front of Alvin.

So there was Alvin, with twenty-five black men forming a semi-circle behind him, and Tenskwa-Tawa, with about as many red men forming a semi-circle behind *him*.

"Is this what it looks like," said Alvin, "when the King of England meets the King of France?"

"No," said Tenskwa-Tawa. "Not enough guns, not enough clothes."

Which was true. Though compared to the black men, the reds looked like they was pretty bundled up, since there were whole stretches of their bodies here and there covered with deerskin or cloth. If I dressed like that, thought Alvin, I'd be roasted with sunburn and ready to serve.

"I'm glad you came," said Tenskwa-Tawa. "I also wanted to talk to you."

"About these fellows?" asked Alvin.

"Them? They're no bother. As long as they sleep on this island, they move freely on the shore. That's where their farms are. We'll be sorry to see them go, when you take them."

"I didn't have no plans to take them," said Alvin.

"But they're determined to become soldiers to fight for you and kill all your enemies. That's why they have to sleep on this island. Because they refuse to give up war."

Alvin was baffled. "I got no enemies."

Tenskwa-Tawa barked out a laugh.

"I mean, none that warriors can fight."

"It's so strange," said Tenskwa-Tawa, "hearing black men speak a red language like they were born to it. The language they speak is not all that different from Navaho, which I had to learn because that tribe was less inclined to give up war than most. It seemed they hadn't quite finished exterminating the Hopi and didn't want to give up killing till the job was done."

"So it hasn't been easy, getting all the reds to take the oath against war."

"No," said Tenskwa-Tawa. "Nor to get the young men to join the oath when they come of age. There's still a lot of playing at war among the young, and if you try to stop it, they just sneak off and do it. I think we've been breeding our boys for war for too many generations for it to disappear from our hearts overnight. Right now the peace holds, because there are enough adults who remember all the killing—and how badly we were defeated, time after time. But there are always those who want to go across the river and fight to take our lands back and drive all the white devils into the sea."

"There are plenty of white folks as dream of getting through the fog and taking possession of these lands, too," said Alvin.

"Including your brother," said Tenskwa-Tawa.

Alvin tried to think which of his brothers had ever said any such fool thing. "They're all farmers or millers or whatnot in Vigor Church," said Alvin. "Except Calvin."

"That's the one," said Tenskwa-Tawa. "It's what I wanted to talk to you about."

He turned to the reds who were with him and spoke a few words, then spoke in a different language to the blacks. Alvin was stunned but delighted when the two groups immediately intermingled and started up two games of cards and some dice-throwing.

"Don't tell me them cards is printed on your side of the river," said Alvin.

"Those black fellows you sent me had them," said Tenskwa-Tawa. "They play betting games, but their money is pebbles. Whoever wins the most struts for an hour, but the next time they play, they all start even again."

"Sounds civilized."

"On the contrary," said Tenskwa-Tawa. "It sounds like childish savages."

His grin had a bit of old pain in it, but Alvin understood. "Well, we white devils would simply regard it as a golden opportunity, and we'd play them with tokens representing all their property and then cheat till we had it all."

"Whereupon we red devils would kill most of you and torture the rest to death because of the power that we could draw from the pain." He held up a hand. "This is what I wanted to talk to you about. Until your brother sailed for Mexico it was not your business, but now it is."

"So he really has joined up with them fools," said Alvin.

"The Mexica have been a problem for us. There's a wide desert between our lands and theirs, but it's not as clear a wall as this river. There are plenty of tribes that live in those dry lands, and plenty of trade and travel back and forth, and stories about how the Mexica rose up against the Spanish and drove them out, except the five thousand they kept for sacrifice, one a day, his heart ripped out of his living body."

"Doesn't sound like your kind of people," said Alvin.

"They live a different way. We remember well when their ancestors came down from the north, a fierce people who spoke a language different from all others. The Navaho were the last wave, the Mexica the first, but they did not trust in the greensong. They took their powers from the pain and blood of their enemies. It's a way of power that was practiced among our peoples, too. The Irrakwa league was notorious for it, and you had a run-in, I think, with others who loved bloodshed and torture. But always we could set it aside and get back into the music of the living land. These reds can't, or don't try, which amounts to the same. And they scoff at my teaching of peace and send threatening embassies demanding that we supply them with white men to sacrifice or they'll come and take captives from our people."

"Have they done it yet?"

"All threats, but we hear from other tribes farther south that once that threat is given, it's only a matter of time before it's carried out."

"So what are you going to do?"

"Not a fog," said Tenskwa-Tawa wryly. "Not enough moisture in that high desert air, and besides, they'd just torture somebody and draw power from his pain, enough to dispel whatever I put in their way."

"So . . . if that *ain't* your plan . . ."

"We live in harmony with the earth," said Tenskwa-Tawa. "They soak their earth in blood. We believe that with a little encouragement, we can waken the giant that sleeps under their great city of Mexico."

Alvin was baffled. "There's real giants? I never knowed that."

Tenskwa-Tawa looked pained. "Their city is built right on top of an upwelling of hot flowing rock. It hasn't broken through in many years, but it's growing restless, with all the killing."

"You're talking about a volcano."

"I am," said the prophet.

"You're going to do to them what was done to Pompeii."

"The earth is going to do it."

"Ain't that kind of like war?" asked Alvin.

Tenskwa-Tawa sighed. "None of us will raise a weapon and strike down a man. And we've sent them due warning that their city will be covered with fire if they don't stop their evil sacrificing of human beings and set free all the tribes they rule over by fear and force."

"So this is how you wage war now," said Alvin.

"Yes," said Tenskwa-Tawa. "We'd be at peace with every people on earth, if they'd let us. As long as we don't come to love war, or to use it in order to rule over others, then we are still a peaceful people."

"So I take it the Navaho weren't just *persuaded* to take the oath of peace."

"They had a long period of drought, where the only rain that fell was on Hopi fields."

"I reckon that got the message to them."

"Alvin," said Tenskwa-Tawa, "I don't have to justify our actions to *you*, do I?"

"No sir," said Alvin. "It just sounds like your brother's way, to fight like that. I just thought of you as being— more patient, I guess."

"Because we bore the slaughter of our friends and loved ones at Tippy-Canoe."

"Yes. You let them slaughter you till they grew sick of murder."

"But what should we do with people who *never* grow sick of it?" asked Tenskwa-Tawa.

"So white folks ain't all bad, is what you're saying."

"The gods of the Mexica are thirsty for blood and hungry for pain. White folks generally want to get rich and be left alone. While they're killing you, the motive doesn't make that much difference. But most white people don't think of war and slaughter as the goal—just the means."

"Well, don't that just put us in a special place in hell."

"Alvin, we're going to do what we're going to do. In fact, it's already under way, and we can't control it or stop it now. The forces beneath the earth are vast and terrible and it has taken all our wise men and women of every tribe many months to teach the earth what we need it to do in the city of Mexico."

"And you needed to tell me because Calvin is headed right into it."

"It would grieve me to cause the death of your own brother."

"Trouble is," said Alvin, "there's no time in recorded history when Calvin has actually done what I wanted when I wanted him to."

"I didn't think it would be easy. I only knew that you would not forgive me if I didn't warn you and give you a chance to try."

Alvin sighed and sat down. "I wish I were a boy again."

"With the Unmaker dropping roof beams on your head and sending preachers to bleed you to death under the guise of surgery?"

"At least then it was only me I was trying to save. I can't go follow Calvin to Mexico and try to bring him back, because I got me five thousand or so runaway slaves and refugee Frenchmen from Barcy that I got to find a place for."

Tenskwa-Tawa motioned with his arm to indicate the island where they were sitting. "If you think you can fit five thousand here, you're welcome to it. But only the runaway slaves. My people wouldn't bear it to have these white Frenchmen you speak of living on our land."

"No," said Alvin. "I reckon not."

"Canada is not such a lovely place that we trust the French to be kinder and less bloody than the English or the Spanish."

"We got some of them, too," said Alvin. "Poor folks who threw in their lot with us. But we don't want to live here."

"Good," said Tenskwa-Tawa. "Because it would be beyond my power to persuade the nations to let you."

"What we need," said Alvin, "is safe passage."

"To where?"

"North. Along the edge of the river. North till we're across the river from the United States. Or, more particularly, the free state of Noisy River. Won't do to cross back into slave territory."

"Five thousand people," said Tenskwa-Tawa. "Eating what?"

Alvin grinned. "Whatever the land and the kindness of your hearts will provide them."

"Five thousand people leave a scar on the land when they pass through."

"It's harvest season," said Alvin. "Fields coming ripe, fruit on the trees. Are times so hard this side of the river that you can't spare enough for folks escaping from bondage and oppression?"

"It would take a great amount of effort," said Tenskwa-Tawa. "We aren't like you. We don't grow the food here and then carry it on wagons or trains or barges to sell it there. Each village grows its own food, and only when famine strikes in one place is food brought from another."

"Well, wouldn't you say that five thousand people with no land or food is kind of a walking famine?"

Tenskwa-Tawa shook his head. "You're asking something very hard. And not just for those reasons. What does it tell all the whites of the United States and the Crown Colonies when five thousand runaway slaves cross over the river despite the fog and then emerge again five hundred miles north?"

"I didn't think of that."

"We'll have them trying to cross into our land by the boatload."

"But they won't make it."

"The fog is fog," said Tenskwa-Tawa. "We instill it with fear, yes, but those with enough greed or rage can overcome that fear. A few try every year, and of those few, now and then a man makes it over."

"What do you do with them?" asked Alvin.

"They wear hobbles and work with the women until they find it in their hearts to take the oath of peace and live among us."

"Or what, you send them back?"

"We never let anyone go back."

"Except me."

"And these twenty-five black men. You can take them with you whenever you want. Because they won't tell tales of this paradise just waiting for the right army to come and drive out the heathen, unarmed savages."

"So maybe we got to make the crossing so spectacular that nobody thinks they could do it in a boat."

Tenskwa-Tawa laughed. "Oh, Alvin, you have a showman's heart."

"You've put on a couple of spectacles in your day, old friend."

"I suppose if it looks like a miracle, the United States Army and the Royal Army won't think they can do the same. The only flaw in your idea, Alvin, is that your crossing of Lake Pontchartrain was pretty much a miracle, and that didn't stop them from sending an army in pursuit of you."

"Once I took down the bridge," said Alvin, "they didn't try to cross the lake."

Tenskwa-Tawa shook his head. "I have a war on my hands with the Mexica, and now I have to help you pull off a miraculous crossing of the Mizzippy, putting the great peaceful nation at risk."

"Hey, that goes both ways," said Alvin. "Here I am trying to save five thousand runaways and you up and tell me my brother is heading into the mouth of a volcano that you can't stop."

"Isn't it good we like each other so much," said Tenskwa-Tawa.

"You taught me everything I know," said Alvin.

"But not everything *I* know."

"And I gave you back your eye."

"And healed my heart," said Tenskwa-Tawa. "But you're a lot of bother all the same."

≈ 11 ≈

Flood

AFTER THE SECOND night, word went on ahead of them and it got harder. Mistress Cottoner didn't talk, La Tia said so, but her son did. And the people at the second house, Arthur Stuart had to use makery to seal the doors and windows of a room in their house so they couldn't get out, because they wouldn't calm down, they kept screaming, It's our life you're taking, you're making us poor, you have no right, these slaves are *ours,* until Marie wanted to fill their mouths with cotton, all the cotton that had ever been picked by their slaves, just stuff it down their mouths until they were as fat and soft as the huge pillows they slept on while their slaves slept on hard boards and straw in filthy rat-infested cabins.

As filthy and rat-infested as the cabin her mother had made her grow up in back in Swamptown. Only her mother wasn't a slave. We're finer people than these scum, her mother would say. We're Portuguese royalty, only Napoleon drove us out and forced us into exile in Nouveau Orleans and then he sold it to the Spanish so that *we* could never go home. Because you are the grand-daughter of a duke, and he was the son of a king, and you should be married to at least a count, so you must learn fine manners and speak French and English very well and learn how to curtsey and stand straight and . . .

And then Marie got old enough to understand that not everybody could see into people's bodies and feel whether they were sick and whether they would die of it. And all of a sudden her mother's story changed. Your father was a great wizard, she said. A maker, they call such a man here. Facteur. Createur. He could carve a bird out of wood and breathe on it and it would fly away. And you have some of his gift, and some of mine, because my talent is love, I love people, my dear Marie, you have that love and it lets you see inside their hearts, and the power from your father lets you see their death because that is the ultimate power, to stare death in the face and be unafraid.

Her mother, such a storyteller. That was when Marie knew that her mother's stories were all lies. In Portugal her name had been Caterina, and they called her *Rina* for short. When she came to Nouveau Orleans they made a joke of it and called her *Rien,* which was French for "nothing." Or even "de rien," which was what the French said after "merci," so it was like the English "you're wel-come." Because now Marie understood that her mother was a prostitute, and not an expensive one, either, and her father had probably been a customer, back in the days before she had a hex against pregnancy that worked.

But she pretended to believe her mother's stories be-cause it made her mother happy to tell them. And Marie was actually relieved, because she had always been afraid that someday Napoleon would fall from power or die, and the Portuguese royal family would be restored to the throne and they'd come looking for them and find them and it would be fine for Mother, she could go back to being what she was raised to be, but Marie wasn't good at curtseying and her French was not elegant and fine and she was dirty and always covered in skeeter bites and they would despise her and mock her in the royal court, just like they did here on the streets of Barcy. Only it would be worse, because it would be fine ladies and gentlemen doing it. So she hated the idea of being royalty. It was better just to be the daughter of a cheap Portuguese whore in Nueva Barcelona.

But now, far from being the most despised people in Barcy, they were actually important. Because Alvin and Arthur Stuart and La Tia treated them with respect, because they were the ones who went to the doors of the houses, everyone looked up to them. They got to wear fine clothes and act like royalty, and even though it didn't really fool people because the clothes weren't fine *enough,* it was still fun to pretend that Mother's story had been a little bit true after all.

The third day, though, as they approached the house La Tia said, "This house is not good. Pass it by." And they would have done it, but then three men came out on the porch with muskets and aimed them and demanded that they surrender.

So Arthur Stuart—such a clever boy, bless him—made the ends of all three of their muskets go soft and droop, so they couldn't shoot anymore. The men threw them down and drew swords and began to run at them, and Arthur Stuart made the swords soft too, like willow wands, and La Tia laughed and laughed.

But there was no pretending this time. The people of this house, of the whole neighborhood, had heard of the huge army of runaway slaves who captured plantations and raped the women and killed the men and let the slaves burn everything to the ground. Of course it wasn't true, not a bit of it—except for the part about how two French women would come to the door and get themselves invited inside, and while they were in there the two slaves that traveled with them, a mammy slave and a young buck, would go provoke a rebellion among the slaves of the plantation and then it was all murder and rape and burning.

There'd be no more deception at the door. Every house would be more like a military campaign from then on.

So that third night, with all the white men tied up in the barn and all the white women locked in the upstairs of the house and not a slave to be found because they had all been sent away, La Tia and Arthur Stuart and Mother and Marie met with the council of colonels to decide what to do.

"If we could hear the greensong," said Arthur Stuart, "we could travel by night and not get hungry—like we did crossing Pontchartrain."

"I don't remember no greensong," said La Tia.

"Yes you do," said Arthur Stuart. "Only you didn't know that's what you were hearing."

"What be in this song?" said La Tia. "What make it green?"

"It's the song of the life around you. Not the human life, that's just noise, most of the time. Not machines, either. But the music of the trees and the wind and the heat of the sun, the music of fish and birds and bugs and bees. All the life of the world around you, and you let yourself be part of the song. I can't do it alone, but when I'm with Alvin, he can catch me up in the song and then I hear it and it feels like my body is running itself, you know what I mean? I can just run and run and at the end I feel like I just woke up from a good long nap. And I'm not hungry, not while I'm running. Not thirsty, either. I'm just part of the world, turning around from night to day, wind blowing over me, plants growing up out of me, animals moving through and over me."

It was lovely to hear him talk about it, his face so lighted up like it got. This young half-black man, he loved his friend, his brother-in-law Alvin, even more than Marie did. Oh, to hold Alvin's hand and run through the trees and hear that greensong and see the bushes and branches bend out of the way and the ground become smooth and soft under her feet. . . .

But La Tia, she didn't get dreamy hearing it. She was

making a list. "Fish, birds, trees," she said when Arthur Stuart was done. "You don't get hungry, you don't get thirsty. Wind. And bugs, yes? Heat of the sun. What else? Anything?"

"You think you can make a charm that does the same thing?"

"I give it a try," said La Tia. "Best I can do." She grinned wickedly. "This my 'knack,' boy."

She immediately sent her friend Michele and a half dozen others who had obviously run her errands before, looking for the things she needed. Feather of a bird, fin of a fish—that was the hardest one—a living beetle, leaves of a tree. A pinch of dirt, a drop of water, ash from a fire, and when it was all in a little sachet she would blow into it and then seal it closed with the hair of a long-haired woman, who happened to be Marie herself.

By morning she had made a sachet for Arthur Stuart and one for herself, and sachets for each of the colonels. "Now we see if we hear this greensong as we walk," she said.

"What about me?" asked Marie. "And my mother?"

"You hold my hand," said La Tia. "Your mama, she hold Arthur hand. I do it otherway, but you get thinking about love, you."

Arthur looked at her and raised his eyebrows as if the idea were ridiculous. Ignorant boy.

She held La Tia's hand and Arthur held Mother's hand and they started walking and . . . nothing happened. It was nothing like what she had felt crossing the bridge.

"I guess we just need Alvin," said Arthur Stuart. "Though you'd think it was something that could be learned. I mean, he wasn't born with it. He learned it from Ta-Kumsaw himself."

La Tia groaned loudly and smacked him softly on the forehead. "You silly boy, why you no tell La Tia this be red man thing, this greensong? Get the colonels, all they, bring they sachet to me."

Soon the march was again halted and the colonels were

gathered while the people mumbled and murmured about another delay in their journey.

One by one, La Tia opened each person's sachet and said, "All right, you. One drop of you blood, right now."

Well, how many people could do *that* without an argument? But Arthur Stuart, he came up and he said, "I can let a drop of your blood go from your finger, and it won't hurt, but only if you say yes." Well of course they all said yes, and sure enough, Arthur held their hand and closed his eyes and thought real hard and one single drop came out from under their fingernail and dropped into the sachet.

Once again La Tia blew into the sachet and closed it, but this time she added a blade of grass to the strand of Marie's hair to tie the top. "Now maybe," said La Tia.

And this time as they walked, the charm seemed to have some effect. Marie couldn't be sure she was actually responding to the greensong—she hadn't heard it, really, crossing the bridge. It had been more like a sort of intensity inside her as she pushed the wheelbarrow, so that her hands never got sore from the chafing of the handles, and her back never got weary, she just stepped on and on.

Well, something like that began to happen now. She had long since given up the wheelbarrow, and she and her mother had taken turns carrying the ball of bloodwater Alvin had created for her. But now she didn't need her mother to spell her off. The burden was still heavy, it just didn't make her tired. Didn't even make her shoulders ache where the straps dug in.

But she did get hungry and hot and thirsty during the day. Yet she didn't *mind* being hungry and thirsty and hot. And her feet always seemed to find the right place to step.

The only person it didn't work for was Arthur Stuart, until he finally took off the sachet and gave it to Mother. "I reckon while I'm spending all my thinking on making this fog stay ahead of us and behind us, and watching for heartfires of them as might mean us harm, this charm just don't affect me."

"Too bad for you, child," said La Tia. "Keep doing what you doing, we all pray for you."

Arthur Stuart tipped his hat to her and grinned and then strode on ahead.

Marie wanted to run to him and hold his hand and walk with him. But that was foolishness. For one thing, she needed the sachet to help her. For another thing, *he* needed to keep his mind on his work. And for a third thing, he probably wouldn't want her to.

As for the rest of the people, the sachets seemed to help. Little children kept up better. Adults who carried babies didn't get so tired. There weren't people constantly dropping out to rest and then losing their place in the company. So even though nobody walked faster than before, they actually made far more progress during the day.

They also waited until later to pick a plantation to be their host for the evening. "We've gone so far," said Arthur Stuart, "maybe the people here will think they're safe and not be looking out for us."

"You think I gonna walk up to no house?" said La Tia. "Wake up from you dream, you."

"What else can we do?" said Arthur Stuart.

"Kill them in their houses."

They all turned at the voice. It was Old Bart, the butler from the Cottoner house. "You heard me. You got this knack, boy. Use it. Reach into they hearts and stop them from beating no more."

"That would be murder," said Arthur Stuart.

"It ain't murder," said Old Bart. "It's war, and they be winning it, less you do what soldiers do, and kill them as would kill you."

"Not here," said Arthur Stuart. "Not today."

"You kill them, *we* win," insisted Old Bart. "Nothing but what they deserve, what they done to us."

"You dead?" asked La Tia. "Your heart stop beating?"

Old Bart whirled on her. "Don't you tell me how angry to be. I was dead inside for all them years, me a man, and couldn't *act* like one."

"Funny way to be dead, you got. Stand there talking. Bet you piss three time a day, too, you! How many dead man do that?"

Old Bart probably had an answer for that, but the laughter of those nearby convinced him that this wasn't the day to argue with her. But Marie saw that he hadn't changed his mind. Just changed his mind about *talking* about it.

"Kill them in they house," La Tia went on scornfully. "We want food. We want a place to sleep. Kill somebody for that in they own house?"

Arthur Stuart shook his head. "If I was in his place, I think I might feel the same."

"You men," said La Tia. "Killing just a thing you do."

"You know that ain't so," said Arthur Stuart. "But when it needs doing, I bet you glad you got somebody to do it."

This had gone far enough. "I know," said Marie. "I go alone."

"No!" her mother cried.

"They look for two women with two slaves. I go alone, and Arthur Stuart and La Tia, they come another way. Arthur, you look out for me, won't you?"

"I will," he said.

"I just go and explain to them. We only want food and a place to sleep. Only . . . maybe you show power to them, while I'm talking. Put fog at every window. Show them it's better just to let us stay one night and go away."

They thought about it, and Arthur only improved on it a little. "All the windows but one," he said. "Clear sky through one window."

"Then we better do it before the sun goes all the way down," said Marie.

Only after everyone agreed and they headed for the house they had chosen did Marie start to realize what she had just done. What if they had shotguns *this* time? How fast was Arthur Stuart?

Just before they got within sight of the house, Arthur stopped them. "There's four grown men in this house, and six women. And no shortage of guns. And no children."

That was a bad sign, Marie knew. The children most likely had been sent away.

"Good sign," said La Tia. "They don't sent away the women. They don't think we come tonight."

"Fog as soon as I get inside," Marie reminded Arthur Stuart.

He squeezed her hand. "Count on me," he said.

Then he let go and she walked alone down the road and turned up the long drive to the house.

Long before she got to the house she had been spotted and three men were on the porch, holding muskets.

"You crazy, girl?" said the oldest of them. "Don't you know there's an army of raping and pillaging runaways coming this way?"

"My papa's wagon overturned up the road, I need help."

"Your papa's out of luck," said the biggest of the men. "We ain't leaving this porch for nobody."

"But he's hurt, when he try to stand up, he falls down."

"What's that accent?" said the youngest man. "You French?"

"My parents are from Nueva Barcelona," she said.

"Being a Frenchwoman in these parts ain't such a good idea this week."

She smiled at them. "Can I change who I am? Oh, you must help me. At least send a couple of servants with me to help right the wagon and bring my father here, can't you do that?"

"Slaves are all locked up, ready to be marched away in the morning, and we ain't letting any of *them* out on the road, neither," said the big man.

"Then I see that Providence brought me to a house with no Christian charity," she said. She turned her back and started back down the road.

It sort of made sense that when she seemed willing to leave, that was what convinced them. "Ain't never turned folks in trouble away from my house before," said the old man.

"Ain't never been no slave revolt, neither," said the big man.

"But even during a time of slave revolt," said the young man, "wagons can still overturn and honest men can still be hurt and need help."

Marie didn't like lying to these men. The old man wanted to be kind, and the young man wanted to trust her. The big man was doing no worse than looking after his people. And since his suspicions were all completely justified, it hardly seemed fair that he was the one made to seem uncharitable. Well, it would all be clear soon enough. She hoped that this one bad experience would not put them off helping their neighbor in the future. It would be a shame if their journey did nothing but make the world worse.

"Come back," shouted the old man.

"No, stay there!" shouted the big man. "We'll go with you." And he and the young man bounded down from the porch and started trotting toward her.

This was not the plan. What would she do with them out here? "But we need to bring him water."

"Plenty of time for that when we've got him to the house."

Now they were beside her, and there was nothing she could do but lead them down the drive.

Suddenly a fog came up. Out of nowhere, and then there was a chill in the air and a fog so thick she couldn't even see the men beside her.

"What the hell," said the big man.

"I can't see my feet on the drive," said the young man.

Marie, however, said nothing, for the moment the fog came in, she turned around and started walking back toward the house.

In a moment she was out of the fog. She did not glance back to see what it looked like, to have a single thick cloud—she wondered if it was like the Bible story, a pillar of smoke.

The old man wasn't on the porch.

And then, as she got closer, there he was, with a musket in his hands. "I know devil's work when I see it, you witch!" he shouted.

He fired the musket.

It was pointed right at her. And the barrel was *not* soft. She thought she must surely die on this spot.

But when the noise of the gunshot died down, she felt nothing, and kept walking toward the porch.

That was when the lead bullet popped out of the barrel of the musket and went maybe two yards and plunked on the ground. It made a pool of lead there, flat as a silver dollar.

"I'm no witch," she said. "And you are a kind and good man. Do you think anybody will hurt you or the people you love? Nobody will hurt anybody."

From inside the fog came shouts. "Who's shooting! Where's the house?"

Now she did look back. Two thick clouds barely taller than a man were moving swiftly across the lawns, but neither one was headed for the porch, and neither one was holding a straight course, either.

"We heard what you done in those other places, you liar!" shouted the old man.

"You heard lies," she said. "Think about it. If we killed everybody, who would tell you there was two French women and two slaves that came to the door? That's what you were watching for, no?"

The old man was no fool. He could listen pretty well.

"We want food," she said. "And we will *have* food from this house. You have plenty, but we don't take all. Your neighbors will help you replenish the lack. And you won't need as much food, anyway."

"Because you're gonna take all our slaves, is that it?"

"Take them?" said Marie. "We can't *take* them. What would we do, put them in our apron pockets? We let them travel with us if they choose to. If they choose to stay with you, then they can stay. They do what they want, like the children of God that they are."

"Abolitionist bastards," said the old man.

"Abolitionists, yes. In my case, also a bastard." She deliberately pronounced the word with a thick French accent. "And you, a man who knows to be kind to strangers, but keeps human beings as property. Even as you do it to the least of these, my brethren."

"Don't quote scripture to me," said the old man. "Steal from us if you want, but don't pretend to be holy when you do it."

She was standing on the porch now, facing the old man. She heard the door swing open behind her. She heard the click of a hammer striking the flint. She heard the sizzle of the gunpowder in the pan.

And then the plop of the bullet hitting the porch.

"Damn," said a woman's voice.

"You would have murdered me," said Marie without turning around.

"We shoot trespassers around here."

"We don't hurt personne, but you with murder in your heart," said Marie, and she turned to face the woman. "What is your food, that you could shoot a woman in the back for asking you to share it?" She reached out a hand toward the trembling woman, who cowered against the door. She touched the woman's shoulder. "You have your health," said Marie. "That's good. Treasure it, to be so strong, no disease in you. Live a long life."

Then she turned to the old man and reached out to him. Took his bare hand in hers. "Oh, you're a strong man," she said. "But you're short of breath, yes?"

"I'm an old man," he said. "Ain't hard to guess I'm short of breath."

"And you have pains in your chest. You try to ignore them, yes? But they come again in a few months, and then a few months. Put your house in order, say your good-byes, you good man. You will see God in only a few weeks time."

He looked her hard in the eyes. "Why you cursing me?" he said. "What did I ever do to you?"

"I'm not cursing you," she said. "I have no such power, to kill or not kill. I only touch a person and I know if they are sick and if they will die of it. You are sick. You will die of it. In your sleep. But I know you are a generous man, and many will mourn your death, and your family will remember you with love."

Tears filled the old man's eyes. "What kind of thief are you?"

"A hungry one," she said, "or otherwise I would not steal, not me, not any of us."

The old man turned and looked down onto the lawn. Marie assumed he was looking at the other two men, or at the clouds that enclosed them, but no. While they were talking, Arthur and La Tia and Mother must have opened the slaves' quarters and now the house was surrounded by black men and women and children. The clouds no longer surrounded the two white men. Unarmed, they were standing inside the circle.

Arthur Stuart stepped forward and held out his hand. As if he expected a white slaveowner to shake with a black man. "My name is Arthur Stuart," he said.

The old man hooted. "You trying to tell us you're the King?"

Arthur shrugged. "I was telling you my name. I'm also telling you that none of the guns in that house is gonna work, and the man waiting just inside the door with a big old piece of boardwood to bat me or Marie in the head, he might as well put it down, because it won't hurt nobody any more than getting hit with a piece of paper or a dry sponge."

Marie heard somebody inside the house utter a curse, and a thick heavy piece of wood was flung out the door onto the lawn.

"Please let us come inside," she said. "My mother and my friends and I. Let us sit down and talk about how to do this without hurting anyone and without leaving you with nothing."

"I know the best way," said the old man. "Just go away and leave us be."

"We have to go somewhere," said Marie. "We have to eat something. We have to sleep the night."

"But why us?" he said.

"Why not you?" she answered. "God will bless you ten times for what you share with us today."

"If I'm going to die as soon as you say, let me leave a good place to my sons and daughters."

"Without slaves," said Marie, "this will finally *be* a good place."

Later, with the family *not* locked up, and everyone safely fed and sleeping, Marie had a chance to talk with Arthur Stuart. "Thank you for giving me the fog when I needed it, instead of waiting till I was in the house."

"Can't expect plans to work out when other people don't know their part," he said with a grin. "You done great, though."

She smiled back at him. She *had* done a good job. But she had never before known what it felt like to be *told* so. Not till this trip. Not till Alvin and Arthur Stuart. Oh, they had such powers, such knacks. But the one that impressed her the most was the power to fill her heart the way their kind words did.

A group of reds took Alvin back across the Mizzippy in a canoe—a much better journey this time. They took Alvin downriver a ways, to a place just upstream of the port town of Red Stick. The river took a deep bight there, so Alvin had only a short walk through pretty dry country to get to the town. Meanwhile the reds got away without being seen by any white man. Up north in the United States, reds were a common enough sight, seeing how they were the majority of people in the states of Irrakwa and Cherriky. But they mostly dressed like white folks. And here in the deep south, where the Crown Colonies had more sway, reds didn't show up much, specially not the ones from across river, who still dressed in the old way. It frightened the white folks to see them, those rare times they showed their faces. Savages, that's how they looked, and people reached for their guns and began ringing church bells in alarm.

But a lone white man, dressed like what he was, a journeyman blacksmith, and carrying a heavy poke slung on his shoulder, nobody paid no mind to him.

Besides, there was bigger news afoot. The governor's expedition had just arrived, and suddenly Red Stick was swollen with hundreds of bored militiamen, some of whom had lost their enthusiasm for slogging through back country and fighting runaway slaves. In fact, their enthusiasm waned in direct proportion to the amount of alcohol in their blood, and Colonel Adan wasn't such a disciplinarian that he didn't see the wisdom of keeping these men just a little likkered up. So they were in the saloons, with Spanish soldiers attempting to enforce a two-drink limit so they weren't too drunk to march. Nobody was looking to see the leader of the very group they came to destroy walking all by himself through the streets of town.

It wasn't much trouble for Alvin to size things up. He was pleased that none of the men from Steve Austin's company were there. Those were hard men who knew how to kill and didn't mind doing it. These men, by contrast, were quick to brag and boast about what they were gonna do, and what they *had* done, but the actual doing wasn't all that attractive to them.

Alvin toyed with the idea of walking right in to Colonel Adan's stateroom on one of the steamboats and telling him, you show up day after tomorrow right *here* and you can see us cross the river and leave you up to your necks in mud. But there was a good chance Adan would simply have Alvin hanged or shot instead of locking him up, and while Alvin could probably get himself out of it, what was the point? Fighting the Unmaker in gator form had taken a lot of the combativeness out of Alvin. The part of him that looked forward to a good rassle was pretty much used up for the nonce, and so he'd find a quieter way of doing the same job.

So he went into a saloon and leaned against the bar right by the Spanish officer who was supervising. "So you know where them runaways actually *is*?" he asked.

"They don't tell me," said the officer, his English thickly accented.

"Well, the thing is, I think I know," said Alvin. "At least I got a pretty good rumor. But I don't want to go tell it to Colonel Adan myself, on account of he's bound to think I look like a soldier and try to jine me up."

The officer looked at him coldly. "What do we care for this rumor?"

"Don't that all depend on who's doing the gossiping? I mean, any of these drunks in here, they can tell you the runaways is on the moon for all it matters, 'cause they don't know squat. Me, though, I got my rumor from a couple of reds who was smuggling furs across the river upstream, and *they* said they seen a bunch of free blacks not far inland."

The officer still looked scornful. "Smuggling furs? And they did not kill you?"

"Well, maybe they would have, except there was only two of them, and I'm not a little fellow, and besides, they wanted me to tell you what they seen."

"And why would they care?"

"Because if them runaways is heading for the river, it might be they got it in their heads to cross it, like they crossed Lake Pontchartrain. They got some wizards with them, I hear. Queen La Tia, I hear. So maybe they can squelch that fog and get across. And them reds don't fancy a bunch of free blacks and scum-of-the-earth Frenchmen trying to set up on their side of the river."

"So you are, what . . . a messenger?"

Alvin shrugged. "I had my say. Who you tell now is none of my howdy do."

The officer reached out and seized Alvin by the arm. The man had a strong grip. Of course, Alvin could have thrown him off without hardly even thinking about it, but he didn't want a fight right here.

"I think you need to come outside and tell me a little more," said the officer.

"And while you're out there, you can bet these men will all get two *more* cups and then they'll be pissing and puking the whole way upriver."

"Come with me."

Alvin went along peaceful enough. The officer had two other soldiers in that saloon, and they came outside, too. At once the noise level inside increased—those forbidden drinks getting ordered, no doubt. The price of rum and whiskey was bound to soar in Red Stick, on account of the scarcity they'd have by nightfall.

Outside the saloon, the officer had the soldiers hold Alvin. "I think you better come tell your story to Colonel Adan yourself."

"I told you before, that's what I *don't* want to do."

"If you do not lie, then he must know this."

"I ain't lying, and I can't think why them reds would lie, but I'll tell you where they said. You go around this first big bight in the river, and then take the second big curve, and where it comes east again, that's the place."

"Telling me is a waste of time," said the officer.

"But you're the only one that's gonna get told," said Alvin. Whereupon he pulled his arms free and elbowed both soldiers in the chin, knocking their heads back against the wooden wall of the saloon. One dropped like a rock, the other staggered away, and Alvin reached out and took the officer's sidearm away from him.

The officer stepped back and drew his sword.

"No no," said Alvin. "If you kill me, *then* what will you tell the colonel?"

In answer, the officer slashed with his sword.

Alvin sidestepped, then took the sword out of the officer's hand and broke the blade across his knee. It pained him to do it with a blade as fine as that—Spanish steel was still a thing to be proud of—and he didn't like smacking those soldiers, either. But he had to get away as a regular fellow might, and not with any obvious makery, or the colonel might realize he was getting set up or maybe just think he was being sent on a wild goose chase.

The officer cried out as if it had been his arm, not his sword, that was broke in two. Alvin jogged away while the officer bawled, "Siga lo! Siga lo!" But his men were in no shape to follow, and in a couple of minutes Alvin was out of sight behind buildings and heading for woodland as fast as he could go.

Arthur Stuart woke up from someone shaking him. "Who's—"

"Shh, don't wake the others yet."

It was Alvin. Arthur Stuart sat up. "Boy am I glad to—"

"What part of shhhh didn't you get?"

"There's nobody nearby," said Arthur. But he talked softer, all the same.

"You think," said Alvin. "But Dead Mary, she's only just over there."

"She wasn't when *I* went to sleep," said Arthur Stuart.

But by now they were both up and walking away into the fog surrounding the camp.

"I just come from Colonel Adan's army," said Alvin. "We got us an appointment at the river tomorrow afternoon."

"We crossing over?"

"Tenskwa-Tawa is granting us right to pass through, and they'll help us get food and shelter without having to take over any more plantations."

"Good," said Arthur Stuart. "I'm sick of it already, folks being so scared of us."

"Guess you're not a natural bully," said Alvin. "And after I tried so hard to teach you."

"Well, it's worked out pretty good so far. Dead Mary's a natural liar, and I'm good at fogging folks and bending musket barrels."

"And La Tia has made some charms," said Alvin.

"They seemed to help. Not like having you march with us."

"Well, I'm here to march with you now. I don't want another stop. I want to get there first. And that means we need to wake everybody now and get moving."

"In the dark?"

"We'll see if it's still dark by the time you get them going."

It took less than an hour to get under way, but that was mostly 'cause Alvin wouldn't let anybody fix any kind of meal. Nursing mothers could nurse, of course, and they could eat whatever bread and cheese and fruit they might have as they walked, but nothing that required cooking or washing or waiting.

Oh, there was plenty of grumbling and some out-and-out surliness, but the past couple of days' marching, with La Tia's charms giving them some good help, had left them feeling hale and ready even with only half a night's sleep.

And now, with Alvin leading the way, the charms worked way better. It really was the greensong now, not just a dim echo of it. Since Arthur Stuart didn't have to mind the fog now, he could join in with it, let it sweep over him.

Before dawn everybody was running along—the adults jogging, the children running full tilt, but everyone keeping up and nobody tired. In the dark they'd run without a soul tripping over a root or straying from the group. Because in the greensong, you always know exactly where you are and where everything else is because it's all part of you and you're part of it.

They ran all morning. They ran all afternoon. They did not stop to eat or drink. They splashed through streams, barely pausing to lift the children who weren't tall enough to ford them. Six thousand people now, with all the slaves at each plantation who had shucked off their bondage to join them. Moving through the woods without need for trail or trace.

The last red of the sunset was just fading from the sky when they came to a low bluff overlooking an eastward curve of the Mizzippy and saw it, more than a mile wide, streaked with red from the sunset.

"We cross in the morning?" asked Arthur Stuart.

"We cross as soon as every last soul is up here on this bluff," said Alvin.

They had spread out a bit during the long day's run, so it was full dark and then some when the colonels reported that everyone was accounted for.

Once again Alvin had Papa Moose and Mama Squirrel and their children at the front, but this time La Tia would be leading them across instead of waiting till last. "Won't be no bridge this time," said Alvin to the council. "We're gonna dam up the river and it's going to look mighty strange, piled up on your right side. Nobody ought to look into it—we got no time for that."

Then Alvin walked to the point of the bluff nearest the water, Arthur Stuart beside him, and raised up a torch.

On the far side of the river, the fog cleared and another torch could be seen, just a wink of light.

"Who's on the other side?" asked Arthur Stuart.

"Tenskwa-Tawa," said Alvin. "He's gonna help me dam the Mizzippy."

"Well," said Arthur Stuart, "I say, dam the Mizzippy all to hell!"

Alvin laughed and then cut open his hand with his own fingernail and *flung* the blood out over the water.

It looked as if the water leaped right back up into his hand, but it wasn't water, no sir, it was the crystal again, and as Alvin held one end of it, it grew, stretching out like a thin sheet of glass right through the river and across it. Halfway there it was met by crystal from the other side and by then the water on the left side of the dam was flowing away, sinking down, gone.

On the upstream side of the dam, though, the water had risen, and Arthur expected it would start to flow over the top any second. But it didn't. Because, he realized, upstream of the bluff it had spilled over the banks and was flooding the land on the white man's side of the river.

Now Arthur Stuart knew why this spot had been chosen. The bluffs on the other side were higher and extended farther upstream. There'd be no flood on the red side of the river.

"I got a job for you," said Alvin.

"I'm game, if it's something I can handle."

"Colonel Adan is coming up the river with a couple of his boats. He's also sent another bunch of soldiers around by land. Well, those boys are gonna be scrambling to climb trees and find high ground for the next while, but what I worry about is the men on them boats."

"Won't they be left high and dry with the river dammed like this?" said Arthur Stuart.

"They will. But they'll be mighty tempted to get out of them boats and come upstream on foot. And when we let go of this dam, they'll all be drowned."

"Like Pharaoh's chariots."

"I don't want any more dead men on account of this trek," said Alvin. "There's just no call for it, if we give proper warning."

"I'll keep 'em in the boats," said Arthur Stuart.

"I was just asking you to give them advice."

"I'll give them such strong advice everybody takes it."

"Well, on your way to showing off for a bunch of men armed with muskets and artillery," said Alvin, "you might want to dry off that bottom mud so nobody gets stuck crossing over."

And indeed it was sloppy going for the first few people to try going down the bank into the empty river bottom. But Arthur Stuart had learned enough these past days that it wasn't hard for him to evaporate the water in the top layer of mud, making a hard-surfaced dirt road about fifty feet wide—broad enough for a lot of people to cross at once. This would go a lot faster than crossing Pontchartrain.

When La Tia saw what Arthur had done, she let out a

whoop of delight and called out, "Everybody move quick! Quick as frogs!" And she began to jog over the new road.

Arthur took only a moment to look at the dam itself. Being such pure crystal, however, it didn't look like any kind of dam. It just looked as if the water simply stopped. Even in the dark, he could see shapes moving in the water. At first he thought it was fish, but then he realized that it was too dark to see anything like that in the water. No, what he was seeing was in the *crystal*. The same kind of visions that had been so disturbing and hypnotic as people crossed over the bridge at Pontchartrain.

"Don't look at the dam!" shouted Alvin. "Nobody look at the dam!"

Which made everybody look, of course. Look once, and then look away, because there was La Tia and Moose and Squirrel and Dead Mary and Rien, urging them on, hurrying them, hundreds and hundreds of them crossing the river bottom on Arthur's road.

Arthur took off at a jog downriver, not running too fast because he had to dry a path before him or he'd sink. All it took was rounding one bend in the river, and there were the two big riverboats, looking pretty forlorn as they rested right on the bottom.

Already dozens of men were out of the boats, slogging along in thick mud.

"Get back in the boats!" Arthur Stuart shouted.

The men heard him, and some of them stopped and looked around to try to find which bank the voice was coming from.

"Vuelvan-se en los návios!" he shouted again, jogging nearer.

Arthur Stuart wasn't careless. He was just starting to scan the boat for weaponry when he heard a shout of "Atiren!" and saw the flashes of a half dozen muskets on board the first boat. Wasn't he out of range?

Well, he was and he wasn't. The musket balls went far enough, but they had slowed considerably, and the one that hit him didn't go into him all that terribly far. But the spot did happen to be right in the belly, just above his navel, and it hurt worse than the worst stomach ache of his life.

He doubled over and fell to the ground. Careless, foolish . . .he cursed himself even as he cried from the pain of it.

But pain or not, he had a mission to perform. Trouble was, with his stomach muscles torn like that, he couldn't work up the strength to shout. Well, he had known persuasion wasn't going to do it, and he already had a plan. When they'd been running with the greensong toward the river, Arthur Stuart had heard and felt and finally seen the heartfires of hundreds and hundreds of gators that lived in the river and its tributaries in this region.

It wasn't hard to call to them. Come to the boats, he told them. Plenty to eat in the boats.

And they came. Whatever they might have thought in their tiny gator brains about the river suddenly disappearing like it did, they understood a supper call.

Trouble was, they had no idea what a "boat" was. They just knew they were getting called and had a vague notion of where the call was coming from and pretty soon they were all headed right for Arthur Stuart. And since he was giving off the smell of blood and looking for all the world like a wounded animal—not unnatural, considering he *was* wounded—he couldn't blame the gators for thinking he was the meal they'd been promised.

This is about as dumb a way to die as I ever heard of, thought Arthur Stuart. I called the gators down on my own self. Good thing I died before I ever fathered children, because this much stupidity should not survive into the next generation.

And then the gators suddenly turned, all of them at once, and headed downstream toward the boats. They walked right past Arthur Stuart, ignoring him like he was a stump. And while they padded by on their vicious-looking gator feet, he felt something going on inside his stomach. He opened his shirt and looked down at his wound, just in time to see the lead ball nose out like a gopher and plop onto the dirt at his feet.

And as he watched, the blood stopped flowing out of his wound and the skin closed up and it didn't hurt anymore and he thought, Good thing Alvin's still watching out for me, because he gives me one dumb little assignment and I find a way to get myself killed twice over.

The gators were rushing toward the boat, but in the darkness it was plain some of the men hadn't realized what was headed their way. "Gators!" he shouted. "Get back in the boats!"

His alarm made them look again, and some of the men nearest to him got a look at what was coming. Now, a man *can* outrun a gator on dry land, but not in thick mud, so Arthur Stuart figured his contribution would be to dry the river bottom around the boats. But it was awfully far away from him and he couldn't be too precise. Still, it seemed to help, and he was relieved that all the men got back to the boats in time. The men onboard the boats reached down and helped haul them up, and the last few had gator jaws gaping wide right under them as they rose into the air, but not so much as a foot was lost, and only a few empty boots.

The gators remained in place, snapping and climbing over each other, trying to get up on deck. Arthur Stuart didn't think it was fair that the gators should get killed just because he told them there was food to be had. Besides, he had something against the muskets on board those boats. So he sauntered closer to the boats and used his doodlebug to find the guns and bend their barrels as fast as he could. They were bound to try the cannons next, but they were so thick-barreled that he found it was easier to melt the fronts just enough to narrow the bore, keeping the gunners from ramming the shot down.

So the men were fighting off the gators using their muskets as clubs. Which struck Arthur Stuart as more of an even match.

With that, he headed back upriver toward the dam, following his own trail of dry ground.

By the time he got back, most of the people were already across. Running twenty or thirty abreast, with the greensong still lingering in their ears, they all ran or jogged across, and kept moving on the other side to clear the way for the ones following after. Arthur went around the flow of people and up onto the bank and in no time he was standing beside Alvin.

"Thanks for taking that ball out of my gut," he said.

"Next time try something more subtle than standing out in the open and yelling," said Alvin. "I'm not trying to boss you around, I just think that's good advice."

"And thanks for getting the gators to turn away from me."

"I figgered you didn't really want them coming to *you*," said Alvin. "And that was nice of you to keep the men from shooting the gators. Not that there's any particular improvement in the world because of having gators in it, but I've never thought it was fair to get animals killed just because they believed a lie I told them."

"It wasn't a lie," said Arthur Stuart. "Plenty of meat on that boat."

"Only a couple of gators have got over the side since you started running back," said Alvin, "and the soldiers managed to throw them back. But I reckon they'll be glad enough when the water starts to flow again."

"Which is when?" said Arthur Stuart.

"Well, I don't see any heartfires up here on the bank aside from yours and mine," said Alvin. "And Dead Mary, seeing as how she just can't seem to stay away from wherever you are."

"Wherever *I* am!" said Arthur Stuart. But when he turned, he saw Dead Mary was indeed clambering back up onto the bank. "Everybody's gone," she said.

"Well, I'll just sit tight here till they all get up on the other bank," said Alvin. "Including, I must suggest, the two of you."

"But I can't leave you here alone!" said Arthur Stuart.

"And I can't worry about you when it's time to take

down this dam," said Alvin. "Now for once in your life, will you just do it my way and *git*? It's wearing me down holding this river back and you're making it take longer the longer you take trying to argue with me."

"I guess I might as well obey the fellow just saved my life," said Arthur Stuart.

"Double-saved it," said Alvin, "so you owe me another obedience later."

Arthur Stuart took Dead Mary by the hand and they skittered down the bank and ran across in front of the dam. They moved fast enough that they weren't far behind the last of the people, and all the way as they ran Arthur Stuart looked for the heartfires of any that might have strayed. But the captains and majors and colonels had all done their job, and not one soul had been left behind.

Papa Moose extended a hand to help Dead Mary up, and La Tia laughed in delight as Arthur Stuart flat-out ran right up the steep embankment without looking for the more gentle slope that most folks had used.

There at the head of the bluff stood Tenskwa-Tawa. It was Arthur Stuart's first sight of him, and his first thought was, he doesn't look like all that much. And his second thought was, he looks like a mighty angel standing there holding back the river with a sheet of crystal partly made from the blood of his own hand.

Tenskwa-Tawa waved the torch he held in his other hand. Then, when he saw that Alvin, far away on the other side, had thrown down his torch and started to run, Tenskwa-Tawa dropped the torch and reached out with that hand as if drawing something toward him.

On the far bank, Arthur Stuart could not see with his eyes, but he could follow Alvin's heartfire and observe with his doodlebug as Alvin ran down the embankment, holding his end of the dam in his hand.

He pulled the dam away from the far bank, and the water burst through behind him. Alvin ran as Arthur Stuart had never seen him run before, but the water was faster, leaping out through the newly opened gap and swirling around the edge of the dam that was now curving behind Alvin as he ran.

"Throw it to me!" cried Tenskwa-Tawa.

Whether Alvin heard with his ears or understood some other way, he obeyed, pitching his end of the dam like it was a stone or a javelin. No way would it have gone as far as it needed to, but Arthur Stuart could see how Tenskwa-Tawa drew it with that one extended hand, even though it was still half a mile away. He drew it toward him faster than Alvin could run, fast enough to outpace the water that rushed to fill the riverbed. Until finally both ends of the dam were in Tenskwa-Tawa's hands, and Alvin was running through a narrow passage between the two walls of the dam as the pent-up river continued to hurl itself through the widening gap.

Arthur Stuart let himself take one look downriver. Again with his doodlebug rather than with his eyes, he saw the first fingers of water flow around the boats, lifting them, starting them moving downstream. But the water came faster and faster, and the boats began to spin in the eddying flood as they hurtled away, completely out of control.

Alvin reached the bank and, as Arthur had done, ran directly up, straight to where Tenskwa-Tawa was standing, and even then he didn't stop, just hurled himself right into the waiting embrace of the Red Prophet, flinging them both to the ground. The ends of the crystal dam flew out of Tenskwa-Tawa's grasp and almost at once the crystal broke up and collapsed and the shards dissolved and became part of the river again. And Alvin and Tenskwa-Tawa lay there in the grass, hugging each other and laughing in delight at what they had done together, taming the Mizzippy and bringing these people to freedom.

La Tia was the only person bold enough at that moment to walk up to men who had just made such a miracle and say, "What you doing acting like little boys? We give merci beaucoup to God, us."

Alvin rolled onto his back and looked up at her. "It's picking which God that gets tricky," he said.

"Maybe you Christians right about God," said La Tia, "maybe me right, maybe him right, maybe nobody know nothing, but God, he take the merci beaucoup all the same."

She had seen Tenskwa-Tawa before, standing there holding the dam as everyone climbed the riverbank, but apparently she hadn't had a good look at him. Because now, as he sprang to his feet—far more energetically than his years should have allowed—a look of recognition came to her. "You," she said.

Tenskwa-Tawa nodded. "Me," he said.

"I see you in the ball," she said.

"What ball?" asked Alvin.

"The ball you make, the ball she carry." La Tia pointed toward Dead Mary, who did indeed have a burden slung over her shoulders. "I see him all the time in that thing. He talking to me."

Tenskwa-Tawa nodded. "And I thank you for helping," he said. "I didn't know you were with this company."

"I didn't know you the Red Prophet."

"So you two met?" asked Alvin.

"He been hotting up under the earth, far away," said La Tia. "He ask my help, wake up the earth there. Help the hot stuff find a way up. I think I figure out how."

"Then I'm as glad to see you here in the flesh as a man can be," said Tenskwa-Tawa.

"Many a man be glad to see my flesh," said La Tia, "but it don't do them no good."

Tenskwa-Tawa smiled, which for him was like a gale of laughter.

And Arthur Stuart thought, not for the first time, that these really powerful people were like a little club, they all knew each other and people like him were always having to stand just outside.

12

Springfield

VERILY COOPER'S KNACK wasn't just fitting barrel staves together to make a tight keg. He could see how most things were supposed to fit, and where the irregularities were that made it so they didn't. Most things—and most people. He could see who was friends and who was enemies, where pride or envy made a rift that few could see. The difference was that when two barrel staves didn't fit, he could get inside them and almost without thinking—and certainly without effort—change them till they did fit.

It wasn't quite so easy with people. You had to talk them round, or figure out a way to change what they wanted or what they believed about the world. Still, it was a good knack for a lawyer to have. He could size people up pretty readily, not as individuals, but how they fit together as families and communities.

Riding into the town of Springfield in Noisy River, Verily got a feel for the place right away.

The people that he met stopped and looked at him— what could a stranger expect, here on the frontier? Or at least what passed for frontier now. With the Mizzippy closed to white settlement, the land here was filling up fast. Verily saw the signs of it every time he traveled through this part of the west. And Springfield was a pretty lively place—lots of buildings that looked new, and some being built on the outskirts of town, not to mention the normal number of temporary shanties folks threw up for summer till they had more time to build something just before the weather got cold.

But these folks didn't just stop and look at him—they smiled, or waved, or even called out a "howdy do" or a "good afternoon" or a "welcome stranger." Little kids would follow along after him and while they were normal children—that is, a few of them could not resist throwing clods of dirt at his horse or his clothes (depending on whether Verily figured they hit their target or missed it)—none of them threw rocks or mud, so there wasn't any meanness in it.

The town center was a nice one, too. There was a town square with a courthouse in it, and a church facing it in each direction. Verily wasn't a bit surprised that the Baptists had to face the back of the courthouse, while the Episcopalians got the front view. The Presbyterians had the north side and the Lutherans had the south. And if Catholics or Puritans or Quakers showed up, they'd probably have to build their churches outside the town. Verily enjoyed the cheerful hypocrisy of American freedom of religion. No church got to be the established one, but you sure knew which ones were way more *dis*established than others.

It was the courthouse, though, where Verily figured he'd have the best luck finding out the whereabouts of Abraham Lincoln, erstwhile storekeeper and river trader.

The clerk knew a lawyer when he saw one, and greeted Verily with an alert smile.

"I was hoping you could help me locate a citizen of this town," said Verily.

"Serving papers on somebody?" asked the clerk cheerfully.

So much for thinking I look like a lawyer, thought Verily. "No sir," said Verily. "Just a conversation with a friend of a friend."

"Then that ain't legal business, is it?"

Verily almost laughed. He knew what type of fellow this was right off. The kind who had memorized the rule book and knew his list of duties and took pleasure in refusing to do anything that wasn't on the list.

"You know," said Verily, "it's not. And I've got no business wasting your time. So what I'll do is, I'll remain here in this public space where any citizen of the United States is permitted to be, and I'll greet every person who enters this courthouse and ask *them* to help me locate this citizen. And when they ask me why I don't just ask the clerk at the desk, I'll tell them that I wouldn't want to waste that busy gentleman's time."

The man's smile got a little frosty. "Are you threatening me?"

"Threatening you with what?" said Verily. "I'm determined to locate a citizen of this fair town for reasons that are between me and him and a mutual friend, doing no harm to him or anyone else. And since this building is at the very center of town—a fine building it is, too, I might add, as good a courthouse as I've seen in any county seat of comparable size in Hio or Wobbish or New England, for that matter—I can think of no likelier place to encounter someone who can help me find Mr. Abraham Lincoln."

There. He'd got the name out. Now to see if the man could resist the temptation to show off what he knew.

He could not. "Old Abe? Well, now, why didn't you say it was Old Abe from the start?"

"Old? The man I'm looking for can't be thirty yet."

"Well, that's him, then. Tall and lanky, ugly as sin but sweet as sugar pie?"

"I've heard rumors about his height," said Verily, "but the rest of your description awaits personal verification."

"Well he'll be in the general store, now that he's out

of the store business himself. Or in Hiram's tavern. But you know what? Just go out on the street and listen for laughter, follow the sound of it, and wherever it's coming from, there's Abe Lincoln, cause either he's causing the laughter or doing the laughing himself."

"Why thank you, sir," said Verily. "But now I fear I've taken too much of your time, and not on proper legal business at all, so I'll step on out of here before I get you in some kind of trouble."

"Oh, no trouble," said the clerk. "Any friend of Abe's is a friend of everybody's."

Verily bade him farewell and stepped back out into the afternoon sunshine.

Abe Lincoln sounds for all the world like the town drunk—or a ne'er-do-well, in any case. Failed at a store. No job to do so he can be found in a tavern or a general store. And this is the one I've been sent to find?

Though a drunk or ne'er-do-well would probably not get such a warm description from someone as precise and well ordered as that clerk.

To his surprise, when he stopped two men coming out of a barber shop—sporting that new clean-shaven look that required a man to spend ten cents a day getting his beard removed—and asked them if they knew the current whereabouts of Abraham Lincoln, they both held up a hand to hush him, listened, and sure enough, the sound of a distant gale of laughter could be heard.

"Sounds like he's over at Cheaper's store," said one man.

"Just straight on down the street," said the other, "kitty-corner from here."

So Verily followed the sound of laughter and sure enough, when he walked into the cool darkness of the store's interior, there were a half a dozen men and a couple of ladies, sitting here and there, while leaning up against the wall was about the ugliest man Verily Cooper had ever seen, who wasn't actually injured in some way. Tall, though, just like they said, a giraffe among men.

Lincoln was in the middle of a story. "So Coz says to me, Abe, isn't the front of the raft supposed to point downriver? And I says to Coz, And so it is. And he says to me, No, Abe, *that's* the front. And he pointed *up*stream, which made no sense at all. Well, now, that kind of illogic always riles me, not a lot, just a little, and I says, Now Coz, that was the front of the raft this morning, I agree, but wasn't it us decided which end of the raft was front? And therefore are we not entitled to change our minds and designate a new front, as circumstances change?"

Now Verily hardly knew what the story was about, and he certainly did not know this Coz fellow Abe was talking about. But when the people in that store laughed—which they did about every six words, on average—he couldn't help but join in. It wasn't just what Lincoln said, it was how he said it, such a dry manner, and willing to make himself the fool of the story, but a fool with a sort of deeper wit about him.

What was most interesting to Verily, though, was the way Lincoln *fit* with the other folks in that room. There was not a soul there who had even the slightest friction between him and Lincoln. They all fit with him like a bosom friend. And yet he couldn't be best friends with every one of them. A man doesn't have time to make more than a couple of friends so close and dear that they don't envy you when you do well or scorn you when you do badly or become irritated with you for any number of little habits you have.

It went way beyond being likable. Verily had met a few who had something of a knack for that—you find them rather thick on the ground in the lawyering profession—and he found that no matter how good their knack was, when you weren't with them, you were really angry at being taken in, and even when you were in that spell, some of that anger remained with you. Verily would sense it, but it wasn't there. No, these people weren't being hoodwinked, and Lincoln wasn't doing it by some sort of hidden power. He was just telling stories, and they were enjoying both the tale and the teller.

It didn't take Verily Cooper much time to notice all this—it *was* his knack, after all. The story continued and Lincoln showed no sign of noticing that Verily Cooper was there.

"Now Coz, he thinks about this—so he's holding really still, because you know when Coz is thinking, it kind of uses up his whole body, unless he has gas—and finally he says to me, Abe, I used to think that way myself, only I found that no matter what you *call* it, you got to put your legs into the *top* of your trousers first."

It took some of them a couple of moments to get the joke, but the thing is, they all *knew* they were going to get it and that the joke wasn't meant to exclude them. Verily found himself liking Lincoln, not just the instinctive liking that came by reflex, but also the liking that comes when you've understood something about a fellow and you admire the thing you understood. Abraham Lincoln doesn't put himself above anybody, but he doesn't lower himself to do it.

"But here we are ignoring our visitor," said Lincoln. "A new fellow, and a lawyer, would be my guess, and so eager to shop at Cheaper's that he hasn't looked for a room or brushed down his clothes."

"Or stabled my horse," said Verily. "But I have urgent business that couldn't wait for such niceties."

"And yet you came to Cheaper's and listened to my story about Coz and me on the river. You must come from a town even smaller than Springfield, if my tale caused you enough wonder to keep you from your business."

"No sir," said Verily Cooper. "Because you're Abraham Lincoln, and my business is to talk to *you*."

"Please don't tell me I've got another creditor I didn't know about."

There was still laughter from the others, but it was rueful—and a bit wary. They didn't want ill things to happen to Mr. Lincoln.

In fact, one of the ladies spoke up. "If your client thinks that Mr. Lincoln won't pay his debts, he can rest assured, Old Abe never leaves a debt unpaid."

"Which I mostly accomplish by never borrowing," said Lincoln.

"Never borrowing for your*self,* you mean," said the lady. A lady considerably older than Lincoln, but Verily ruled out the possibility that she was related to him. No, she had probably come here simply to buy something.

"Mr. Lincoln, my name is Verily Cooper, and we have a friend in common—Alvin Smith, whom I believe you met on a trip down the Mizzippy not more than a couple of weeks ago."

"A good man," said Lincoln—but added nothing more.

"What," said one of the men. "No story about this Smith fellow?"

Lincoln grinned. "Why, you know I don't tell stories on other folks, only on myself." He strode toward Verily and offered a hand. "I'm pleased to meet you, Mr. Cooper. Though I got to fess that's a strange name for a lawyer."

"I was raised to be a cooper," said Verily, "and when the lawyering business is slow, I can always support myself by making a keg or two."

"Whereas my family could never get over the shire they came from back in England," said Lincoln. "Which, judging from your speech, is where you're from."

"I am, but a citizen of this country now," said Verily. "We're none of us very far from the boats that brought our people over."

"Well, I'm eager to talk to you," said Lincoln, "but I'm the clerk of this store right now, working for Mr. and Mrs. Cheaper, and I've been keeping these poor customers waiting for their purchases while I listened to myself talk. Can you wait your business for a half hour?"

Verily could, and did. In fact, he used the half hour to get his horse stabled and fed, and when he returned, there were no customers in the shop. Lincoln did not look so jovial now.

"Mr. Cooper," he said, "there ain't been time for *good* news to get from Barcy to here, but I heard some bad stories about yellow fever breaking out there. I hope you're not here to tell me that Alvin or his young friend with the royal name has took sick."

"Best of health, as far as I know," said Verily.

"Also there's a strange tale came upriver on a steamboat and got included in the daily lie collection known as the *Springfield Democrat*. About all the slaves in Barcy walking on water and the Spanish Army coming upriver to fetch them back. I got to say, some folks—the ones foolish enough to believe a tale like that—are now worried that Spain is going to invade Springfield, and I've been trying to get Mr. Cheaper to order some Spanish grammars to get us ready for the occupation, but he won't do it."

"And you guessed that Alvin had something to do with this exodus."

"I hoped," said Lincoln. "Because if a man's going to get in trouble, it ought to be in a good cause, and Alvin has that air about him, that whatever he does, somebody's going to be mad at him for doing it."

"I came here because he needs some help, and you're the only person we could think of who might be able to handle it."

"Well, I'll help him if I can. I owe him something, you know."

"That's not why we're asking," said Verily. "This isn't a debt, because whatever you think you might owe him, what he's asking is way bigger."

"What could be bigger than saving my life?"

"The lives of five or six thousand French folks and former slaves, who have no place of safety to which they can repair in their time of trouble."

"I can put up three of them in my room over the tavern, but not one more, and that's if they don't mind getting stepped on if somebody has to get up in the night to use the privy."

"They're coming up the river and they need a place that will take them in and protect them. Alvin's wife, Margaret Larner—you may have heard of her . . ."

"Highly thought of among abolitionists," said Lincoln, "though not by those who think the only way to free the slaves is by war."

"Margaret is, as you may also have heard, a torch."

"That doesn't get mentioned even in the pro-slavery press, and you'd think they'd make a big deal of it."

"She retired from the public use of her knack," said Verily. "But she still sees what she sees, and what she saw was this: The only way this expedition of runaway slaves and Frenchmen is going to find any peace or safety is with your help."

Lincoln's bony face suddenly looked sad. "Mr. Cooper, I hope your friend is ready for disappointment."

"You won't do it?"

"Oh, I'll do whatever I can. But you got to understand something. Everything I turn my hand to fails. I mean everything. I think I've got a knack for failure, because I manage it no matter what I undertake to do."

"I don't know," said Verily. "You tell a good story."

"Well, that's not something a man can make a living at."

"I do," said Verily.

"Telling stories? Forgive me for saying it, but you don't look like the humorous type."

"I didn't say my stories were funny, but it wouldn't hurt a bit in my profession if I had a little more humor from time to time."

"You're saying that lawyers are storytellers?"

"That's our main job. We take a set of facts, and we tell a story that includes them all and doesn't leave out or contradict a one of them. The other fellow's lawyer then takes the same facts and tells a different story. And the jury believes one story or they believe the other."

Lincoln laughed. "Why, you make your profession sound almost as useless as loafing around in a general store telling silly stories to help folks pass the time of day."

"Do you really believe that's all you do?" asked Verily.

"I think the evidence of your own eyes should confirm that story, sir," said Lincoln.

"My eyes see what your eyes can't," said Verily Cooper. "This town is a happy place—one of the happiest towns, house for house and man for man, that I've ever seen."

"It's a good place to live, and it's good neighbors make it that way, I always say," said Lincoln.

"A town's like a living thing," said Verily. "It all fits together like a body—not an attractive body, because there's a head of this and a head of that, and all kinds of arms and legs and fingers, but you get my analogy, I'm sure."

"Everybody's got his place," said Lincoln.

"Ah, but most towns have people who can't find their place, or aren't happy with it, or are trying to take a place that they're not suited for, or hurt somebody who belongs there just as much as they do. But from the feel of this town I'd say there's not too much of that."

"We got our skunks, like any other town. When they get their tail up, folks know to duck for cover."

"This town has a heart," said Verily.

"I'm glad you could see that," said Lincoln.

"And the heart is you."

Lincoln laughed. "Oh, I didn't see that coming. You *do* have a sense of humor after all, Mr. Cooper."

Verily just smiled. "Mr. Lincoln, I think if you set yourself to figuring out where these five or six thousand souls might find refuge, you'd not only come up with a good answer, but you'd be the very man best suited to persuading folks to let them go there."

Lincoln looked off into the distance. "I'm a terrible salesman," he finally said. "I always tell the truth about what I'm selling, and then nobody buys it."

"But how are you at pleading for the downtrodden? Especially when every word you'd say about them would be true?"

"In case you haven't noticed, Mr. Cooper, the downtrodden get less popular as their numbers increase. A man approached by one beggar is likely to give him a penny. A man approached by five beggars in one day won't give a thing to the last one. And a man approached by five beggars at once will run away and claim he was being robbed."

"Which is why we need to have a refuge for these folks before anybody can see with their own eyes how many they are."

"Oh, I know how many five thousand is. It's about four times the population of Springfield, and about equal to the population of this whole county."

"So there's not room for them here," said Verily.

"Or any other town along the Mizzippy. And I reckon if they're being carried on boats up the river, you'll want a place for them that's near a landing."

"Not on boats," said Verily.

"Walking? If they can make their way to Noisy River, with the militia of every slave-owning county roused against them, they don't need any help from *me*."

"They're not walking up the east bank of the river."

Lincoln grinned. "Oh, now, you're telling me that Alvin got them reds to let his people pass through."

"Pass through, but not linger."

"No, I reckon not," said Lincoln. "You let in five thousand one day, you'll have to let in ten thousand the next."

"Mr. Lincoln," said Verily, "I know you don't think you can do the job, but Margaret Larner thinks you can, and from what I've seen of you, I think you can, and all that is lacking at the moment is your agreement to try."

"Knowing that I'm likely to fail," said Lincoln.

"I can't fail worse *with* your help than I'm bound to fail without it," said Verily.

"You know that Coz will want to help, and he's even more of a blockhead than I am."

"I'd be happy to have the help of Coz, whoever that might be, as long as I can rely on you."

"I'll tell you what," said Lincoln.

"There's something you want in return?"

"Oh, I'll do it anyway," said Lincoln, "or try my best, I should say. But since you and I will be together for a while, and likely to have many an hour on the road together, what would you think of using your time to start teaching me the principles of law?"

"You don't talk law," said Verily Cooper, "you *read* law."

"You read law after you've decided that a lawyer's what you want to be," said Lincoln. "But before you decide, then you talk law so you find out just what it is you're getting yourself in for, and whether you want to spend your life doing it."

"I don't think you'll spend your *whole* life doing any one thing," said Verily. "I don't think that's in you, if I know anything about a man. But I think if you set your mind to lawyering, you'd be a good one. And not least because there's no chance under heaven that you will ever, for a single moment, *look* like a lawyer."

"You don't think that's a drawback?"

"I think that for a long while, every lawyer who comes up against you in court will think you're a country bumpkin and he won't have to work at all to beat you."

"But I am a country bumpkin."

"And I'm a kegmaker. A kegmaker who wins most of his cases in court."

Lincoln laughed. "So you're saying that by simply being myself, as I am, not pretending to be anything else, I'll fool those highfalutin lawyers better than if I tried to lie to them."

"You can't help what other people choose to believe about you, before they have all the evidence in hand."

Lincoln reached out his hand. "I'm with you, then, till we find a place for this tribe that Alvin's recruited. Though I have to say, he ain't gonna need some camp on the outskirts of a town. Lessen he's figuring to split those folks up among twenty towns or more, nobody's going to want them."

"Splitting them up might be necessary," said Verily. "But it might also be dangerous. You know there'll be slave catchers here as soon as it becomes known where they are."

"So you need them all to be in a place where slave catchers won't be able to cart them all back south one at a time."

"A place that will afford protection, yes," said Verily.

"A completely abolitionist county, then, is what you need. With its own judge, not a circuit rider, so you know how he's going to rule on every slavery issue."

"A strong enthusiasm for habeus corpus would be an advantage, yes."

"A county where every justice of the peace can be relied on not to cooperate with the catchers."

"Is there such a county?" asked Verily.

"Not yet," said Lincoln, and he grinned.

≱ 13 ≰

Mission

IT WAS ALL as well planned as a church party, and Arthur Stuart plain admired how they done it. All the stories about reds that folks told these days was about savages living a natural life picking fruit off the trees and calling to deer and they'd come right up and the red man would clunk them on the head. Or else stories about savages murdering and raping and scalping and capturing white folks and keeping them as slaves till they got away or till some soldiers find them and they refuse to go home. Or about how if you give a red man likker he'll get as drunk as a skunk in five minutes flat and spend the rest of his life devoted to getting more.

Of course, Arthur Stuart knew in the back of his mind that this sort of thing couldn't be the complete story. Alvin's time with the reds had been back before Arthur Stuart was born, but he knew Alvin was friends with the mystical Red Prophet, and he knew Alvin had known and traveled with Ta-Kumsaw, and had even got himself known as a renegado because of the time he spent with the reds during the war.

And Arthur had seen plenty of red men, from time to time—but they were Irrakwa or Cherriky and they wore business suits just like everybody else and stood for Congress and supervised railroad construction and ran banks and did all kinds of other jobs so there wasn't no difference between them and white folks except the color of their skin and how fat they got when they grew up, because some of them reds could get huge.

Alvin got kind of sad sometimes, after meeting one of them. "A good man, as men go," he said to Arthur Stuart once. "Prosperous and clever. But what he gave up to get rich."

Arthur Stuart figured what Alvin was talking about was the greensong. He sort of had the idea that maybe red men were supposed to live inside the greensong all the livelong day, and that's what that Irrakwa railroad man had give up.

But when you thought about the red men living out beyond the Mizzippy, you sort of thought they'd be living the old way, hunting and fishing and living in wigwams. So it plain irritated Arthur Stuart at first to find out that they built log cabins and laid out their towns in streets, and that they planted acre after acre in maize and beans.

"This don't feel like no greensong to me," Arthur Stuart said to Dead Mary. "This just feels like a town."

Dead Mary laughed at him for that. "Why shouldn't red folk have towns? Big cities, too? You think only white people know what a city is?"

And when it came to feeding all these six thousand runaways, why, the red men was as organized as a church picnic. There was fifty tables set up, and each colonel and major would bring their fifty households and they'd pass along the tables and pile up food on baskets and carry them off to the pastures that had been designated as their campsites and it was so smooth that everybody got their breakfast before the sun even got hot. And all the while, there was red women hauling more food to the tables— corn bread and flat bread and bean mash and cider and apples and pawpaws and big bunches of grapes.

The grapes he just had to ask about. "Iffen red folks got grapes, how come they didn't invent wine?"

"They didn't have grapes," Alvin told him, "till they learned how to grow them from white folks."

"So what are they doing, making wine now?"

"Their cider and their wine have so little alcohol that you'd have to pee it all out long before you got drunk," said Alvin. "Tenskwa-Tawa sees to that. But it's the safest way to store water that got no disease in it, and besides, he wants to build up the reds' tolerance for it, so his people don't get enslaved by alcohol the way he was and so many others were."

"Hard to think of that man being slave to anything," said Arthur Stuart.

"But he was," said Alvin. "Slave to likker and slave to rage and hate. But now he's at peace with everybody that wants to, and he spends his life reading and studying and learning everything he can about everything."

"So red folks got books?"

"He gets them from our side of the Mizzippy," said Alvin. "And from Canada and Mexico. He travels widely, the way his brother used to do. That's why he speaks English so well. And French and Spanish and about thirty red languages, too. He says that someday the barrier won't hold, and white folks and red folks will have to mix, and he wants his people to be ready so they can do it without losing the greensong the way the Cherriky and Irrakwa did."

All that morning, Tenskwa-Tawa was holed up with La Tia and about a dozen old red men and women, and when Arthur asked what they were doing, Alvin told him to mind his own business.

But at noon—when they started in on yet another meal, this time with meat in it—mostly smoked turkey, which the reds seemed to herd like sheep—Alvin was invited in to the big hall where the red council and La Tia were meeting, and in a few minutes he came back out and fetched Arthur Stuart inside.

It was a cool, dark place, with a fire in the middle and a hole in the roof, even though the reds knew perfectly well how to make a chimney, as every cabin in town proved. So it must have something to do with keeping up the old ways. The reds sat right on the ground, on blankets, but they had a chair for La Tia, just like the one she sat in back in Barcy. So she was the tallest thing in the room, like one lone pine standing up in the middle of a stand of beeches.

"Sit with us, Arthur Stuart," said Tenskwa-Tawa. "We have a mission for you, if you're willing."

This was about the last thing Arthur Stuart expected. A mission for him? He'd expected to follow along with Alvin as he led the company north along the river. The days he'd spent as a second-rate maker barely keeping the fog around the camp had convinced him that he was *not* ready to go out makering on his own. Nothing terrible had happened, but it could have, and he had never been more than barely in control. He was proud that he'd done OK, and perfectly relieved if he never had to do it again.

"I'll do my part," said Arthur Stuart, "but you do know that I'm not a maker, I hope."

"It's not makery they need you for," said Alvin. "Or at least not mostly. It's your own knack with languages, and the fact that you're smart and dependable and . . . you."

That made no sense to Arthur Stuart, but he was willing to listen—no, he was eager to hear what it was that they actually needed *him* for, himself.

Tenskwa-Tawa laid out for him what was going on in Mexico, about how the volcano was going to blow up, especially now that La Tia was on the case. "I already planned to send some of my own people to give warning to the Mexica, and they will still go," said Tenskwa-Tawa. "Already some of them are there. But there's a complication. A group of white men is heading for Mexico City and they will surely be killed, either by the Mexica or by the volcano."

"Or both," said La Tia. "Some men has to die two times to get the point."

"So we need you for two things," said Tenskwa-Tawa. "You have to go warn the white men and help them get out, if they're willing."

Arthur Stuart laughed. "You gonna send a half-black boy my age to warn *white* men to get out?"

"My brother Calvin's with them," said Alvin.

"But he don't like me."

"But he'll know you came from me," said Alvin. "And it's up to him to persuade the others."

"So this is about saving Calvin's life," said Arthur Stuart dubiously. He knew perfectly well that his sister Margaret had no high opinion of Calvin and Arthur Stuart kind of suspected that if Calvin died it might ease her mind. But Alvin wouldn't feel that way, of course. He still thought of Calvin as nothing worse than a foolish little brother who would grow up someday and became a decent man.

"And all the others," said Alvin, "if they're smart enough to be saved."

"But how am I going to get there in time to warn them?"

"Two things," said Alvin. "First, you'll run with the greensong."

"But it's desert between here and there."

"The greensong doesn't depend on the color green, really," said Alvin. "It comes from life, and you'll see, the desert is packed with living things. They're just thirstier, is all."

"But I can't do the greensong alone."

La Tia spoke up. "I give you a charm like I made before, only better."

"And I'll run with you the first hour or so, to get you started. Arthur Stuart, you've passed the threshold, don't you realize it? You're the first one to do it, but you're a man who wasn't born to be a maker, but he's learned makery all the same."

"Not as good as you. Nowhere near."

"Maybe not," said Alvin, "but good enough—and the greensong's not makery anyway. I learned it as surely as you will, and you get better at feeling it the more you do it. You'll see."

"And somehow I'll find the way?"

"The closer you get to Mexico, the more folks will know how to point out the road."

"And if somebody decides my heart would make a dandy sacrifice?"

"Then you'll use the powers you've learned to get away. I don't just want you to deliver the message, I want you to come back safe and sound."

"Oh," said Arthur Stuart, realizing. "You want me to bring these white men with me."

"I want you to bring them as far as it takes to make them safe," said Alvin, "but on no account is that to be here with us. Get them to the coast and put them on a boat—as many as will come—and then you come on back."

"I don't think a soul's gonna listen to me," said Arthur Stuart. "When did Calvin ever listen to *you*?"

"Calvin will do what he wants," said Alvin. "But I won't let him die because he didn't know something I could have told him."

"I just hope I get there before the volcano blows," said Arthur Stuart. "What if I get lost?"

"Don't you worry," said La Tia. "You be carrying the volcano with you."

The other part of the errand? "How can I do *that*?"

Tenskwa-Tawa answered. "We have awakened the giant under the earth," he said. "It flows now hotter and hotter. But what we couldn't do was control the moment when it erupted. Or where. But La Tia, she knows the old African ways of calling to the earth. She's made two charms. They won't work until they're burned. But where they're burned, and what you say when you burn them, you'll have to memorize that and teach it to my people who are there."

"Why two charms?" asked Arthur.

"The one she call smoke from the ground," said La Tia. "The other one, she call the hot red blood out of the earth."

"My people," said Tenskwa-Tawa, "will tell the Mexica people what day the smoke will first appear, and when it happens, they'll believe. We want to give them plenty of time to leave. The idea isn't to kill Mexicas. The idea is to show them that a greater power rejects their lies about what God wants them to do."

"We're trying to break the power of the priests who sacrifice human beings," said Alvin.

"Three days after the first charm," said Tenskwa-Tawa, "they'll use the second one."

"And the volcano blows up."

"We don't know how bad it will be," said Tenskwa-Tawa. "We can't control what the giant does, once it's awake."

"What about the reds who work the charm?" asked Arthur Stuart.

"We hope that they'll get away in time," said Tenskwa-Tawa.

"I don't know how fast she work," said La Tia. "I never make this kind before."

"How do you know it'll work at all, then?" said Arthur Stuart.

It seemed a practical question to him, but La Tia shot him a glare. "I be La Tia, me," she said. "Other people charms, they maybe don't work."

Arthur Stuart grinned at her. "I hope I grow up to be perfect like you."

She apparently didn't detect the irony in his words. "You be so lucky," she said.

Arthur Stuart spent the next hour studying the charm

to learn how it was put together—"in case she come apart on the road," La Tia said—and learning the words and the motions.

"What if I don't do it exactly right?" said Arthur Stuart. "What if I forget some bit? Will it just work a little slower, or will it not work at all?"

La Tia glared at him again. "Don't forget any. Then we never find out how much she go wrong when stupid boy forget."

So even after she was satisfied that he knew what to do, Arthur Stuart went off by himself, to a stand of trees near the river, to go through it all again.

That's where he was when Dead Mary found him. But he was asleep by then, exhausted from all that he'd been doing for days. The greensong helped him and everyone else stay vigorous all through the night and into the morning, but the need for sleep had caught up with him and there was no denying it.

Arthur Stuart felt a hand on his shoulder and sat bolt upright. He was confused to see that it was Dead Mary who was kneeling beside him, because she had also been in his dream.

"Alvin sent me to look for you," said Dead Mary. "Sorry to wake you up."

Arthur shook his head. "That's all right," he said. "I didn't mean to fall asleep."

"What's that you were lying on?"

Arthur Stuart looked down and was horrified to see that he had rolled over on the smaller charm and bent it. He said a swear word, apologized for it, and when Dead Mary said it was all right, he thanked her and said it again. "She's gonna kill me if I don't get this back together right."

"La Tia?" said Dead Mary. "Sometimes I think she might kill someone for practice. The power she has!"

"I'm just glad she's on our side," said Arthur Stuart.

"She is for now."

"Same could be said for you," said Arthur. "When we

get to safety, what then? Where will everybody go?"

"Where *can* we go?" said Dead Mary. "All these run-away slaves, where will they be safe? And my people, the French—we don't speak the way they do in Paris, you think they'll want us in Canada? We will be strangers wherever we go. Maybe we stay in the United States. Maybe we stay with Alvin."

"Alvin wanders all the time," said Arthur Stuart. "He hardly sleeps in the same bed twice."

"Then maybe we wander."

Oh right, Alvin was bound to want her along on his journeys. "He's married, you know."

She looked at him like he was crazy. "I know that, ignorant boy."

"Is that what I am?"

"When you talk like that, yes," said Mary. "You think I want a *husband*? You think all women, they want a man for a *husband* or not at all?"

"Well, you ain't *got* a husband," said Arthur Stuart.

"And when I want one," she answered, "I will tell him and it will be none of your business."

So much for Arthur Stuart's dream. "It's none of my business now." He looked at the small charm from every angle. There was nothing wrong with it that he could see, and yet it still didn't feel quite right.

"Was this supposed to be part of it?" said Mary. She held up a grain of dried maize—a red one.

"Yes, yes, thank you." He inserted it into its place between two pieces of birchbark. "It's hard to remember what you're *not* seeing. I'm going to mess this up, I just know it. This is important, and they're crazy to send an ignorant boy to do it."

She laid a reassuring hand on his shoulder. "You are not really an ignorant boy," she said.

"No, you had it right."

"You are an ignorant boy when you try to guess what a woman is thinking," said Mary. "But you are not an ignorant boy when it comes to doing a man's work."

"I guess *then* I'm an ignorant *man*," he grumbled, but he liked having her touch his shoulder, even if she *was* sweet on a married man.

"I saw you in the crystal ball," she said. "I saw you running and running. Through desert, up a mountain. To a great valley surrounded by tall mountains, with a lake in the middle, and a city on the lake. I saw you run to the middle and light a fire and it turned all the mountains into great chimneys giving off smoke, and then the earth began to shake and the mountains began to bleed."

"Well, the plan is for me *not* to be there by the time that stuff happens."

"The ball does not show what will actually happen," said Mary. "It shows the *meaning* of what *might* happen. But you will run, yes? And thousands of people will be saved from the fire."

"A fire that wouldn't happen except for this." He held up the bigger charm. "You want to know how scary La Tia is?"

"I have seen my mother ride the back of a shark," said Dead Mary. "I have seen her swim with sharks, and play with them like puppies. I am not afraid of La Tia."

"Why are some people so powerful, and other people barely got a knack at all?" asked Arthur Stuart.

"Why can I see sickness and death, and do nothing about it?" asked Mary. "Why can you speak any language you want, but you don't know what to say? To have a knack is a burden; not to have a knack is a burden; God only cares to see what we do with the burden we have."

"So now you're speaking for God?"

"I'm speaking the truth," said Mary, "and you know it." She got up. "Alvin wants you and I came to bring you."

"I remember," said Arthur Stuart. "But I wasn't coming back till I got this fixed."

"I know," she said. "But now it's fixed, and here we are. What are you waiting for, Arthur Stuart?"

"We was talking is all," he said.

Then, to his surprise, she put her hands on his shoulders, leaned up, and kissed him right on the mouth. "You were waiting for that," she said.

"Reckon I was," he said. "Was I waiting for maybe two of them?"

She kissed him again.

"So you're telling me you're *not* sweet on Alvin?"

She laughed. "I want him to teach me everything he knows," she said. "But you—I want to teach *you* everything *I* know."

Then she ran off ahead of him, toward the red city.

When Arthur Stuart got back to camp, La Tia immediately demanded to see the charms, and though she clucked and straightened a little here and there, she did it as much on the one he had *not* crushed as on the one he had, so he figured she was just fussing and he had done OK at putting it back together.

Alvin took him out of the city right after supper. "You had your nap," he said, "and anyway, the greensong will sustain you."

"You're going to get me started," said Arthur Stuart, "but I'm gonna have to stop along the way, if only to ask directions, and then how will I get started again?"

"You can stop without losing the greensong," said Alvin. "Just hold on to it, keep hearing it. You'll see. It's easier, though, if you stay away from machinery."

"I'll keep that in mind."

"It's one of the things that makes it hard for me," said Alvin. " 'Cause I love machinery, and I love the greensong, and a lot of the time I just can't have them both at once. Tenskwa-Tawa sneers at the Irrakwa for choosing railroads over the music of the earth, but I tell you, Arthur Stuart, the railroads got a music of their own, and I love it. Steam engines, wheels and gears, pistons and fires and speed over the rails . . . sometimes I wish I could settle down and be an engineer."

"Engineers only get to go where the tracks have been laid," said Arthur Stuart.

"There you have it," said Alvin. "I'm a journeyman, and that's the truth."

"That's why you should be making this trip, not me," said Arthur Stuart. "I'm gonna mess this up, and folks are gonna wish it had been you all along."

"Nobody wished it had been me leading that exodus across the delta lands."

"I did."

"You'll do fine," said Alvin. "And now we ought to stop talking, and get your journey started."

They began to run, and soon Arthur Stuart was caught up in the greensong, stronger than he'd ever heard it before. The red farmland wasn't like white men's farms. The maize and the beans grew right up together, all mixed in, and there were other plants and lots of animals living in it, so the song didn't go silent where the ground had been plowed and planted. Maybe there was a way that machines could be made harmonious with the earth the way these farms were. Then Alvin wouldn't have to choose between them.

After a while Arthur Stuart noticed that Alvin wasn't with him, and he fretted for a moment. But he knew that worrying wouldn't change a thing, except maybe to draw him out of the greensong, so he gave himself over to the music of life and ran on and on, steadily southwest, over hills and through copses and splashing through streams, as directly as the land allowed, all living things making way before him or helping him along his path.

It occurred to him that he might move even faster, and then he did. Faster yet, and now he fairly flew. But his feet always found just the right place to step, and when he leapt he cleared every hurdle, and every breath he took in was filled with pleasure, and every breath he let out was a whispery song of joy.

⚒ 14 ⚒

Plow

"WHY WON'T YOU look in the crystal ball, Alvin?" asked Dead Mary one morning.

"Nothing there that I want to see," said Alvin.

"We look into it and see important things," she said.

"But you can't trust it, can you?" said Alvin.

"It gives us an idea of what's coming."

"No it doesn't," said Alvin. "It gives you an idea of what you already expect is coming. Distorted by what you *fear* is coming and what you *hope* is coming. But if you don't already know what you're looking for . . ."

"For someone who refuses to look," said Dead Mary, "you know a lot about it."

"I don't like what I see there."

"Neither do I," said Dead Mary. "But I think that is not why you refuse to look."

"Oh?"

"I think you do not look because it is your wife who sees the future, not you. And if you ever looked into the ball, then you would not need her any more."

"I think you're talking about things you don't know anything about," said Alvin, and he turned away to leave.

"I also don't like what I don't see," said Dead Mary.

Alvin had to know. He could not leave yet. "What don't you see?"

"A good husband for me, for one thing," she said. "Or children. Or a happy life. Isn't that what crystal balls are supposed to show?"

"It ain't no carnival fortune telling ball."

"No, it's made of water from the swamps of Nueva Barcelona," said Dead Mary. "And it shows me that you love your wife and will never leave her."

He turned around to face her again. "Does it show you that it's wrong of you to toy with Arthur Stuart and lead him to think you're in love with him?"

"It is not wrong," said Dead Mary, "if it's true."

"True that you're toying with him? Or true that you're in love with him?"

"True that I am drawn to him. That I like him. That I wanted to kiss him before he left."

"Why?"

"Because he's a good boy and he shouldn't die without ever being kissed."

"The crystal ball showed you he was going to die, is that it?"

"Isn't he?"

"The ball tells back to you what you already believe," said Alvin. "That's why I don't look in it."

"Let me tell you what the ball shows *me*," said Dead Mary. "A city on a hill over a river, and in the center of the city, a great palace of crystal, like the ball, water standing up and shining in the sunlight so you cannot bear to look on it."

"Just one building made of crystal," said Alvin. "And the rest of them are just ordinary city buildings?"

She nodded. "And the name of the city is The City of Makers, and The City Beautiful, and Crystal City."

"That's a lot of names for one dream."

"This is where you are leading us, isn't it?" said Dead Mary.

"So maybe the ball *doesn't* show you only your own dream," he said.

"Whose dream did I see, then?"

"Mine."

"Let me tell you something, Monsieur Maker," said Dead Mary. "These people don't need some fancy building made of crystal. All they need is some good land where they can set a plow, and build a house, and raise a family, and they'll do just fine."

In Alvin's poke the plow trembled.

When Verily Cooper met up with Abe Lincoln in Cheaper's store at noon, there was someone else waiting for him. The precise little clerk from the courthouse.

"Out of your territory, aren't you?" asked Verily.

"I'm on duty, as a matter of fact," said the clerk.

"Then your list of duties is longer than I thought," said Verily.

The clerk walked up to him and handed him a folded and sealed paper. "That's for you."

Verily glanced at it. "No it's not," he said.

"Are you or are you not the attorney for one Alvin Smith also known as Alvin Miller, Jr., of Vigor Church, state of Wobbish?"

"I am," said Verily Cooper.

"Then in that capacity papers to be served on Mr. Smith can be served on you."

"But," said Verily, touching the man on the shoulder to suggest that he should not rush out of the store as he seemed to be in quite a hurry to do. "But, we are not in the state of Hio, where I am licensed to practice law, or the state of Wobbish, where I am licensed to practice law. In those states, I am indeed Mr. Smith's attorney. But in the state of Noisy River, I am an ordinary citizen, engaged in private business with Mr. Abraham Lincoln, and nobody's attorney at all. That's the law, sir, and these papers have not been legally served."

He handed them back to the clerk.

The clerk glared at him. "I think that's pure horse piss, sir."

"Are you a lawyer?" asked Verily Cooper.

"Apparently you aren't either, in this state," said the clerk.

"If you're not a lawyer, sir, then you should not be offering a legal opinion."

"When did I do that?"

"When you said that what I said was pure horse piss. It would take a lawyer to offer an opinion on the degree of purity of any particular sample of horse piss. Or are we to assume you are practicing law without having been accepted at the bar in the state of Noisy River?"

"Did you come here just to make my life a living hell?" asked the clerk.

"It's you or me," said Verily. "But let me tell you something that it was my pleasure once to say to the Lord Protector and all his legal officers in England."

"What's that?"

"Good-bye."

Verily clapped his hat on his head and strode out the door into the street.

The clerk stomped out immediately after him, and kept on stomping, which raised something of a dust cloud behind him, the day being quite dry and hot.

Then Abe Lincoln sauntered out, followed by his faithful companion, Coz. "What do you think, Coz? I think we got to agree that was sharp lawyering. But then again, any time a lawyer says he ain't a lawyer, isn't that some kind of improvement to the general condition of humanity?"

Coz grinned and then spat into the dirt, which made a little ball of mud that actually rolled a few inches before it settled down and disappeared. "But we like Mr. Cooper," said Coz. "He's a *good* lawyer."

"He's a good *man*," said Abe. "*And* he's a good lawyer. But is it possible for him to be both at the same time?"

"You keep this up," said Verily, "and I won't teach you any more about lawyering."

"I think Abe is already a fine lawyer," said Coz.

"What do you mean?" said Verily.

"Well, look at you," said Coz. "You're just walking around, right? And nobody's paying you, right?"

"Right," said Verily.

"That's what Abe does most of the time."

"You know I'm a hardworking man, Coz," said Abe. "I split half the fence rails in Springfield, working odd jobs to pay off my store debt. And dug ditches and hauled manure and any other work that I could get."

"Aw, come on, Abe," said Coz. "Can't you let another man have his joke?"

"Just wouldn't want Mr. Cooper to think I was a lazy man."

Since Verily had spent the last few days trying to keep up with the long-legged, fast-walking Mr. Lincoln, he really hadn't got the impression of laziness from him.

Today, though, they were not walking. At Lincoln's request, Verily had hired two horses for him and Coz to ride, though in truth Verily could not think why Coz's company was worth the rent of a second horse. But Lincoln wanted it, and so Verily paid for it out of a dwindling wallet. They checked the saddles and harnesses, and then Verily checked Coz's and Lincoln's again, because from the look of it, they had no idea what to look for when checking a horse's saddle and harness. "You two don't ride much, do you," said Verily.

"We're poor men," said Abe.

"I'm poorer," said Coz.

"Because you spend every dime you make on riotous living."

"A man in love is inclined to buy gifts for his lady."

"And drinks."

"She was thirsty."

"And then she was unconscious," said Abe. "And then you paid for a room in the tavern for her to sleep it off, hoping no doubt that her gratitude in the morning would be greater than her headache, only in the morning . . ."

"My love life ain't none of Mr. Cooper's business."

"Your love life is imaginary, except for the amount of money you lose at it," said Abe.

And so it went all the way from Springfield to the Mizzippy.

They left the cornfields behind them after a couple of hours and forded Noisy River itself, and then passed along an ever-narrowing track through prairie land dotted with trees, where nobody was farming except here and there. A reminder that this *was* the frontier after all. And also that farmers tended to prefer not to locate near the foggy Mizzippy.

They reached a tree-covered bluff overlooking the great river just before dark. There wasn't much to see. A lot of trees below them, and beyond the trees, a glimpse of the river reflected scattered moonlight. And then the fog that obscured all vision of the land on the other side.

"Here's where we spend the night," said Lincoln.

"And eat supper, I hope," said Coz.

"Supper?" said Verily.

Abe looked at him sharply. "I said we'd need provisions."

"You didn't say we'd need *food*," said Verily.

"Well I'm blamed if provisions don't *mean* food!" said Abe, sounding a little cross.

"If you meant food," said Verily, "you should have said food."

"If you think I'm going to hunt for rabbit this time of night on an empty stomach, you're looney," said Coz.

"Myself," said Abe, "I'm thinking of maybe turning cannibal."

Verily grinned. "Now I know why you brought Coz along."

Coz put his hands on his hips and glared at them both

by turns. "Now see here, there ain't nobody going to eat nobody, least of all me. I may look stout, but I assure you it's all fat, every bit of it, not a scrap of muscle on me, so if you tried to fry me up like bacon you'd end up gagging on account of there being no lean in it."

Verily sighed. "It's hard to play a joke on men who refuse to notice the jest."

"We were joking back," said Coz. "We knowed you had food all along."

"Oh, no, I don't have food," said Verily. "The joke was the part about eating you."

They both uttered disgusted noises and then Verily laughed. "All right, then, I suppose I might have something left over from my journey here in my saddlebags."

He was getting the waybread and corned beef out of the saddlebag when Abe said, "You know, I'm a mite uncomfortable that the campfire that was going down by the river when we got here has since been put right out."

"Maybe they got done eating," said Coz.

"I didn't see a campfire," said Verily.

"Maybe they don't want a fire 'cause it's a hot night," said Coz.

"Or maybe they took note of some travelers on horseback coming out of the wood at the crown of this bluff and decided that we looked like easy folk to rob."

A powerful voice came from the brush off behind the horses. "Fine time to think of *that,* sir." And out from the bushes stepped a big man, who looked like he'd been in a lot of fights but hadn't lost any of them. And he had pistols and knives all over him, it seemed, with a cocked musket in his hands.

It was the first time Verily had seen Abe Lincoln look scared. "If you were hoping to rob somebody easy," said Abe, "you're half right. We'll be easy, only we ain't got nothing to steal."

"Speak for yourself, Abe," said Coz. "I bet Mr. Cooper's got everything he owns on that horse."

Abe gave Coz a shove. "Well, ain't that a fine thing,

drawing this man's attention to our friend Mr. Cooper!"

"Well *Mr.* Cooper was planning to fry me up like bacon!" said Coz, shoving Abe back.

"That was a joke, Coz," said Abe, shoving him harder.

"He says *now,*" said Coz, shoving Abe back, even harder.

But when Abe flung himself forward to shove again, it wasn't Coz he shoved. He took a flying leap at the stranger and down they tumbled into the bushes.

"Don't you worry, none, Mr. Cooper," said Coz. "Abe's a pretty bad fighter, but he puts his whole self into it and he don't give up early."

"Verily!" called the big man from the bushes. His voice sounded like somebody was pounding on his chest.

"He knows your name?" said Coz.

"Verily, are you going to say something, or am I going to have to kill your big ugly friend!"

"He oughtn't to call Abe ugly like that," said Coz.

"Abe," said Verily, "this man is not here to rob us."

The fight quieted down. "You know each other," said Abe.

"Abe Lincoln, meet Mike Fink. Mike Fink, vice versa."

"Leave off that legal talk, Mr. Cooper," said Mike. "It just riles me up and then I have to kill somebody."

"Well, don't kill Mr. Lincoln," said Verily. "He hasn't yet told me why he brought me to this godforsaken spot."

"I don't know either," said Mike, "but this is where Peggy said you'd be on this very evening, so this is where I came to meet you."

"Don't tell me you rowed upstream the whole way from Hatrack River," said Verily.

"I'd never tell such a lie," said Mike Fink, "but it's kind of flattering you'd think it was a possibility. Also kind of stupid, since half the journey would have been down the Hio, which ain't upstream."

"Ah. You didn't start in Hatrack River," said Verily.

"Vigor Church, and I took the train west to Moline and then I got a boat and came *down* the river. Got here this morning. You took your time coming. Springfield ain't *that* far."

"My butt says it was far enough," said Coz. "They made me ride the uncomfortable horse."

"Any horse with you on it's gonna be uncomfortable," said Abe.

"So Peggy knew that we'd be here," said Verily.

"Who is this Peggy," said Abe, "and how did she supposedly know days ago a thing I didn't find out about till yesterday?"

"A man who fights like a big-armed baby oughtn't to imply that a man that just whupped him is a liar," said Mike.

"Didn't accuse a soul," said Abe. "I asked a question."

"Peggy is Margaret Larner," said Verily. "Alvin's wife. I told you about her."

"She didn't happen to say," said Abe, "whether the plan that brought us here is a good idea."

"I'm not here for you," said Mike. "No offense. Nor for Verily Cooper, neither."

"Well I sure hope you ain't here for me," said Coz, "cause I peed my pants just looking at you, and if you rassle me it'll get all over you."

"I appreciate the warning," said Mike. "But I'm here for Alvin."

"I thought Peggy sent you," said Verily.

"Peggy sent me," said Mike, "to *meet* Alvin here. And Alvin's coming here because *you're* here."

Coz was delighted. "Alvin's a-coming here! Did you have any idea of that, Abe? Or was that your plan?"

"That makes this a right propitious spot," said Abe.

"No it doesn't," said Verily. "Margaret wouldn't have sent Mike Fink unless Alvin was in danger."

"What Peggy says is, when neither Alvin nor his lawyer showed up in court, the judge put out a summer judgment against Alvin and demanded that he be arrested for theft and brought back to Carthage City where he will either produce the gold item in question or be jailed for attempt of court."

"Let me guess," said Verily. "Is there a reward?"

"Somebody put up five hundred dollars," said Mike.

"And you're here to help Alvin resist arrest?"

"I'm here to take anybody who tries to earn that reward and grind him into flour and bake him like bread."

"We ain't looking to do that," said Coz.

"Five hundred dollars is a lot of money," said Abe.

Mike took a step toward Abe—who, to his credit, did not flinch.

"Calm down, Mike," said Verily. "Abe Lincoln is a man who likes his joke. He's a trusted friend of Al's."

"Ain't trusted by *me*," said Mike.

"My question is," said Coz, "if he's got you willing to protect him, how come he runs around all the time with that scrawny brother-in-law of his?"

"He don't need me to protect him from the kind of danger you meet on the road," said Mike. "He can defend himself just fine against that. It's when they come to him with legal papers and he gets all honorable and starts believing that he should let them haul him off to jail and then he *stays* there even though we know there ain't no jail can hold him—that's when he needs *me*. Because I don't mind beating in the face of a man who's just doing his job."

"Or biting off his ear," added Coz, hopefully.

"Gave up ear-biting long ago," said Mike. "And eye-gouging. Alvin made me promise."

"*Made* you?" asked Abe.

Mike looked embarrassed. "He's a blacksmith, don't you know. Look at them shoulders he's got. Not to mention that he could just look at my leg and break it."

"I think the fight, which is legendary, was equally unfair on both sides," said Verily.

"Oh, that's so," said Mike. "I wasn't accusing Alvin of nothing, I was just explaining how he could beat a fellow as mean as me." He took a step and loomed over Coz. "I *am* mean, you know. It ain't all show. I like that scrinchy sound a man's face makes when I'm grinding it into the ground."

"Ha ha," said Coz lamely. "You're such a joker, you are."

"When's Alvin getting here?" said Verily.

"Well, you know how Peggy gets kind of vague when it comes to Alvin's doings. I don't think she knows, except he'd get here while you were here, so here I am."

"Came by train," said Verily. "Would've been nice if *I* could've done that."

"So I wondered if you folks already et," said Mike. "Because I just couldn't see no point in hotting up a pot just for me, and I also didn't much care to eat my beans cold."

Soon they had a fire going right on the bluff, with two pots beside it, one full of stew, the other full of water, waiting to come to a boil.

"I reckon we're putting this fire right out in the open like this," said Abe, "so anybody seeking a reward won't waste time tripping over foxes and beavers in the dark."

"Alvin ain't here yet," said Mike, "so there's no reward, is there?"

It wasn't that Mike Fink was completely incautious, though. He volunteered for the first watch of the night, and warned Verily that he was next.

So it was that a groggy Verily Cooper was the one leaning against a tree looking out over the river when suddenly there was a man standing beside him. "River's beautiful at night," said Alvin softly.

Verily didn't even bat an eye. "Someday I'd like to see it with no fog."

"Someday," said Alvin. "When there ain't no need for it."

"Glad to see you," said Verily.

"Glad to be seen."

"Where's your company of five thousand?"

"Six thousand now. They're coming north. I ran on ahead to meet you and see if you're doing what I hope you're doing."

"Finding a place for your people to come."

"Have you? Found a place?"

"Abe Lincoln and I have been up and down, here and there," said Verily. "There are abolitionist towns that'll take a hundred or so. But I don't think there are sixty such towns in the whole state."

"Bad news," said Alvin.

"So tell me some good news, Alvin," said Verily. "Tell me that there's nobody near us, so we don't have to keep watch and I can go back to sleep."

Alvin grinned. "There's nobody near us," he said. "Go back to sleep."

"Before I do," said Verily, "tell me this. Did you come here tonight because this is the right place for us to be?"

"I came here tonight because tomorrow I need you to make the handles for my plow."

When Dead Mary told Alvin about her vision of the Crystal City, it filled him with hope. He hadn't told her about the Crystal City, had he? And what she described, it wasn't like what he saw in Tenskwa-Tawa's whirlwind. Or rather, it was *more* than what he saw.

All he had ever seen or thought of was the part of it that was made of crystal, the part of it that would be filled with dreams and visions like the ball, like the bridge, like the dam. And he had always thought that to live in such a place, all the citizens would have to be makers, like him. That's why he had been teaching them, or trying to teach them, all these eager people who simply couldn't do it. All had accomplished something, some slight increase of awareness or ability. Verily Cooper, of course, already had something of makery in his knack, and Calvin *was* a maker, after his fashion. And Arthur Stuart—now, *he* was a marvel, all these years and suddenly he makes his breakthrough and he sees it. But that's what, four people? And Calvin none too reliable. You don't make a Crystal City out of that.

But that's why Dead Mary's vision of the Crystal City

changed everything. Because they weren't all living in the palace, as she called it. In fact, probably *nobody* was living there. They lived in regular houses on regular streets, and most of them did regular jobs and had regular lives, except that for a few hours a week they helped to build this extraordinary palace or . . . or library, or theater, or whatever the building was supposed to be . . . and when it was built, then for a few hours a week you go inside and look at what you see there, what the walls of it show you, and you learn from it what you can and try to understand what it means. Not some grand, earthshaking thing, maybe just . . . who your wife really is, or what your children might be, or some danger to avoid, or why the suffering in your life is bearable after all. Or why it isn't. Not everything would be happy. But you'd know things that you didn't know otherwise. Even if all you saw was your own hopes and dreams and fears and guilt and shame thrown back in your face, even *that* would be worth going inside to see, because how else can you come to know yourself, unless you have some kind of faithful mirror that can show you more than just your face?

It's a city of makers, not because everyone in it is a Maker, but because the whole city cooperates in making the Making possible, and the whole city participates in the good thing that they have made.

So obvious now. Who is the builder of a great cathedral? The architect can truly say, I built this, even though he never lifts a stone. The stonecutters can say, I built this, even though it was not their hands that put the stones in place. The masons, the glassmakers, the carpenters, the weavers of rugs, they are all part of the building of it. And the bishop who caused them to build it, and the rich people who donated the money, and the women who brought the food to the workers, and the farmers who grew the food they serve, all the people of the city caused that building to exist. And fifty years later, when all the people whose hands did the work, they're all dead now, or old and doddering, their grandchildren can walk inside that building and say, "This is our cathedral, *we* built this," because it was the city that built the building, and the city that goes inside to use it, and each new generation that keeps the city alive, and walks into the building with veneration and pride, the cathedral is theirs as much as anyone's.

I can still teach makery to those who want to learn, thought Alvin. But I don't have to wait until they master it. Because I can make the crystal blocks one by one, and others can set them into place. Verily Cooper can set them into place, because he'll know how to make them fit. And other people, with other knacks, they can help. It might even be that Arthur Stuart can make some of the building blocks.

And since everyone will have contributed in one way or another to the crystal edifice, then they are part of it, aren't they? Part of the Crystal City. And a maker is the one who is part of what he makes. So . . . they are all makers, then, aren't they? Makers of the Crystal City.

Which means the Crystal City will truly be the City of Makers.

Through the morning he watched and then tried not to watch and then watched again, as Verily Cooper stroked the wood and with his bare hands made it into what it needed to be. Verily did not set a tool to the wood. Nor did he choose a fallen log or fell a tree. He found two saplings that were of a size, and stroked them until they separated from the tree. He didn't exactly knead the wood like clay, but the effect was the same. Bark stripped away from the living wood, and the wood shaped itself, bent itself until each of the saplings was now the shape of a plow handle.

Abe and Coz and Mike watched too, for a while. In awe, at first. But miraculous as it might seem, it was a slow and repetitive process, and after a while they wandered off to do other things—survey the area, Abe said.

So it was that when Verily was done, it was just him and Alvin there. The two saplings were now joined at the base as completely as if they had grown that way.

"Time to take that plow out of the sack," said Verily.

"The wood is still alive," said Alvin.

"I know," said Verily.

"Have you made anything out of living wood before?" asked Alvin.

"No," said Verily.

"Then how did you know how?"

"You asked me to do it, and I didn't have any tools," said Verily. "But all this work you've had me doing, learning how to actually see and understand what was going on inside the wood when I made barrel staves and hooped them—well, Al, did you think I wouldn't learn *anything*?"

Alvin laughed. "I knew you were learning, Very. I just . . . didn't know it would happen like this."

"So let's see if it'll fit."

Alvin set down the poke and rolled back the top until it made a thick cloth circle around the top of the golden plow. Then he picked up the plow and knelt down before the handles that Verily had made.

"Gold is soft," said Verily. "It'll wear away quickly in hard ground, won't it?"

"A living plow don't fit into the world the way ordinary ones do, and I expect it'll be as hard as I need it to be." Alvin rotated the plow this way and that, trying to figure out how to do the job with only two hands. "So do I fit the plow to the handles, or the handles to the plow?" he asked.

Verily laughed. "I'll hold the handles in place, and you work it out from there."

Alvin laughed, too. Then he brought the plow closer to the end where it was supposed to fit. His intention was to see how close a fit it was, and how exactly to insert it into place. But this was a living plow, and the handles were made of living wood, and when they got near enough, it was as if they recognized each other the way magnets do, lining themselves up in exactly the right way and then leaping together.

Leaping together, joining, the plowshare sliding into exactly the right spot, the wood flexing a bit to let it in, then closing back down over it, so it looked as if the handles had been carved from a tree that had the golden plow already embedded inside it.

Neither of them had a chance to marvel and admire, though, for the moment the plow leapt into place, there came such a music as Alvin had never heard before. It was the greensong—the song of the living wood, the living world, he recognized it, and felt how the handles vibrated with it. And yet it was another music, too. The music of worked metal, of machinery, of tools made to fit human needs and to do human work. It was the beating throb of the engine in a steamboat, and hissing and spitting of a locomotive, the whine of spinning wheels, the clatter and clump of power looms. Only instead of the cacophony of the factory, it all blended together into a single powerful song, and to Alvin's joy it fitted perfectly with the greensong and became one music that filled the air all around them.

Even then, he scarcely had time to realize what the music was before the plow started bucking and bouncing. It was clear that it no longer intended to be still, and Verily, far from controlling it, was barely able to hang on as the plow lurched forward—no ox or horse pulling it, nothing at all but its own will. It skipped a few feet and then dug into the thatch of the meadowgrass, cut through it like a hot knife through butter, then raced forward, Verily hanging on for dear life, running and twisting to keep up with it.

Whatever else this plow might want, it had no respect for the idea that the best furrow is a straight one. It twisted and turned all around the meadow, as if it were a dowser's stick searching for water.

Which, when Alvin thought about it, it very well might be. Not searching for water, but a dowser's wand all the same. Hadn't Verily shaped it into a single piece of living wood? Wasn't it shaped like a dowser's wand, with the two handles joined at the base?

"I can't hold on any longer!" cried Verily, and he fell to the ground as the plow lurched forward another yard and then . . . stopped.

The plow just stood there in the ground, unmoving.

Alvin ran over as Verily got up off the ground.

Gingerly, Verily reached a hand out to it. The moment his skin touched it, the plow bucked again and moved forward.

"I have an idea," said Alvin. "You take the right handle, I'll take the left."

"Both at once," said Verily.

"One," said Alvin. And Verily joined in on "two" and "three."

"Wait a minute," said Verily. "How high are we counting?"

"I was thinking of three, but looks like that won't be it after all."

"When we *say* three, or when we would have said four?"

"When we say three, we should be grabbing right then," said Alvin.

One.

Two.

And away they went.

Only this time there was no bucking. The plow moved, all right, cutting deep into the ground and turning up the soil just like a plow should do. But its path was no longer so crooked.

And its purpose seemed to be to get out of the meadow, move through the trees, and climb back up onto the bluff.

It was steep going—this wasn't all that gentle a slope— and there were low branches that looked like they were designed to take the head right off anyone foolish enough to be hanging on behind a living plow.

But the greensong in the music of the plow was powerful, and the branches seemed to rise up or bend back, and neither Alvin nor Verily suffered so much as a scrape or scratch or bump. Nor did they get weary as they ran up the hill behind the plow.

When it reached the top, the plow turned a little and ran across the face of the bluff. That was when Alvin became vaguely aware of the voices of Mike and Abe and Coz, somewhere in the distance, whooping and hollering like little boys. But there was no waiting for them to catch up. For the plow was zeroing in on its destination and speeding up as it grew closer.

Closer to a stony outcropping some twenty yards back from the front of the bluff, a spot where no trees grew because the stone continued under the meadow, leaving too little soil for any tree to root deep enough to withstand a storm.

They headed straight for the bare rock in the middle of the clearing, and Alvin was not altogether surprised when the plow cut right through the stone without so much as a stutter. It cut a furrow into the rock just as it had with the soil, only where the soil behind the plow had been loose and warm, the upturned stone hardened in place, like a sculpture of a furrow.

And when the plow got to a spot where a puddle of water had formed in a depression in the stone, it went straight to the middle of the puddle and stopped.

The water drained down the furrow the plow had made. A thin stream of pure water being guided by the stone furrow, and then the furrow in the soil, to the edge of the bluff and along it down to the meadow where Verily had made the handles.

The plow did not move.

Alvin and Verily took their hands from the handles.

The music faded.

"I think we're done here," said Alvin.

"What is it we did?" said Verily.

"We found the spot for the Crystal City," said Alvin.

"Is that what we've been looking for?" asked Verily.

"I think it's what this plow has been looking for since it was first made."

Alvin knelt beside the plow that he had carried for so long. All these years of toting it, and now its work was done, and wild and joyful as the trip up the hill was, it hadn't taken long. Just a few minutes. But when Alvin reached out and touched a finger to the golden face of the plow, the thing quivered, and the handle came loose and fell away. Fell to the ground.

Verily picked it up. "Still alive," he said.

"But no longer part of the plow."

The music was gone, too. The greensong still lingered, as it always did in Alvin's mind. But the music of machinery was completely still.

Alvin tugged on the plow and it slid easily out of the stone. He put it back in the poke. It still quivered with life, no more nor less than it always had. As if it had no memory of what it had just done.

They all drank from the spring that now welled up from the end of the furrow. The water was sweet and clean. "We could keg this up and sell it for wine," said Abe, "and nobody'd say we cheated them."

"But we won't," said Verily.

Abe gave him an I'm-not-an-idiot look. "So you reckon this plow of yours has picked this spot for your city."

"Might be," said Alvin. "If we can figure out who owns the land and figure out a way to buy it."

"Well, you're in luck," said Abe. "It's why I brought you here. This is part of what the Noisy River government calls River County. It's the wild land along the Mizzippy between Moline and Cairo. There's an old law from territory days that offers to make a county out of any part of River County that can prove it has two thousand settlers and at least one town of three hundred people."

"A county?" asked Verily.

"A county," said Abe.

"But a county has the right to elect its own judges," said Verily.

"And its own sheriff," said Abe.

"So when somebody comes into Furrowspring County

with a warrant from some court in Hio," said Verily, "the Furrowspring County court can vacate the warrant."

"That's how I figured it," said Abe.

"You were really listening when I explained about the law."

"And I remember my old dad trying to farm boggy land along the Hio, and somebody come along and told him all about River County, and how the land was there for the taking if just two thousand folks would join up and go, and Dad said he had a hard enough time farming a swamp, the last thing he needed was fog on top of it."

"If we have our own county," said Alvin, "then we can build a city here, and populate it with black people and French people and anybody else we want to invite, and nobody can stop us."

"Well," said Abe, "it's not that simple."

"You mean there's some law against folks moving in here?"

"There is against runaway slaves," said Abe, "but I think we got that solved, since the same judge can vacate a lot of other orders, and the same sheriff can run any slave-catchers out of town or at least make it real hard to find any former slaves. But what I was getting at was, *anybody* can move in. Not just folks that you invite."

"Well, we invite everybody," said Alvin.

Abe laughed. "Well, shoot, word gets out about this golden plow that cut right through stone and brought water out of the rock like Moses, and your six thousand won't be but a drop in the bucket for all the thousands of gold hunters and miracle seekers who'll be tramping all up and down this country. And I reckon *they'll* be the ones electing the sheriff and the judge and maybe somebody'll get that reward after all."

"I see," said Alvin. "It ain't all that easy after all."

"If I kill you all," said Mike, "won't be nobody to tell about this place."

"Except you," said Alvin.

"Well, I didn't say it was a perfect plan."

"What we need," said Verily, "is a charter from the state. Granting us the boundaries that we want for our county, and then we got to make sure we control all the land so it only gets sold to people we choose. People who are with us and won't cause trouble."

"People who are willing to help build this place as a city of makers," said Alvin.

"I know how to write such a charter," said Verily. "But I don't know that I'll be able to find my way around the state government."

"Well don't look at me," said Abe. "I'm no politician."

"But you're from around here," said Verily. "You don't talk like a highfalutin Englishman. And you have a way of making people like you."

"So do you," said Abe.

"You know everybody hates him," said Coz.

"Well, yes," said Abe, "but only because they know Englishmen are smarter than other folks and they resent it."

"Will you help me get that charter for Furrowspring County?" said Verily.

"I notice you took it upon yourself to name the place," said Abe.

"Do you have a better one?" said Verily.

"I was partial to Lincoln County," said Abe.

"How about Lincoln-Fink County?" suggested Mike.

"Now that's pure vanity," said Abe. "Naming the county after yourself."

"What were *you* doing?"

"Naming it for the county in England, of course," said Abe.

"Furrowspring it is, then," said Alvin. "The voting is unanimous." He turned to Abe. "But in the meantime, settlers can come freely into River County lands, right? And farm and build wherever they want?"

"That's the law," said Abe. "Don't need permission. As long as you don't step on somebody else's farm, and I don't see any around here."

"You know," said Alvin, "I was wondering why there wasn't at least one or two farmsteads, belonging to the kind of folks who think six houses make a city too big to enjoy living in."

"Maybe because this is land meant for something better than a stumpy little farm," said Verily.

"And who's doing the meaning?" asked Alvin.

"Maybe the stone itself was ambitious," said Verily. "Or maybe it was the water, begging to be let out from under the rock."

"Or the sun that wanted this patch to have no trees to make shade," said Alvin. "Or the wind, needing a little meadow to blow across. Gentlemen, I don't think any of the elements have a *plan*."

"The plow did," said Verily.

Alvin had to concede the point.

They put the plow handles on the back of one of Verily's steeds and instead of anyone riding they led the three horses back to Springfield together. They moved with the greensong, all of them, and got there in only an hour of steady running, and the horses weren't lathered or winded, and the men weren't hungry or tired, and as for thirsty, they had all drunk from that clear spring, and they were loath to taste any other water, because they knew it would taste like tin or mud or nothing at all, instead of sweet, the way they knew now water ought to be.

⚔ 15 ⚔

Popocatepetl

IT WAS SUCH a lovely ride from the coast to Mexico City. Everything went just as Steve Austin had predicted—which was not at all how Calvin expected it to go. Their ship put into the free port of True Cross, where whites could come and trade without fear of being taken for sacrifice. They took three days finding interpreters and buying supplies and pack mules, and then they went to the inland gate of the city.

"You are not safe to go outside," said the door warden.

"We're going," said Steve Austin. "Out of the way."

"I will not let you go. White people die out there, give bad name to port of True Cross."

Austin raised a pistol to shoot the man in the head.

"No, no," said Calvin impatiently. "What did you bring me for, anyway, if you're just going to go shooting people. What if we need to get back here and thanks to you they shoot us on sight?"

"When we come back we'll be the rulers of Mexico."

"Fine," said Calvin. "But let me do this."

Austin put his pistol away. Calvin studied the gates for a few moments, trying to decide whether it was worth the effort to make this a truly spectacular event or merely a practical one. He decided that something showy, like making the gates burst into flame and burn down to ash, would be wasted here. It was the reds outside this city that they'd need to impress.

So he dissolved the linchpins in the hinges and then, with a gentle nudge, made sure the gates fell outward instead of inward.

The door warden—with no more door to ward—shrugged and turned away. And out they rode, a hundred heavily armed white men, to take on the Mexica.

Almost at once they were confronted by Mexica soldiers. These were not the club-wielding warriors that Cortez had faced three centuries before. They were mounted and carried new-model muskets that had probably been bought from the United States, where Philadelphia—the city of brotherly love—had quite a munitions business going. Immediately they surrounded Austin's army, which bristled with weapons at the ready.

"Patience," said Calvin to Austin. It wasn't hard to make fire, but it was tricky to make a ring of it, and he singed quite a few of the Mexica horses when the flames didn't go quite where he'd planned. But that only made the demonstration more effective. The Mexica backed off, the horses shying and neighing, but then dismounted and prepared to fire through the flames.

Calvin was ready. He knew how Alvin handled this sort of thing, bending the end of the gunbarrels so the enemy wouldn't bother firing. But Calvin wanted them to fire. So he pinched off each gunbarrel inside, not tightly, but enough to keep the ball from coming out. It was quite a scramble to find all the muskets and close them off before the firing started, but it helped that the Mexica commander kept shouting for them to surrender, while the panicky horses kept the Mexica in an uproar long enough for Calvin to finish the job.

"Don't shoot," said Calvin.

"But they're about to lay a volley into us," said Austin.

"They only think they are," said Calvin.

The Mexica captain gave the command, and the soldiers pulled the triggers of their muskets.

Whereupon every single one of them exploded, killing or blinding almost all of them, and blowing the heads right off more than a few.

The Mexica captain was left standing there with his ceremonial obsidian-edged sword and only a few of his men still alive enough to writhe on the ground moaning or screaming in agony.

"Shoot him!" cried Austin.

"No!" cried Calvin. "Let him go! You want somebody to tell the story of this, don't you?"

Austin didn't like being contradicted, but it was plain that Calvin was right. What good was it to put on a show like this, if there wasn't somebody left to go tell the rest of the Mexica about these white men who came with irresistible power. So if it bothered Austin that Calvin had countermanded his order, well wasn't that too bad. If he didn't want that to happen, he shouldn't give stupid orders. And besides, it wasn't a bad thing for Austin to remember who actually had the power here. Austin might plan to be the emperor of Mexico, but if he achieved it, it would be because he had Calvin Maker with him.

Calvin had thought he'd have to do several more demonstrations, but it all went better than he'd hoped. The first city they came to, the alcalde came out to them and insisted that the people of this place were not Mexica and begged the mighty priest they had with them not to harm them.

Austin gave a speech about how they had come to restore good government to these lands and free them from the rule of the bloodthirsty, murderous, savage Mexica. Whereupon the people cheered and the alcalde insisted on sending five hundred men along with them to Mexico City. Since these were not real soldiers, but only ordinary men, many of them old, and armed only with ceremonial clubs and swords, Austin agreed to let them come. But he insisted that they provide their own food and promise to obey his orders.

So when they came to the next city, they weren't just a hundred white men, they had a brightly costumed troupe of reds with them, singing and chanting. Again the alcalde came out and begged them to pass on through, giving them food and water and another five hundred men to accompany them. Calvin was getting a little frustrated, so this time he crumbled part of the stone wall of the city so there'd be more to the story. The alcalde fell to his knees and offered them anything they wanted, but Austin only glared at Calvin and told him that there would be no more city walls when he ruled in Mexico City, because all the land would be at peace.

"What did you do that for when they'd already surrendered?" said Austin afterward.

"They've got to *see* that we come with power," said Calvin.

"Well, what you showed them was that we come to tear stuff down."

"I'll find something better to do next time," said Calvin. "Nondestructive."

"Thank you kindly," said Austin, his voice dripping with sarcasm.

So it went all the way up to the high Mexican plateau and through villages and cities, and by the time they got within sight of the great volcanic mountains that ringed Mexico City, they had at least fifteen thousand reds with them, a mighty army indeed, marching ahead of them and behind them and singing and chanting and dancing at every opportunity.

It was a glorious entrance they made into the valley of Mexico. But Calvin was getting more and more uneasy. "Where are the Mexica soldiers?" he asked Austin.

"All run away, if they've got any brains," said Austin. Jim Bowie was riding close by, and he seconded Calvin. "This is all too easy," he said. "I don't like it."

"We raised up the conquered people against the oppressor. The Mexica soldiers aren't going to waste their lives resisting the irresistible."

"There's a trap waiting for us here," said Bowie.

So while Austin beamed and waved now and then, as if he was in a parade, Calvin and Bowie and a handful of others kept their eyes open, looking for some lurking army in hiding. Calvin sent his doodlebug ranging ahead as far as he could, but all he found were civilians, and most of them were in plain sight, standing outside to watch this army pass along the wide avenue that led to the lake in the middle of the valley.

Not until they actually reached the long causeway that led to the ceremonial city in the middle of the lake did they finally see any kind of Mexica opposition. And while there was plenty of pomp and color, lots of flags and feathers, there weren't many that looked like soldiers. In fact, there weren't many of anything—maybe three hundred men in the whole group that came down the causeway to meet them.

"Do they think this is going to be a picnic?" asked Bowie.

"How many men do you think it takes to surrender to us?" said Austin. "Calvin Maker, you are worth your weight in gold. We didn't have to fire a shot, and here we are, victorious!" Austin kicked his horse and moved forward through the throng, the other white men following. Soon they were lined up near the front of the vast army, within earshot of the dignitaries coming from the city.

"We demand that you surrender!" shouted Austin. "If you surrender your lives will be spared!"

He turned to look for an interpreter, but apparently they hadn't kept up when the white men had ridden forward. No, there was one, and Austin beckoned him over. "Tell him to surrender," said Austin. "Tell him what I said."

But before the interpreter could go forward with the

message, a befeathered Mexica standing on a huge litter borne by a dozen men began to speak.

"What's he saying?" asked Austin.

The interpreter listened. "He is the high priest and he thanks the people of . . . all these tribes . . . for bringing so many fine sacrifices for the god."

Austin laughed. "Does he really believe these people came to offer sacrifice?"

"Yes," said the interpreter.

"What a fool," said Austin.

"There's a fool all right," said Bowie, "but it ain't him."

All at once, the reds who were surrounding them gave a great shout and dragged the white men off their horses. Bowie managed to get knives into a couple of them before they got him down. And Calvin was trying to work up some flames, but he couldn't get anything going before they had him down on the ground and hit him in the head with a club.

Calvin woke up in pain, and not just from his head, which was throbbing. He was also tightly trussed, and lying on a stone floor. He was also blindfolded.

He could make his bonds break apart, but he figured he ought to find out first where he was and what was going on. So with his doodlebug he worked on the threads of the blindfold and soon he had an opening he could see through. He was lying on the floor of a large dimly lighted room—a Catholic church of some kind, from the look of it, but not one that was used much. A couple of statues of saints stood against one wall, and there was an altar near the front, but everything looked shabby and dusty.

All the white men were sitting or lying on the floor, and at the doors stood heavily armed Mexica soldiers.

Calvin sent his doodlebug to see behind him, and sure enough, there were four soldiers standing over him. He was the only one of the white men with a special guard. Which meant the Mexica knew he was the powerful one.

He was surprised they hadn't just killed him outright—but no, he was the prize, he was the one they'd be proudest to sacrifice.

Ain't gonna happen, he told himself.

He continued to lie still, checking the condition of the other men. It might still be possible to bring this thing off and snatch victory from the jaws of defeat.

Then a door opened, putting a wedge of light into the room, and four women came in, carrying golden cups. They began offering drinks to the men, who took them eagerly, some of them even thanking the women. Calvin almost called out to warn them that the drink was drugged, but decided it was better to deal with it himself. One by one he went into the cups and separated the water from the drug, making it sink to the bottom of the cups and stay there, under the pure water. Except for the first few who had drunk, none of the others were getting any of the drug at all.

So when they got to him, Calvin offered no resistance. He pretended to be groggy—which wasn't hard, with his head hurting so bad. Pain shot through his head when he sat up, and he wished he'd paid more attention when Alvin tried to teach him how to heal injuries like this. But after the mess he had made of Papa Moose's foot, he wasn't about to start fiddling with his own head.

They put the cup to his lip and he drank eagerly.

No doubt they'd become complacent soon, thinking that even the great white wizard was under control.

Except, of course, only the first few men were *acting* drugged. The women were beginning to be confused, talking to each other, probably wondering why most of the men were still awake.

So Calvin put them to sleep, one by one, until they all lay unconscious on the floor. That was what the women wanted, and out they went. Out, too, went the Mexica soldiers, even the ones guarding Calvin.

As soon as they were gone, Calvin woke all the ones he had put to sleep. The drugged ones, though, were another matter. It was simple to separate the drug from the water in the cups, but impossible to do anything of the kind when the drug was already in somebody's blood. So they slept on while the others sat up and looked around.

"Talk softly," said Calvin. "There are still guards outside the door, and we don't want them to hear us."

"You bastard," said a man.

"Don't tell us what to do."

But they talked softly.

"Are you so stupid you blame *me* for this?" said Calvin. "I never claimed to be a mind reader. How should I know we were prisoners the whole way here? Did any of *you* guess it?"

No one had an answer to that.

"But I'm the reason the poison didn't work on you, once I realized the water was drugged. So don't get pissed at me, let's plan how to get out of here."

"Better plan fast," said Bowie. "Since you're the one they plan to sacrifice this afternoon."

"I'm hurt," said Calvin. "I would have thought they'd save me for last."

"They're not stupid," said Bowie. "And just so you know, they also told us—using our own interpreters—that if you didn't go willingly to be sacrificed, they'd kill all of us without even sending us to the god."

"Won't happen," said Calvin.

"The way we figure it," said Bowie, "we'll make our break for it while they're cutting your heart out."

"Good plan," said Calvin. "Of course, without me you won't know where your weapons are stored. You won't know how to get out of this room without getting caught. I think a few of you might make it as much as a hundred yards from this place."

They were thinking about this when suddenly the ground shook under them. At once, from the city outside this building, they could hear screaming and shouting.

Calvin broke open his bonds and stood up. None of the others were tied, so they also stood. But the windows were too high in the walls to see through.

The ground shook again.

"I think we ought to lie down again," said Bowie. "In case they come in and see us."

"They aren't going to," said Calvin.

"How do you know?"

"Because the guards at the door just ran away."

The door opened.

Bowie was in the middle of a snide remark about how reliable Calvin was when they realized that the man who stood in the doorway was not a Mexica. It was a half-black young man dressed like an American.

"Get ready to go," said the young man. "We got about a day to get out of the city before Popocatepetl blows."

"Before what?" asked a man.

"Popocatepetl," said the young man. "The biggest volcano. All that screaming out there, the ground shaking, it's because we just caused it to start spewing smoke and ash. And tomorrow, anybody who didn't get out of the city will be killed when the thing erupts all the way."

"Who's 'we'?" asked Bowie.

"My guess is it's my brother Alvin doing all this," said Calvin. "Cause this is his brother-in-law, Arthur Stuart."

At once there were cries of protest.

"Your brother is married to a black woman?"

"Somebody named him for the *King*?"

"We're supposed to listen to a slave tell us what to do?"

But Arthur Stuart's voice cut through the noise. "It's not Alvin," he said. "It's Tenskwa-Tawa. He's making the volcano erupt to stop the Mexica from offering human sacrifices. It's between reds, Tenskwa-Tawa against the Mexica."

"So what are *you* doing here?" asked Calvin.

"Saving you," said Arthur Stuart. "And anybody else who wants to come with us."

"I don't need you to save me," said Calvin contemptuously.

"I know you don't need me to get you out of this old church," said Arthur Stuart. "But how are you going to get out of the city? I speak Spanish, which most of the folks here speak well enough, and I also picked up quite a bit of Nahuatl—that's the Mexica language. Any of *you* know how to ask for directions or food? And good luck finding your way out of this valley with all the panicky people filling the roads. Plus I reckon a lot of folks'll think you brought this down on their heads, and they won't be too glad to see you."

"But why should we leave at all?" said Calvin.

"So you don't get burnt to a crisp and covered over with lava," said Arthur Stuart. "This don't take no Aristotle to figure out, Calvin."

"Don't you talk to a white man that way!" shouted a man, and a couple of others got up to do him some kind of violence.

And Calvin was perfectly willing to let them get started. Arthur Stuart needed to learn who was in charge here, and how to show proper respect.

But the men never reached Arthur. Instead, they started sliding and tripping over themselves just as if the floor was suddenly smooth marble covered in butter, and after a minute it became clear that anybody as started after Arthur Stuart would end up on his butt.

The boy had really learned some makery—but not as much as he probably thought. Calvin toyed with the idea of having an all-out wizard's war with him right here on the spot, to show him just how far he had to go—but what would be the point? There was no time to waste.

"Forget him," said Calvin. "He came to save us, so great, anybody who wants to run away, go with him, right now. He's not much of a maker but he's got a knack with languages and maybe he can get you to safety. But me, I think we can turn this to our advantage. We came here to rule over Mexico, didn't we? So let's let the volcano kill the Mexica and then claim we did it and rule over the country in their place!"

"What does Steve say?" asked a man.

It was only then that they all realized that Austin was one of the ones who had been drugged.

"You know what he'd say," said Calvin. "He didn't come here to quit. He didn't come here so he could run away after a black boy who thinks he's hot stuff cause he can make a floor slippery. We came here to take over an empire and I aim to do it."

"Everybody already knows it's Tenskwa-Tawa's doing," said Arthur Stuart. "His people are already here, they said when the smoke would start coming, and it came when they said."

"But Tenskwa-Tawa ain't going to come down here and rule over Mexico, is he," said Calvin. "No, I didn't think so. Well, somebody's gonna do it, and it might as well be us. And after this is over, and we're telling folks that it was my brother Alvin who was telling Tenskwa-Tawa what to do, and they've left me here to see to it Steve Austin is made emperor of Mexico . . ."

"Anybody who wants to get out of this valley alive, come with me now," said Arthur Stuart.

"I'd rather die than trust a slave for anything!" shouted one of the men he had put on the floor.

"That's the choice," said Arthur Stuart.

The ground trembled again, and then again, and a third shock was so strong that several of the men fell down.

"You're not doing that, are you?" Bowie asked Calvin.

"I can do it whenever I want," said Calvin.

"You're such a humbug," said Arthur Stuart. "It took a council of shamans a year to get this volcano at the point of eruption. Even Alvin couldn't make a volcano erupt whenever he wants."

"Maybe there's things I can do that 'even Alvin' can't do," said Calvin.

Arthur Stuart turned to the rest of the men. "How fast can any of you run? How far do you think you'll get? When Popocatepetl blows up tomorrow, it won't matter where you are in this valley, you'll be dead. Do you understand? If we leave today, now, we'll make it out of here in time. *If* you have me to help you move fast enough and get far enough. As for him—do you think he cares whether you live or die? Do you think he has the power to save you from a volcano? He'll be lucky if he can save himself."

A few of the men were wavering. "We can't take over Mexico if we're dead."

"We can do it from outside this valley."

Calvin laughed. "You saw what I did back in True Cross, didn't you? Have you forgotten who and what I am? This boy is no wizard, he's nothing, my brother keeps him like a pet, to do tricks." And with those words, Calvin made the door behind Arthur Stuart fly from its hinges and burst outward onto the street. And then he made a wind that picked up Arthur Stuart and flung him through the door.

"Anybody who wants to," said Calvin, "is free to follow him. Seeing how he has so much power."

Arthur Stuart appeared in the door. "I never claimed to be more powerful than Calvin. But all his power doesn't give him a single word of Spanish or Nahuatl. And he knows nothing about the red man's way of running faster than a man can run. Come with me if you want to live. I can get you back to True Cross, and from there you can get safely home. Look at him! He doesn't care about you!"

"All I care about," said Calvin, "is the lives of these men." Now he started talking to the men directly. "You trusted in me and I will give you what I promised—Mexico. All the gold and wealth of Mexico. All the people as your subjects, all the land as your estate. And when you hear of us ruling in splendor, while you sit in your miserable cabin on a bayou in Barcy, then make sure you thank this boy for saving you."

Jim Bowie strode toward Arthur Stuart. "I know this boy," he said. "I'm going with him."

Calvin didn't like that. Bowie had enormous prestige with the other men.

"So it turns out Steve Austin couldn't rely on you after all," said Calvin.

"He's asleep," said Bowie, "and as for you, you're the one got us into this place. Who all is coming?"

"Yes," said Calvin, "who are the cowards who refuse the chance to rule an empire?"

"Now," said Arthur Stuart. "No second chances. Come now, if you're coming with me."

About a dozen men got up and came over to join, not Arthur Stuart, but Jim Bowie.

"What about the ones they poisoned?" asked one man.

"Their bad luck," said Bowie.

But Arthur Stuart looked at the men near the door, the ones who drank first and were drugged. And as he gazed at them, one by one, they woke up.

Calvin was mortified. This stupid knackless boy had somehow learned how to counter the poison in their blood. And now he had to show off and rub Calvin's face in it. Didn't he know that Calvin could have learned how to do anything if he had wanted to? But why should Calvin bother learning how to wake up men who were stupid enough to get themselves drugged?

In the end, though, not one of the drugged ones decided to go; in fact, one of them was able to persuade his brother not to leave with Arthur Stuart and Jim Bowie. So when the boy left, he had ten men with him. The others all stayed in the church. With Calvin.

"Now all we've got to do," said Calvin, "is find out where they took our weapons."

"How you gonna do that?"

"By watching where that boy goes. Do you think Bowie's going to let him lead them out of the valley without taking him first to his lucky knife?"

Several of the men laughed.

And sure enough, as Calvin kept track of Bowie's heartfire, he saw when they got to a nearby building and Arthur Stuart opened the door and Bowie picked up his knife and the other men armed themselves.

"It's only one street over, just outside the walls of this church," said Calvin.

"Then let's go," said Steve Austin. "But let's get organized first."

"Let's get armed first," said Calvin.

"Doesn't do any good to have guns if we don't have a plan!" said Austin.

Ten minutes later they were still talking when the Mexica soldiers poured in through the open door.

"Fools!" shouted Calvin. "I told you to go!"

Two of the Mexica aimed their muskets at Calvin and fired.

Their guns blew up in their faces.

But the others were bringing their weapons to bear too fast for Calvin to plug them all.

So he did the only sensible thing. He stepped backward through the wall.

He'd done it before, back when Napoleon had him imprisoned in Paris. Softening the stone enough to slide through it, like pushing his hand through clay, and then letting it harden again behind him. He heard the bullets hit the wall just as it was hardening, so they sank into the stone with a soft thunk and the wall hardened behind the bullets without so much as a dent.

And there stood Calvin on the outside of the church.

Where was Arthur Stuart? Calvin found the boy's heart-fire, though it took some hard searching, and he was at the limit of Calvin's range. Well, the boy said he knew how to get out of the city, and that's what Calvin needed, now that these fools had wasted the opportunity Calvin gave them. They didn't *deserve* to live.

He took off at a run. He had to pass near where the Mexica were dragging the white men out of the front of the church, but he didn't even have to make up some kind of fog—nobody saw him.

And why should they even be looking? With him gone, there was nothing these unarmed men could do. And waiting for them there in the plaza in front of the church was that same high priest who had met them on the causeway. One by one the men were dragged to him and thrown onto a wooden altar that had been placed in the square. Two priests cut their clothing open and laid bare their chests, and Calvin could hear the screaming as one by one they had their hearts torn from them and held up as an offering to whatever god the Mexica thought might prevent the eruption of Popocatepetl.

What a stupid end to Steve Austin's dream. But that's all the man was, a dreamer, a planner. Even now, when he could have turned this all to victory, he chose planning instead of action and now he'll die for it and ain't that just too bad.

Calvin turned his attention to the streets of the city. There were people running every which way, and with Arthur Stuart so far away, it was all Calvin could do to keep track of where he was. Nor did he know which of these labyrinthine streets would take him there, so there was always the danger that Calvin would guess wrong and make a turn that took him out of range.

Instead, though, he was lucky and chose right every time, or at least right enough, and instead of getting weaker, his vision of Arthur Stuart's heartfire got stronger. He was gaining on them.

When they reached the wall of the city, they stopped, and Calvin's running was now pure gain. Arthur Stuart was opening a gap in the wall, and in his clumsy way he was making it take ten times longer than it needed to. Well, good for me, thought Calvin. And he got there just as the last of them was passing through an opening in the wall. Calvin ran straight up to it and plunged through.

Outside the wall at this spot was an orchard, and Arthur Stuart and Bowie and the others were running through it. But running oddly—they were all holding hands, for heaven's sake, which was about as stupid a thing as Calvin could imagine. Nobody made his best speed holding hands.

Only they were running awfully fast. No one tripped. No one stumbled. And they gained speed and kept speeding up and no matter how hard Calvin ran, he couldn't catch up. Nor did the ground prove as smooth for him as it had for them. Branches whipped his face and he stumbled over a root and fell and by the time he got up, they were out of sight. And when he looked for Arthur Stuart's heartfire, he couldn't find it. Couldn't find any of them. It was like they had ceased to exist. There was only the trees and the birds and the insects, and the distant sound of shouting from the city and the roads.

Calvin stopped and looked back. The ground outside the city had sloped up enough, and he had run far enough, that he could see over the walls, though not down into the streets. Somewhere back there most of the men he had journeyed with were having their hearts ripped out, while in the other direction Arthur Stuart had run off with the ten best of them—the ones who were smart enough to act instead of plan. Why do I always get stuck with the fools on my side? thought Calvin.

Beyond the city, Popocatepetl spewed thick plumes of white ash into the air. And now it was beginning to fall onto the city like hot grey snow. It got into his lungs almost at once, and it felt like it was burning him. So Calvin turned his attention to keeping the air in front of his face clear of ash, as he began to jog on in the direction that he had last seen Arthur Stuart's group going.

He ran and jogged and, when he was too tired to do more, he walked and staggered and never once caught a glimpse of Arthur Stuart's group or saw any sign of what path they took. But he climbed ever higher up the slopes of the valley into the hills, and when darkness came he found an adobe house with nobody home. He sealed it to keep ash from seeping in, except for a few airholes through the thick walls. Then he fell onto cornstalk mat on the floor and slept.

When he woke it was still night. Except it wasn't. The sun *was* up—but it was only a dim red disk in the ashes that filled the air. Morning. How long till the eruption? What time of day had it been when the smoke first started?

Doesn't matter. Can't control that. Keep walking. There was no running in him today, especially since his path led inexorably uphill, and the ground kept shaking so much that if he'd been running he would have fallen down.

He was still far from the crest when the volcano blew up. He only had time enough to burrow his way into an outcropping of rock, which took the brunt of the shock-wave. It struck with such force that the rock he was hiding in would have given way and crumbled and collapsed into the valley, but Calvin held it firm, kept all but a few shards and slivers of rock in place. And when the hot fiery air blew past, incinerating all life in its path, Calvin kept a bubble of air around him cool enough to bear, and so he did not die.

And when the shock wave passed, he stepped out into the burning world, keeping that cool bubble around him, and turned back to see lava pouring down the slopes of the mountain like a flood from a burst dam. Only it wasn't heading toward the city, because there was no city. Every building had been blown flat by the blast. Only a few stone structures stood, and then only in ruins, most of the walls having been broken down. There was not a sign of life. And the lake was boiling.

Calvin wondered, for a moment, whether any of the men of Austin's expedition had lived long enough to be killed by the eruption. Probably not. Who was to say which was the better way to die? There was no good way to die. And Calvin had come *this close*.

But close to death was still not death.

Cooling the ground under his feet so his shoes didn't burn, he slowly made his way up the slope until, before nightfall, he reached the crest and started down the un-burnt side. Ash had fallen here, too, but this land had been sheltered from the blast, and he could eat the fruit from the trees, as long as he got the ash off it first. The fruit was partly cooked—the ash had been that warm when it fell—but to Calvin it tasted like the nectar of the gods.

I have been spared alive yet again. My work is not yet done in the world.

Might as well head north and see what Alvin's doing. Maybe it's time I started learning some of the stuff he taught to Arthur Stuart. Anything that half-black boy can learn, I can learn, and ten times better.

⇒ 16 ⇐

Labor

TENSKWA-TAWA WATCHED from the trees as Dead Mary, Rien, and La Tia uncovered the crystal ball.

"We got to do something good for Alvin, all he do for us," said La Tia.

"Maybe we should ask him what he wants," said Dead Mary.

"He not here," said La Tia.

"Men never know what they want," said Rien. "They think they want one thing, then they get it, then they don't want it."

"Your life story, Mother?" asked Dead Mary.

"I name her Marie d'Espoir," said Rien to La Tia. "Marie of hope. But maybe Marie de la Morte is the right name. She the death of me, La Tia."

"I don't think so," said La Tia. "I think men be the death of you, and that don't come from the crystal ball, no."

"I'm too old for men," said Rien.

"But they never too old for you, Caterina," said La Tia.

"Now we look to see what Alvin want the most in his heart."

"Can you command it to show what you want?" asked Dead Mary.

"It always show me the right thing," said La Tia.

"But I would still find a way to *do* the wrong thing," said Dead Mary.

"You see?" said Rien. "My fille n'a pas d'espoir."

"I have hope, Mother," said Dead Mary. "But I have experience too."

"Look," said La Tia. "Do you see what I see?"

"We never do," said Dead Mary.

"I see Alvin with a son. That what he want most."

"I see him with a woman," said Rien. "That is what he miss the most."

"I see him kneeling by a child's grave," said Dead Mary. "That is what he fears the most."

"I can make a charm for this," said La Tia.

Tenskwa-Tawa stepped out from the tree. "Don't make a charm for him, La Tia."

"I knew you was there, Red Prophet."

"I knew you knew," said Tenskwa-Tawa. "That crystal shows you want *you* want to see, not always the truth."

"But the truth what I want to see," said La Tia.

"Everybody thinks they want to see the truth," said Tenskwa-Tawa. "That's one of the lies we tell ourselves."

"Him heart more dark than Dead Mary, him."

"Alvin knelt by the grave of his firstborn," said Tenskwa-Tawa. "The child came too early to live. Don't meddle this time."

"Give him the woman he love," said Rien. "I know you have the charm for this."

"He has the woman he loves," said Tenskwa-Tawa. "She's carrying his child right now."

"Give him the power to keep the child from dying," said Dead Mary.

"He has the power," said Tenskwa-Tawa. "He figured out what the baby needed. He just couldn't do it fast enough. The baby suffocated before he could get its little lungs to breathe."

"Ah," said La Tia. "Time what he need. Time."

"You have a charm for this?" said Rien.

"I got to think," said La Tia.

"Leave him alone," said Tenskwa-Tawa. "Let his life be what it is. Let it be what he makes of it."

"Did he leave our lives as they were?" said Dead Mary. "Or did he heal my mother?"

"He heal me better than I was before," said Rien. "I had the Italian disease, long time, long before the yellow fever, but he fix that too."

"Did he leave black people in chains, him?" asked La Tia.

"But *he* knew what he was doing," said Tenskwa-Tawa.

La Tia reared back and roared with laughter. "Him! He don't know what he do! He do the best thing he think of, and when that go wrong he do the best thing he can think of *then*. Like all us, him!"

Tenskwa-Tawa shook his head. "Don't meddle with his baby or his wife," he said. "Don't do it."

"The Red Prophet command the Black Queen?" said La Tia.

"Lolla-Wossiky was a slave to hate, and blind with rage, and Alvin made me free, and Alvin let me see. I never set *him* free. I never gave *him* sight. He is in the world to bless *us*, not the other way."

"You do what you think with him," said La Tia. "I gonna bless him back, me."

Margaret spent all day preparing for her journey to Vigor Church. Not that she owned that much—packing was the least of it. But she had letters to write. People to summon from here and there. Those who should know that Alvin was going to build the City of Makers now. People who should come and take their place beside him, if they wanted, if they could get away.

And then there was the carriage to arrange. She had seen many paths in which the journey was too much for her, and caused the baby to come early. This baby must not come early again. Already it had lasted longer in the womb than their firstborn, but not long enough. If he was born on this journey the child would die.

So she hired the finest carriage in town, the one belonging to the young doctor. He tried to refuse, telling her that any carriage was out of the question in her condition. "Stay here and have this baby," he said. "To travel now would only endanger you *and* the child. Do you think you're made of iron?"

No, she had no such fancy. Nor did her torchsight show her everything clearly. The futures of this child were as foggy and confused, almost, as Alvin's futures. There were great gaps. So even though the child had nothing like Alvin's gifts, it was caught up in the same mystery, the same defiance of the laws of cause and effect. She did not know with any kind of certainty what would happen to the child if she stayed or went. But she knew that Alvin needed her in Noisy River, and on the far side of the fog, she saw a few paths that had her holding a baby in her arms, standing with Alvin on a bluff overlooking a fog-bound river. Those were the only paths where she saw herself holding that baby. So she was going to Vigor Church, to Alvin's family, to invite them—and any others from the school of the makers—to come to Noisy River to help Alvin build the Crystal City. And with them traveling with her, she would go the rest of the way well accompanied.

Alvin's brother Measure was the one in the world most like him. Not in power—though Measure was a good student of makery, within his limits. He was like Alvin in goodness. Perhaps he was Alvin's better in compassion and patience. And far Alvin's better in judgment about other people's character. Let Measure stand beside Alvin, and Alvin would never lack for wisdom. Who could know better than I that foreknowledge is a poor chooser, for it

gives too great a weight to fear. While a generous heart
will make choices that, at the very worst, do not poison
the heart of the chooser.

Perhaps that was why she was sure she had to go to
Vigor Church and on to where Alvin was. Because fear
told her to stay, but hope told her to go. Her hope of
being a good wife to Alvin and a good mother to her baby.
A good mother being, at the very least, one that gave birth
to a living child. As a woman who had given birth to a
child too soon born to live, surely she should be a one fit
to make such judgment.

So she spent her day cushioning the carriage while
workmen resprung it. Choosing a team of horses that
would pull evenly and not run faster than she could bear.
Packing her few things, writing her letters. Until at the
end of the day she was ready to drop with exhaustion.
Which was good, she would sleep without fretting, she
would rise early and refreshed and set out to meet her
husband and put a baby in his arms.

She was just undressing for bed when the first labor
pain came.

"No," she cried softly. "Oh, please, God, no, not yet,
not now." She laid her hands upon her own womb and
saw that the baby was indeed coming. He faced in the
right direction, all was well with him, but she saw no
future for him. He was going to be born, like his sister,
only to die.

"No," she whispered.

She walked to the door of her room. "Papa," she called.

Horace Guester was serving the last round of drinks to
the night's customers. But he had an innkeeper's ears, to
hear all needs and wishes, and in a few moments he came.

"The baby is coming," she said.

"I'll fetch the midwife," he said.

"It's too early," said Margaret. "The birth will be easy,
but the baby will die."

Tears came to her father's eyes. "Ah, Peggy, I know
what it cost your mother, those two tiny graves on the hill

behind the house. I never wished for you to have two of your own."

"Nor I," she said.

"But I should fetch her anyway," said Father. "You shouldn't be alone at such a time, and it's not fitting for a father to see his daughter in labor."

"Yes, fetch her," said Margaret.

"But not in here," said Father. "You shouldn't do this in the room where the baby's father was born."

"There's no better place," said Margaret. "It's a room where hope once triumphed over despair."

"Have hope then, my little Peggy." Father kissed her cheek and hastened away.

My little Peggy, he had called her. In this room, that's who I am. Peggy. My mother's name. Where is she now, that fierce, wise, powerful woman? Too strong for me, she was, or anyone else in this place, I see that now. Too strong for her husband, a woman of such will that even fate would not defy her. Perhaps that's why I was able to see the way to save baby Alvin's life—because my mother willed it so.

Perhaps it was losing two babies against her will made her so indomitable.

Or perhaps she simply imprinted her own life on mine so indelibly that I, too, must bury my first two babies before giving birth to a child who might live.

Tears flowed down her cheeks. I can't go through this again. I'm not as strong as Mother. It will not make me stronger. It took all my courage just to let Alvin give this second child to me, and if I lose this one, too, how can I try yet again? It isn't in me. I can't do it.

The midwife found her weeping on the bed. "Aw, Mistress Larner, what have you done? Stained the bedclothes, and your own fine underthings as well, couldn't you have taken them off? What a waste, what a waste."

"What do I care about my *clothing,*" said Margaret savagely. "My baby is going to die."

"What! How can you—" But the midwife knew exactly

how Margaret Larner could say such a thing, and so she fell silent.

"Grieving on your own childbed," grumbled the woman, "grieving for the baby before it's had a chance to live, it's not right."

"I wish I didn't know," said Margaret. "Oh, please God, make me wrong!"

And with a single push, the baby, small and thin, slipped out into the midwife's waiting hands.

The emptiness in her own body hurt more than the pains of labor. "No!" cried Margaret. "Don't cut the cord! Don't tie it off, no!"

"But the baby needs to—"

"As long as the cord is still connected to my body then he isn't dead!"

They were starting to cross over the river now, but not with any spectacular show. The people might have expected otherwise, but Alvin insisted that they would come by boat, by raft, by canoe, by something that floated by itself.

"That'll take weeks," Verily told him.

"I know," said Alvin.

"Then why—"

"The first to come will fell logs and make shelters. A place for the children when they cross over the river. Six thousand souls, all in a place where there's nothing standing, nothing cleared? It's not too heavy a burden on Tenskwa-Tawa's people, to keep most of them on his side of the river for a while. They can spare the food—and the time. And on our side, well, Verily, you're the man who knows how things should fit together."

"But I should be with Lincoln, working on the charter."

"Who will I put in charge, if not you, Verily? You drew up the plat of the city. Who else knows it the way you do? Arthur Stuart isn't back from Mexico yet and besides, he's too young to be telling folks where to build their houses and where to farm. La Tia's no town-builder. Mike Fink? Rien? Who can I trust?"

"You can trust yourself," said Verily.

"I can't," said Alvin. "It's not my job."

"It's your city."

"Not today," said Alvin. "I have no city today. The baby's making ready to be born."

It took Verily a moment to register what baby he was talking about. "Now?"

"Soon," said Alvin. "Do you think I care about a single one of these six thousand souls, when my baby's going to die?"

Verily looked as if he had been slapped.

"Die," he said. "And you, who've healed so many . . ."

"Many but not all," said Alvin. "The first one died. This one isn't quite so early, but . . ."

"But you'll try."

"I'll do what I do," said Alvin. "You get the city started, Verily. It's as much yours as mine. You held onto the plow as much as I did."

The truth of that sank in and Verily nodded gravely. "So I did." He turned and left.

Alvin sat alone on the stone outcropping just above the spring. He reached down and filled his hands with water. He lifted the water to his face and started to drink, but then splashed it onto his skin and wept into his hands.

And then, in the far-off place where his attention really lay, in the very room where he himself had come out of his mother's womb, his wife gave a mighty push and all at once the baby was out in the open air and there was no more time for grief because even though he knew he could not save the baby, he had to try.

This time, at least, there was no fumbling and searching. He knew exactly what was wrong—the lungs, not yet fully formed inside, the tiny structures not yet ready to filter the air through into the blood. The tissue was a little better formed this time; some air was passing. And for some reason the baby's umbilical cord had not yet been tied off. The placenta would soon detach itself from the wall of the womb, but for the moment, there was still air passing into the baby's blood. So there was a little time. Not enough, it would take hours and hours to prepare the lungs, and the placenta could not last that long.

But he did not brood on what he could not do. Instead he simply did it, told each tiny part of the lung what to do, helped it do it, and then the next part, and the next, each time a little easier because the tissues could more easily change when they were adjacent to tissue that had already matured enough to transform the air into what the blood needed it to be.

It was almost as if the baby's very heart slowed down—indeed, for a moment Alvin thought that the heart had stopped. But no, it was beating very, very slowly, and he worked with feverish intensity, wishing he could slather on the mature tissue the way a painter slaps whitewash on a wall instead of doing it the way he had to do it, like a tatter making knot, knot, knot, and only gradually turning it into lace.

"I've got to tie this cord," said the midwife. "You know your business, I'm sure, but I know mine, and you don't wait for the afterbirth to come out of itself!"

"Look how he breathes in the air," said Margaret. "Look, almost as if he had a hope of life."

And then, as she watched his quick breathing, as she felt his rapid heartbeat, she began to see paths emerging out of darkness. He would not die. He would live. Mentally damaged from the lack of air at the time of his birth, but alive. She was not afraid of such damage—maybe Alvin could fix the problem, yes, if Alvin was watching he could . . .

More paths opened, and more and more, and now there were a few where the baby was not damaged, where it would learn to walk like any other child, and talk, and . . .

And now all paths were open, like a normal life, except

that there was something that she needed to do.

"Cut the cord," she said. "He can breathe on his own now."

"About time," said the midwife. She strung a thread around the cord and tied it tight, then another about two inches away, and then passed a sharp knife under the cord between the knots and pulled upward.

The afterbirth slid out onto the clean rags covering the bed.

The baby cried, a whimpering sound, not the lusty cry of a full-term baby, and the poor lad was still as scrawny as could be, but he could breathe, and now almost every path in the child's life showed him in his father's arms, as the three of them, father, mother, and son, stood on the bluff overlooking the river.

The sound of an axe chopping against wood rang out and Alvin came out of his deep concentration. It had been hours and hours, working on the baby's lungs, but somehow the child had stayed alive through all of it, and now it was done. The child was breathing on his own. The cord was cut. And Alvin was surprised that it was still light. Surely it had taken him all day.

He got up from the stone, his body stiff from resting in one position for so long. He walked to the edge of the bluff, expecting to see many trees fallen.

Instead, there was Verily making his way down the hill. What had he been doing, coming up and checking on Alvin all day? Couldn't he do this by himself? And instead of teams of axemen toppling trees, only the one axe was being wielded, and by a man who seemed to be no part of an organized plan.

What had Verily been doing all day, while Alvin wrestled to keep his baby alive?

Only as he was about to cry out to Verily impatiently did Alvin take note of the fact that Verily's shadow still fell long beyond him, down the hill, toward the west.

It was still morning. Early morning. Only minutes after Verily had left Alvin. Somehow, all those hours of work—and as sore as his body was, it *had* to have been hours—had been compressed into only a few minutes.

"Verily!" he called. "Wait!"

Verily turned and watched as Alvin leapt and slipped and slid down the hill to join him.

"What is it?" said Verily.

"How long ago did we talk?"

Verily looked at him as if he were crazy. "Three minutes."

"I did it," said Alvin. "Somehow in just those minutes, I did it."

"Did what?"

"The baby's born. He can breathe. He's alive."

Only then did Verily understand. "Thank God, Alvin."

"I do," said Alvin. "I do thank God."

Then he burst into tears and wept in the arms of his friend.

⚔️ 17 ⚔️
Foundation

ALVIN LEANED ON the fireplace, watching Margaret nurse little Vigor. "Got a mighty good suction in him," said Alvin.

"Like a tick," said Margaret. "Can't pry him loose till he's full."

"He's getting strong, don't you think?"

"Getting some muscle on him," said Margaret. "But I don't think he'll ever be one of those fat little babies."

"That's fine," said Alvin. "Don't want to raise a spoiled child."

"You'll raise him whatever he is," said Margaret. "And if anyone's likely to spoil him, it's you."

"That's my plan, more or less," said Alvin.

"Don't want him to be spoiled, but you plan to spoil him."

"Can't help it. Only way to save this boy is to have another child to divide up my doting."

"I'll do my best," said Margaret.

"Do you mind, not traveling now, not being in the world of affairs?"

"I don't look beyond this town now," said Margaret. "I try to forget that the world outside is maneuvering itself toward war. I pretend that somehow it will stay beyond the borders of our little county."

"Not so little. Very and Abe got us good boundaries. Lots of room to grow."

"I'm more concerned about how much our people grow inside them."

"Can't make them," said Alvin.

"I know."

Vigor was done with breakfast, and now Alvin cracked the boiled eggs and sliced them onto a plate for his and Margaret's breakfast.

"Mayor of the fastest-growing city in Noisy River, and you have to fix your own breakfast."

"I'm fixing *your* breakfast, and that's all the difference."

"My but we're in love," said Margaret.

Old pain and ancient loneliness hung in the air between them.

"Alvin," said Margaret. "I always tried to do what was best."

"I know," said Alvin.

"And sometimes what was best was not to tell you all that I knew."

Alvin said nothing.

"You never would have gone to Barcy," she said. "We never would have had all these people, the core of this City of Makers."

"Might have gone to Barcy all the same," said Alvin.

"But you would never have gone near Rien."

"You sure that saving her was what spread the fever?"

"In all the paths where you never met her, she died without a single other soul catching the disease."

Alvin smiled a wan smile and stuffed an entire egg into his mouth. "At least I've got good manners," he said, spraying bits of yolk onto the table.

"Yes, I can see that all those lessons I gave you have paid off. I can't take you out in company."

"Guess we'll just have to stay in."

"You'll never listen to me again, will you?" she said.

"I'm listening right now."

"But you'll never do something just because I tell you that you ought to."

"Have you changed?" asked Alvin. "Or do you still think you're the one best able to decide whether I should know the consequences of my deeds?"

"I've already promised a dozen times over."

"But I don't believe you," said Alvin. "I believe you mean it now, but in the moment, when you're deciding what to tell me and what not to tell, I think you'll hold back the things I most want to know, if you're afraid that knowing will cause me harm."

"You're not the most important thing in the world to me now, you know," said Margaret.

"Am so," said Alvin.

"The baby is."

"The baby's just little and he can't get into much trouble yet."

"*You* did."

"You got the habit of looking out for me too deep set. I can't trust you to let me decide for myself."

"Yes you can," said Margaret. "Besides, you don't need me to tell you everything now."

"I can't control what the crystal ball shows me. It's not like your knack."

"It's better."

"I think the blood and water make more of a mirror than a window."

"I think it shows good people how to do good, and bad people how to do bad. You won't come asking me what to do, when you can see what's good and right in the walls of the house you're building."

"Don't know if we should rightly call it a house," said Alvin.

"It's not a chapel—nobody's going to preach."

"A factory, maybe," said Alvin. "Or a house of mirrors, like in that carnival in New Amsterdam."

"Then it's a house after all," said Margaret. "And I was *right.*"

"Didn't say you weren't *right,*" said Alvin. "Just said I'd like to have chosen for myself."

"You'd rather have chosen wrong, knowing, than chosen right, not knowing."

"Well, when you put it that way, it makes me sound like a dunce on purpose."

"Indeedy," said Margaret.

"Do I have to be mayor?" said Alvin. "I'd rather just spend my time building the . . . crystal."

"They all look to you, anyway, whether you have the title or not. You're the one who looks out for them, who watches the borders. You're the one who causes the slave-catchers who come near here to keep losing their way. You're the one who figured out that draining the swamp would stop the malaria."

"It was Measure who suggested it," said Alvin.

"You're the one who watches over everybody like a mother hen."

"Then let me run for mother hen."

"Alvin," said Margaret. "So what if you don't care for the title? You're going to be doing the job anyway, and it would be quite unkind of you to make someone else take the title, when everybody will know you're the real leader. Take the name upon you, and don't burden someone else with it, when they'll never have the authority."

"Didn't think of someone else having to do it," said Alvin.

"I know you didn't," said Margaret primly. "Because you're still a hopelessly ignorant journeyman smith."

"I am, you know," said Alvin.

"You know I was teasing," said Margaret.

"But I am," said Alvin. "'Cause the thing I'm building, it's not some cathedral made of visionary crystal. It's the city. It's the people. And I can make the blocks of crystal water as pure as can be, I can make the wcbs of blood that hold them up strong and true, we can plumb the walls straight, we can dwell inside it all the livelong day and see great visions and small memories according to our own desires. But I can't make one bad person good."

"You can make many a good person better."

"Can't," said Alvin. "They have to do it their own selves."

"Well, of course, but you help."

"I'm trying to knit everybody together as one people, and I don't think it can be done. Now that the journey's over, the French folks suddenly don't want much to do with the former slaves. And the former house slaves lord it over the former field slaves, and the blacks who were already free in Barcy lord it over all of them, and the ones who still remember Africa think they're the kings of creation—"

"The queens, more likely," said Margaret.

"And then there's all the folks who've been close to me for years, they come here and think they know everything, but they weren't on the journey, they didn't cross over Pontchartrain on that crystal bridge, they didn't camp in a circle of fog, they didn't run before the face of the Mizzippy dam, they didn't live being fed by reds on the far side of the river. You see? They think they're closest to me, but they went down a different road and there's nothing but divisions among the people and I can't make it right. Even Verily can't do more than patch up some of the tears in the fabric here and there, and that's his knack!"

"Give it time."

"Will it last, Margaret?" asked Alvin. "Will the things I'm building outlast me?"

"I haven't looked," said Margaret.

"And you expect me to believe you?"

"I can't always see, when it comes to you and your works."

"You've looked, and you've seen. You just don't want to tell me."

A single tear spilled over one eyelid, and Margaret looked away. "Some of the things you're building will outlast you."

"Which ones?"

"Arthur Stuart," said Margaret. "You're building him, and you've done a fine job."

"He builds himself."

"Alvin," she said sharply. Then softer: "Alvin, my love, if there's anyone in the world who understands this, it's you. Everything you make builds itself, or thinks it does. That's what making is, isn't it? To persuade things to *want* to be the way they need to be. People are the hardest to persuade, that's all."

"Is Arthur Stuart the only thing I've created that outlasts me?"

She shook her head. "I see now that you were right. I can't keep my promise. I can't tell you everything." She faced him, and now her cheeks were striped with tears, and her eyes were full of longing and regret. "But not because I'm trying to manipulate you or control you or get you to do something you wouldn't otherwise do, I promise that, and I'm keeping that promise."

"So why won't you tell me?"

"Because I hate knowing the future," said Margaret. "It robs the present of its joy. And I won't make you live the way I do, seeing the end of everything when it's still young and hopeful to everyone else."

"So the city fails."

"Your life," said Margaret, "is a life of great accomplishments, and the best things you make will last for as many lifetimes as I can see." Then she raised the baby higher in her arms, and though little Vigor was sleeping, she buried her face in the blanket he was wrapped in and wept.

Alvin knelt beside her and put an arm around her and nuzzled her shoulder. "I'm a bad husband, to plague you like this."

"No you're not," she said, her voice muffled by the baby, by weeping.

"Am so."

"You're the husband I want."

"Your bad judgment."

"I know."

"You tell me what I need to know to be a good man," said Alvin.

"But you are one, always, whether I tell you anything or not."

"You tell me that much, and I won't ask for more." He kissed her. "And I'm sorry that you carry the burden that you do."

"I'm not sorry for it," she said. "It's who I am. But I wouldn't wish it on anyone else, that's all."

Arthur Stuart watched the men digging the foundation of the observatory—for so Verily insisted on calling it, and Arthur liked the name. They dug deep to bedrock all the way around the outcropping of stone where the water came out. That would not be touched—it would remain inside, forever pouring its water out to flow in a clear, cold stream down the bluff and into the Mizzippy. It was the dry season now and other streams had slackened or gone dry, but this one flowed exactly as it had all summer.

The men digging the foundation trench—did they know that Alvin could have cleared this all away in just a few minutes? That he could have made the topsoil and the rocky subsoil flow upward and pour out onto the outside of the trench just by showing the dirt what he wanted it to do?

It was one of the perverse things Alvin had always done, making Arthur Stuart labor with his hands to make things that Alvin could have made in a moment. Like the time Alvin made him work half the summer making a canoe, burning and digging at a thick log until it was hollowed out. Now Arthur had learned enough makery that he could do it in ten minutes; it hardly mattered that Alvin could do it in ten seconds, ten minutes was good enough for Arthur Stuart.

But now Arthur was beginning to see what Alvin had been after, all that time. It wasn't that digging the canoe helped Arthur learn how to use the hidden powers of makery, not at all. It was the deeper, truer lesson: That the maker is the one who is part of what he makes. If Alvin had simply made the canoe, then it would have been Alvin's canoe. But because Arthur Stuart worked so hard to make it, it was *his* canoe, too. He was part of it. And if he had not gotten to know the wood—the shape of it inside the tree, the hard and soft of it, the way it burned slow and held its strength and even got harder where it had been scorched—then would he now be able to send his doodlebug through it and understand the virtue of the living wood? Could he be the maker that he was, if he had not been the clumsy boy with sweat pouring down his face and back, laboring with his hands?

These men who were putting in their day, digging the foundation, they couldn't drip their blood into the Mizzippy and come up with blocks of visionary crystal. But they could dig into the earth, so when the finished observatory rose into the sky and people went inside to see what they could see, to learn what they might be, these men would be able to say, that building stands on the foundation I dug. I helped make that miraculous place. It has my sweat in it, along with Alvin Maker's blood.

There was a man standing on the far side of the cleared land, watching, not the diggers, but Arthur Stuart. It took a moment for Arthur to realize who it was.

"Taleswapper!" he cried, and he ran full tilt right toward him, leaping over the trench just as a man was about to pitch a spadeful of earth, earning Arthur an irritated curse as the man had to stop himself in midswing and spill half the dirt back into the hole. "Taleswapper, I thought that you were dead!"

Taleswapper greeted him with an embrace, and his

arms were stronger than Arthur had feared, but feeble indeed compared to what they had been, years before, when last they met.

"You'll know when I'm dead," said Taleswapper. "Because suddenly all the jokes will run dry and all the gossip will go silent and people will just sit and look glum because they got no tales to tell."

"I reckon you heard what we were doing here and had to come and add it to your book."

"I don't think so," said Taleswapper. "I filled it already." He slid a thick volume from inside his deerskin jacket. "Every page in it, full, and I even added a few scraps to make more pages than the blamed thing had. No, I think I'm here because what you're building, it'll take the place of books like mine."

"I hope not," said Arthur Stuart. "I hope never."

"Well, we'll see," said Taleswapper. "You've grown a lot taller, but not a whit smarter, as far as I can see."

"Can't see smart," said Arthur Stuart.

"I can," said Taleswapper.

"Come on, then," said Arthur Stuart. "Even *I'm* smart enough to know Alvin and Peggy'll want to see you *forth with*."

"Forthwith?" asked Taleswapper.

"Abe Lincoln is reading law with Verily Cooper, and they let me listen in."

"I'd rather you kept on speaking English like the rest of us."

"Law is the biggest mishmash of languages. Two kinds of Latin, two kinds of French, and three kinds of English all made into a soup that nobody can understand except a lawyer."

"That's what it's for," said Taleswapper. "It's how lawyers make sure they'll always have work, cause nobody can understand what they wrote down except another lawyer."

Arthur led him down off the bluff to the flatland leading to the river. The trees were mostly gone from this area, cut down and turned into cabins and fence rails. "Eight thousand people living here now," said Arthur.

"Still more than half of them runaway slaves, though, right?" said Taleswapper. "And therefore subject to being taken back south?"

"All citizens *here*," said Arthur Stuart. "Ain't no catcher been able to claim a soul yet."

"Word outside is that Furrowspring County is in virtual rebellion against the laws of the United States, refusing to accept the Supreme Court ruling that slaveowners can recover their escaped property."

"I reckon *so*," said Arthur Stuart proudly.

"There's war fever, and those as want to prevent the war, they might decide to sacrifice this town."

"As if they could," said Arthur Stuart. "With Alvin watching out for us!"

Taleswapper only shook his head.

They found Alvin down by the river, up to his knees in mud, helping with the sinking of posts to support a riverboat dock. "Howdy, Taleswapper!" cried Alvin. "About time you got here! You've missed all the best stories already, poor fellow. Too old to keep up with us boys, I reckon!"

"Reckon so," said Taleswapper. "But I got sense enough not to stand up to my neck in mud."

"This ain't just ordinary mud," said Alvin. "This is Mizzippy clay. It gets ahold of you and steals the boots right off your feet."

"Well, that's a recommendation for it. Make a cup out of such clay and it'll suck the tea right out of your mouth, is that the way of it?"

Alvin and all the men laughed. "Make a jar from it and it'll collect water from dry air."

"So you carry a bit of the Mizzippy with you even into dry land," said Taleswapper. "Why, with advertising like that, I reckon you could sell such jars for a dollar each and make fifty bucks in every town, as long as you high-tailed it out before they found out the jars don't work."

"They'd work if Alvin made 'em!" shouted a man. That was enough to rouse a bit of a cheer for Alvin Maker, much to his embarrassment.

"Well, if you're gonna waste time cheering a man covered in mud, I reckon I'll leave you to your own work and go show my good friend just what a perfect baby looks like."

"Show him your son, too, while you're at it!" shouted one of the workers, which was good for another laugh and another cheer for Alvin.

Alvin clambered out of the water and up the bank, and Arthur took due note that the mud just slid off his clothes and the water dried while he was watching and thirty steps from the river you'd never guess what Alvin had been working on not two minutes before. He won't use his knack to spare these men a moment's work, but he'll use it to spare himself a bath! Or at least to spare Peggy the task of cleaning up after a muddy husband . . . so that was all right.

They passed Measure, who was leading a team of men and horses doing stump removal. Arthur Stuart knew perfectly well that Measure was using as much makery as he had mastered to help free up the roots from the deep soil. But since there was still plenty of hard work for the men and teams to do, Alvin didn't say anything about it to him, and Arthur Stuart figured that as long as Measure kept his makery secret, nobody would give him the credit for how fast the clearing of the land was going.

But Measure left the work and came along. And when they got to Alvin's cabin, there inside it were a gaggle of women. La Tia seemed like the president of the women of Furrowspring County, and what had gathered here might have been the great council: the leading women of the exodus, including Marie d'Espoir, Rien, and Mama Squirrel, and some of the women who had known Alvin and Peggy in years past, come to be part of the long-awaited city. Purity, a young preacher against Puritanism from New England, who still seemed to be in love with

Verily Cooper—who hardly noticed she was there—and Fishy, a former slave from Camelot who had become something of a great woman among the abolitionists of the north in the years since her escape. And, of course, Peggy.

"I can't stay in this room," said Taleswapper. "So many glorious women, I have no choice but to be in love with all of you at once. It'll tear me apart."

"Live with it," said Peggy dryly. "I think you know them all."

"Them as I don't know, I hope I soon will," said Taleswapper. "If I don't die in the next few minutes from pure happiness."

"That man talk some," said La Tia appreciatively.

"I didn't know there was a meeting," said Alvin.

"You wasn't invite," said La Tia. "My meeting. But you welcome a stay."

"What's the topic?" asked Alvin.

"The name of that thing what you build," said La Tia. "I don't like what Verily call it, me."

Peggy laughed. "Nobody likes what anybody calls it," she said. "But La Tia was reading in the Bible and she has a name."

"You lead us out like Moses," said La Tia. "And Arthur Stuart, he lead us like Joshua when you gone. Not like Aaron, no! We got no golden calf! But we the book of Exodus, us. So this thing you build, I find out in the Bible, she a *tabernacle*."

Alvin frowned. "Makes it sound like a church meeting place."

"Oui!" cried Rien. "Only instead of you go and a priest pretend to be God, we go inside and find out where he live in our heart!"

"For a building that don't exist yet, everybody's got a good idea of how it's gonna work," said Alvin.

But of course they did. Alvin had already made thirty-two of the crystal blocks—big ones, heavy, hard to haul. They were stacked up waiting to be laid down as foundation stones, but there was hardly a soul in Furrowspring County what hadn't walked the corridor between those blocks and looked into their infinite depth. You walk among them and it feels like you're in a place larger than the whole world, with all of what was and is and is yet to come beside you on either hand, and the ordinary world looks so small and narrow, when you see it at the end of that glistening corridor. But then you walk away from the stacked up blocks and they get to looking small, and quite plain. Shimmery, yes, reflecting the trees and the sky, the clouds and the river, if you're standing where the reflection of the Mizzippy could be seen. Small on the outside, huge on the inside—oh, they all knew what this building was going to be like, when it was done.

"In the Bible," said Marie d'Espoir, "the tabernacle was a place where only the priest could go. He'd come out and tell everyone what he saw. But our tabernacle, everybody's the priest, everybody can go inside, man and woman, to see what they see and hear what they hear."

"It suits me fine," said Alvin. "I know I don't want it to be a church or school or such. Tabernacle's as fitting a name as any, and better than most. Though I know Verily's gonna be disappointed to find out you didn't like 'observatory.'"

"I *like* it," said La Tia. "But I don't can *say* it, me."

That issue decided, the women went on talking about which families didn't have clothes enough for their children, and which houses weren't big enough or warm enough, and who was sick and needed help. It was a good work they were doing, but the men weren't needed in the discussion and soon Arthur Stuart found himself outside. But not with Alvin and Taleswapper—they were off looking at the big house where Papa Moose's and Mama Squirrel's family were living even as the house was still being built. "Fifty-seven children," said Taleswapper. "And all of them born to this Mama Squirrel herself."

"We have the legal documentation," said Alvin. "Not only that, but we know of another half dozen on the way."

"A remarkable pregnancy," said Taleswapper. "And such a small woman, she seemed, from what I saw of her."

Arthur Stuart stood outside the house and looked up at the bluff. The house was well placed. At the back door, you could look out onto the river and see any boat that might tie up at the new dock. And out the front door, you could see where the . . . *tabernacle* would stand, and even now you could see the two rows of stacked up crystal blocks waiting to be laid in place.

He felt a hand on his shoulder.

He jumped. "Marie," he said. "You startled me."

"I meant to," she said. "All your makery, but you still don't notice a woman at all."

"Oh, I notice you," said Arthur Stuart.

"I know," said Marie. "You notice me all the time. You make sure you know exactly where I am, so you can always be somewhere else."

"Oh, I don't think that's what I'm . . ."

But it *was* what he was doing. He just hadn't realized it.

"You afraid I kiss you again?" asked Marie.

"I didn't mind it, you know," he said.

"Or you afraid I won't?"

"I can live without it, if that's how you want it."

"Ignorant boy," she said. "You are supposed to say, I can't live without your kisses."

"But I can," said Arthur Stuart.

"All right," said Marie. She playfully slapped his shoulder as if brushing dust from it. Then she started to walk back to the house.

"But I don't want to," said Arthur Stuart.

He wasn't quite sure where he had found the courage to say it. Except maybe the fact that it was true, that he hardly went an hour without thinking about her and wondering whether she had kissed him to tease him or whether it meant something and how would he go about finding out. And so the words just spilled out of him.

She turned around and came back to him. "How much do you *not* want to live without my kisses?"

He gathered her into his arms and kissed her, with perhaps more fervor than skill, but she didn't seem disposed to criticize. "Enough to do that in front of God and everybody," he said.

"Ah, look what you've done now," said Marie.

"What?"

"You kiss me so hard, now I'm going to have a baby."

It took him a moment to realize that she was joking, but in the meantime he'd been standing there with such a stupid look on his face that no wonder she laughed at him. "Why are you always so serious?" she said.

"Because when I kiss you," he said, "it's not a game to me."

"Life is a game," she said. "But you and me, I think we can win it together."

"You proposing something?" asked Arthur Stuart.

"Maybe," she said.

"Like marriage?" asked Arthur Stuart.

"Maybe a man should propose such a thing."

"And if I did, would you say yes?"

"I will say yes," said Marie, "as soon as Purity says yes to Verily Cooper."

"But he ain't asked her," said Arthur Stuart.

Marie laughed gaily and darted back into the cabin.

Leaving Arthur Stuart convinced that something really deep was going on between him and Marie d'Espoir, and he didn't have the least idea what it was.

He turned around and looked back at the rows of crystal blocks up on the bluff, and saw two men standing between them, looking into the walls. He knew them at once, without even sending his doodlebug out to confirm their identity. Jim Bowie and Calvin Miller.

"Alvin," he murmured softly, then jogged around the cabin to where he could see the new house of Moose and Squirrel. Alvin and Taleswapper were out front, with Papa Moose talking all about this and that—he had so many

plans for the house that now and then people had to remind him it was just a building—but Arthur Stuart could
see that Alvin was looking up at the blocks and seeing
just what Arthur Stuart had seen.

Alvin started moving away from the others and jogging
toward the bluff. Taleswapper and Papa Moose followed
behind, more slowly.

Arthur Stuart ducked inside the cabin again. "Peggy,"
he said, and beckoned.

"No, don't do that way," said La Tia. "You take her,
all we talk about is why she go. Take us all!"

"Calvin's back," said Arthur Stuart. "And the man
that's with him, he's a killer. I knew him on the river and
in Mexico. "I should've known when I left him in True
Cross that he'd join up with Calvin again."

The women started out of the house behind him, but
Arthur Stuart didn't wait for them. He ran up the bluff
and arrived just as Alvin did. They stood at the end of
the corridor between the blocks.

"Calvin," said Alvin softly. "Glad to see you here."

"Could you lend a hand here?" said Calvin. "Seems old
Jim Bowie here just can't tear himself away from whatever he's seeing in these mirrors of yours."

"He's seeing himself," said Alvin. "Like you did."

"I think he's seeing more than that," said Calvin.
"Though I can't think what."

Was it possible that Calvin saw nothing but his own
reflection, as simple as a mirror, when he looked into
these walls? Arthur Stuart thought it might just be possible—Calvin wasn't known for being a deep thinker, and
maybe the walls had no more depth than the person looking into them. But it was more likely that Calvin saw the
same kinds of visions as everyone else, but just couldn't
bring himself to tell the truth about it, any more than he
could tell the truth about much of anything else.

Alvin walked between the blocks, and when he reached
Jim Bowie, put a hand on his shoulder. Immediately
Bowie looked at him, grinned. "Why, I was seeing you

in there, and seeing you out here, it's like the same vision. With just one tiny difference."

"I don't want to hear about it," said Alvin. "Come on out of here, both of you." He began to lead them along.

"The difference was, in the wall there I saw you full of bulletholes," said Jim Bowie. "But how could a thing like that happen? Imagine the bullet that could hit *you*!"

"Just wishful thinking on your part," said Alvin.

"Bulletholes!" said Calvin. "What a cheerful mural to put on public display, Alvin."

They reached the end of the corridor where Arthur Stuart was waiting.

"Howdy, Calvin," said Arthur. "I see you made it out of Mexico City after all."

"No thanks to you," said Calvin. "Leaving me there to die like the others."

Arthur didn't bother to argue. He knew Alvin already knew the truth, and would not be inclined to believe Calvin's version, which was naturally designed to pick a fight between Alvin and Arthur Stuart.

"I know Alvin's glad you lived," said Arthur Stuart. No need to say that Alvin was about the only one, apart from their mother and father.

"And I've forgiven Jim here for leaving me to have my heart ripped out."

Jim Bowie didn't rise to the bait, either. His attention was directed entirely toward Alvin. "Calvin told me what you're building here," said Bowie. "I want to be part of it."

"Yes," said Calvin. "If it's a city of makers, how could you think to do it without the only other living maker." He grinned at Arthur.

"We're all makers here," said Alvin, ignoring the fact that Calvin already knew how offensive his words were. "Come on along, my house is just down here."

They met the women on the way, and Alvin introduced everybody to everybody. Jim Bowie was, to Arthur's surprise, quite a charmer, able to put on elegant Camelot manners when there was someone to impress. Calvin was his normal saucy self—but Rien seemed to enjoy his banter, much to Arthur's disgust, and when Calvin showered flattery on Marie d'Espoir, Arthur Stuart thought about causing him a subtle but permanent internal injury—but of course did nothing at all. You don't start a duel with a maker who has more power and fewer scruples than you.

They got to the house and Alvin invited them inside to sit down. The furniture, except for Peggy's rocking chair, was all rough-hewn benches and stools, but they were good enough to sit on—and Arthur had heard Peggy say that she didn't wish for more comfortable furniture, because if the chairs were softer, company would be inclined to stay longer.

Calvin seemed to want to talk about his narrow escape from Mexico City, but since Tenskwa-Tawa had already told Alvin and Arthur Stuart all about it as soon as Arthur got back from his mission there, they were not inclined to hear a version of the story that made Calvin out to be something of a hero. "I'm glad you got out all right," said Alvin—and meant it, which was more than Arthur Stuart could say for himself. "And Jim, I think you know that your going along with Arthur Stuart here probably saved the lives of all the other men who went with you, since they might not have gone if you had refused."

"I don't plan to die for any cause," said Jim Bowie. "Nor any man, excepting only myself. I know that ain't noble, but it prolongs my days, which is philosophy enough for me."

He expected, Arthur thought, a bit more amusement or admiration for his attitude—but this wasn't a saloon, and nobody here was drunk, and so it rang a little hollow. There were people here who *would* die for a cause, or for someone else's sake.

It was Peggy, bless her heart, who came right to the point. "So where will you go now, Calvin?"

"Go?" said Calvin. "Why, this is the city of makers,

and here I am. I had some experiences—I was just about to get to them, but I know when it's not time for a tale—I had some experiences that made me realize how much I wished I'd paid more attention to Alvin back when he was trying to teach me stuff. I'm an impatient pupil, I reckon, so no wonder he kicked me out of school!"

Even this was a lie, and everyone there knew it, and it occurred to Arthur Stuart once again that Calvin seemed to lie just because he liked the sound of it, and not to be believed.

"I'm glad to have you," said Alvin. "Whatever you're willing to learn, I'll be happy to teach, if I know it, or someone else will, if it's something they know better than me."

"*That's* a short list," said Calvin, chuckling. It should have been a compliment to the breadth of Alvin's knack—but it came out sounding as if it were an accusation of vanity.

Arthur didn't have to be told that his sister was furious that Calvin was staying and Alvin was welcoming him. He knew Peggy thought that Calvin would one day cause his brother's death. But she said nothing about that, and instead turned to Jim Bowie. "And you, sir? Whither now?"

"I reckon I'll stay, too," said Bowie. "I liked what I saw up there. Well, no, not what I saw in the glass— don't misunderstand me, Alvin—but the manner of seeing. What an achievement! There's kings and queens would give up their kingdoms for an hour in that place."

"I'm afraid," said Alvin, "that you won't be welcome inside when the tabernacle is built."

Bowie's expression darkened. "Why, I'm sorry to hear that," he said. "Might I ask why?"

"There's some as finds the future in there," said Alvin. "But a man who kills his enemies shouldn't have access to a place that might show him where his future victims might be."

Bowie barked out a laugh. "Oh, I'm too much of a

killer for your tabernacle, is that it? Well, here's a thought. Everybody here who has ever killed a man in anger, stand up with me!" Bowie rose to his feet and looked around. "What, am I the only one?" Then he grinned at Alvin. "Am I?"

Reluctantly, Alvin rose to his feet.

"Ah," said Bowie. "Glad to know you admit it. I saw it in you from the start. You've killed, and killed with relish. You enjoyed it."

"He killed the man who killed my mother!" cried Peggy.

"And he enjoyed it," Bowie said again. "But it's your place for visions, Al, I won't dispute you about it. You can invite whoever you please. But that only applies to the building, Al. This is a free country, and a citizen of it can move to any town or county and take up residence and there ain't a soul can stop him. Am I right?"

"I thought you were a subject of the King, from the Crown Colonies," said Peggy.

"You know that an Englishman has only to cross the border and he's a citizen of the U.S.A.," said Bowie. "But I've gone them one better, and taken the oath just like a . . . Frenchman." He grinned at Rien. "I think I know you, ma'am," he said to her.

She looked at him with eyes like stones.

"I'll be your neighbor like it or not," said Bowie. "But I hope you like it, because I intend to be a peaceable citizen and make a lot of friends. Why, I might even run for office. I have a bent for politics, having once made a try at being emperor of Mexico."

"As you said," Alvin answered quietly. "It's a free country."

"I will admit I thought I'd get a warmer welcome from old friends." He grinned at Arthur Stuart. "This lad saved my life in Mexico. Even though he surely would rather not have done it. I'll never forget that."

Arthur Stuart nodded. He knew which part Bowie would never forget.

"Well," said Bowie. "The good cheer and bonhomie in this room is just too much for me. I'll have to find a place where I find less cheer and more alcohol, if you catch my drift. I hear it may take going into Warsaw County to get that particular thirst satisfied. But I'll be back to build me a cabin on some plot of land. Good day to you all."

Bowie got up and left the cabin.

"An obnoxious fellow," said Calvin loudly—Bowie could certainly hear him, even outside the door. "I don't know how I managed the journey from Barcy to here without quarreling with him. Maybe it was his big knife that kept the peace." Calvin had a remarkable ability to laugh at his own jokes with such gusto that one could miss the fact that he was the only one laughing.

Calvin turned to Arthur Stuart. "Of course, I could have got here sooner if somebody had bothered to take me along the way you did with Jim and his crew. He says you were able to make them run like they were flying, as if the ground rose up to meet their feet and trees got right out of their way. But I suppose I'm not worthy of such transportation."

"I offered to let you come along," said Arthur Stuart—and then immediately regretted it. Arguing with Calvin's lies just made him more enthusiastic.

"If you'd told me about this—greensong, was it?—I'd have come with you in a second. But to come along just because the Red Prophet was making threats—well, I reckon he wanted to conquer Mexico as bad as we did, and he got there first. Now he's got the empire, and I'm just an ordinary fellow—well, as ordinary as a maker can ever be. You, Alvin, you pretend to be ordinary, don't you? But you always manage to let people see a bit of what you can do. I understand! You want to be thought modest, but at the same time, nobody thinks a man's modest unless they know what great things he's being modest about, eh?" He laughed and laughed at that one.

*   *   *

The baby was fussy tonight, and since Margaret had already fed him and Alvin had changed his diaper, there was nothing for it but to carry him around and sing to him. Alvin had long since learned that it was his voice that Vigor wanted—something about the deep male tones vibrating in Alvin's chest, right next to the baby's head. So he let Margaret go back to sleep and walked outside in the air of a warm September evening.

He expected to be the only person abroad in the night, except for the night watchmen with their lanterns, and they'd be more on the outskirts of town, one along the river and the other along the edge of the bluff. But to Alvin's surprise, someone else soon fell into step beside him. His brother, Measure.

"Evening, Al," said Measure.

"Evening yourself," said Alvin. "Baby was fussy."

"I was the fussy one in my house. I sent myself out so I wouldn't cause any trouble."

"Calvin's staying with you, then?"

"I never could figure out why Ma and Pa felt the need to have the one more child. Not like there was a shortage."

"They didn't know what he'd be," said Alvin. "There's never too many children in the house, Measure. But you're not responsible for what they want, only for what you teach them."

"Alvin, I'm afraid," said Measure.

"Big man like you," said Alvin. "That's just silly."

"What we're doing here, it's wonderful. But how folks hate us and fear us and talk against us, that's pretty fierce. The law's against us—oh, I know, that charter is mighty fine, but it'll never stand up, not with us resisting the fugitive slave law. And with Calvin here—I don't know how, but he's going to cause trouble."

"It's the Unmaker," said Alvin. "It always is. No matter how fast you build things up, he's there, trying to tear it down even faster."

"Then he's bound to win, isn't he?"

"That's the funny thing," said Alvin. "All my life, I've

seen that all I can build is just a little bit, and he tears down so much. And yet . . . things keep getting built, don't they? Good things. And I finally realized, here in this town, watching all these people—the reason the Unmaker is gonna lose, in the long run, isn't because somebody like me or you does some big heroic deed and knocks him for a loop. It'll be because of all these people, hundreds of them, thousands of them, each building something in his own way—a family, a marriage, a house, a farm, a sturdy machine, a tabernacle, a classroom full of students just a little wiser than they were. Something. And after a while, you come to realize that all those somethings, they add up to everything, and all the Unmaker's nothings, you put them all together and they're still nothing. You see what I mean?"

"You must be smarter than Plato," said Measure, "because I can understand *him*."

"Oh, you understood me," said Alvin. "The question is, when we go down this dangerous road, with so many hands against us, will you be there with me, Measure? Will you stand beside me?"

"I will, to the end," said Measure. "And not just because you saved my life that time, you know."

"Oh, that wasn't much. You were trying to save mine, as I recall, so it was a fair trade on the spot."

"That's how I see it," said Measure.

"So why *will* you stand beside me? Because you lo[ve] me so much?" He said it jokingly, but he thought tha[t] was true.

"No," said Measure. "I love all my brothers, you k[now.] Even Calvin."

"Why, then?"

"Because the things you make, I want them to b[e.] You see? I love the work. I want it to *be*."

"And you're willing to pay for it, right along [with me.]"

"You'll see," said Measure.

They stood facing the rows of crystal bloc[ks that would] become the gleaming tabernacle of the Cryst[al City.]

baby was asleep. But Alvin tilted him up anyway, just enough that his little sleeping face was pointed toward the blocks. "Look at this place," he said to Vigor—and to Measure, too. "I didn't choose this place. I didn't choose my life, or the powers I have, or even most of the things that have happened to me. But for all the things that have been forced on me, I'm still a free man. And you know why? Because I choose them anyway. What was forced on me, I choose just the same." He turned and faced Measure. "Like you, Measure. I choose to be a maker, because I love the making."

we
it
how.

made.
with me?"
ready to
City. The